"It's near," he muttered. "So near."

Then I heard it too. On the very edge of perception, a keening wail that made the hair on my arms stand up.

Something like a cloud but darker and swifter passed over the sun, dimming the bright day, turning the green grass to dun.

Sudden pain made me look down. Phandros' bony fingers gripped my wrist. "We must get inside. If it sees us while hunting, nothing will keep it off."

"Have you seen it?"

"Only as a fell shadow across the moon when first it came. And I have seen what is left of the sheep after it feeds."

"Only sheep?" I asked. "That's unusual."

"So many have fled to the sea or the hinterlands that it may well have killed half a dozen people and we'd not know of it."

It is true that in such confusion, given a monster, a king who had shown no leadership, and absconding citizens, the ordinary bonds between people would shatter. Captain would break faith with king, husband flee from wife, mother abandon child, mankind would turn from their Gods. Anyone might be destroyed and, without those bonds that tie us to one another, no one would pay attention to anything but saving their own necks.

But if the harpy had killed anyone, I felt it would become known. Harpies are not neat in their habits. Entrails in the trees would be the least of it.

HERO FOR HIRE

Book One

Eno the Thracian

C.B. Pratt

To my family

Author's Note:

To avoid tedious scenes of bartering, I have moved the existence of the coin back in time. The Dorians/Greeks had no coinage; everything -- goods, the services of a hero-for-hire -- was 'paid for' with other goods and different services. It was not until approximately four to six hundred years after the time of this book that some clever Lydians, in what is now Turkey, invented the portable, easily recognized, and easily degraded coin.

Copyright Notice:

CHAPTER ONE

Jori, my favorite Phoenician pirate, understood everything about my latest mission except for two things. The how and the why.

"To hunt a harpy is a good and noble act but to capture one and bring it across the sea...this is madness."

"Probably. But it's the best way I know to get five hundred drachma together in a hurry."

He shook his head as if giving me up for lost and toyed with a couple of loose stones atop the sea-wall where we sat. "This cage you mean to build, I have never heard of such a thing. Will it be strong enough?"

"I don't really know. No one has ever tried this before."

"Other people are wise, sometimes. No, no, Eno, my friend, it is madness."

"But you'll take me there?"

Jori tends to fidget when he doesn't want to give a straightforward yea or nay. It's the merchant in him. He always wants to make a deal and you don't get what you want as a trader by saying yes or no without every detail hashed out. That's why, when he gets fed up with negotiations, he turns back to piracy. Piracy is simple.

"Surely you must know someone who can lend you this money?"

"Like who?"

"You have done much work for important people. What about that rich merchant from Carthage? Or King Lycymon? He was very grateful."

My turn to shake my head. "A king's gratitude lasts as long as the walk from the steps of his throne to his front gate. I've never had one yet hand me a basket and the keys to his treasury with orders to help myself."

"But you saved him from poison!"

"Poison administered by his favorite concubine. He was glad to know what was behind all the vomiting, but he hated giving her up. The Queen was pleased."

"Maybe she'll give you the money."

"She wasn't that pleased." She'd offered something, all right, but after witnessing what the king did to his would-be poisoner, I didn't wait around to find out what he did to men who committed adultery with his queen. I told her I was for hire, but not interested in that kind of work, and slipped out a window when the king came in through the bedroom door.

A couple of months ago I got a message from her, reminding me that Lycymon had gone off to Troy with most of the other rulers of Greek city-states and wondering if I was still available for 'hire.' I told her my rates had gone up and am waiting to hear whether it was a real job or just more fun-and-games.

In the loose conglomeration of states, alliances, defeats, and victories that is Hellas, there's a definite pecking order. Astride the top of the heap stand the Olympian Gods, family of Zeus the Mighty. Quarrelsome, proud, immortal, their family troubles often affect the mortal population, almost never to the benefit of the poor working slob who just wants to get his catch in or the harvest safely under cover. There are more gods beyond the Olympians, gods of rain, of wind, of dreams, of sleep. Naiads live in water, dryads live in trees, maenads roam the mountains, any one of which can trip a man up and ruin his life.

Between Gods and mortals are the heroes, men of might and valor clad in supernatural armor and unending self-satisfaction. They are usually related in some degree to the Olympian they are fighting against or for. The Gods admire them as the finest examples of human-kind, though that doesn't always prevent heroes from coming to a sticky end. Their stories are the stuff of legend, told and re-told around countless fires. Emulating them is an excellent way to wind up dead.

So what is a farmer or petty king to do when all the heroes are off fighting somewhere else? Somewhere like Troy, for instance.

The Battle for Troy has been good for my business. With most of the big-name heroes off salvaging Menelaus' pride, wounded by a wandering wife, who are you going to summon to battle the monsters rampaging through your vineyards and carrying off your maidens? What about the guy who'd posted the following in the marketplace?

Hero for Hire. All monsters dispatched from carnivorous geese to Minotaurs. Special rates for multiples. Eno the Thracian at the sign of the Ram's Head, one flight up.

But, to be a bit vain myself, I'm more than your average sword-swinger. Let's say you're a nice young prince, new to the ruling game, and you've got this chief vizier with a square beard and a twisted mind. Sure, you could just hack off his head and hire a fresh face but there's something about the job that turns an ordinary civil servant into a gibbering, war-whooping maniac with eyes for your wife, your daughter, or your throne.

Throw in a few magical powers, and you're going to find yourself in need of some muscle. Muscle alone is all very well but muscle that can outthink the traps, monsters, and mental trickery old Weird Beard has thrown around his Fortress of Death is easily worth an extra five drachma per day. Plus expenses.

I'm getting a reputation for being that man. It doesn't pay all that well but I'm in demand more than ever recently. Business has been picking up as preternatural creatures seem to be on the increase. I'd just gotten back from a nice little job in Syria where...well, another time.

"After all you have said about women, about Queen Helen, now you want to do this because of some girl?" Jori clicked his tongue chidingly.

"I can't very well get married if I can't afford to keep her."

"Keep her? A man does not keep a woman; she keeps him. Come back with me to Tyre. My mother has many fine girls in her eye. She will choose you one. One that can cook. Even pretty if you must be so picky."

"Why doesn't she choose one for you?"

"Oh, she says I am too young to marry."

Jori is maybe three years older than I am, though I admit he doesn't look it. His smooth brown face is hardly weather-beaten at all, considering his profession. He has a few lines around his quick brown eyes, peering under a fringe of smooth hair, that hair enough to mark him out as xeno, Not-Greek. He doesn't seem strong enough to do the heavy work of a ship. I know of at least one sailor, now dead, who thought that a slim, youthful-appearing captain meant an easy mutiny. I didn't see the end result myself, but these stories get around. Sailors gossip more than washerwomen.

He has his own ship, the *Chelidion*, not the biggest or the fanciest but enough to take him around the rim of the known world. Not all the goods she carries appear on a manifest. I travel with him when I happen to be going in the same direction. He claims that his grandfather did a favor for some sea-god or other but says he doesn't know the details. It's why the sea is always calm for him.

I have no quarrel with any supernatural being, from the Olympians down to the weakest sand-sprite, so far as I know. But they can be an easily offended bunch, so I am careful with my lustrations and sacrifices. At the moment, I was wooing Hymen and Aphrodite, all because I'd glimpsed a face in the marketplace.

I'd been buying eggs, a homely pursuit, and turned away just as a girl, an ordinary girl, let the corner of her veil fall. She'd been holding it to her face to keep out the dust and donkey smells. Maybe if she'd been barefaced, I wouldn't have noticed her. As it was, I caught a glimpse of a pink cheek and a pair of eyes that, though dark, were bright as the flicker of a star.

The power of one of Zeus' thunderbolts is nothing compared to Aphrodite's.

I forgot about the eggs, though I'd already paid for them, and turned to follow her. But it was the harvest festival and there were more women in the streets than at any other time so I lost sight of her in the crowds. When I came home, a broadly-grinning messenger boy was waiting on my steps with the eggs and word of her father's name, occupation and directions to his home. There are no secrets in the Piraeus agora.

Her father is an oil merchant, doing good business for himself. Well-enough that he can pick and choose a suitor for his third daughter. A near-penniless hero for hire is not his first choice. But a man with acquaintances among royal houses and strength of arm and head might make a useful son-in-law. And even if Minthe hadn't hit me with a thunderbolt, I might still be interested in marriage into a family like Karoli's. Even heroes have to think about retiring sometime.

So, after a wink and a nod and an introduction from the local matchmaker, I was informed that if I had five hundred drachma tucked away, I could consider myself a son-in-law. There were, however, a couple of other suitors in the hunt, both of whom were younger, better-looking, and didn't have to kill anything or anybody for a living. Sometimes I'd comfort myself with the idea that they were weedy specimens without a good tale to tell between them. But for all I knew, that's what simple, home-loving girls like Minthe preferred.

I would have liked to ask her. But nice girls like that never talked to their future husbands. Or saw them. Or even knew there was such a man until her father told her otherwise.

Fortunately, a day or two later, when I was wracking my brain for a way to come up with the money, I received a messenger from the king of Leros, a small backwater island, with word that his herdsman were being menaced by a harpy.

Over a glass of wine, the messenger mentioned that the harpy seemed to be both small and confused, no doubt in the hope of getting me to lower my prices. I made him a good deal for I knew that the King of Troezen had a standing offer of four hundred drachmas to anyone who could bring him a harpy alive and undamaged.

The King of Troezen loved the hunt and was especially keen on fighting monsters in the good old heroic style, face-to-face, carefully ensuring that the monster was hamstrung or drugged before he risked himself in front of his guests.

So I'd solve the Leronian Harpy issue by capturing it, charging a couple hundred drachmas, and then delivering it to King Pavlos for another four hundred. Everybody's happy and I'm rich enough to marry Minthe and live without working at least until our first baby was born.

I should have remembered that coincidences are always unlucky for me.

* * *

A week later, the *Chelidion* came dancing up to the quay. The cage I was having built was about done and I thought it was just more good fortune that Jori showed up to take me along to Leros.

"Yes," he said at last. "I will take you and your crazy idea there. I will do more. I will wait for you and, if you live, take you to Troezen."

"Have more wine," I pushed a beaker towards him across the sticky table. "How soon can we leave? I don't want anyone else getting there ahead of us."

"What would you have done if I hadn't arrived?"

"Drunk that wine myself," I said, watching the last of it disappear down his throat, "and hired Telamon."

"That fool? He gets lost every time he puts his nose out of port. And his crew are all cut-throats."

"Safety against piracy. I hear a lot of that goes on, this time of year."

He hiccupped when he wanted to laugh and looked cross-eyed at the beaker. Before he fell over, we agreed to meet in two days' time at the boat. He was having her bottom tarred and I needed the time to finish the cage.

It had cost a bit more than I anticipated, as is usually the way with custom work. No ropes tied these corners together. Harpies have sharp claws. The blacksmith had protested the impossibility when I said I wanted the wooden bars joined with iron but on my last visit to the agora, I saw that he'd put up his own placard, describing his new 'method of ironwork, revealed in a dream from the master-contriver, the god Hephaestus himself.'

When I mentioned this questionable advertisement, playfully twisting a few left-over bars of iron into decorative shapes, he threw in the use of a cart to get the thing to the quayside free of charge. Idle boys ran along behind it, any excuse to scamp off school or work. I threw a few hemi-obols among them, remembering my own boyhood craving for sesame honey candy and jellied quince.

Jori had picked up a new crew since I'd last traveled with him. They seemed shy of me. It's the muscles. And maybe my reputation. Lifting the cage into the boat without using the winch might explain their attitude too.

I kept up my exercises during the voyage, having little else to do. Prudently, I skipped my usual swims. Though the sea was flat as my hand, the water was somehow uninviting, greyish-yellow foam scumming the water-line and an oily sheen sliding from one small wave to the next. There was some muttering among the crew at this but Jori soon set them tasks to take their minds off any evil omens they might invent.

"Lazy men," Jori said to me. "It's the last time I take men from Ithaca. King Odysseus took the best with him and all that's left is the dregs of the port. It is the same story all over Hellas these days."

"Do you still run supplies to Troy?"

"No," he said, curling his lip. "The blockade is very strong, like a wall of wood. Now I run supplies to the Greeks."

"The city can't hold out forever." I was only repeating what everyone else said. It had been the better part of two years since Queen Helen had run off with Prince Paris. No one seemed to know if she'd gone of her own free will, or if he'd ensorcelled her somehow. If he had, it was with Aphrodite's contrivance and I wasn't about to utter a word against the Lady. Not with the plans I had in mind.

Thinking of my future wife made the time sweep by. Soon we were looking at the rising coast of Leros. The white houses tumbled like a child's blocks down to the water's edge. Somewhere there was a famous shrine to Artemis, goddess of the hunt among other things, where I would make a sacrifice to implore her good wishes. First stop, however, was the palace.

As we approached the dock, we saw a man waving two red cloths warningly. The keenest-eyed crewmember went to the prow and reported that the dock was half-tumbled into the sea. Jori frowned.

"Your harpy, perhaps?"

"She's not mine yet. Can you get closer?"

"Bad shoals here," Jori said, pointing to where the white water foamed and broke.

I nodded and headed to the waist where our midday meal of bread, oil and dry sausage was being laid out. I emptied the beaker of oil over my best armor, put on that morning, always impressive for the first visit to a new client, and ignored the cook's surprised curse.

One step up to the rail and I dove into the sea.

After a week without much chance to get clean, the warm water was welcome. I turned onto my back to wave at Jori. He shouted over the water, "You are a madman, my friend. When you sink, we'll fish you out!"

I turned the wave into a rude gesture, rolled over, and set as fast a pace as possible toward shore. My ceremonial armor isn't as heavy as the stuff I wear for business but it slowed me down nevertheless. Besides, even with the oil to protect it, I didn't want it to get rusty.

Pulling myself up by the two remaining upright pilings, I shook all over like a wet dog, then promptly drew my short sword.

The signal man, a beardless boy really, gave a squeak of alarm and backed away, shaking his head, "No, no..." he keened.

To him, I must have look like an avenging minion of Poseidon.

Keeping an eye on him, I snatched one of his cloths from his weakened hand and wiped the seawater from my blade before it rusted. It was good bronze, stronger and more expensive than the long one at my side. I figure that if a battle reaches the point where whatever was trying to kill me got past the long sword, I'd want a really, really good short one.

I picked up the other cloth and ran it over my dripping hair, face, and arms. It felt good to have something solid under my feet again.

"Palace up there?" I asked the boy.

He nodded and raised a trembling hand to point up the hillside. I clapped him on the shoulder as I passed, buckling his knees. "Keep up the good work."

"The King won't see you," he piped.

"Eh?"

"He won't see anybody now. Not since it came."

"The harpy?"

He nodded, and looked up at the sky, his large eyes rolling.

"He'll see me, boy. He sent for me."

"Are you...Eno the Thracian?"

I retraced my steps. "I'm Eno, right enough. Who are you and who told you I was coming?"

His round young chin came up. His fear was passing off. I gave him credit. At least he hadn't wee'd himself.

"I'm Prince Temas. This is my island."

"And your father's holed up in the palace? Were you waving those for help or to keep us off?"

"My father...told me to keep ships off. He thinks...he says we are cursed by this thing that has come to us. He's barricaded himself in with a few servants to pray and make sacrifices. I haven't seen him since."

"Well, I'll just go pay a call on him anyway. You come along to show me the way."

It didn't take a whole lot of intellect to notice the gaps in his story. A curse doesn't just happen. Most men have to make a real effort to be worthy of a curse. Murder on a large scale and incest being prime examples of foolishly piquing the attention of the Gods. Even then, the Gods often wait to until someone dies to give some everlasting Underworld punishment, not ordering a beast to curse a whole island kingdom. In any case, why send for me?

The seaside village seemed deserted. Our sandals slapping – or in my case squelching – was the only sound yet I felt the weight of stares on the back of my neck. The prickling feeling in my muscles told me that some part of me was expecting an ambush.

"What of your father's guards? Where are they?"

The prince did not answer. I pivoted and pinned him by his thin neck to a white-washed wall.

He was scarlet-faced, his eyes filled with tears of anger and helplessness. "The...the captain is in the woods on the other side of the island. He says he is king now and will come soon to take over the palace. I'd fight him but how can I? He has men and I have nobody."

"He has not moved against you already?" I slacked the pressure on his neck. "That's bad tactics."

"He doesn't want the harpy to follow him for the crime of killing his sworn king."

"Sensible fellow. How do you know what he's thinking? Or is your father already dead?"

"No! One of the maids comes out to bring back food. She says Father is trying to propitiate the Gods with prayers."

I released him. He rubbed his throat and coughed. "You have no reason to believe me," he said.

I began to have some respect for Prince Temas. Most boys of his age – I'd trained a few during my brief stint in King Cademus' Army before we'd parted ways over a small matter of Dragon's Teeth – would have shown resentment. Temas either didn't feel it or was gifted in concealment. I'd have to bear that second possibility in mind.

"When did the maid last come down for provisions?"

"Two days ago. She should come again today."

"I'll need to get in to see your father. To finalize my contract."

Just then, the shriek of the harpy shredded the air. Partly the scream of a brutalized woman, partly the screech of an eagle spying prey, it dug into the mind like claws into the back of your neck. Though it faded away, some echo remained, rattling in my head like a stone in a dry skull.

The boy clapped his hands over his ears, bending down low, his own cry of agony a faint imitation of the harpy's shriek. "Do you see it? Do you see it?"

I scanned what I could see of the clear blue sky. "No, there's nothing."

I looked at the boy, seeing him sweating and shaking. "Come now," I said, shrugging off my own unease. "It's just the cry of a mindless beast."

"You don't know. It grows worse with every repetition. You start to think you hear it even when no one else does."

I made a mental note to acquire some wax before leaving Leros. Wax pellets in the ears should keep the crew from panicking. Pirates have their own sign language, useful for night attacks so temporary deafness shouldn't impair the running of the ship.

The boy sniffled and wiped his hands over his face as though he were awakening from a dream. His eyes were glazed. I had to repeat my question twice to get his attention.

"The palace?" he murmured.

"Yes, the place you live. Where the king is?"

He seemed to have to think about it. "Past the olive grove and the spring. That way."

"Come on; you'll show me."

He hung back. "He doesn't want to see me."

"I want you to tell the maid to let me in." I had to grip his arm to get him to move. The cry of the Harpy seemed to have sucked the spine right out of him.

The white walls of the seaside village seemed to magnify the silence as we heading out on the single road. Though it was nearly noon, there was no smell of cooking coming from any house. No face peeped around a door and no shutter opened but the feeling I had of being watched persisted.

Outside of town, signs of life at last. Two dogs dug listlessly at the edge of a garbage dump only to slink away without barking as we passed. The boy stared after them. "I think those were two of my father's dogs." If I hadn't tightened my grip, he would have wandered off after them.

"Later," I said. "Show me the palace."

Temas turned sulky. "I already told you! Keep straight on and you can't miss it."

I'd heard that before, usually just before getting lost. "I want you to show me the way. The maid will be frightened of me. You can talk to her first."

The road was hard-packed dirt. Our sandals kicked up no dust. A trickle of water grew louder as we passed through some trees. It was probably refreshingly shady before the branches had been lopped for firewood.

A drink from the spring, bubbling up in a stone basin, seemed to restore the prince's rattled brain. "Father's going to be pissed about the trees. But the people are scared to go any farther for wood than they need to."

He clasped his hands together reverently and said to the water, "I will bring you a libation and sacrifice for the desecration of your grove, oh Lady of the Spring."

The tops of the trees rustled in a breeze that had not blown before. A sweeter scent seemed to arise around us, though no flowers bloomed there. I coughed to draw the nymph's attention. "I have seen bright tiles in the Athenian agora, brought all the way from Gaul. Should my task prosper, I send some to this prince to add to your fountain."

The breeze grew stronger, caressed my cheek, and faded away. It was, therefore, with a bit of added confidence that I approached the palace. A two-story, four-square building, it stood on a smoothed prominence overlooking the sea-road. Jori's ship was far below, tiny, seeming not to move on the sea which lay spread before me like a wrinkled blanket.

An enclosed balcony overhung the sea cliffs. The air shimmered as though heated by a brazier, a hair-thin plume of smoke curling up from a corner.

"My father has retreated there," the Prince said, pointing.

"We couldn't have missed the maid?"

"No, Nausicaa always comes this way. There is no other path."

A locked door, even a palace door bound with brass, wouldn't have stopped me. But battered wood hanging from a hinge, while impressive, tends to annoy prospective clients when it is their front door.

So we hung around for a while. The boy showed me a half-finished statue of the Sea-God standing in what might one day be a fine arbor. The head, one arm and a massive torso, as yet lightly modeled, seemed struggling to be free of the encompassing marble. The chippings were piled around the base, a chisel and a hammer half-buried among them.

"Where's the craftsman?"

"Gone...on the first boat after the harpy came." Temas glanced skyward. "This garden used to be full of butterflies. My father liked to sit here while a harpist played." He sighed. "There was this one dancing girl who had this way of bending backwards.... It's all gone now. Ever since the harpy came."

Though the bushes were losing their shapes and the paved walks were dirty and leaf-strewn, I could sense the peace that had once bloomed here like the small white flowers. I shook off the spell. "None of this is getting me my commission."

I turned to see a woman, her hair shrouded by a cloth, come out of a side door. The prince called her name. "Nausicaa!"

She saw us. Even from a distance, we could see the start she gave as she recognized the Prince. She threw up a hand as if to block a sudden beam of bright light and immediately turned back to the door.

"Come on," I said. "Something's wrong."

CHAPTER TWO

At a jog, I reached the side door before she could shut it fully.

She cowered back as I entered. I was blinded for a moment in the contrast between the brightness of outside and the dimness within. An oil lamp burned before an altar to one side. I smelled baking bread and burned meat and I heard the whispers of startled women and their movements in the gloom. I confess my hand was clamped to my sword though I did not draw it.

Prince Temas entered behind me and called the maid's name. "What's wrong? Why did you run from me?"

I could see her now. She had the worn and weary strength of a life spend in service to others. Her cheeks were fallen in, her hair twisted into a wiry knot. Her lips worked soundlessly. She sank to her knees, hands high, open palms in supplication. "Forgive, lord. Forgive!"

As though her keening summoned them, the other servants appeared, all dropping to their knees, some crawling forward to grasp at the hem of the boy's chiton. A few of the younger maids were bawling, their tears dripping onto their shawls.

I guessed what it all meant while Temas was still gaping around. He knew these people well but he'd never seen them behave with this mixture of grief and terror. I'd seen it often enough. I'd even caused it a few times. Death had visited this house today.

I headed to the stairs at the back of the kitchen. The maid called out, "No, no, no!" an expression more of pain than of denial. "Stop him, lord."

"Eno, maybe you...what's this all about, Nausicaa?"

The smell of smoke grew sharper as I climbed. At first, it reminded me of the yearly sacrifice of an unblemished white bull to the Thunderer. I'd met the wrangler at the last year's ceremony. He told me how they hand-raised the bulls from birth, and how they'd every day draw a blunted blade along the bull's throat until the animal grew to expect it, raising its head for the treat. They would suspect nothing then when the priest cut their throats on the altar. Most people think it is a miracle that the bulls lift their heads for the stroke. I wish I still thought that.

As I climbed the stairs though, the smell began to remind me of something else, darker yet than the betrayal of the bulls.

I'm about thirty, according to my mother. My first experience in the hero business was when my village was plagued by man-eating horses the spring I turned sixteen. Several hunters had gone to rout them out but none had returned. Being big for my age always, when a more organized group went up into the hills, I went along.

What we found were not horses but men; a family of cannibals, traveling from place to place, seeking what they might devour. We attacked their cave stronghold with fire and sword, slaughtering them as they'd slaughtered others.

For days afterwards, I could smell the greasy odor of cooked human flesh that had permeated their hiding place, their clothing, even their skin. I'd wrestled one of their grimy, mad-eyed boys when he'd leaped on me, teeth clinking together as he snapped for my throat.

I'd never killed before but rage burned my heart when I'd seen the half-devoured carcass of my mother's brother, my favorite uncle. An upward stab with the knife I'd almost forgotten I carried ended the boy's life and then another, the female who came at me to avenge him. I seemed to feel the stickiness of their blood again on my right hand as I reached the top of the stair. I gagged as the filthy smell reached me. Nothing else smells like a burning human being.

I had guessed the King of Leros was already dead. But I felt a dread apart from that when I kicked open the door to the room where the king had hidden himself away from everyone.

Long curtains flew, beckoning me through the room and out onto the enclosed balcony. My sense that I approached something vastly unclean grew stronger. Dark magic had been done here. Symbols were scrawled on the floor and ceiling, symbols that seemed to move with fetid life of their own.

The fire smoldered in a wide copper-lined pit in the center of the tiled floor. A bundle of sacking or old clothes had fallen across it, smothering the fire even as the fire consumed it.

Covering my nose, I thrust open the shutters, my palm landing in something sticky. Turning with the light behind me, I saw the 'sacking' was the body of the king. A bloody knife, the handle a leering satyr's head, lay where it had fallen from his hand. Blood had sprayed the wall and the shutters. I didn't need to look to know my palm was red.

"Father?" Prince...King Temas called from the chamber beyond.

"Here. He's here. He's dead."

Temas came through the curtains, his face the same dingy white as his chiton, and stopped short. "By the Gods...what happened to him?"

"Sacrifice, I think. But to who and why?"

"Sacrifice," he echoed, staring at the body.

"What cults did your father follow?"

"Zeus, of course, and Artemis. We have this temple. It's famous. But for the rest...human sacrifice is abhorrent to the Gods. Everyone knows that."

He took a step forward and one of the symbols lifted a hooded head. Temas had all but put his foot on it. The snake hissed and bobbed its head, preparing to strike.

Temas stood statue-like, the angle of his thigh between my knife and the snake. I took one slow, gliding step and then another. The cobra was too focused on Temas to notice me.

Seizing it behind the hood, I lifted three feet of thrashing, twisting muscle straight up into the air. A stroke of my knife separated head from body. The long body fell, writhing. I threw the head, fangs still a-drip, into the coals. It was the largest snake I'd ever killed thus far.

Temas paid little attention. He dropped to his knees, pushing the corpse of his father off the remains of the fire. It had devoured the king's chest, leaving it like a half-burned log on a campfire. The smell of burned human flesh arose stronger than before. I was reminded again of sacrifice. His throat was cut, open like a smiling second mouth, gleaming white and red, butcher's work.

He lay now face-up in the shaft of sunlight. It showed clearly the two shallow cuts high on the left side, under the jaw, as well as the deep crimson cut that exposed the severed vessels in his throat. The gout of blood had stopped the fire from consuming the upper part of his clothes. They were of a style strange to me, a flowing robe with a wide embroidered collar and cuffs tight to the wrists. The symbols were soaked with red but those that escaped the deluge looked much like the ones drawn on the floor.

I spoke my thought aloud. "This room reeks of dark magic."

"My father knew nothing about such things."

"Well, for an amateur, he's done very well."

"I don't understand any of this. It isn't like him. What was he trying to do?"

"Propitiate some god by the looks of it. Or expiate some sin. A sin big enough to punish him and his people with a harpy?"

"There was nothing, I swear," he said passionately, tears starting in his eyes. "He was a good king, wise and loved. And a good father too."

"No man can ever answer for another's soul."

His straining eyes stared at the great wound in his father's throat. "Could the harpy have done this?" he asked, pointing with a trembling finger. "I see marks like claws there."

"Most men make a couple of tries before slitting their throats, sire." I laid a hand on his shoulder and felt the jolt that went through him as I became the first to call him that. "Call your servants to prepare the body for the funeral."

While he was gone, I built up the fire to burn the snake's body, and tore a strip off the curtains to bind up the late king's throat. I didn't want his head falling off when the servants lifted him up.

Then I vomited out the window.

Downstairs, I found a boy to carry a message to Jori, telling him that the situation had grown more complex and that I doubted I'd be back on the ship tonight. Having been on cases with me before, I knew he would not be too surprised by any of it.

With a sigh, I went, again, in search of a king.

* * *

He sat on the ground near the half-created statue as though his knees had failed him just there. His eyes were red. He knuckled them roughly with a boy's shame, the tear marks like creek beds down his cheeks.

I had grabbed a straw-covered jug as I'd passed the kitchen altar. Tugging out the cork with my teeth, I took a sniff. My own eyes watered at the harsh bouquet of the local wine.

"Drink deep. It'll help."

He swigged it as though he'd been given it in his cradle. The color surged back into his face.

"Better?"

He nodded, wiped the lip of the jug with a grimy thumb and handed it back to me. "It's our best yet."

"The Goddess won't grudge it," I murmured. He hadn't realized where I'd gotten from 'til then and he cast a glance skyward as I drank.

One sip and I saw I'd wasted my efforts upstairs. To anyone used to the wine of Leros, cobra venom was a mild tonic suitable for peaky children and sickly kittens.

When I could use my voice again, I asked the question I'd wanted to ask his father. "So...this harpy problem. Your father's man offered...."

"Whatever Phandros offered, I'll double! All our misfortunes fell on us when this thing came upon us. My father would never have committed suicide except for that!"

I was tempted - a double fee would mean I could just kill the creature instead of transporting it across the sea. Easier all around.

But I'd already paid for the cage. That, and the Hero's Code, decided for me.

"I couldn't do that. Your representative and I already worked out a price. Speaking of which, where is Phandros? Didn't he come back ahead of me from Athens?"

"He's down at the taverna most days. He's been drinking a lot since my father threw him out. He'll be back as soon as he hears the news."

No doubt the boy I'd sent to Jori would be at pains to tell everyone he could find about the old king's death. Bad news travels on the wind as effortlessly as a bird.

I'd given Temas three swigs to every one of mine. So he was nicely blurry when Phandros came up, long beard blowing in the breeze. The prince hailed him even as the newcomer hesitated. "Phandros! Come to mourn or celebrate?"

"I cannot guess your meaning," Phandros said, bowing austerely. He nodded to me, in brief recognition. "I grieve for your loss, King Temas. Your father was a great and noble king and shall be long remembered. But now we must look to the future."

I hadn't cared much for Phandros when we'd worked out our deal. He was thin and pale, with a greenish tinge like a reed dipped in fat. It had been dark in the bar and I'd had a hard time resisting the urge to light his head. He had a high arched nose, ideal for sneering down. I now knew why it was so very red at the tip.

For the rest, his hair was dirty white and swept off a high brow over eyes too small for his face. He was missing an eyetooth on the right. I wondered who had tired of his permanent sneer and tried to knock it off. Whoever it had been, I liked him already.

Temas pointed at me. "He's going to destroy the harpy for me."

"I hold to our bargain, Master Phandros."

"No doubt," he said, running his hand down his beard, "but does my lord forget that there are other, nearer, dangers? Mortal dangers?"

"He means the guards," Temas said in an aside to me.

"Word will reach them soon of your father's passing. They will not long delay their attack. They know we are defenseless."

Temas seemed to be squinting down the neck of the bottle. "What would you have me do, counselor to my late father? What wise words made him kick you downstairs?"

The bony face showed two pink patches on the cheekbones matching the wine stains on his tunic. "I spoke true. We must leave, seek assistance from another kingdom. Your uncle, Scoros of Phyros, would grant you ships and troops. Leave Leros to this captain and return in force to rout him out. There is a ship in the Roads now; take it."

Temas seemed now to be attempting to balance the bottle on one outstretched finger. It fell, of course, but did not break thanks to the stone chips littering the ground. He stared at it, his eyes round as an owl's. He glanced at me. "What think you of wise, frightened Phandros' counsel, Eno the Thracian?"

"I don't think he's a coward, or he would have run away in Athens."

Phandros bowed to me with gracious irony. "Praise indeed."

"It's your kingdom now," I said, ignoring him. "I'd not give bits of it away to anyone else. Scoros is known as a hard bargainer. He does nothing from kindness, not even for close family. He might help you and leave you penniless, prey to the next renegade."

"There are other kings to aid you if you don't trust Scoros. But if you do not seek aid, sire, Captain Eurytos and his men will overwhelm you."

Temas stood up, swaying slightly. "My father was a good king before these trib-trib-troubles came on us. I haven't his wisdom. But I can rec-hic-ernize a gift from the gods when it appears before me. Phandros...where are you...Phandros...."

"My lord?"

"Persuade Eno the Thracian to send the Captain and his fellows to Hades."

"Sire," Phandros whispered. "He is but one man."

"Then you help him." Temas walked away, his left sandal not knowing what his right sandal was doing. He didn't seem to hear Phandros' gargling protest. I knew the boy was weeping again.

I turned to Phandros, staring him down. "What villagers have experience in arms?"

"Few indeed." Holding his elbow tight to his hip, Phandros extended his hand, flat, in the ancient sign that bargaining had begun. "I am prepared to offer three hundred for this task. In addition to our agreement regarding the harpy."

"How many guards are with this Captain?"

"Ten. They killed two, including the lieutenant, when they refused to betray the...er...late king."

"Only ten some guards for a place this size?"

"Our other soldiers went to Troy to honor our treaty with Menelaus."

"Then the Captain has not held his place for long?"

"No, indeed. Had our prince been older, he would have taken the command. Being but a lad, however...."

"And now he is king and no older than he was."

Phandros looked grim. "He has always been a sensible boy. I have known other princelings who have run wild, chasing nymphs, racing chariots, torturing their slaves. When I was tutor to the forty-seven sons of Pharaoh...no matter. Yet even a careful boy may make unwise choices in such dark times."

I thought of the hacked trees of the sacred grove, of desperate men, of the unseen villagers. "Twelve hundred," I said boldly and added, "And I'll recruit some new troops for Leros when I get home. At no extra charge." Though they'd pay for transporting and feeding them.

"Twelve! Absurd. Six hundred."

When we'd negotiated before, he'd gone up in increments of no more than fifty. That he made a two hundred drachma leap told me he had no faith in the outcome. He might have as well agreed to my first – admittedly overlarge – demand as a promise to a walking dead man but there was always the slimmest chance that I might come back alive. Then he'd have to pay up. He might not like the House of Leros much but he was the kind who hated to pay out anybody's money.

"This Captain...where'd you find him?"

"He came highly recommended from King Cadmus."

"Cadmus? I wonder if I know him. What's his name?"

"Eurytos, or Eurytacles. Something of that sort. Our late king hired him while I was away on business for him. The fellow seemed to understand his duties well enough but he and I had little to do with each other. Not a man of letters...or numbers. He'd be hard pressed to count to ten, I fancy, even if he had both hands."

"Missing a hand, is he? Ten-fifty."

"Nine hundred. Yes, he wears a claw fashioned like a crab's."

"Doesn't sound familiar. Nine-fifty and I bring back both head and claw."

"Done," Phandros said and spit to seal the bargain. I spit into the same dirt to bind our words together.

I felt pretty pleased with myself. Nine-fifty in addition to my other fees and I could perhaps realize a long-held dream. More than one father had offered a younger son to me as an apprentice. I'd always refused, having seen more than enough brave but badly trained men die. But if I could found a school, a school for heroes, then they wouldn't be prey for the first Caledonian boar or Nemean lion they came across. And

I could pass on what I had learned, not just sword-work or spear-throwing, but the little details. How to get ichor out of leather, how to refuse a sorceress without waking up with two heads, how to ask for a blacksmith or a well-grilled octopus in four languages including Upper Egyptian.

"Any of the villagers have military experience?" I asked again.

"Not one.' Phandros shook his head, then touched it gently as though to be sure it hadn't fallen off. He held his wine well but the signs still showed in his yellowed eyeballs and lightly tremulous hands.

"What about you?"

"I? I am a scholar, not some vulgar brawler."

I drew my knife and threw it at him in a forward pass, the blade whistling toward his eyes.

He snatched it by the hilt as it passed his face, reversed it and drew back to return it. Then his thought caught up with his body and he let the knife roll off his fingers. "I abhor violence."

"But you are not unfamiliar with it? Come on, Phandros.   What's   the   story?"

He did not answer me, though he opened his mouth as if to speak. A shudder broke over him. "It's near," he muttered. "So near."

Then I heard it too. On the very edge of perception, a keening wail that made the hair on my arms stand up.

Something like a cloud but darker and swifter passed over the sun, dimming the bright day, turning the green grass to dun.

Sudden pain made me look down. Phandros' bony fingers gripped my wrist. "We must get inside. If it sees us while hunting, nothing will keep it off."

"Have you seen it?"

"Only as a fell shadow across the moon when first it came. And I have seen what is left of the sheep after it feeds."

"Only sheep?" I asked. "That's unusual."

"So many have fled to the sea or the hinterlands that it may well have killed half a dozen people and we'd not know of it."

It is true that in such confusion, given a monster, a king who had shown no leadership, and absconding citizens, the ordinary bonds between people would shatter. Captain would break faith with king, husband flee from wife, mother abandon child, mankind would turn from their Gods. Anyone might be destroyed and, without those bonds that tie us to one another, no one would pay attention to anything but saving their own necks.

But if the harpy had killed anyone, I felt it would become known. Harpies are not neat in their habits. Entrails in the trees would be the least of it.

At this appetizing moment, we were called in to eat.

The maids washed our hands and feet while Nausicaa made formal apology for Temas' non-appearance. I acted as though I believed the excuse of sudden illness and apologized in turn for remaining in the house during their mourning for the king.

After some minutes of this, we were served. The bread and cheese were excellent, the lamb rich with onions and spices in a recipe new to me. I stayed away from the wine, despite Nausicaa's pressing me, except to pour a libation on the household altar.

I felt guilty at having snatched the goddess' flagon, even if it was in a good cause. I promised her a new stola as the red one around her shoulders had seen brighter days.

But I sighed a little. So far this job had cost one cage, one sea journey, some tiles and now a stola. And

I'd only had a small sum down on deposit. I'd have to hit Phandros up for an increased advance on the new job.

Nausicaa showed me to a small chamber, pleasantly scented with verbena and herbs. Her voice was low with a rough note. "Lay aside your armor, master, and take your afternoon rest."

I thanked her but made no move toward hasp or strap. "What can you tell me of the king's mood this last day?"

"I? Nothing. I am but a maid servant here."

"But of long service. All your life, perhaps?"

"Not so. I came here with my mistress from Lesbos when she arrived as a bride to the King."

"She is dead?"

Nausicaa inclined her head. Even the lowest women of their island bore themselves like queens. This one looked over my head like a queen ignoring a dirty servant. "Four years ago of a summer fever. It struck suddenly and hard."

"Yet the king did not remarry. Why not?"

"I was not in his confidence regarding such personal matters."

"But you were about other things?"

Her gaze flickered to meet mine for an instant. Those black eyes held no humility, no consciousness that she was a mere servant. Pride ran through her like a vein of gold in white quartz. You'd have to break her to get it out.

"What did the symbols on the floor mean?"

"I saw none."

"Come now! You washed the floor or the others did. I'll ask them."

"We did our duty but we saw no such marks."

"I suppose there were none on the robe he wore either. Did you sew it for him? Did you embroider the collar and the cuffs?"

"My Lord King was naked but for a loincloth when we carried him away. I saw no such robe." She turned toward the shuttered window. "Will you have this open? It is stuffy in here."

I knew she was lying but such women would face torture sooner than say anything of discredit to the families they serve. I've never kept one myself who wouldn't blab my every action all over the marketplace. Maybe you have to born into the right kind of family.

There was only one thing that surprised me. When she turned from the window, the light caught her face. I looked at her more closely. I saw that her face was as white and wet as curds. Maybe she wasn't lying to protect the King's memory. She was terrified and I thought I knew what it was. In plenty of royal households, if the king should die, his servants were put to torture to determine whether they'd had a hand in the death. Some new kings even slaughtered staff wholesale just to ease their suspicions. As it turned out, I was quite wrong about that. Nausicaa wasn't afraid of being killed.

I dismissed her, telling her I would nap for a time but wished to be awakened before dusk so I might go up to Artemis' temple to beseech a blessing on my work.

"The Temple? It is closed...for repairs."

"I wish only to offer a prayer," I said. "I won't bother anyone or stay long."

She caught her lower lip with her teeth. I felt that I'd caught her off-guard but a woman like that was never off-guard for long. "Besides, it is a holy day."

"It is?"

"Our priestesses hold to an older worship than you might find in a larger city. It is ancient and must not be defiled by men."

That was three excuses for why I couldn't go to the Temple. In my experience, the truth never needs more than one. What was this maid trying to keep from me?

"The goddess and I are old comrades. I invoke her aid on my every hunt. Against this harpy I will need her more than ever. Surely the priestesses cannot object to a truly reverent visit...even from a man."

"I am going there myself, ere long," Nausicaa said slowly. "I will ask if you are to be permitted to enter. Do not take it amiss if they say no. They are very old and set in their ways."

Four excuses? Something was definitely up. "That is all I ask," I said.

After a few minutes, I opened my door and stopped a girl carrying a bucket. She looked at me with eyes so wide I could see the whites all around. I didn't question her. I had no doubt Nausicaa had been before me. Nobody would talk now about what had happened to the king. "Get me a cloak, girl. A dark one."

She must have run both ways for she returned breathless. Pretty thing; I chucked her chin and won a smile.

I flung the cloak over my head and left the house. Just in time too. Nausicaa had just slipped away into the grove beyond the palace.

She too wore a cloak but I am used to tracking and she was not used to being followed. There was hardly a twig to crack under my feet. As in the sacred grove, frightened villagers had picked up all the available wood.

After a time, Nausicaa came out onto the road. As I expected, she stopped and cast a nervous glance around. I stood still, hidden in shadow. She walked on, away from the village and the palace. I kept to the verge in case she turned again.

Nausicaa should have been at home, bringing the mourning clothes out of verbena-scented chests, hunting out gold coins for her master's eyes, driving underlings to distraction and preparing to pour dust on her head in the funeral procession. Something more important had drawn her from her kitchen and I wanted to know what it was.

The trees on this side of the island leaned over as thought straining to escape a fierce and relentless wind. But the treetops were still, not a leaf rustled. I heard no birds, either, and saw no life, not even a spider.

As I followed the maidservant towards a sunlit clearing, my cloak was caught by crooked branches like grasping fingers. Shaking free, I almost tripped over a vine crossing my foot, though there had been none there a moment before. Even as I watched, another shoot crawled up to clutch lightly around my ankle.

Strangely, I felt no sense of threat. Something here did not want me to follow the woman but prevented me more as a nurse blocks a child's impetuousness for its own security rather than in anger.

Through the last, straggling trees, I saw Artemis' temple. Much the same size as the palace but with a cluster of smaller buildings nestled around its skirts, shrines to the other gods. Nausicaa hurried up the main steps, taking her cape from her shoulders and, swinging it wide, turned it inside out. I saw a flash as of gold from the folds even as I heard the clang of the large brass doors as she entered.

I felt it was safe to follow now despite there being no more cover. Gently picking off the vine entangling in my sandal, I crossed the border between trees and clearing.

Instantly, I was driven to my knees by a malevolence as strong and startling as the blare from ten thousand ill-tuned battle trumpets. Every sense was blinded. A blast of malice that seemed made of every evil thought ever directed at me ripped at my mind and body. I could all but feel the poisoned claws pierce and tear my skin.

I confess I crawled back to the shelter of the woods. Instantly, the pain passed. I stood bent over under one great tree, hands on my thighs as I fought for breath and for control of my galloping heart. A passing breeze rattled the leaves over my head. A whisper seemed to speak my name and to say, "You should not stay here...."

I was alone but stood in a landscape where any tree might hide a spirit. "I must go on," I said aloud.

"Fool...."

Delicately, two branches dipped as though to shelter me. I looked up into the shifting play of light through the golden-green leaves. "What lies beyond those temple doors? What have you seen?"

"Death..."

As the dryad whispered to me, I could feel the whole tree shiver with something that was not the breeze. What could frighten a tree-spirit so much?

Looking about me, I saw that the grass stopped growing right at the point where I'd felt the scourging hatred rip at my body and mind. It was as if a line had been drawn with acid. What could hate even the grass?

CHAPTER THREE

This time, teeth gritted, I ran straight toward the temple doors, feeling as though I dodged a flight of arrows. I was doing well, head up and lungs working, until I tripped and landed sprawling in the dirt.

The hatred flattened me at once as if a boulder had tumbled off a cliff, crushing me to the earth. My tongue clove to the roof of my mouth and began to swell. The swelling spread to my throat, cutting off my air. I felt a rope tightening, though there was nothing there. I forced my hand down lest I strangle myself.

I could not go back; my pride would not let me flee a second time. I had either to go on or to die here in the dirt like an exhausted animal. I fought with the part of me that wanted to turn back, ordering it to keep faith as though it were a cowardly soldier deserting in the heat of conflict. I had faced men and monsters; a mere feeling had no power over me. I would not be so constrained.

I got painfully onto one knee, straightened my legs, and rose up, feeling the implacable hatred burning on my skin as though I passed through an acid-cloud from the heart of a volcano. In a crouch, my breath coming short, tears and sweat mingling, I pressed on slowly, step by dragging step. The malice seemed to increase with each strike of my boot until I felt as though I were pushing a huge rock before me. A moment's inattention and it would roll back to crush me into paste.

I looked up to find my foot on the first white marble step of the temple entrance. I drew my first full breath since leaving the woods. The horrible malignity that had tortured me had ebbed. I could not tell if it was gone or merely withdrawn for the moment.

I laid one hand against the temple door and the other on my sword.

Inside, all was dark and cool. My bursting lungs eased, though a faint scent of rot seemed carried on a chilling breeze over the floors. Tall columns lost their capitals in the darkness of the timbered roof. A lamp burned in the peristyle, its many-paneled red glass sides doing nothing to illuminate the space. A basin of water stood to one side. I staggered to it, wishing to test whether my throat really had grown closed. Perhaps it was just the red light, but it looked as if the basin were filled with blood.

I decided I wasn't that thirsty, though a moment before I would have sold my mother for a drink.

Directly in my ear, a woman laughed softly. I turned, sword out. No one was there, though I had distinctly felt breath tickling my skin.

Anger strengthened me. No matter how sick I felt, I wasn't about to let invisible women laugh at me.

I could see the altar now, the massive statue of the goddess gleaming twenty feet tall, her face far above the reach of mortal hands. Only prayers could reach her. Floating veils of smoke obscured her face, thickening into blankets exactly wherever I wanted to look. There seemed to be something not quite right about the goddess, especially the shape of her head.

I slashed with my sword in frustration. The veils dropped, falling to the floor in pieces like solidified grease on a pot of cold soup. It reliquefied as it hit the stone floor. A nauseating smell arose, like a garbage pile on a steamy summer's day, worsening to gag-level when I inadvertently stepped in a puddle.

I strode up to the altar, imagining that here, if anywhere, there'd be sanctuary. Forever fleet and young, Artemis had little to do with men except in her role as goddess of the hunt. I'd meant to implore her aid in my primary quest but my new mandate had taken me far beyond that purely selfish pursuit. She might have helped me hunt a harpy but now I had men to hunt as well.

"Oh, virgin inviolable...guide of arrows, huntress, Artemis...."

The laughter came again, muffled as though by a hand. It came from the goddess herself, far above my head.

"Come nearer, insignificant creature." The voice was harsh with a hiss in it as of snakes.

Torches flared into life and light. I leaned back to look upwards and yet more upwards.

The head of the statue had been hacked off. In its place, joined to the marble neck, was block of roughly carved black wood. Three hideous faces, with mouths obscenely open and starting eyes, had been carved into the sides, blending one into another. By some sorcery, the head slowly revolved upon the neck, showing each grimacing horror in turn.

I am not particularly religious but I know Blasphemy when I see it.

Then all three pairs of eyes snapped open their lids and living eyes focused down on me. The malice I'd met outside was like a tossed bouquet of spring flowers in comparison. The intensity of their malevolence could have flayed the skin right off me. The chuckle came again, harsh but sweeter, like poison cloaked in honey.

"Who are you?" I demanded, only my voice came out in treble squeak.

"I am She Who Opens the Gate."

"What gate?"

"The Gate between your world and the dark on the other side. Look upon me. I judge all...and will judge you."

For a long, long time I stared up into those red eyes, eyes both frigid and burning, that looked into me without pity or even justice. I felt she hated me and all human things with a hatred all the more implacable for its eternal coldness that no feeling or thought could ever touch. I thought I bore it for an hour, but it was hardly thirty beats of a thundering heart before I couldn't bear it another instant.

I held up the flat of my sword like a shield between my gaze and that hideousness. But my curiosity came back, stronger in me than fear. I peered over the edge. The cruelty that had pinned me down was withdrawn for a moment. "I had high hopes of you, for you are reputed to be brave. I see now that you are a child afraid of a nightmare," the harsh voice said with infinite contempt. "Die in one now."

I took a fighting position, crouching to minimize vulnerable areas, knees bent, feet planted firmly but lightly for balance and mobility.

Nothing happened, except the foul smell grew stronger.

After a moment more when nothing happened, I stood up and went to look for the entrance to the interior rooms. Her mocking laughter followed me.

As I thought, the door was behind the statue for ease of access by the priestesses. I wondered where they were and was afraid I knew. No true daughter of the Moon would have permitted such a travesty to stand in her lady's place while breath still moved her body.

Just as I put my hand on the door, I heard a knocking. At first, I thought it came from the door before me but quickly realized someone was knocking on the entrance door to the temple. Thinking perhaps

Phandros or Temas had followed me, I called out to them, warning them not to enter.

The door opened and in walked The Dead.

The King was first as the most recent to die. He held one hand, nails already blackening, to the makeshift bandage around his throat and moaned as he came on.

Following him, two men in dusty armor, dried blood crusting on their necks and faces. Their eyes were rolled up so only the whites showed but they shuffled toward me as if they could still see.

The next, of many, was a child, a naked baby boy, hardly able to toddle. His stomach was grossly distended. He trailed one hand along the temple wall for balance. Where his tiny fingers dragged the stone crumbled away.

The door behind the statue was false sanctuary. For all I knew, it was locked and I didn't want to be pounding on it when those questing hands touched me.

Sheathing my longer sword and clenching my short one in my teeth, I turned to the statue and began to climb. My knee on the stone thigh, a quick slightly blasphemous grasp of firm marble breasts, and I was up, standing on smooth white shoulders. I hoped Artemis wouldn't mind; as I said, she's been known to be touchy about such things.

The horrible rotating head was between my thighs. I gripped it about the ears with my knees, stopping the movement though I felt the unseen force resisting my strength, trying still to turn. "They're coming for you, Thracian," it said, laughing again. The voice echoed weirdly, coming from three mouths at once.

I glanced down at the dead ones, milling about, moaning as they touched each other, ripping away putrid flesh. Several women, still pregnant with the infants that had killed them, were clawing at the base of the statue itself. I felt it rock as one took a stronger swipe at the pedestal. One way or another, it was coming down.

With my sword now in one hand and my dagger in the other, I began to scissor away at the joining of wood and stone. The power that had called out the dead was centered here. Destroy it and, with luck, they'd fall quiet again.

A good theory but my progress was slow. I tried not to look down a second time. I was already working as hard as I could. But a gurgle of happy laughter in that setting so surprised me that I couldn't help but glance down.

One of the women had snatched up the gray-skinned little boy and was cradling him to her bosom. She was rocking back and forth, crooning something that might have once been a lullaby. He was pressing a gentle hand to her sunken cheek, leaving no wounds. They had forgotten about everything else. Something infinitely sweet had survived not only the grave but even the dark power that animated their bodies.

The head between my knees shuddered and ceased its struggle to turn. Shaking off my amazement, I struck a blow and chips began to fly from the statue instead of flakes. Though the eyes fluttered and the mouths gaped, the monstrosity was at least silent now.

None of the other walking dead had paid any attention to the touching reunion. They continued to claw at the statue, though their strength seemed to have grown less.

Hearing a hiss, I glanced down below me. One of the dead guards had dug his fingers deep into the statue's backside and was attempting to pull himself up to me. I kicked him in the head and he tumbled down, knocking over both former king and comrade.

My arms were aching and the sweat kept dripping into my eyes. The dead were causing the statue to totter but they had no idea of teamwork. The women scrabbled at the front, trying to reach me but unable to do more than dig at the plinth, the king and his men were doing better but unable to come at me more than one at a time. I couldn't be sure that I was doing any more damage than they were. I could, however, feel confident that if I were to fall, my life would be done one way or another. They must not have had any such comfort.

A new fear reinforced all the others. Would I die? Or would I lurch to my feet and wander, blind, grasping fingers destroying everything they touched? I started to hack with greater violence at the neck, grunting with every blow, trying to achieve some kind of proper sword position so that I could cut even more deeply. There wasn't really enough room to get a good swing going.

More of the dead had come in, old men, a maiden or two, more children, some things hardly recognizable as once human dragging themselves over the threshold. The smell was growing worse by the moment, nastier than a battlefield on the third day of a heat-wave.

The ceiling was just above the statue. I braced myself, arms above my head, and began kicking at the nearest face. Again and again I hit the same spot, hoping I'd hacked out enough of the neck to make the head topple over like a half-cut tree in the woods.

Finally, though I jarred loose several of my teeth, I put all my strength in such a violent kick that the thing flew off, ricocheting from one pillar to the next, bowling over some corpses and splattering two or three others into fragments. The instant it rolled to a stop, however, out of sight behind a curtain, all the walking Dead fell down, empty of all will, all life, once again.

My troubles weren't over. The headless statue began to lean forward inexorably. I had nothing to hold onto; besides, being left hanging twenty-five feet up in the air wasn't an attractive prospect.

I dropped, sliding down the goddess' marble back to wrap my arms desperately around the remains of her slender throat. I shut my eyes tight in anticipation of a bone-shattering fall.

The echoes of the crash banged around from one side of the temple to the other. Dust, more dust than one would have thought possible, flew up and sifted down. Coughing, I sat up and slid off the statue. It had broken in several pieces, arms off, legs snapped at the ankles. Luckily, I'd been on the most solid bit.

I looked around at the Dead, pitiable, huddled things now that the will that had driven them to attempt my destruction was withdrawn. I couldn't see the mother and child whose coming together had altered the spell.

I'd always heard that death severed all bonds, that one died and drank from the River Lethe, causing one to forget all mortal ties. Could some loves survive even that? I put aside philosophy for the moment. She Who Opened the Gates had perverted these honorable dead, twisting them to an evil cause.

I strode over to where the ghastly head had rolled. I wanted to examine it closely, to understand who had made it and what it was supposed to be. It did not belong in any sacred place, let alone one dedicated to the purest of all the Olympians.

Acid ate black holes into the edge of the curtain. I pushed the fabric back gingerly, rattling on its rod, and saw a bubbling pool of gleaming black slime, emitting small popping noises as it seethed. The last eye was just melting into the viscous mess as I watched. Then, as though it had some rudimentary life of its own, the black mass slid away into a crack in the floor and was gone, leaving behind no trace beyond a foul smell like a latrine used by a large army suffering a mass outbreak of bad hummus poisoning.

I remembered that I was there to search for Nausicaa and now had more reason than ever to find her.

The door to the inner chambers swung inwards a few inches then stopped, blocked by something that gave only a little when I pushed. I wasn't about to poke my unprotected head into the gap to be target practice for some long-dead archer. So I slashed through the soft brass hinges, picked up the door as a shield, and went in low.

Just enough light came through the doorway to show a body lying at my feet. One glance told me the woman had been dead some time. I didn't take a second look. She must have been pretty once.

I continued in toward the rooms toward the back of the temple. High windows let in plenty of light, now, but I still peered into rooms before entering them and kept my ears sharpened for any noises. A door banging to and fro almost wound up wearing my sword as a knocker.

Finally, at the extreme end of the building, I found the other priestesses. They lay in pathetic, jumbled heaps around the base of an oracle's throne. One's fingers, twisted and swollen with rheumatism, clutched at the stone as though to tear it to shreds.

Nausicaa sat there, as upright as a caryatid holding a roof, her cloak thrown back over the chair. The same symbols that the king's cloak had borne were embroidered lavishly over the red lining. The brilliant gold thread still glittered in places, though much of it was tarnished and blackened as though burnt.

I was so interested in these details that I hardly noticed that, like the king, Nausicaa was naked. Her white sagging flesh showed long scarlet scratches and deep purple bruises, clustering most thickly around her throat as though someone had nearly succeeded in throttling her.

She lifted her head and tried to focus on me. "Hail, Thracian," she said, her voice soft and delicate. Her eyes were wide with pupils so dark I could see my reflection. Blood stained her teeth and had trickled from the corner of her mouth, turning shiny as it dried.

I knelt down beside her but she still looked at me as though I stood a long way off. "Is it you doing these things, Nausicaa? How are you doing them?"

"A test, that's all. New powers need to be tested...and such powers. Like nothing I've ever known. I have been given my birthright. Justice at last." She sighed as though replete with some vile pleasure, though she still did not move.

"Where did you get these powers?"

"Wouldn't you like to know?" Her soft voice died away. She smiled shyly like a young girl, her eyelids fluttering as she tried to keep me in focus. Then she spoke again, in the same harsh voice I thought I'd just silenced.

"This is only the start of it. Soon all my armies will flood the world, making my daughters their queens, and the terror of their coming will make me stronger yet. I will stand where I belong, Queen over All as I was promised. No one can stop me now. I have been kept from it too long already by a fool like you. You foolish men think you know so much...."

She coughed and then sighed, a long breath that smelled of the grave. The blood cracked and fell from her chin. But blood dries only when it has stopped flowing.

"Queen of where? Queen of what?"

"You will know! You will bow down to me, Thracian. And when you do, perhaps I shall spare you after all. You may be more useful to me than you think!" She began to laugh, the low insane sound I'd heard coming from the triple-mouthed head. I jumped up and grasped her by the shoulders. Her head fell back limply, her eyes glazing. She was dead. One of the reanimated priestesses must have done for her before I ever got there.

But if that was true....

"Who, then, have I been talking to?"

* * *

Perhaps only the need to reclaim their wandering dead could have brought the villagers out so far from their homes. They had seen the graves open and, though many cowered inside their homes, some had followed their loved ones. Their weeping was more pitiable than the dead.

Some blamed me and a fisherman ran toward me with hard fists clenched. I made no attempt to defend myself. After all, he hardly came up to my shoulder and he was only in danger of bruising his knuckles on my armor. But bruised knuckles take one's mind off a bruised heart.

After the fisherman threw few more wild swings, Phandros, of all people, persuaded the poor fellow to see to his late wife and to take a swig of the local wine which the king's clerk had brought along, showing great forethought.

"What did happen here?" young King Temas asked. The evidence he'd seen had sobered him more quickly than a dunk in the cold sea.

I explained as concisely as I could. My task was all the easier as I couldn't explain much. "I wish I had more answers for you but I've never seen anything this loathsome before. I deal in magical creatures and figuring out what crimes mortals commit but this...this smells of witchcraft."

"As does my father's death?"

The young king had seen his father's body carried out from the temple, but had given no more sign of distress than a shake of his head. "My father had been odd of late, Eno. Taciturn, hardly eating, but drinking heavily. He did not share his thoughts with me. He considered me little more than a foolish boy, playing at being a prince, not yet worthy to serve as his right hand."

"I think he was wrong," I said. "You're no weakling."

He shrugged off the compliment. "There must be a reason for these nightmarish happenings. What did she say to you, again?"

I told him.

"It makes no sense. I've known Nausicaa since I was a...since I was born. She wasn't a warm-hearted woman by any means but she never seemed interested even in ordinary religion let alone any occult matters. She used to say 'let the Gods take care of their own business; I have beds to make.'"

"How long has it been since regular temple services have been held?"

"We had extra prayers and sacrifices when the harpy came but most people have been too frightened to come here lately. There have been reports that the harpy has been seen hovering in this area."

"Really? That might be useful."

He didn't seem to hear me. "I wonder who killed the priestesses. Their deaths grieve me almost as much as my father's. They were good women; they didn't deserve this."

"It may have been Nausicaa. They would have trusted her, a woman like themselves."

"They would have trusted my father as well. They weren't strangers; they were born here. I will ask among the servants whether any of them accompanied him up here."

I put my hand on his shoulder. It was thin, a boy's, but the expression on his face was that of a man facing a sad reality. "I doubt it was your father. As virgin priestesses of Artemis, they would never see him alone."

"True. Then you think it was Nausicaa?"

I had not mentioned my idea that Nausicaa had left her body sometime before I reached her. I now wondered just how long ago Nausicaa had departed. An illness, a poison, could leave a husk of a body all ready for someone, or something to move in. When questioned, the prince recalled that Nausicaa had suffered a fall and a blow to the head in the winter, just six months before the king had changed so much in his ways. I had known strange alterations to take place in men after receiving a strong blow to the head, almost strong enough to cause death. I'd never heard of such changes spreading to other people, though.

"I hope that with both Nausicaa and your father dead, these strange happenings will stop." I suppose I could have been more tactful.

"I hope you are right," Temas said after the color returned to his face.

"The thread between them, whatever is was, is broken. The creature I saw in the temple is gone and if it was indeed Nausicaa bringing this ruin on Leros, she is dead now."

"We will know for sure if the harpy leaves. I shall ask if anyone has heard or seen it lately."

I took the renewed outbreak of weeping from the villagers when the bodies of the priestesses came out as a sign that my room would be preferred to my company, I returned to the woods beyond the clearing, glad to get out into the fresh, moving air.

Magic always gives me a headache, clustered right between my eyes. It's the same sort of strain I might feel at a party, when the host and his best friend have quarreled but are trying not to show it. The veiled hints and splashes of venom make everyone uneasy, even those who aren't sharp enough to pick up on the reason until too much wine makes everything clear. Secrets, hidden power, twisted emotions turning the commonplace into vileness. I breathed deeply, shook all over like a dog, and went to find some place quiet to think.

I had no more sense of the dryad's presence, though I stopped a moment by her tree. She'd known that death waited in the temple, feeling it in the same way she felt the warmth of the sun or the coolness of the earth beneath these roots. But it had not been my death, after all. I wanted her to see that.

I went deeper into the woods, picking my way through the questing roots until I could no longer see the temple. The sighing of the wind in the branches mingled with the whisper of the sea, not far from here. I must be near the cliffs but I wanted rest more than I wanted a glimpse of the sea. I yawned, wondering if Jori was still there.

I unlaced my armor and lay back into the warm green embrace of the earth. What I really needed was a water-butt to sink into or at least a few dippers of spring water but I was still on edge. I knew I was half-listening for someone to start screaming.

What was going on here on Leros? Was Nausicaa the font of these magic events and would they indeed cease now that she was dead? I couldn't believe it despite my suggestion to King Temas that it was so.

This whole affair wore witchcraft like a tribal tattoo. Who had been master and who was the disciple in the rituals that Nausicaa and the late King had performed? Considering that the King had died first, I felt that Nausicaa had led him into it, not the other way around. Whether she killed him herself or induced him to do it was of less importance than the reason. Had he served his purpose?

The problem was that I didn't know enough about these dark things. My field is sword-swinging, bone-crunching, and monster-mangling. Magic traps and tricks could often be overcome by the use of force and those that couldn't were, at least, created by a fellow human mind and so were comprehensible. This didn't feel like that. That triple-head, for instance...that was big magic. Not even the Egyptians could pull off something like that.

I was trying not to say the word 'Goddess' even to myself. But it kept recurring to me, while I tried to think of other possibilities. It was like having a bad tooth which twinges even when left strictly alone.

So far in my career, I'd met monsters, human and otherwise, and a good few minor supernatural creatures, like the dryad and a centaur I'd met once in a house of ill-fame. I'd managed thus far not to tangle with the Gods. I wanted to keep it that way.

I certainly didn't want to deal with a God gone mad, yet I was afraid, desperately afraid, that might have been what I had met in the temple. But which one? Who was She Who Opens The Gates? It had a grandiose sound but I'd never heard of any Hellenic God or Goddess using that title. And what gates, where?

A little motion caught my eye. A field mouse, sleekly white and brown, was trundling across the grass. He or she stopped to look at me, going up on hind legs to sniff the air, whiskers twitching. Deciding I was harmless or perhaps only thinking I was a new kind of rock, it hurried away.

Somehow, I felt better. Whatever horror had inhabited the temple would be cleansed away and the proper Goddess would again inhabit it. No doubt the island would return to normal after I finished the job I'd come to do. One harpy, captured; one kingdom back to the proper business of 'beggar my neighbor' and 'it's a fine bright Tuesday morning; who do I want to make war on today?'

I listened to the wind playing tag in the grass and decided a little nap was in order.

I woke up at dew-fall, a deep sigh escaping my chest. The nearly-full moon turned the whole sky to silver, framed by the tops of the trees. I took it as a good omen for the return of Artemis to her temple.

Then I yawned widely, stretching out my arms to their maximum reach, and touched feathers.

CHAPTER FOUR

Harpies are bird-women, often sent as a punishment against those who have offended the Gods. Zeus is especially fond of sending them to pursue some poor soul. They snatch food from the hands of their victims, leaving just enough to keep alive but never enough to satisfy the gnawing of hunger. They despoil all the rest of the food with vomit and excrement. In the end, with luck, the victim goes insane before he starves to death.

The last ones I fought were like bats with leathery wings and curving sharp teeth. They were less interested in the buffet-trap I'd spread than in biting my neck. But I'd worn an iron-collar anointed with the juice of some garlic flowers and they hadn't harmed me, though I will never forget the pungent swamp-gas smell of their breath.

I believe, in fact, that there are two classes of harpy – some created when a dragon's blood splattered on burning rocks from a volcano. Others came into being when the bright brass blood fell on clouds.

So a feather was good news to me. I hate fighting in an iron collar.

Nevertheless, I was glad I'd only unlaced my armor, not taken it off. I didn't want to reenact the liver-gnawing punishment of Prometheus today or any day.

The moon had set but there was no feeling of dawn at hand. The darkness seemed to huddle on the ground in pools. Yet here, among the thickly clustered trees, a little patch of light flickered like the play of sun through leaves, just where I'd put my hand. I drew it in and the light came too.

I examined the feather by its own light. It was the color of burnished bronze lit by pale flame, like a lamp burning low. The light that shone from it brightened near the tip. Yet it was a genuine feather, light, hollow and flexible.

No one had mentioned that the harpy glowed in the dark. Maybe they'd all been too afraid to come out at night since it arrived.

I ran a finger along the delicately serrated edge then quickly stuck my finger in my mouth, tasting my own blood. The feather was sharp!

Getting up, I went to investigate. The more concentrated glow turned out to be fluffy down and several full feathers, one bent and another missing about a third of one side. There was a faint, greasy smell like chicken cooked in oil.

I looked around. Where had the feathers come from? It took me longer than I like to admit to look up as one would logically do.

The tree nearest to the little glowing pile of feathers had a massive trunk. A patriarch of tree-kind, probably the tallest in Leros. The bark looked like plates of armor fitted together, thick seams running between the joins. I squinted up the length and saw, dimly, another glow about three-quarters of the way up.

Even I could not quite reach all the way around the massive trunk. Slipping off my sandals, I dug my toes and fingers into the bark and climbed up to where I felt a thick branch over my head. From there it was easy, even in the dark. A reach, a pull, a swing with extended legs and I soon reached my goal.

About halfway up, I'd begun to hear a low, rhythmic rumble, growing louder as I climbed. With that in mind, I'd worked my way around to the far side of the trunk from the glow. I'd shared enough barracks to know snoring when I heard it.

The pine needle clusters didn't offer much cover as I peered through them. A nest as large as a human's bed took up the space where three branches came together. It was built from a variety of leaves, a sheep's fleece, and feathers all laid together more or less neatly in a hammock made from the twisted ropes of a fishing net.

In the center, curled up, lay a strange figure, much smaller than I would have guessed. I had no trouble seeing details in the soft glow that emanated from the creature. The harpy slept with its head tucked under a wing, the feathers spread wide.

Traders with Africa report strange flightless birds with long naked legs whose kick can disembowel a man. The harpy also had long legs, covered with small shell-shaped feathers, ending in narrow feet with five gleaming claws. Longer feathers covered the rest of it, shading from a deep bronze, almost crimson, to the palest gold.

If I had the cage waiting down below, with Jori standing by to slam the door closed, I might have made a play right then. As it was, now that I knew where to find it, I could come back in a few days, right after taking care of the rogue guards. This job was going to be easy money after all.

Then someone bellowed my name.

It shattered the silence like the roar of a minotaur. The urgent, buzzing note in it set up echoes in my head of all the other times I'd been called in desperation.

"Eno! Eno!"

This cry was followed by another sound, one that made the hair on the back of my neck stand up and wave. A softer sound, wordless but interrogatory. The sound of a creature roused suddenly from sleep and wondering what all the fuss was about.

Not really wanting to, I looked down into the nest and a pair of eyes looked back.

The face was pale and fair with a nose, not a beak, and lips. Close-fitting feathers covered the head but the face and neck were human...more or less. The feathers rose again from the abdomen to cover the bosom, tightly following undoubtedly feminine curves as though the creature had been dipped in gold.

It got its legs underneath it, spreading immense wings up and out as though to leap into the sky. But it stared at me, unblinkingly, trying perhaps to figure out what kind of animal I was. I'd seen owls look like that but never with long-lashed blue eyes.

I could have stabbed it to the heart with a single blow but I did not even think of it until later. I stared back, my mouth as dry as a castaway's after three weeks at sea. I'd seen many weird and wonderful things in my life, but I'd never felt the power of enchantment so strongly as I did at that moment. She looked as though she might speak; there was so much emotion in her face.

Then whatever blasted soul was calling my name did it again, louder and closer. The harpy gave an answering cry, less piercing, less lonely, than before, at least to my ears. Then it took flight, with one powerful beat of those huge wings. The backwash of air nearly shook me from my hold.

I watched the golden glowing shape rise like a flaming arrow into the first light of dawn and wondered if it would ever return.

I wouldn't have cared to descend while it was still dark but with the fast-brightening day to help me, it was a simple matter to come down. "I'm here," I said, when my feet touched the ground.

There was no reply but the sighing of the morning breeze.

A rustle behind me made me turn abruptly, hands spread for combat.

A pile of leaves was pushed aside and Phandros sat up, brushing off those that clung to his arms and beard. "I heard the harpy. Did you see it?"

"How did you bury yourself so quickly?" Even if he'd begun the moment I'd begun to climb down the tree, I couldn't see how he managed it in the time.

He didn't answer, though his face reddened. He bent down and retrieved something about as long as his foot from the leaf mold. I took it from his hand. It was a cone, a roughly rolled piece of papyrus paper, punctured with a piece of twig to hold the edge of the paper closed. The buzzing sound must be caused by the passage of the air setting the edges to rattling.

"Clever," I said,

"Just a child's toy, really, but useful sometimes. Makes a sound like a ram's horn if you play it right. And, of course, it amplifies the voice."

"Fascinating. Why were you calling me?"

Behind his beard, Phandros looked grave. "There's been a challenge sent to you."

"To me?"

"Word of your deeds has spread throughout the island like fire. There were actually vendors in the market this morning; they are so certain you will be the one to kill the harpy."

I decided to keep my recent failure to do just that a secret for now. "Your chance to buy pickled eggs again relieves my mind," I said. "What about this challenge?"

"Eurytos shows you his thumb and declares you his enemy. Leave Leros by noon and you will be permitted to leave unharmed. Stay and you will face your doom."

"And Eurytos is....?"

His graying brows lifted. "The former guard captain."

"Oh, yes. Sorry, hard night. How did you come by these   sweet   words   of   welcome?"

"His second in command waylaid a fisherman in the woods on the far side of the island and passed on his master's words. The fisherman told a goat girl who told her mother as they gathered mushrooms. She told her husband who told me."

"Busy woods for so early in the day. That fisherman wouldn't happen to have been visited by a miracle...say, his fish turning into cash just after meeting this brigand?"

"You have guessed correctly, Eno," Phandros said. "Some villagers have been supplying the rebels, it's true. Extra obols are not easy to find on Leros these days. I have wondered where Eurytos is getting his funds."

I was thinking. "With so many mouths chewing on this message, its possible Eurytos did no more than send me civil greetings. Warlike words, worthless deeds. I should pay him a visit."

"He is no courtier," Phandros began.

"After breakfast, I think," I said. "I did not dine last night. I could eat a Leviathan. Raw!"

As I fastened my sandals, I found my thoughts less busy with the truculent captain and more focused on Phandros. I had heard soldier's tales of men who could silently and swiftly dig hiding places out of bare earth, concealing themselves in less time that anyone could believe possible. They could stay hidden for long periods without moving, without hunger or thirst. I'd never met anyone who'd actually witnessed this feat; it was all third or fourth hand. A man's grandfather had told a tale or the friend of a cousin had sworn on his mother's grave that he'd seen it. Now I wondered if I had become one of those who are the 'they' in 'they say'.

I had sat down on the root of the large tree on purpose. Stealthily, I slid the unbroken feather into my short scabbard, behind my sword. It might be worthless except to shave with but I wanted a remembrance of what other wonders I had seen that morning.

Starting the walk back, I glanced curiously at Phandros. He really was a weedy specimen, the sort of man who went on getting drier and thinner year by year until he either splintered like a twig or turned into leather. He could have been thirty-five; he could have been sixty. "Just how long have you served here, Phandros?"

"Almost six years, though it seems less. I came as tutor to the prince."

No old family retainer, he. I wondered again why Phandros had chosen to return here from Athens. Loyalty? It seemed like a lot of loyalty for six years' service. No family or ancestry bound him here.

"The king put much trust in you, then?"

His slightly pop eyes wandered from path to sky. "Some, some. He was not a trusting man. Leros being a small island, there was no need for dozens of hangers-on. A pleasant court, though. Always someone about to drink or dice with. Then, of course, when the harpy came, even the best of those fled."

"But you stayed on."

"I had nowhere else to go. No money. No acquaintance. There may be some pupils who will give an honored place to their old tutors but most turn on their heel the moment their scholarship is done. Few indeed wish to be reminded of their schoolboy days once they are grown."

Probably true. Being self-taught, I could never escape from my teacher.

"You came here during the late Queen's time, then?"

A smile moved in his beard. "Ah, Queen Amymone. Delightful woman. Kindly, beautiful...really an ideal woman in every respect." He proclaimed some poetry, stopping and taking a rhetorical pose as taught in the best academies.

I idly scratched the back of my neck and waited for him to finish. With a decent semblance of modesty, he broke off, adding 'Written on the occasion of her last anniversary. She was pleased to offer me a word or two of praise for it."

"I'm not much of a poet," I confessed. "Some people like it."

"The king preferred music to poetry. He was a fine harpist. He could have made a good living at it, had the Fates not chosen to make him a king. Indeed, the Queen deigned to tell me once that it was their shared love of music that changed their marriage -- arranged by their fathers, of course -- from a mere royal match into something richer and more rare."

"A love affair?"

"Assuredly. As passionate as any from legend. You would not, perhaps, have understood my reference in the fourth line without knowing that the king often referred to himself as Orpheus and his queen as Eurydice."

Orpheus whose god-like gift of music had charmed the birds from the trees and maids from their clothing could have had married any woman but he'd chosen the radiant Eurydice, only to lose her within a short time to the sting of an adder. He'd tried to rescue her from the world of Death, charming the triple-headed Guard Dog Cerberus with his lyre and slipping past the shaded dead. But he'd ultimately failed, as he perhaps had always been fated to fail.

"The king must have been devastated by her death," I said.

Phandros nodded heavily, his beard like a wave on his chest. "For a time, we feared for his reason. Even after he ceased to weep, it was long before he recovered the tone of his mind. Even so, I cannot recall him ever laughing again. Well, not until his last night."

"His last night?"

"How melancholy to think of it so! I had come back from the taverna...I had been spending the nights there of late. But I wanted a change of robe. The servants were huddled in the kitchen and we could hear the king laughing. We thought perhaps he'd finally gone quite mad...well,   you   understand."
"Yes. Go on."

"But when he came down, he was cheerful, quite his old self. He pinched a girl's cheek, drank wine with me, and asked after the boy. I told him that Temas was standing to the duty he'd been set, warning away the ships, and the king laughed and said there would be no more need of that. I thought he'd found a way to rid ourselves of the creature but he seemed not to regard it as important."

"No?"

"He dismissed it with a wave of his hand...like that." He showed me, a careless wiggle of his fingers. "Then he drained another cup of wine and said he had some work to finish before the night was through. I asked him what it was he was doing but he only touched his finger to his lips and dashed away upstairs." He sighed. "That's the last time I saw him alive."

I walked on in silence, my mind busy with a thousand questions. What had the king been working on and had he achieved his goal? I could not think what other reason there might be his being in such merry spirits. Had he'd learned from Orpheus' mistakes and tried to retrieve his adored wife from the Underworld in another way? Such efforts are doomed. People don't return from the other side of the River Styx. We are given the water of forgetfulness and leave this world behind forever. It is one of the hardest lessons we mortals have to accept.

Had the king opened a door into the Darkness Beyond? If so, Nausicaa must have helped him but why? To bring back Amymone? That did not fit with her dying words...if her words they had been. Someone else wanted to come into this world and rule it but it hadn't sounded like a gentle and musical woman. It had sounded like a monster, a monster with many children, and if it could make the dead walk, perhaps it came from somewhere that had a lot of dead people. But was that door closed for good, now that both the king and Nausicaa were dead?

I doubted it. The tools had been disposed of but you only drop tools when you don't need them, when the work is finished.

Perhaps I had one answer. If the king and Nausicaa had been meddling in matters of life and death, the Gods would punish that trespass without mercy. They'd sent a harpy to harry similar criminals before this, often. But I couldn't reconcile that explanation with the beauty of the creature I'd seen asleep in the tree. When the Gods send a punishment, there is no mistaking it for anything else.

Without Nausicaa's steadying hand, the Palace staff were utterly confused as to what should be done next. Not even the death of the king had been so confounding. A king may run a kingdom but a good housekeeper runs the king.

The little one who had brought me a cloak before I'd followed Nausicaa was doing her best. Her hair was coming down in wisps, dirt smudged both cheeks, but she gave orders crisply. Little Iole, who hardly came up to my elbow, organized two girls to wash our feet though the water was cold.

"I beg your pardon, lord," Iole said, her voice clogged with tears. "The fire went out last night and the tinder did not light."

"It's a curse!" someone howled in the kitchen.

Iole flinched. "If you will overlook this fault, please?"

"It doesn't matter," Phandros said before I could give her chin another chuck. "Cold or hot is unimportant. I feel the same about food. So long as it is plentiful."

"I prefer it hot, though," I added. "But fast is best of all."

"Yes, my lord. This way, my lord."

I don't know when I was raised to the nobility in her eyes but I followed her into the kitchen. There was food on the table, left there from a dinner no one had eaten. A cat walked daintily across the tabletop, browsing at leisure among the plates. Iole swept in, scooping it up, and cuddling it close to her thin bosom.

"Heat this up," she said to one of the other girls, handing her a plate of cold mutton. "Isn't the porridge ready yet?"

"It's cursed! Cuuuurrrsssed, I tell you! I've been watching it and watching it but it won't boil!" screeched a crone nearest the fire. The leaping light showed her broken teeth in a cackling smile. There is always someone pleased by chaos and disaster. It confirms everything bad that they believe about the world.

"Yum," I said. "Cursed porridge. My favorite. Does it have raisins in it? If it doesn't, then it's just mildly unlucky porridge and that's not nearly so tasty."

Iole smiled, her lips trembling as if she'd sooner weep. "We are like scattered reeds this morning, my lord."

"It doesn't matter." I saw that Phandros was already digging in, a plate of honey-cakes held close to his chin.

I wanted something more substantial so reached for the sliced pork. After dredging it in a little savory sauce, I didn't mind the toughness. Even the wine, well-watered, tasted better when I was really thirsty.

"How's the prince...how's King Temas this morning?"

Phandros had to get his beard unstuck from his mouth before he could speak so little Iole got in first. "After he came back last night, he started going through all his father's notes and papers. He's up there now," she added, rolling her eyes toward the ceiling. "Where it all happened."

"You've worked in the Palace for a while?"

"Since I was a child, my lord."

"And you're such an old lady now, of course."

The crone cackled again and dished up some glutinous mess from a pot. I am pretty sure even lentil porridge isn't supposed to be green, at least not that color green, shiny and greasy like a wound turning bad. Nor, I am sure, is it supposed to suck at the spoon with a sound like questionable digestion.

I decided I'd had enough to eat and invited Phandros to come talk to Temas with me. He eyed the porridge as well. "Yes, I think that's the wisest course"

"Just like a man," the crone screeched. "Ask for something special and then turn his nose up at it!"

"Don't be like that, Grandmother," Iole said. "I'm sure they're just full of other things."

"You said it, sweetie, not me!"

* * *

The choking smell of cold ashes filled my nose as I entered the upstairs room. Seeing Temas there, squatting in nearly the same spot where his father had died seemed a dangerous omen. Phandros apparently agreed.

"Come away, my king," he said, standing over the boy. "This is no place for you."

Temas' eyes were bloodshot and red-rimmed. He rubbed them hurriedly, removing traces of tears. "I'm going over a few papers."

There were heaped up scrolls just beyond him. "Anything interesting?" I asked, jerking open the curtains. I saw that the one I'd ripped hadn't been repaired yet.

"Yes, quite a bit. Of course, I can't read all of it. I think there's some Egyptian here and maybe some Chaldean characters as well."

The fresh air drove off the memories. Temas, blinking in the sunlight, seemed less the eldritch inheritor of a black fate and more a young man with an air of responsibility that sat oddly on his shoulders. Remembering my youthful visits from the Hangover God, I could sympathize. He stood up like an old man, all hinges and creaks.

"Have you eaten?" he asked, fulfilling his duty to a guest. Or was I his servant? Heroes for hire occupy a strange half-world when it comes to etiquette. Still, Temas was a gentleman.

"Yes. Have you?"

A slight tint of pale green washed into his complexion. "There was this cold porridge...."

"Yeah, I saw it. I think I would rather face those things from last night again than eat that."

The boy hastened to the balcony, the same that I had found so useful for the same purpose. After a few distressing minutes, the king called me.

"Sire?" I stepped out to join him.

"I think you'd better tell me what did happen last night. There are some very strange tales flying about and I must know the truth of what I myself saw."

"These scrolls are most interesting," the scholar said, appearing in the doorway. "If I may study them further?"

Temas nodded his permission. "But stay and listen to what Eno has to say. The incidents of last night are so peculiar that I can hardly accept all I saw myself."

Phandros' cool eyes studied me. "I have no doubt, sire, that Eno the Thracian comported himself entirely in your interests. There are strange portents and powers at work in this land but they will never overcome men of valor. I will study these papers and guard the way so you may speak freely and without interruption." ·

I felt as if someone had hung a golden chain around my neck. On the one hand, I was grateful for the compliments, which I felt Phandros did not hand out like sprigs of mint on a festival day. On the other hand, however, I now felt even more closely bound to the King of Leros and his problems. Even if I'd wanted to, how could I sail away without satisfying the terms of my contract?

After I filled him in on all the details of last night's adventures, reserving only my discovery of the harpy's nest and my guesses about his father, Temas stood swaying in the sunlight, his hands pressed to his eyes. "We are cursed, indeed. How can such things be?"

"We live in a time of mysteries," I said, not wanting to share my surmises till I had a chance to think things through. "The Gods work their will as they see fit."

"What God could do such horrible things? What I saw last night...the pity of their faces, faces I knew well. My father. Those guards, men I knew and fenced with. And the poor women."

"It's over now, my lord. Whatever caused it won't happen again."

"How can you be sure? If they walk again tonight, everyone will leave the island. I might as well abandon the palace to Eurytos right now."

"Nausicaa is dead. It was working through her, whatever it was, and that doorway is shut. Permanently."

"I pray so. What will you do now?"

I rubbed my bristly chin thoughtfully and caught myself starting to scratch. "I'd like a bath and a shave. Then I should pay a visit to my friends waiting in the harbor."

"I'll go with you. If I and my household must flee..."

"Oh, Jori will take you, for a price." I should have told him then, I suppose, that I'd seen the harpy, that I had a feather from it on my person, and that I knew where it nested. I knew I should and even got so far as opening my mouth when I noticed Temas looking at me with extra intensity in his young eyes.

"Do you...do you think I should grow a beard?"

In the bright morning light there gleamed the faintest hint of down on the young king's chin. Remembering back to my own chest-bursting pride in that first public sign of manhood, I pretended to ponder the question. "That's something each man must answer for himself."

"You don't choose to wear one?"

"I fight for my living, sire," I explained. "I don't care to give my enemies something easily grasped. It's why I clip my hair close as a sheered sheep." I ran my hand over the short growth, just long enough to show black. "Besides, have you noticed how men with beards scratch all the time?"

I mimed with both hands a thorough scratch of jawline and chin. "Like a dog scratching after fleas. Or a man digging for gold."

Temas grinned and pointed discreetly past my shoulder. I turned to see Phandros in the room beyond, enjoying a vigorous scrubbing with both hands among the thicket on the lower slopes of his face. He looked up and smiled in answer to our laughter without knowing the cause.

Temas turned back to me. "I suppose it's as my father was fond of saying, 'as bad as things are, they could always be worse. At least it isn't raining.'" Seeing that I didn't understand, he shrugged. "It was just something he used to say in bad times. It didn't make much sense during droughts though."

"One day you'll say it to your sons."

"Yes, I suppose. I imagine they'll roll their eyes and make faces just as I did. Now I'd give anything to hear him say it one more time."

I didn't want to see him grow melancholy once again. "You know," I said, "it won't matter what you decide about a beard. When you marry, it's your wife that will choose for you."

"I don't think so." Temas said confidently.

"Oh, believe me. If she says it itches, you'll shave it off quick enough. And if she says it tickles, you'll grow it to your knees if she likes it that way."

He chuckled, somewhat sadly. "You remind me. My father had a list of suitable king's daughters. We discussed my marrying often before he grew so changed. I wonder where it has gotten to." He turned and went inside. "Phandros, have you seen that list?"

I inhaled a great bushel of morning air and let it out in a long sigh. Though I'd spoken confidently to Temas, I was worried. I ran through all the rumors I've heard lately. Business is proving to be good for a lot of us independent heroes. I hadn't thought much of it, except the money side of things of course, but now I wondered what was really going on.

Working outside the usual parameters of 'I hear and obey' had been a good move for me. But there were factors involved in going independent that you don't understand until you are thigh-deep in new troubles. Just getting the dents beaten out of armor could eat up half my profits, or did until I bought a second-hand anvil. The vendor had thrown in half-a-dozen smithing lessons for free.

Add in the paperwork, receipts, sub-contracting for big jobs, and funeral expenses when said sub-contractor failed to duck, and a lot of freelance heroes go back to a third-shift night watch at the local acropolis just to make it easier on themselves.

So when business had picked up, I figured that, between the war in Troy and the accounting hassles, I was just getting the overflow. Now I wondered if there wasn't more business because more dark forces were stirring. If that was true, did Nausicaa's last words explain why? How far did this nightmare reach?

I found myself scanning the sky for the harpy, not in any fearful way, but just because I wanted to see her -- it -- again. I wondered if it would burn across the sky like a comet, pale against the sunlight, but a portent of evil days to come.

CHAPTER FIVE

Rather than a bath, which would only make more work for the disorganized household, I asked Iole for some hot water to be brought out to the stables. Of course, life being what it is, Iole didn't bring it herself. Nor could she spare any of the young and active maids.

The crone brought it, her thin shoulders bowing under the weight as she shuffled forward. But she shooed me away with hissing noises when I tried to take the buckets.

She perched on the end of the horse trough. Muffled in dusty black draperies, she looked like a molting crow with eyes just as black, shiny and inquisitive. Black bands bound brow and chin, white hairs sprouting from both. She rocked a little on her uneven perch and screeched, "Go on, go on! You have nothing I haven't seen before. I've buried three husbands and have another one on the string any time I say the word!"

"The men of Leros are valiant," I muttered. Well, if she didn't care, neither should I. The men of Athens often walked through the streets wearing little besides their short capes. It was times like these that reminded me that I remain just a country lad at heart.

I stripped and upturned one bucket over my head. The soap was scorchingly strong, pumice and lye mixed with goat's fat. Some hopeful soul had added verbena flowers but they had long-lost the battle to overcome the goat smell. It worked though. I felt I'd added significantly to the local topsoil and seemed at least two shades less tan when I was done.

I rinsed while the crone cackled. "A well-set up fellow indeed. Brave too, I hear. Fighting the dead...and other things."

Hearing some undertone in her voice, I cast her a sidelong glance. One of her eyes was buried in puffy flesh, the other surrounded by a web of wrinkles. I decided she wasn't actually screwing up her face in a leering wink but that this was her usual appearance.

Every case, it seems, must contain at least one cryptic crone. I'll teach a whole class on them in my school someday. What is so frustrating is that they never come right out and say what they mean. I suppose once you are old, with all your intense emotions behind you, you have to find your fun where you can.

They want careful handling, the crones. Show your impatience or try to awe them with your authority and they'll tell you nothing, or worse than nothing. They seem to enjoy sending busy men on wild goose chases. Be especially cautious if they start calling you 'dearie' or complaining about their feet. It's like the warning rattle of a snake. It means trouble.

While pondering the right approach for this ancient creature, I picked up my discarded clothes.

I sniffed gingerly at the sweat-stained crumpled pieces and decided that they'd do for another day or so. Doing battle in the nude has never been my choice. I had no reason to assume today would not end in a fight. It would be pleasant to get to grips with something reliably human for a change.

The crone cackled again, less like a mocking crow, more like a setting hen. "Men," she said, in a tone of indescribable knowingness.

After fumbling in the depths of her robe, she drew out an oblong length of crisp white fabric and, from her sleeve, a tunic actually long and wide enough for me. They were so white, especially in comparison to the others I'd worn since leaving Athens, that they seemed to sparkle as they passed from her hands to mine.

"Now you are dressed as befits the emissary of our new king."

"Thank you, good mother."

She snorted wetly and spat. "Call me Doris."

"Doris?" It was the name of mother of many sea-nymphs, lithe, beautiful, and full of joy. Everything she wasn't.

"Aye. I was nurse to the late king and favorite handmaiden to his mother. My own children are scattered to the four winds."

"That must grieve you."

She shrugged or perhaps she merely hitched at her robe. "They are good children and follow their paths. I even have a son and grandson fighting now in Troy for good King Priam."

"Good luck to him," I said, and spat.

"Aye." She spat again. "You try to help the young ones but they don't listen, think they know it all."

"I'll listen."

She peered at me, plucking at one of the long hairs that grew from her chin. It came out and she flicked it away. "Will you, dearie? You want to know about last night? About the temple?"

"Whatever you want to tell me." I smiled down on her, trying to imagine that I had nothing better to do than listen to the meandering tales of the old ones.

She impatiently motioned me closer. "That Nausicaa was bad clear through, like an apple with a canker. I would have watched over the boy but she never let me near him. Still, she couldn't do much with him while I was always on the watch. So she turned her wicked ways upon the king, made him kill himself."

"What 'wicked ways'?"

"Telling him things men shouldn't know. Divulged the Mysteries, got him hooked like a fat eel, and then drew him ever deeper in. Why did he buy a lock for his door and only she had the other key? What rites did they perform during the black of the moon? I could say more, but I will not corrupt your heart."

Having seen the remains of the king, I didn't really want to hear more. "What were they trying to do?"

"She told him he could bring back his wife, with certain rites. But whether those were the rites she taught him...ah, that's another question, isn't it?"

"At least Nausicaa is dead now."

She laid her hand on my arm. I expected it to be hot but it was as cool as the clean cloth laid on a fevered man's brow. "Did you kill her, Thracian?"

"No, one of the Dead did for her. One of the priestesses."

"They were good women. Their service will not be forgotten. Others will come to rededicate the temple." Her voice was fainter, as though she were speaking to herself or to someone I could not see. "All must pray to the Fearful Goddess that no harm will come to Leros itself through being used in such a way."

"I'm sure Artemis will protect her people."

"Artemis? She'll do her best, I'm sure. We shall see. But I am glad you are not guilty of any crimes."

"Thank you, mother. Why did the king kill himself?"

"What else could he do? How else could he turn the spell back on she who sent it?"

"What spell?"

She didn't answer that. "He cast her out, didn't he? He repented all they'd done, all the terrible things. They made the women miscarry and the crops wither. They made the sky turn green and the spring dry up." The cackle had come back.

"Temas didn't tell me his father had dismissed Nausicaa."

"How could he know? He was down by the pier. And that foolish tutor was drunk in the tavern. But I...we of the household...we know all that happened."

"She was here when I came. She was running the household."

"We saw him thrust her down the stairs so that it's a wonder she didn't break her neck, and more's the pity that she didn't. But he gave no orders to the rest of us and who was brave enough to tell her she must go after the king died? She could shrivel a woman's womb or rot a penis off with a look."

"Mine's all right," I said. I thought she was going to choke with laughter.

"So I saw...."

I felt relieved. Whatever the late king and housekeeper had summoned from the dark pits of Hades had been dispatched. Perhaps the king's sacrifice had made it easier for me, the way the mother's embrace of her dead child had eased my task last night. Everything would return to normal, I hoped, not just on this one island but throughout Hellas. Less business for me, maybe, but somehow I didn't mind.

"What do you know about this Eurytos fellow?"

Her hand slipped from my forearm. "A paltry blowhard, one would say, and yet I have felt some stronger force within him. Perhaps the same force that moved Nausicaa. Perhaps another. Not even the Gods know everything, let alone one old woman." She coughed juicily, pressing her hand to her thin breast. "Be wary of him."

"I will, never fear. Tell me one thing more, good mother."

"Aye?"

"What Gods does this Eurytos worship?"

That was one of the side benefits to having a Pantheon. You could tell a lot about a man from the temples he frequented or never visited.

She shrugged again. "None, perhaps. Or all. The snake, the hyena, the lion...he kept a talisman of each one, the deadliest and the most cowardly. No woman would go near him with that claw of his and he never bent his knee to any goddess." Doris straightened her back. "Oh, me poor old bones," she said. "No rest for us women-folk, not even today."

I bent my arm and offered it to her. She laughed and slapped my wrist. "You're a gallant fool, Thracian. Go carefully as you well know how to do and may the blessings of an old woman go with you."

* * *

As we'd discussed, Temas and I went down to the ruined dock. I still tried to reassure him that leaving wouldn't be necessary. But he wanted to have an escape plan in reserve which made a certain amount of sense. This Eurytos fellow might prove tricky.

Some shutters were open in the town and a few goods were exposed for sale. People were still spooked, though. If so much as a gull flew over, they'd crouch down, making themselves small and unappetizing. Some drew courage enough from the presence of their young king to come out to greet him. I got mostly sideways glances and crooked fingers held to brows to ward off the Evil Eye.

A few strong pulls of the oars on a borrowed dinghy and King Temas and I were stepping aboard the *Chelidion* to a graceful welcome from Jori. He claimed to have done nothing but fished and lazed about since I'd left. "A most pleasant anchorage," he said, bowing to the king.

"You've heard nothing strange?" Temas asked.

"Strange noises? None, lord. Should we have noticed something?"

Temas glanced at me. I shook my head and went forward to inspect the cage. It looked just the same. I kicked the cook forward with a few delicacies for refreshment.

As I thought, Jori was perfectly willing to take on as many passengers as Temas' treasury would permit even if it meant stacking them like cordwood in the hold.

Then he said something that surprised the moussaka out of me. "This ship, my fleet little Swallow, will take you wherever you wish, lord, but I see no need for you to be alarmed into thus fleeing. You cannot do better than to trust my old friend Eno, here. He will not fail you."

"How much money do you want to borrow?" I asked.

Jori laughed, as did the king after an uncertain moment. "No, indeed. You have arranged many such troubles, have you not? What I have not seen with my own eyes, I have heard with these ears. The tales they tell in the marketplace of Athens alone, lord, would entrance a sorceress. Have faith in Eno. I do."

Temas eagerly voiced his agreement and reiterated it when I took him back to shore. I thanked him, refusing his hesitant yet gallant offer to go with me to deal with Eurytos. I set off, waving to him as I entered the woods.

Jori's vote of confidence should have lightened my heart as I walked over the stony spine of the island. Instead, I was so puzzled I hardly noticed which way I went. Jori was never one to ladle praise over someone like a cook basting tough mutton with oil. About the only answer I could find was the outside chance that he'd suffered some kind of prophetic dream in the night and had been thus convinced of my invincibility. I wished such a dream had come to me, though all too often such things are more a snare than a promise.

As I started down between some large boulders toward the far side of the island, I became more alert. None too soon, either.

Though lost in thought, I had heard the calling of small birds, the rustling of this creature and that through the grasses, the skittering of lizards, and always, flowing through and around all other sounds, the rasping of the cicadas in every tree. From time to time, I heard the far-off lowing of a sheep, though I couldn't see where they rested in the shade. All the usual sounds of the beautiful, peaceful Attic countryside sleeping under the beating heat of the noonday sun.

So when I distinctly heard the hoot of an owl, echoed immediately by another a little farther away down the hill, my ears pricked like a hungry dog's.

Of course, I whispered a fast prayer to Athena, the All-Seeing, whose herald and avatar is the owl, just on the off-chance she was putting in an appearance. The Gods are often nearer to us than we knew, or so the priests say.

More likely, however, was that Eurytos, trained in Cadmus' service, still used the owl's hoot as a signal between sentries. As much as anything, it had been the incessant hooting that drove me away from that army. Ghost owls, tawny owls, scoops, every soldier was sure that he and he alone could imitate the birds better than anyone else. As an officer, I'd had to referee more 'my sleepy owl at the first touch of Rosy-Fingered Dawn is better than yours' arguments than I cared to remember.

I walked on more slowly, letting anyone who wished to have a good look at me. When you are built like the lighthouse at Rhodes, this is often a useful technique. No doubt their suppliers had delivered to the rebel guards all the gossip along with their fish. It is natural to discount such tales by half, but I fancied I live up to even exaggerated reports. I paused for a moment where the sun shone strongly and pretended to yawn and stretch, letting the spread of my muscles ripple and gleam.

A few minutes later, after I'd hardly gone another couple hundred yards, I heard a mix of raised voices and then the crashing, yelping sounds of someone breaking through underbrush and falling down. I turned to scan my surroundings. The hooting got louder.

I saw a youth, a sheepskin tied with a thong over his shoulder, crouching among the white boulders. He saw me looking at him and his eyes widened. Then he sprang to his feet, running away down the hillside, rocks and stones bouncing down in front of him. Somehow he kept his balance. He started yelping, "Captain! Captain!" foolishly, as though Eurytos were waiting around the next rock.

"He'll be too out of breath to deliver the message," I said out loud. I knew there was at least one more pair of eyes watching me. I yawned again, stretching my arms wide then bringing my fists in to make all the muscles along my back and shoulders bulge up like melons on a vine.

"Hercules...." someone said, his whisper echoing off the stones. I couldn't see him but knew that here was one guard who wouldn't be joining the fight.

"There'll be amnesty for anyone who returns to the Palace by nightfall," I said idly to the shadowless stones. "King Temas knows you are not evil, even if your heads were weak."

There was no answer. I walked on. After a bit, I looked back toward the top of the hill I'd just come down. A figure stood there, dark against the chalky path. He hesitated, then gave a half-wave. I saluted him with two fingers waved in the air and he turned to go back toward town.

"One down, nine to go."

Though the hooting had been intended to alert the next two guards, the shouting, falling and yelping would have worked just as well. The next two were waiting among some trees that shaded the path where it leveled out. My eyes took an instant to adjust but my ears were fine. I heard the creak as an arrow was drawn back on the string and the knock of a spear-butt against a tree trunk and the soft, involuntary 'damn' that went with it.

I drifted easily to the side to avoid the arrow which whistled over my left shoulder. The spear-wielder came out with an ululating yell and a six foot spear. Not the best choice for close-quarter fighting. I felt no need to take the sword from the scabbard resting between my shoulders.

I grabbed the base of the metal spearhead and yanked, forcing him to continue his charge right past me into the sunlight, his legs flying out in front of him.

Reversing the spear in one cartwheeling motion, I threw it straight, pinning the archer's cloak to a tree with it. He fainted, hanging from the neck-strap.

Walking back, I picked up the former spear-carrier in one hand, dusting him off with the other as if he were a fallen-down child. I told him to tell his unconscious friend about the amnesty. He faithfully promised he would.

"How much farther is it to your camp?" I asked. "Am I right in assuming your captain is there?"

He nodded, his teeth chattering as if with cold. "A-another mile, down by the coast. There's a-a kind of fortress. The rocks piled up all around there."

"Sounds like a good place to hole up." I put him down gently.

By now his comrade was awake again, twisting violently to rip himself free of the spear, choking himself uselessly. It had penetrated past the point, leaving a large hole in his cloak. "Ask a nice lady named Doris to mend that," I said as I broke the shaft and yanked him free.

"Doris?" he asked.

"Old woman, wears black." I helped him up. "If you hurry, you'll make it back before the harpy starts flying around again." I picked up his bow from the ground and snapped it over my knee and handed him the bits dangling from the string. "Hurry up."

Maybe that was a bit cruel but it got them moving.

So far, I'd only met young men who had chosen badly when deciding to rebel against their rightful leader. I could see in their eyes their desperate desire to return to the past, to set things right. I never knew a youth who didn't regret big decisions like that almost the moment they were made. They probably had been praying every night to Father-Zeus to make everything go back to the way it had been before Eurytos had killed those first two guards, boys like themselves but with the courage to say 'no', foolhardy though it had proved.

I'd come now to once-plowed fields which should have been golden with sprouting wheat. But the fields were overgrown, poppies drooping and bind-weed crawling up and over stalks. Some places the wind or the rain had beaten down the stalks; other places deer or sheep had trampled and chomped.

A bit further on and the smell of burning lingered, reminding me of other fields, other sunny days turned dark with smoke. I didn't know if it was a lightning strike or the hand of man that had set these fields alight.

Then I heard a crackle, a burning roar and a scream and I had my answer as to the cause of the fires.

There were three of them, one a bald hulk with a face like a burlap sack. He was laughing, standing back a little from the others, having a grand time, urging on the other two to evil deeds. At first, I hoped this was Eurytos but I saw both his hands were human.

They'd captured a girl, a peasant, her hair bound close to her head with a cloth. Her hands were tied to a stake so she had room to run a few steps either way but no chance at freedom. She twisted her thin body and tried to bring one hand to free the other from the rough ropes even as they cut mercilessly into her wrists.

A fire had been kindled, just a small fire. The two younger men were busying themselves there and at first I couldn't make out what they were doing. All three men's attention was fixed on it so they never noticed me as I came up behind them. The shepherd boy had been wise enough not to come this way. These louts wouldn't care if his message was urgent. They were out to play nasty games.

"Now you take the rocks and flick 'em at her. Go on!" the big bald one said. "With luck, you'll set her dress on fire! That's a sight worth seeing!"

"But they're hot...." One of the younger ones had the kind of whining voice that make you long to drown the owner in a bucket to make up for parental oversight. "They're too hot. I'm not burning my fingers for sport!"

"Dog! Cowardly dog! I'll show you!" The other stood gilded by the firelight, with a straight profile and the tight curling locks sculptors give to statues of Adonis. He bent and fumbled, swearing, for one of the stones resting on the edge of the firepit. He stood up, juggling the too-hot stone between his hands and looking around for applause.

He saw me about one instant before I closed my fist over his. I'd caught his right, the one with the rock in it. I squeezed, holding on despite his thrashing.

The whiny one stared, opening and closing his mouth in much the same way he probably chewed, as pasty as if he'd seen a nightmare in the daytime. I hoped to haunt his dreams for a long, long time. He backed away fast, tripping over his own sandal lacings. I let go of him. He fell to his knees, keening over his crushed and burnt fingers.

The big one leapt on me, trying to wrap his arm around my throat. I grappled on to his hairless, tight arm with my free hand. An elemental throw, catching him on my hip, tossed him over my head to land on the other side of the fire.

Even the girl stopped struggling to stare.

I dismissed the snuffly one from my thoughts, concentrating on the big man. His girth was mostly gut which meant a blow there would dissipate into the fat. As for wrestling, I already knew he'd be slippery. I'd caught a whiff of his greasy skin as he'd flown past. I wiped my hand on my side.

"Who are you?" he demanded.

"I'm the one you're supposed to be watching for instead of playing these sick games. Why not send these boys to tell Eurytos I'm on my way?"

"Nobody needs to bother Eurytos. I can take a dozen overgrown monkeys like you and never break a sweat. Let 'em stay and get an education."

He started to circle around the fire like an experienced fighting man, one foot feeling out the ground before he lifted the other. He crouched low to present less of a target. He held his hands in the classic 'grasping an iron-ball' form, ready to grab onto me no matter what hold I tried first.

"Come on, you bastard!" he cried, showing his pointy teeth in a fierce grimace but his eyes shifted behind me to where the pretty one stood. That glance betrayed his worst fear, the fear of looking like a fool in front of his accomplices. Any pain I'd inflict would be nothing compared to the agony of that humiliation.

I jumped right through the fire at him, hitting him in the neck with my elbow to stop blood flow, sweeping a leg behind his to steal his balance, and coming around with my other fist to snap his head back. He went down hard, the air going out of him in a whoosh. I stood on him a moment, thoughtfully wiping my feet on his belly.

"What kind of wrestling rules are those?" the whiny one asked as I stepped off the body.

"Mine."

I took two steps toward him and he scrambled away on his hands and knees. "It wasn't me," he gasped out. "I just did what they said. I didn't want to!"

Then I heard the slithering ring of a sword being drawn behind me.

CHAPTER SIX

The biggest and bravest man can be brought down by any coward with a rock. But not by some idiot with a sword.

This sword must have been the property of the bigger and balder villain. In the hands of this younger one, the tip wavered like a bird drunk on fermented figs. His farm-trained arms shook so that he had to use both hands to hold it even so steady as that. It showed a tendency to point down even as he used all his strength.

"Never hold it like that," I said, coming closer.

"What? Stay back. I'll run you through! I will!" His voice went high, a plucked string on the harp of hysteria.

"All right, then. I'll just stand here while you saw at me. Should take you about a week."

"Don't you laugh at me!"

He decided that now, while I stood at least a dozen feet away, was a good time to take a swing at me. Despite the effort of just holding the sword, he lifted it a little higher and tried one of those swirling, two-handed exercises that look so very impressive. I confess I was in something of a sweat, worried that he might lop off a limb...one of his.

When he finished, he had just about enough breath to say 'aha!' After a moment of self-admiration, he remembered to point it at me again.

By then, however, I was close enough to slap it out of his hands. I wasn't about to pay him the compliment of crossing swords with him. It fell blade-flat on the ground, giving off a dull ring.

With one hand around his skinny throat, I lifted him up to look me in the eye. His cavalry boots, ridiculously ornate for field conditions, kicked uselessly around my knees. "Now, you listen to me, you pipsqueak...."

"Oh, don't hurt him!"

Amazed, I turned around. The girl, her arms at full stretch, leaned toward me, imploringly. "Don't hurt him, please. Please don't."

I had involuntarily tightened my fingers when she'd spoken. The boy scrabbled frantically at my hand, his pretty face turning blue and his eyes bulging. I let go. He fell to the ground, gasping.

I picked up the sword and released the girl. Still trailing the cut ropes, she ran to his side and flung herself down, her hand resting tenderly on his back. She leaned down to see his face. "Oh, Yanni! Are you all right?"

"Yanni?" I looked heavenward. "I bet he's the only son of a widowed mother, too."

He was sitting up and coughing now, his hands to his bruised throat. But his scornful eyes told how little he appreciated the girl's concern.

When I came closer, she spread her arms around him defensively. "Don't hurt him anymore!"

"How did you get here, miss? Did he bring you?" I gave him a little dig in the thigh with my foot.

"Yes...but he didn't mean to hurt me. It was just...it was all that one's idea," she cried, pointing to the bald one, who still lay flat on his back, cradling his middle. Seeing us looking, he rolled away from us, making noises as if he were choking up his last meal.

Yanni pushed the girl roughly aside. "It wasn't his idea; it was mine, all mine. You're a fool for me, like all you silly girls. But what do I want with some filthy little peasant who reeks of goats?"

"You don't mean that, Yanni!" she said, clasping her arms around him.

"Oh, don't I!" He put a hand under her chin and shoved her over. He stood up, tears of rage and pain tracking down his face. "I'm going to get away from this rotten island. King Eurytos has promised to make me an ambassador. He says I'd be good at it. I'll marry the first princess I see, if she's as ugly as Hekate, and then I'll be a king myself. Then I'll show you...I'll show 'em all!"

He looked the part, I'll grant him that. As he stood there, his head thrown back as he posed like a statue of some young athlete, I could almost see a wreath of laurel or olive decorating his smooth brow. But a strange expression of surprise and dread wrinkled his forehead and aged him in an instant. His face distorted into a mask of terror. A deep shudder rippled through his body, like a palsy-shake.

The girl looked past me and screamed so violently that it seemed to surpass mere sound. At the apex of it, her eyes turned white and she fainted.

Only my instinct made me dive to the side, hurling me down onto my hip in the dirt. Above me as I rolled, rearing up against the noon-time sky, was the flat, triangular head of a pure white snake, as long as three horses, its poison spittle already flying through the air.

If I had not dodged, it would have splattered me. I writhed in the dirt to smother any that might have struck my back but I felt no burning. I had been in time.

Yanni, poor bastard, turned to run too late, his mouth still wide open. The greenish-yellow froth had hit him all down the left side and clung to him like a wet cloth. He raised one slime-covered hand before his eyes, an expression of horrified wonder replacing his fear.

"Drop and roll, boy!" I shouted.

If he'd obeyed, he might have survived, though without his good looks.

Instead, he drew breath to scream again as the pain hit him. Some of the venom went in with the air. The pus-colored froth turned red, then black, spreading tendrils to wrap around and consume his flesh.

With a hiss like the rising steam from the poisonous waters of Lake Aegina, the snake uncoiled, segment after segment flowing past above me. It unhinged its jaws in mid-spring and swallowed Yanni whole before the boy's body had time to do more than sag.

"Yum!" it said, whipping around to face me. "You're a big second course, Monkey, but I can always save half of you for breakfast!"

I fought the urge to turn, to look to see whether the fat, bald guy had genuinely transformed. I knew he now stood before me, balancing on his tail, weaving back and forth to keep me hypnotized and unsure. There was no need to confirm it but I found it surprisingly difficult not to do so. Evil had not yet departed from this island.

The girl moaned, coming awake. Her eyelids flickered and she opened them sleepily, trying to focus on what she saw. When she realized there was a sixteen-foot-long snake not three rods away, she bit her lip til it bled, knowing that any further screaming would be useless. She looked at me, but I didn't dare even nod at her. I had to keep the beast's attention on me.

I raised the sword and it laughed, ripples running up and down the long body. The girl started to crawl away but the tail came around, knocking the props from under her. "I mustn't forget dessert!" the snake declared.

It bent over her. "Such a fresh morsel...how can I bear to wait?" The long tongue, forked and dripping, flickered through the air above her. "Mmmm, the smell of fear! So delicious, like the best cheese!"

"You'll love me, then," I said loudly. "I'm turning to jelly."

The head twisted toward me, the body following, coil upon coil. Though it was very definitely a snake, there remained some vestige of the man he'd been in the eyes. The pupils were not entirely elongated and there was more of an eyebrow than is usual in reptiles. Not that I've spent a lot of time studying them.

What was completely reptilian was the thing's speed. It could twist and change direction without a pause and cover the ground faster than a running horse. The ground was too open to give me cover by leading it through trees and we were a long time away from the comfort of concealing night. It was going to be a stand-up fight but I couldn't match his reaction time.

"Don't run away," it said. "It makes the thighs tough."

"Hera knows I'm sorry about that. Nothing worse than tough thighs," I said. "What were you before? A cook in a Carthaginian whore-house?"

"I was a snake, sunning myself on the rocks in the southern sun. I devoured all that came, insects, mice, my own children. I grew. I continue to grow."

It snapped at me. I jumped aside and stumbled on the loose stones piled near the fire. It laughed. "Men came to slay me. I devoured them too and found I knew all that they had known. I wanted to see this world of men."

"Do   you   know   any   cats?"
"Cats? Cats? I have eaten them; what of it?"

"Just curious." So far, I hadn't swung the sword, merely holding it in front of me to keep off the great head. I knew I was only going to get one chance. If I missed, I was going on the bill of fare.

This sword was heavy, ill-made, and I could see that the edge was much too dull for my liking. There was no time to drop it and draw my own. I couldn't leave myself open against a foe that moved so fast it almost seemed to be in two places at the same time.

"How did you come to be walking around in human guise?" I asked both to gain a few minutes and because I really wanted to know.

"Eurytos has been given the power to change creatures like myself into humans, for a time. He came before me, bearing such delicious gifts, young, fresh and sweet. While my belly was full, he told me all the wonders that awaited me. So I agreed."

"How's that working out for you?"

The forked tongue flickered again as if to be rid of a foul taste. "You eat very delicious things, cream sauce and pomegranate jewels and those wonderful, wonderful stuffed grape leaves. But for the rest -- ugh! How can you stand it? You all smell so bad, and those tiny, cramped bodies, always too hot or cold...."

With a sudden slashing leap, it curved around me so that I had to jump quickly to continue to face the giant head. It was studying me with even greater intensity than hunger. "Eurytos offered me that ugly body, the body of a friend of his. He had nothing better on hand. But you...you, Monkey, can never be cramped in that body."

"I'm not as big as I look."

"Big enough." It struck again, throwing another loop. I jumped high, pulling in my legs to clear the coil. As I came down, I slashed, but the sword merely bounced off the overlapping scales along the outside.

If I hadn't much cared for the idea of being eaten, I liked being replaced inside my own body by that creature even less. Where would the collection of ideas, prejudices, and memories known to me as 'Eno' go? I had no interest in finding out. Metaphysics is not my arena.

We were both breathing hard now, ready for battle. But it couldn't spit for fear of wrecking my body and I couldn't cut because it wouldn't do any good anyway.

"I don't need sleep," it said. "I have eaten well. I will run you to exhaustion then take the shell to Eurytos. He will re-animate your body and it will be mine."

"I'm not that kind of a fellow," I said but I knew what it said was true. It could kill me that way.

"Already your muscles are burning," it said, weaving that great head back and forth, fixing me with those half-human, half-slitted eye each as big as my face. "Your heart is thundering like the cattle of Geryon across the plains. And your thirst is a torment which cannot be slaked but which grows greater with each breath."

I laughed. "Save it," I said. "I dined very well with much to drink and my only failing right now is a need to relieve myself. Which I will do as soon as your head lies beside your body."

Of course, this was just boasting. The sweat beaded along my hairline had already begun to gather and run down to my jaw. My tongue felt swollen and tended to stick to the roof of my mouth. I'm stronger than most, capable of great endurance, but I am mortal.

The snake knew it and gave another hissing chuckle. "You are a poor liar. You'll do better once I have mastered your form."

Apollo seemed to have parked his chariot close overhead for the heat of full noon poured down upon us. Time seemed to slow like resin dripping down a tree trunk. Even the buzzing of the cicadas had died. There was only the hot gold of the wheat-field, the weight of the day, and the pitiless glitter of my enemy's eyes willing me to fall, to fail, to surrender. No friendly spirit of tree or waterfall appeared to save my skin as it had before the fight in the temple. Neither of us dared move now for the first strike would mean victory or defeat.

Infinitely distant, infinitely lonely, almost beyond the gift of hearing, the harpy's keening shriek tore the sky.

And the snake flinched!

"Damn that beast!" it snarled, which, to my mind, was the pot calling the kettle hard names. "As soon as that idiot boy Temas is dead, I'm doing to hunt that thing down and choke it."

"A pity you won't have the chance."

It eased itself a little, side to side, never blinking or looking away. "Why doesn't it bother you?"

"Does it bother you?"

"Of course it does. Beastly sound. We can hardly sleep at night in the camp. It seems to infest the air over there."

That was good information but it didn't gladden my heart. The bride-money seemed no closer to my hands. First, I had to get out of this. If the harpy cried again, I would have to be ready to act.

Naturally, now that it would be useful, the harpy went silent. But as everything else was also hushed, the snake and I soon heard another sound, small and muffled. It was the sound of weeping, muffled as though someone were trying desperately to stifle the rattling sobs, but still audible to a man and a creature with nerves on the stretch.

"Boy," the snake said, voice dripping with the venom of contempt. The sobbing stopped but through fear, not comfort. "Boy, is that you? Weeping like a woman...I expected nothing better of you."

A few stalks of wheat shivered. I could imagine the whiny boy crouched down there, hoping against discovery, knowing it was too late. Perhaps he was praying for the kindly earth to open and swallow him up, a far better fate than Yanni's.

Still the snake didn't take its eyes off me. "Come out, boy, come out, come out wherever you are."

The voice had less of a hiss in it, sounding more like the human being it had pretended to be. "Poor little boy wanted to be a man and all you really are is meat, just cold meat. At least I appreciate you for that!"

The rock that bounced off its head did not come from the wheat field. Nor did it come from the hand of a coward.

The girl stood astride the road, her hair unbound, her eyes bright with clean tears. They didn't impede her aim. She swung a second stone in the sling she'd improvised from her head-cloth. "What are you waiting for?" she shouted.

The snake reared back, ready to spit at her.

I woke up from my own astonishment. Dropping the useless sword, I reached behind my head and pulled my own. All the energy pent up in my body let loose as I jumped forward with a yell that rivaled the harpy's in volume. I sank my sword deep into the creature's neck, at the angle of the jaw.

It hissed and twisted, sucking down its own venom deep into its throat. It tried to bite me but if there's one place you cannot bite it is under your own lower jaw. It reared up, up and up, almost the entire length of the body, then fell backward, thrashing as violently as the snake that had nearly bitten Temas.

Only this time I was riding athwart the ridged muscle of the body. Where does a snake's neck end and the body begin? My sword cut a jagged line through the white skin and spurting flesh as the creature twisted and writhed.

It heaved over onto its belly and began beating its head on the earth, trying to kill me with its own death throes. Dazed, I leapt off but not so dazed that I stood where it could still spit its hatred at me with its dying breath. I whirled my sword up and over, cleaving the head off in a blow so hard it went right through to the ground.

The eyes glazed over, the white membrane falling over the half-human pupils. My sword was smoking; I shoved it under the dirt of the road.

I sank to one knee as the girl came closer. I wish I could claim it was in homage but the truth is that the snake had been right. I was exhausted. But I had three more men to fight, four if you counted Eurytos himself. The Fates alone knew what vile abominations Eurytos' remaining little friends would prove to be. What other creatures had he found on his travels, converted like the snake into some new thing neither honestly animal nor entirely human? A wolf, a bear, a boar?

The girl produced a wineskin full of well-watered wine. I could have drained it in a breath but remembered in time that someone else had been out in the heat as well. After she'd drunk, I said, "That was a well-thrown stone."

"When I was a little girl, they set me in the fields to keep off the crows. I had nothing else to do but practice rock-throwing. Then when my brothers were born, I had to learn to weave instead."

"If you throw a shuttle as skillfully as you throw a rock, you must weave better than the spiders. You saved my life."

"I didn't do it for you; I did it for Yanni. And Pacci."

"Pacci?"

The whiny boy came out from the wheat, dirty, disheveled, dragging his feet with shame. His brown eyes looked like a scolded puppy's. "Where is Yanni? Did he run away?"

The girl dug her foot scornfully into the dead snake's side. "He's in here, eaten at a gulp like a pelican downing a fish."

The boy shivered and turned white. I had a feeling he had nothing more to be sick with. "Shouldn't we let him out?"

The girl and I just looked at each other. She handed him the wineskin. "Drink that. We'd better be getting home."

"What's your name?" I asked.

"Omphale, daughter of Demos, farmer and smith. That is my brother, Paculi. He wants to be a hero."

"No, I don't. I want to be a blacksmith and never, never look at another sword. I'll make pitchforks and shovels and horseshoes forever and a day but I won't ever make a sword or a knife longer than my finger! I swear by Hephaestus Himself!" It was the kind of fervent prayer that finds its way at once to Heaven and the ears of the Gods. I had no doubt it would be recorded there. Perhaps with time and much labor, he could erase the memory of his cowardice. It would help if his sister wasn't always there to remind him of her courage.

"Has your father arranged your marriage?" I asked. It's the sort of polite question we old, worn-out men ask young and lovely maidens when we met them.

She shook her head and drew down her scarf from where she'd flung it over her shoulder. With deft fingers she bound up her hair again. "Come on, Pacci. You'll have to apologize to Father but he'll forgive you. He always does."

She walked away, her back straight. There'd be no more tears on that face, not where anyone could see them. At night, under the eye of the moon, perhaps. I hoped Artemis would turn her tears to pearls.

Pacci lingered behind a moment, shifting from foot to foot nervously. "It was him," he whispered with a frightened glance at the snake's body. "Yanni. She was supposed to marry Yanni. His grandfather's the second richest man on the island, next to the King."

"She's well out of it, then. He was a...." there didn't seem any words that would do him his proper justice.

"Oh, he was bad, I guess, but good company. I'll never have another friend like him."

"You're well out of it too, then."

He shot me a glance full of dislike, the sort that should accompany an out-thrust thumb or tongue. I hoped his father would sweat the brattiness out of him behind a plow or an anvil. It would take more than work to make a man of him, though. Strange how a girl could inherit all the balls in a family.

Like most men, I don't really understand women. According to the ancient story of the Flood, after Deucalion, son of Prometheus, and his wife Pyrrha drifted to safety over the surface of the waters, they repopulated the earth by throwing stones over their shoulders. The stones thrown by Deucalion became men; those thrown by Pyrrha became women. But how can men and women be made of the same stuff, from the 'bones of the earth', and yet be so utterly different from one another?

I'm glad I'm a hero and not a philosopher. These kinds of questions make my head hurt.

I rested a while not far from the corpse of my fallen foe. I felt as though I'd been beaten, slowly and expertly, by teams of tiny men with large hammers. The wine had helped but I didn't want to meet the next enemy looking like I'd come off second best from the last encounter. Besides, I had a lot to mull over.

First of all, I had to get off this island. I was getting too involved, too interested in what was going on here. I felt an urge to stay, help Temas to clean up and set things right. I wanted to know more about that girl and her brother, talk to their father, get the kid's feet set on a better path. Even drinking down in the tavern with Phandros had a cozy sound. It was a pretty place, Leros, or would be once the evil that festered here was gone. Maybe my future bride would like it too.

I rubbed my head vigorously, putting those dreams aside for a better time. The foes I had to face next might be stronger and more fell than the snake-creature. I was beginning to take Eurytos' measure. If I'd been defeated by any of the guards I'd met so far, well and good. He could hold his stronger forces in reserve. But if I won out, as I had, he'd need to throw something more powerful yet at me.

Was Eurytos in league with the three-headed thing in the temple? It had been more dangerous than the snake, commanding strange powers. This big fellow whose remains lay beside me had been something more than mortal. Evil had been done to it. It had been an animal, twisted into a semi-human with a bad attitude, but the thing in the temple had seemed like a manifestation of something else, something capable of far-reaching sorcery. Was Eurytos the font of all the evil on the island or just another tool, like Nausicaa and the late king?

I sat on, gripping my forehead as if squeezing it would help, trying to remember everything the evil three-headed creature had said. I felt that there was a clue there, if I could tease it out. It couldn't be under Eurytos' control because it had said it wanted to be Queen. And the dead boy had called Eurytos 'King' and talked about his plans to take over Leros. The thing in the temple had talked about ruling everything. Eurytos must be working for that unknown queen as I had a hard time believing in the coincidence of two evil magicians at work at the same time in the same place.

Be that as it may, I knew at least Eurytos had some supernatural creatures at his command. What did I have to use against him? A sword or two, twigs, rocks, my strength? None of it particularly useful until I got a look at my opponents.

The wind had picked up, drying my clothes. The monotonous song of the cicadas had started again, as soon as the snake had fallen. I could do with another drink. Pity the wine-skin was dry.

When the wings beat over my head, I mistook them for the rising wind. But when a soft down puff floated before my very eyes, I glanced up.

She was there, hovering with long strokes of her wings, floating with a strange grace. Her claws weren't ten feet above my head, cruel as the hooked barbs on an arrow, designed to rend flesh from bone. The sun threw rays of light over her bronze body, receiving her radiance in return. I could feel her looking at me but she was far too bright for me to gaze long upon her.

The hilt of my sword was near to my hand. I could have snatched it up, clipped her wings and brought her crashing to earth. I could have bound her with the ropes young Omphale had dropped and returned later to deal with Eurytos. I did nothing of the kind and it was not the thought of the claws that stayed my hand. Perhaps it was a recompense for her timely cry during my fight with the snake. Perhaps it was the soft cooings she was making now.

When it changed suddenly to a snarl, I did glance up. She'd moved away from me, to hover effortlessly above the snake's body. Her claws flexed as a human might tighten and ease a fist.

She dove down over the head, digging her claws in to the thin flesh that covered the skull. With powerful beats of her large wings, she lifted it off the ground. The cut neck trailed a thin dripping of blood as she flew off with it. Thankfully, she did not fly over me.

With renewed strength, I followed her. She was going in the right direction, toward Eurytos' natural fortress. From what the snake had said, I knew the harpy was no friend to my enemies.

She led me up into the cliffs above the sea by a secret path that only one who could see from the sky would know. When I stopped or turned in the wrong direction, she would come back, drop the head and rest on it, watching me. I found myself talking to her, the way I would explain my actions to a dog, knowing it understood nothing but the tone of my voice. Yet it is a comfort to speak sometimes, especially while working hard on something that requires much bodily labor.

Just before I poked my head for the second time over the ridge that ringed the men's hideout, she left me, still clutching the snakehead in her sharp talons. I watched her fly up, getting some altitude. I wished her good appetite, though why she'd chosen the head was beyond me. Maybe she liked brains.

Bordered on one side by the ocean, the sandy clearing was about a hundred yards across, encircled by embracing arms of stone. There was a tunnel below me, through the ridge. I could, by leaning out, see the tall wooden doors bound with iron that closed off this side. The heads of the nails were still gleaming in the sun from Eurytos' recent repairs. They'd made their natural fortress stronger with all the tricks of military men. It seemed odd that the doors were open, however, unless it was a trap for me.

For the rest, they had a few tents, enough for ten men, and two piles of arms, some swords and bows, one quite near the tunnel entrance, the other closer to the high-tide mark. A fire burned between the two, a large shining perch suspended on a spit above it. My stomach rumbled as I caught the smell of the grilling fish. I'd been working hard without time to eat. Two men stood by the fire, talking with their heads close together.

Then, with wings outspread, the harpy dove into the bowl of the camp, a gilded figure of heavenly vengeance. I watched in gape-mouthed admiration as she glided so low that the two men threw themselves flat to avoid her, and then she powered out again with a few strong, almost lazy wing beats. Her terrifying beauty so drew my eyes that I almost forgot to watch my enemies.

Her cry echoed off the stone walls, magnifying their terror until it seemed as if a hundred harpies shrieked.

I heard shouts of consternation and saw two more men run out from the tunnel into the middle of their camp. For the first time, I saw their leader. He wasn't the tallest, or the most muscular. He wore a simple leather vest over his burly chest and, true to report, his right hand ended in a claw like a crab's. One could almost overlook that macabre touch. Eurytos walked as if he were king already.

The harpy flew twice around the camp, her cry at its most piercing. Only I could hear the note of triumph underlying the bloodcurdling blare. The second pass saw three of them, including Eurytos, flat on the ground, their hands over their ears. The fourth figure stood unmoved, his face hidden under a broad-brimmed straw hat. None of them, however, seemed to have enough wits left to seize one of the bows lying about.

Then she dropped the snake's head, right amongst them all. It only seemed a pity that it had stopped dribbling an hour or so earlier.

From the increasing horror of their shouts, it was obvious that they recognized their fallen comrade, even in this guise. It was only then that Eurytos himself hurried to grab up a bow and a quiver of arrows. His claw didn't seem to impede him much.

It was time for my entrance. He'd no sooner fitted a notch to the string when I jumped over the cliff and landed, one knee down, in the sand. The harpy gave one last cry and flew away.

I stood up and greeted him, quite civilly under the circumstances.

He couldn't decide for a moment where to point the bow, at me or at the fast-flying harpy. I ignored his indecision and bowed.

"I felt sure that after such an introduction," I said, pointing after the harpy, "I would meet with a warm reception."

For a moment, the arrow point stayed focused on my eye. "Are you Eno the Thracian?"

"Are you Eurytos the...Renowned?"

"I am." He lowered his weapon. "It is good to see you again, my friend."

CHAPTER SEVEN

Despite his warm greeting, I didn't recognize him and said so.

"I know you largely by reputation," he admitted, tucking the bow under his arm. "But we have met before. It was on the docks at Kalithanos."

"I don't recall it," I said.

"I'd just been hired on as a first mate aboard our mutual friend's ship. How is Jori? Still up to his old tricks?"

Kalithanos is one of my favorite ports, nicely central to some of the mountainous city-states owned by the Hittites. The wine is good, the women clean, and there is always someone ripe for gambling even if you arrive in the middle of the night in nothing but your tunic. It must have been three years since I was there for I'd been keeping busy closer to Athens. The last time I'd taken passage there aboard the *Chelidion*, I'd been heading up to handle some bandits haunting the trade route between Themiscyra and Troy. It was a tricky job. I vaguely remembered Jori chattering away about some new mate he'd picked up who had plenty of experience with sailing into danger. Maybe I'd met him. I meet a lot of people.

It had been shortly after leaving Kalithanos that Jori had dealt with mutiny for the first time. Some members of the crew, deceived by Jori's apparent youth, had tried to take over ship and crew. It had ended badly for the mutineers. Jori had killed the ringleader...or had he? The man who'd told me the story had mentioned a name. I was certain it had not been Eurytos but where an honest man's name is an asset, it is nothing but a liability to a criminal.

"Maybe I have heard of you."

"Ah," he said, "so nice to be remembered. I certainly remember him clearly...very clearly." He raised his claw and rubbed it as though it pained him.

I saw that the pincers were hard as rock with a sharp inner edge. He saw my glance and raised the thing up. "I owe this and so much more to Jori. Tell him I haven't forgotten the next time you see him."

Didn't he know that the *Chelidion* was loitering not a half-mile off shore? Maybe not. If he'd questioned people at all, it would have been about me and my appearance here, not about the ship I rode in on.

The claw was odd and drew my attention, but it was by no means the only noticeable thing about Eurytos. Despite his attempt at regal bearing, the sad truth was that the man had no neck. Usually when people describe someone this way they mean that he is unusually muscular around the shoulders, giving the perception of a shorter neck. Or sometimes they mean that a man's jaw is heavy, again giving a false impression. People have even said that I have no neck but it isn't true. If it were, I would not have come so close to having my throat cut so often.

What I mean is that Eurytos had quite truthfully no neck. His earlobes rested on his shoulders. His chin would have hit his collarbone if he yawned. He looked as though he'd been hit on the head until his upper spine collapsed.

"You are fortunate to have so many friends," he said. "The harpy, it seems, for one."

"You have a few odd friends, yourself, if it comes to that." I pointed at the snake's head lying a few feet away.

"Poor old snake. Well, he had a good few runs around the stadium. And he was getting fearfully hungry cooped up in here while we waited for you. Fish and bread weren't what he liked best to eat."

"Will it relieve your grief if I mention he had a good meal just before the end?"

One of his eyes swiveled toward me while the other stayed fixed on the snake's head. "Which boy did he eat? The whiny one or the pretty one?"

His fleshless lips split into a grin at my surprised expression. "It was just a matter of time. They were getting on everybody's nerves. Want-to-be villains are just as irritating as want-to-be heroes. I saw Snakey here watching them and biding his time."

"He ate the pretty one," I admitted.

"Hmmm...good choice but he shouldn't have done it. Snakes get slow when they've eaten."

"He was fast enough for me."

Eurytos gave a short bark of laughter, went to slap me on the back but thought better of it. The claw dropped to his side. His quick eyes took in more details about me. "Your hands are bleeding, my dear fellow."

"The rocks up there are sharp," I said, hiking a torn thumb back toward the place I'd come down.

"Indeed they are. That's why we were expecting you to come through the gate. It's a good lesson to me not to expect the usual from an unusual opponent. Erm...." he smoothed thumb and forefinger over the straggling mustache that half-hid his mouth. "You are our opponent, yes?"

"It's why I'm here."

"That's what I imagined you'd say. You don't mind dropping your sword, do you?" His hands moved fast for all their inequality. The arrow point covered me again.

"Not at all," I said, and unbuckled the strap to throw it down away from my reach, sword and scabbard together. I regretted it; I liked the sword, though it was now more notched that it had been that morning, and the scabbard had been expensive, but it was best to allay whatever suspicions I could. Not that I felt Eurytos was a wide-hearted and easy-going kind of guy. He'd probably kept a close watch on his mother when she changed his diapers to make sure she didn't cheat him.

"You wouldn't like to reconsider your position? No doubt the boy-king has offered you a tidy sum to fight his battles for him but consider me as an alternate employer. As a fighting man myself, I know your worth far better than a beardless youth could ever do." He smiled at me like a traveling merchant does when offering genuine snips of Aphrodite's hair and medallions made by Hephaestus himself. "And the size of the shares have just increased!"

His wave took in the four men left to him.

I looked at them too, at least the two I could see without turning my back on Eurytos, which would be a short-lived error. I couldn't tell if they were some kind of animal turned into a man or just men. They stood with their backs to the firepit, with swords drawn, legs braced for attack at a word from their leader. One wore a deep-brimmed hat, hiding his face. The other had tiny eyes and a pert nose that would have looked charming on a girl. Once the bristly chin and snot were added, it turned him into something from a traveling fair. I didn't know where the other two were, exactly. Somewhere behind me, waiting for the signal to cut me down.

Eurytos' eyes had a roving cast. Neither seemed capable of looking in the same direction at the same time. I had counted on some kind of hint from him, a glance, or a nod, to show me where his men would be standing behind me. I'd have to manage without it.

"You know I sent the first three boys back to Temas?" I asked.

"Why do you think I made them our sentries? They'd only be in the way here. The shepherd boy reported you were on your way but he wouldn't come in. I shall have to look him up later. I don't like people who don't trust me."

Behind me, I heard a thrumming growl, deeper and richer than a dog's. A big cat sounds that way just before it lunges. "I don't like him," a throaty voice said from my immediate left. "He smells of blood."

Eurytos showed him the palm of his human hand. "Down, Leander. Give the man a chance to decide."

A gruff voice added, "He's not much to look at, is he?" Then his voice broke into laughter, a half-hysterical, half-threatening sound I'd last heard at Cyprus where the king thought keeping hyenas beside his throne lent distinction to his court. He was right too, though perhaps not in the way he thought.

If I turned to fight the lion-man and the hyena, Eurytos could stab or shoot. If I fought Eurytos for the bow, either one of them could kill me. I didn't know the exact properties of the other two but I could guess they were not now and never had been Cretan dancing girls.

"Your offer is flattering," I said, "and I really want to know how you are doing the things you've done. But I have a reputation to maintain. You know how it is."

"Yes, I know. I have the same problem."

I hit him in the mouth before he could give the word. It was like punching a mountain. His head hardly rocked back at all. His independently functioning eyes could focus on one thing after all, focus with intense, burning hatred. "Get him."

It looked as if I'd have to do things the hard way after all. If Eurytos had dropped the bow...but he hadn't. I'd have to get another one.

Leander had leapt onto my sword which I'd already given up for lost. Hyena dodged and weaved, indecisive without his partner. But he wouldn't attack on his own, not until I was wounded by one of the others.

I spun away from my own weapon and sprinted across and back to the cache by the tunnel door. Thinking that I was trying to escape, one of the other two 'men' ran that way to block my access to the tunnel. He snorted as he ran, turning his head to grin at me through protruding teeth like the jagged rocks above my head.

I skidded through the sand to the weapons cache. They were all stacked up together in an approved military style, swords on top, shields all around. I flung the shields aside like skipping stones, hardly caring where they went. A grunt and a groan told me they'd hit someone but that wasn't my intention or objective.

As I'd hoped, there were a few greasy goat-skin bags, legs taut at each corner, looking life-like if headless. I snatched one of those and a bow. The full quiver of arrows was right beside it.

As I turned, the lion was racing toward me, half-transformed. I hit him right in the still-human jaw with the bag. The cork stuffed in the opening flew out under pressure. I'd like to think it hit someone but I have no proof.

The sand made it hard to run for them as well as for me, though they had the advantage of four paws. It flew out beneath my feet and I could not zig-zag very well. When the lion leapt upon my back, I went down hard, scraping off skin.

The arrows scattered from the quiver as I hit. My hand went to my small scabbard and I pulled my short sword. If he'd been completely transformed, I would have been completely dead. But no lion can bite through a man's skull with a human mouth. It had to back off to have enough room to disembowel me with its giant paw. When it did, I rolled over.

It sprang on me again. I buried the sword and a good bit of my arm between the ribs. Throwing the dying thing aside, I flipped up onto my feet. The boar was closing in, followed by the hyena. Though changed, it seemed to recognize that its hunting partner was mortally wounded. There was no hesitation now in its savage eyes.

I pelted toward the fire, my heart all-but pounding through my side. Though I'd had only hope that my idea would work, and that the necessary ingredients would be present, I moved as though I'd never been anything but certain. It was too late for a change of plans.

I threw the arrows down beside the firepit, spilled the black liquid from the goat-skin over the arrow points, grabbed one up, set it to the bow, and thrust the iron point into the fire. The combination of tar, naphtha and sulphur blazed up with a crackle like a forest fire.

The animals held back from me as the arrow flared between us. It might have been the smell as much as fear. Even to my mere human senses, the stuff had reeked like all the rotten eggs ever laid before it started burning. Now it was all the eggs plus all the maggot-ridden meat.

"Stop!"

Eurytos came down the sand, limping, followed by the fourth man. "Stand back, all of you."

The hyena whined and pawed at the beach. "I know," Eurytos said as if in answer. "Go to him and wait there. We must be obedient." The boar and the hyena slunk off, though the look in their eyes was eloquent.

Eurytos squatted down on his haunches, the fourth man standing behind him. "Put out the arrow, Eno. You don't need it now."

I extinguished it in the sand. "What do you want?"

"It's what you should want that matters. I have just been sent a message regarding you."

The jocularity had faded from his tone. He huddled down as if he were cold, his teeth chattering together. He did not look at me, while the man behind him never took his eyes off me. It began to bother me, that steady stare. He wore a hat like a farmer's with a brim so deep I couldn't see his eyes but I could feel them.

"Sent a message? Who came here?"

"She doesn't need mortal mouths to speak to me, her faithful servant."

"She?" Doris the Crone had spoken of a goddess. I'd assumed it was Artemis. She had domination over animals and had been known to turn men into them from time to time, usually after a spied-upon bath in the woods. But she wouldn't turn animals into men. She liked them better than us, not that she had much opinion of the males of any species.

Eurytos dropped his hand and began idly drawing figures in the sand. "Do you know what it is to die? You who have dispatched many a soul to the Underworld?"

"Not yet." This conversation had taken a strange turn.

"I died...once. A sea-captain cut off my hand, thrust his knife into my heart and threw me overboard. I sank down into the sea, deeper and deeper, colder and colder, for what seemed forever. Do you know there are fire-filled cracks at the bottom of the ocean, great fissures that run for miles? You fall through the blackness and the cold then suddenly you see below you light and fire and heat. The cracks are deep, so deep they open into Hades itself! There I fell, time out of mind. There She found me, made me her servant...made me? I begged her to let me serve her and she sent me back. But not as I had been. She gave me power over the beasts, to change them as I had been changed."

"What is he?" I asked, nodding toward the silent one.

"My brother," Eurytos said. "He died when he was but a boy of seventeen, a chattering, singing lad who was my dearest friend. My lady let me bring him back to life, though he doesn't have so much to say now."

Suddenly, the lingering aroma from the burnt arrow didn't smell so bad. I definitely didn't want him to take his hat off or do anything besides stand there.

"So what's the message?"

"What?" Eurytos looked up, his hand hesitating above the last symbol.

"You said there was a message?"

"Yes, there is. Listen well for She will not ask you again."

Behind him, his dead brother opened his mouth and there emerged a voice that seemed to come rumbling from the ground like an earthquake. "This land was opened to her will by her servant, Nausicaa, and is promised to her servant, Eurytos. Leave and hide yourself away in some small corner of the earth. We will not seek you further. Or stay and serve her as we all serve her. She offers you wide dominion, leadership over her deathless armies and eternal life."

The dead jaws creaked shut. They had not moved except to open, forming no words.

Eurytos smiled at me, his own cheerful identity reasserting itself. "Take the advice of an old campaigner like yourself, Eno. Accept this offer. The Dark Lady will keep faith with you, if you keep faith with her. Think of it. General over an army that can never be killed, never be beaten. Look at me. I started out as a sailor, now I will be a king."

"Why does everyone want to be a king?" I asked. "It's nothing but kissing smelly babies, smacking the backs of sheep and hogs, and endless paperwork. Sign here, seal there, count this, go to war, make peace, and die at the hand of a son, a wife or a friend. It's not much of a life to my way of thinking. Better to live and die a shepherd."

"You lack ambition. I do not. She has given me much power and will give me more. If you refuse her, she will turn to me. I shall not be king of only this island for long. Soon with her will, I unite all of these lands into one force, one power. From Leros, under her midnight standard, I will lead an army of the living and the dead. No one will stand against me. Egypt, Syria, Mesopotamia and the wild lands of Africa will all be mine."

You run into people like this from time to time in my line of work.

"Take your share of this power," Eurytos offered. "Do you desire the northern lands? Thrace could be the heart of your empire and onward until the world ends where the pine forests go on forever. No army could withstand yours. Every man you kill is a new recruit when the Dark Lady rules."

"Who is this Dark Lady?" I asked.

"Join us and you will know."

For a moment, I was indeed tempted. Every man thinks in his heart that he could out-general Theseus given half a chance or half an army. I have been witness to enough bad military decisions to know how an army should be run.

For a moment, a vision rose up before my eyes, as real and sharp as a sword. I rode at the head of a vast force, greater than all the soldiers and ships now besieging Troy. Every face, dead-eyed and obedient, turned to me, awaiting my orders. With a sweep of my arm, they drove down upon the white walled cities of the Inner Sea, forcing the weeping hordes to the water's edge. I heard the cries for mercy and laughed with a brutal delight. I could taste the metal of blood on my lips...

I squeezed my eyes tight shut, forcing the image from my mind. Eurytos, in thrall to his bitter Goddess, waited my answer when he could have slain me then and there. I had to cough and spit before I could speak again.

"We both know my part in your plans would last right up until the moment you decided you can't trust me. Tomorrow? Next week? I don't like the long-term prospects because there are no long-term prospects. I'm staying independent."

"You are probably right. You have a nasty moral streak that would undoubtedly cause me nothing but headaches." He drew one last curved line in the sand. "My Lady said you would not accept so she granted me a new power to show you. Look on and marvel as you die!"

The sand around us began to bubble and to seethe like cursed porridge. Two areas remained calm, the other side of the fire where Eurytos and his silent brother stood, and farther back, where the hyena and boar waited by their fallen comrade. There wasn't much calmness where I stood but I didn't dare give up those arrows.

The bubbling subsided for a moment, only to grow more localized. Half a dozen or more mounds rose from the sand, cracking open to spill out colonies of confused ants. They scurried about in black streams, seeking for the danger that had roused them from their endless industry.

Within a few heartbeats, they changed from standard ant size to the size of small dogs, with saw-like and formidable jaws. They made a high-pitched chittering sound, bunching up together, rubbing their antennae. They began to range themselves in serried ranks, as neatly as though they'd trained for years, while Eurytos chuckled.

"My new army!" he declared. "There are thousands upon thousands, Eno. Die without hope, brash fool!"

The power-crazed people I meet in my line of work often say things like that. It's like a secret code or something. As if you couldn't join the villainy league or be an all-around pain-in-the-butt without the magic words.

The ants were still growing, some already as large as the hyena. I hadn't planned on fighting an army today, let alone an army that came equipped with natural shining black armor and scimitar-like jaws that could snap a man in two.

Rank by rank, their elongated heads, and each eye as large as a pumpkin, turned toward me. I didn't have to worry about the ranks in the back. I'd be chopped up into ant-food long before they'd have a chance to reach me.

With a shake of my head for the strangeness of it all, I snatched up three arrows, thrust them into the fire and put them to the string at the same time.

"It's useless yet see how he fights on! Brave, doomed, absurd Eno!"

"Great, now you're a bard," I said, and fired. Not at the approaching ants but over the top of the tunnel. Then I gathered up another three arrows and fired above the curtain of rocks to the left and once more to the right. I only prayed I'd chosen timbers dry enough to burn swiftly all my hope lay in speed.

I turned and ran toward the sea. The giant ants, now as big as the late lion, raced after me, their multiple legs coping with the sand far better than I could. Even above their screeching noises, I could still hear Eurytos' laughter, echoed by the hyena's.

I also heard Eurytos when he shouted, "What is that?" as I dove headlong for the sea.

He'd noticed that my hands were scraped and bleeding but hadn't asked me why. I'd spent the time between killing the snake and arriving in the camp chopping down timbers with my sword, dragging them into interwoven piles and adding stones on top. Stones is perhaps too small a word...most of them were boulders. Finding the liquid fire had been lucky. Otherwise I would have had to shoot out the wedges that held my careful constructions together and I really hadn't had time for fancy marksmanship once Eurytos had conjured up his latest horror.

The intense fire burned away the dry wood, releasing the boulders. By the time they poured down into the natural fortress of stone, they had collected enough other stones and dirt to be avalanches. Nothing could escape.

I turned over onto my back in the cool water to observe. The few ants that had been close enough to follow me into the water had drowned already. They would have floated if they'd been their natural size but their armor had proved too heavy when scaled up to lion-size.

The rim of rocks above the tunnel had collapsed inward just about where the hyena and boar had been. I felt sorriest for them. They had been beasts, free and without conscience, until Eurytos had turned them into something far worse.

I headed out toward the deeper water to swim around the island until I could reach some place to drag myself out for a rest. I was tired as I thought I could never be. Mostly, though, I was hungry. It had been a long time since my last meal and I'd been busy.

Something brushed my leg under the water. A rogue wave broke over me, sweeping me under. The water was clear, the beautiful blue-green of chrysoprase. Clear enough to show me the giant crab propelling itself toward me, nine sets of pincers at the ready, and one human hand.

CHAPTER EIGHT

Weaponless, literally out of my element, losing my breath from second to second, I broke the surface, gasping. The salt burned my eyes and filled my mouth with brine. The waves slapped at me, like a trainer in the gymnasium trying to rouse a battered boxer. They were not high or fierce but they were relentless.

I had only seconds to realize the hopelessness of my situation. How could I fight a crab, a thing perfectly at home in the water? Even if Eurytos in this form needed air, which I couldn't be sure of, I couldn't out-swim him. Fleeing, therefore, was out.

I inhaled deeply and threw myself back underwater. Diving deep, I evaded his first grab at my arms. With a hard kick, I took my legs out of range and swam under him and up. His hard shell was slick with seaweed but I clutched onto a couple of projections where his shoulders would have been.

A vast fore-claw, bulging with barnacles, snapped a few inches from my face. I threw myself back to the furthest extend of my arms. After a moment, I realized that his crab-arms couldn't reach his own back.

He realized it too. Turning turtle, he started to dive. I couldn't hang on, didn't dare leave the air behind. I kicked for the surface, knowing Eurytos would follow the instant he figured out I was no longer clinging to him.

I had found out one weakness of his, but my own were even more obvious.

I glanced around, pawing the water from my eyes, seeing nothing but waves and sky. There was no way to orient myself. I had no idea where I'd entered the water or even whether I was swimming toward the land or out to sea.

Peering down, I could see my own pale body and, underneath it, a rising darkness. Eurytos had come back.

I dove again. It was a little calmer under the surface, where the waves did not break. In that greenish world, the white parts of Eurytos' shell gleamed yellow and the hand that was all remaining of his human side looked as dead as his doubly-late brother.

He tried to catch me with it. I dodged, only to be grasped by one of the smaller pincers. He clenched hard, bruising but not cutting, trying to bring up the big claw to dispatch me. All the others flexed and reached, rippling in the water.

The one that held me was the kind you don't even bother to get the meat from, the reward not being worth the effort. How I wished I had some boiling water now. Even a little melted butter would be a big help.

Using my free hand, I twisted off the small claw, and kicked off against his inner shell. A large claw came up and though it missed me, the rough inner side scraped my foot. My red blood bloomed like a flower in the water.

I was so cold, I hardly felt it.

The problem was simple. If I had time and plenty of breath, I could twist off all his claws, rendering him harmless. But, as the fisher folk know, the limbs of crabs grow back. I didn't want to neutralize him; I wanted to kill him. Nothing else would protect the people of Leros...or me.

My chest was on fire. Even on rising into the air, I couldn't seem to draw a full breath. Opening my mouth to help just earned me mouthful of water, making me cough and spit.

He caught me by the ankle. Pulling me down, he began to swim deep. He didn't want to snip me limb from limb. He wanted to drown me, or drag me off to be another slave to whatever dark force he served.

This was it. I could pound in the general area of his sunken head but I had no force with the weight of the water chaining my limbs. Half-panicked, I clutched at the small scabbard at my side, forgetting that I'd buried my last weapon in the side of the lion, remembering only that once I'd kept a weapon there.

Yet, there was something held in the leather. Small, harder to grasp than a stylus, it pricked my fingers as I drew it out. The fire in my chest was all-consuming now, spreading throughout my body. I could hardly focus on the thing I held between my thumb and fingers.

The harpy feather gleamed like lost mermaid gold in the green light of the underwater world. It had not gone spiky or bedraggled as most feathers will when wet. The form was as crisp as when I'd found it that morning.

And as sharp.

It took forever for this observation to travel the short frozen distance between my eyes and my mind. Meanwhile, Eurytos was taking me ever deeper.

Almost lazily, I drew the feather across the joint of the claw that held me. It separated from the arm as though they had been but lightly joined together. The claw remain clasped around my ankle.

I began to fight my way to the surface, battling not only the cold and the weight but my own desire to stop the struggle, to let the fire in my chest rage until I was ashes, to rest.

The sun shone down, making a brilliant cross above my head, showing me the way out. With renewed strength in my heart, it was as if I were climbing up a ladder, not swimming at all.

The painless breath I drew then was the sweetest I had known since my very first.

Unfortunately, it was my last. No sooner had I drawn it into lungs no longer burning, than a great force yanked me down under the water again.

The little bit of damage I'd inflicted hadn't fazed him. He still had plenty of claws to catch me with and water was still his element. He needed air but not the way I did.

All I had was the feather and desperation. My fingers were numb, wrinkled into insensibility. I couldn't even be sure I still held the feather.

But I wanted another of those painless breaths. I wanted it so much I attacked madly, without thought or plan. I did not fight now for Leros or the king or my own anger. I fought for breath and breath alone.

I slashed at the chitinous underbelly, slicing through that thin but tough membrane as if it were silk. Even through the water, I could hear Eurytos scream. I dug my hands into the opening and wrenched it wide, splitting him in half with a jerk that seemed to tear my own muscles from my body.

The water clouded with his fluids. I broke the shell with a snap. Without a second glance at my destroyed enemy, I pushed one last time for the air above.

I exploded upwards half my own length. Gasping, choking, strangling, I fell back, floating upon the surface of the waves like flotsam from a wrecked ship. I let the sea have its way with me, washing me wherever it would. I had no thoughts and hardly any sensation left.

Even when the long gray shapes swam so near that they brushed against me, I could not rouse my thoughts. Even the triangular fin on the back could not awaken me to a sense of danger.

* * *

Sand gritted between my teeth and I found myself spitting it out before I was even aware I was awake. A dream-echo lingered in my mind. Someone had been laughing. I looked around for the crone. I thought it had been her in my dream, though the laughter had been that of a young girl.

There were gulls crying and wheeling overhead. Perhaps I'd heard them and the sound had carried over into my dreams.

I sat up, feeling the back of my head. It was hot from the sun, but otherwise as hard as ever. My hands, though, were cramped. The cuts were white bands of stickiness, soon to be more scars.

I found myself below the tidemark on a beach where the white sand lay in a sweep as pure and unmarked as a length of new linen. The sea danced with a swirl of foam a dozen yards away but I was not tempted to dive in to rinse off the sand crusting on my body.

The breeze blowing in from the sea felt clean on my nakedness. My clothes must have either come off in the fight or while I'd been tumbling around in the surf. I was glad not to remember landing here, though, judging by my relatively unscratched skin, it had been an easy landing.

Beyond the shallows, a large object broke through the surface, landing with a splash. I jumped up, tensing, unsure for the moment whether Eurytos' defeat had been part of my dream or real. Or had he been reborn yet again by the will of his dread mistress?

The dark grey dolphin powered up again, did a flip, followed by half a dozen others, shadowing his every move. Their seeming joy in the very act of being, their playfulness, reassured me that nothing vile was about to emerge from the water. They clicked and sang, performing for me or for themselves alone.

Had they brought me to shore? The Minoans have lots of legends about swimmers saved by dolphins. Down at the docks in Knossos, they sell souvenirs of one god or another riding around on their backs. They can't keep the ones of Aphrodite in stock. Not only does she protect sailors from shipwreck, she's depicted in the moment of her birth, fully-grown and naked, being brought to shore by two dolphins.

I wished I could recall if they had saved me. It would be something to tell my grandchildren about, now that it looked as if I might actually live long enough to have some. For a few moments there, grappling with the giant crab, I hadn't been sure.

I drew in several deep, fully conscious breaths. I was alive.

"Of course you are, you silly man."

Spinning around, instinctively crouching, I scanned the beach as far as the trees. I was alone. The light, lilting female voice must have been in my head. Yet it had sounded close. It had sounded like the laughter that had awakened me.

Suddenly this quiet sunlit stretch of beach seemed less pleasant. It was too open. I wanted to get out of the eye of the sun before it baked my head any more.

It was a long walk in bare feet to the small village near the summit of the island, made all the longer by my searching high and low for the harpy. Why had she done so much and then left me to face Eurytos? She'd carried the snake's head for me, dropped it off at the most distracting moment, and then she'd gone. I had not heard her since.

I looked at the tops of the trees, even whistling and making other enticing noises as if I were trying to call a dog. All I found were lizards and some birds who startled me far more than I scared them.

The sun was setting, turning the sky to flame, before I'd reached the village. The sight of the yellow lights in the windows was like a vision of home.

I knocked on the first door I saw. In the back of my mind, I'd been hoping to see Omphale again though I knew it was foolish to think I'd pick her house out of the seven or eight that made up the little community.

A quavering voice called out. "Who's there?"

"My name's Eno. I work for the king."

"Eno?"

There came the sound of a wooden latch squeaking open. A shadow fell toward me as I stood in the thin strip of light shed through the tiny width that he'd opened the door. "Hmmmm...."

The door opened wider. An old man stood there, bent down with years or the weight of a truly remarkable beard. Thick and white, it flowed from his chin to his wide belt like the tail of a horse. He peered at me. "You did say Eno? Eno the Thracian?"

"Yes, venerable sir."

He pursed his lips and frowned at me as if trying to bring me into focus. For a moment, he looked like a petulant baby and I was reminded of the boy Pacci.

"I never expected to see you. You were given up for lost," he said. "No one knew what had become of you."

My heart faltered. I didn't want to believe the wild idea that occurred to me. How long had I been washing around in the sea? Strange stories of lost men, returning after what seemed minutes only to find that they'd been gone for years. Could this be Pacci after the passage of forty or even fifty years? Would Omphale walk in, twisted with age, with nothing of me in her mind but half-memory, half-tale?

I suppose my combination of hunger and exhaustion made this bizarre idea seem not only true but inevitable.

I collapsed across the threshold. Wisely, the old man didn't even try to catch me. I would have flattened him.

My second waking was more pleasant than the first. I lay before the fire, wrapped in a sheepskin rug. A red and black jug of oinomel, that delicious mixture of honey and wine, stood beside me, the clay inscribed with wishes for a long life. The drink soothed my throat but could have been water for all the flavor it had.

At the far end of the single room, a woman turned from the roughly cobbled table. "You're awake? Good. Eat this."

"Omphale?"

"Don't talk; eat. Oh, I forgot the bread."

Eggs and lamb's kidneys mixed with herbs could have been the rocks fed to Kronos for all the notice I took of their flavor. Savoring food seemed to belong to another Eno.

She brought me bread, and stood gaping at the empty skillet. "That was quick. More?"

"That old man...who was he?" Even now, looking at her in the firelight, I couldn't shake off the feeling that this was Omphale's granddaughter, not Omphale herself. The hair, the eyes, the mouth were the same but something had changed. Her spine drooped where the girl I'd known had held herself with pride and determination.

"He is my grandfather. He came to find me when you fainted. Everyone else is celebrating my brother's return as if from death."

"Not you?"

Her mouth firmed. "I have someone to mourn, if you remember."

My fears of having been gone for years faded back into the realm of nightmare. I smiled at her for the first time.

"I remember that I didn't thank you for a well-timed and placed rock. If you hadn't done that, I'd be dead too."

"I doubt that." She took the skillet and gave me the plate with bread and salt. "I have some crab ready if you'd like it."

I laughed. "No."

Once I started to laugh it was hard to stop. The perplexed expression on Omphale's stern face made me laugh even harder, despite the pain in my ribs. A healthy swig of the wine helped dull both the pain and the laughter.

She took the jug from my hands and lifted it to her mouth, tilting backwards to balance the weight. I could have counted to twenty before she took it away.

Her eyes were bright. "What else can I offer you, hero?"

I was suddenly keenly aware that an old rug was not an ideal covering for a naked man. "Another drink?" I said, and hoped my voice stayed steady.

She held the jug against her hip. "Of course." She made me reach up to take it.

"A very handsome piece," I said, caressing the thick glaze on the shoulder.

"It was a gift from our late king on the occasion of my grandfather's fiftieth birthday, twenty years ago."

"A generous gift. Um...where is your grandfather?"

"Tending to the beasts. He'll be some time."

She reached up, her breasts rising against the simple white draping of her gathered dress. Freeing her hair from the thong that held it, the locks tumbled over her shoulders, deep black and so rich it looked moist.

My senses, deadened since my first waking, roared back to life, like a river bursting through a dam. I could smell the oil she rubbed on her skin, the boiling resin in the wood on the fire, the fleabane strewn on the floor.

When I took another drink, the sharpness of the wine mingling with the sweetness of the honey rushed through me like a madness.

She touched her shoulders, her fingers fumbling a little, and the bronze clasps that held up her dress fell to the floor. She clutched the fabric to her body. Her eyes were huge as she stared down at me. "What do you want, hero?"

"What do you want, Omphale, and why do you want it?"

"I will never marry now and you will be gone in a day or so. I want to have a memory to take away what I saw today. Every time I close my eyes, I see that thing eating...." She swayed.

I took her hand and pulled her down beside me. She looked startled, surprised that I'd taken her offer. Sliding my arm around her smooth young shoulders, I said, "That isn't the worst thing I saw today. Believe me, the only cure is time."

Omphale tilted her head back, her eyes wide, her lips parted. Her hair curled over my arm as cool as water. I struggled to maintain my gallantry. She felt warm and firm against my chest.

"You're turning me down?"

"Nobody walking in here right now would believe it, but yes, I am. You are young, brave and good. I have no doubt that you will indeed marry one day."

"And still I must face the night alone," she said forlornly. The tears gathered and slipped down her golden-ivory cheeks.

"Even if you slept in my arms, you would still sleep alone. I cannot by my strength keep the nightmares away. Have you told your father or grandfather about what happened?"

"I didn't know how without making Pacci sound like the fool he is. They are so glad to have him back again. He knelt at my father's feet and begged his forgiveness. How could I say anything after that?"

I could be certain that she'd always protected her brother at the expense of her own soul. Coming from a village not unlike this, I knew how little importance would be given to the feelings of a woman, even one as conscientious and strong as an Omphale.

Now that she was soothed, I gently moved to a safer distance. I looked into the fire as she refastened her clothing. "Tomorrow," I said, "I want you to accompany me to the palace."

"The palace? Me?"

"They need extra help now that the head-housekeeper, Nausicaa, is dead. They pay well and you could use a change of scene. You'll like Iole or do you know her already?"

"Iole? She's one of the taverna keeper's daughters. We've met at weddings and such but I don't know her well. We don't associate much with the townspeople. And I've only ever seen the palace from the outside."

"You'll like that too. It's a handsome building." I would make a special point of introducing Omphale to Temas. I had a feeling those 'suitable princesses' would hear no more of him.

Matchmaking...just another service I offer.

When her grandfather returned, we were playing noughts and crosses on a piece of old slate with half-burned sticks from the fire. Seeing us playing like children seemed to allay his surprise at finding his granddaughter there, alone, with a man not of their family. Nevertheless, as he untied the worn fleece from around his shoulders, he said, "You should not be here alone, child."

"I'm not alone; I have a hero. Besides, now that I have won again..."

"What?" I exclaimed, studying the board.

"I'll be on my way home."

"You'd best stay here tonight," the old man said gruffly. "Strange portents in the air tonight. I saw yet another star shoot low across the sky, a ball of fire trailing a golden vapor. There have been many such of late. It is a bad omen."

"Did you hear anything?" I asked. No wonder no one had reported the harpy glowed in the dark. They hadn't realized what they'd seen.

"Nay, naught but the wind. Yet there has been so much evil walking abroad in this island, it is best to be cautious. I have warned the others not to go home alone. You have done much, good sir. But there is more yet to do."

CHAPTER NINE

I reported to King Temas first thing the next morning.

Well, first I borrowed a tunic from Demos, Omphale's father, the blacksmith and largest man in the village. It covered the essentials but hardly anything else. Many Greek men will walk around wearing only their himation, the long length of cloth that serves as cloak, scarf or what have you. I remember my surprise and shock the first time I saw a man swaggering around Athens dressed in little more than his skin. We Thracians are more modest or, as we prefer to think of it, sensible. Besides which, it is far colder in my northern country. I hate drafts.

Nobody in the village had sandals big enough.

The smith greeted me civilly, holding a metal bar in his hands, not in a threatening way. More as though he found the feel of the metal to be a comfort. "I am grateful to you."

"You have little reason. No doubt Omphale would have taken care of matters herself given a few more minutes." He'd asked me what had happened yesterday and I felt I owed him the truth. If he didn't know his son was weak and his daughter strong, it was time he learned.

"She has always been a good girl. She got her head turned, that's all, and without a mother to talk sense into her," Demos said, running his finger over the metal. "That Yanni...." He spit into his bosom to ward off ill-luck.

"Do his people still live here?"

"His mother married again when Yanni was a boy. There was the timber yard to run. She has other sons, steady lads. Yanni was wild, wild as his father. He was just such another, sending all the girls mad about him. Blood runs true."

Tactfully, we neither of us made any further mention of Pacci. I hoped his fright-fueled reformation would stick, for his family's sake as much as for his own. Yet I wouldn't be shocked to return to Leros someday, only to find that he'd been lured away into the train of the first stronger character he met.

Demos reluctantly agreed to my idea of taking Omphale from this high village down to the palace. "They'll look after her well?"

"There's some sensible women there. Another Yanni wouldn't make it past the front door."

"That's what we all need in this life, isn't it? A sensible woman. If her mother were still alive, maybe things would be different."

He shook his head, a burly, grizzled man who could beat hot iron into submission but had no notion how to handle anything delicate like hopes or dreams. He probably hadn't talked about anything deeper than chores to be done with his children in their lives. Like so many of his kind, he was content to leave those seemingly unimportant matters to his wife. With her gone, he had no idea how to cope.

"You've done a fine job with the girl," I said. "I'll see her safely down to the palace."

Demos nodded. I pretended to be absorbed in some unassembled kettles while he knuckled his eyes like a child.

"Shall I bring her here to say farewell?" I asked.

"No, you say it for me. You'll know what to tell her."

"Very well."

I'd gone not much above twenty steps when I heard
Demos call my name. I turned as he came hurrying up.
In one hand, he held a small bag. In the other, a short
sword threw back the light of the torch burning outside
his forge. I raised an eyebrow as I waited for him, toying
with the idea that he'd changed his mind and had
decided to kill me. A strange ambush, to call a man's
name, in order to stab him and leave a gift of money
behind.

He held out the small bag first. "A few coins for the
girl. She'll see things she'll want to buy, fancy goods,
hair combs...um...things."

I realized he'd probably never been more than a
couple of miles from his forge in his life. The simple
village by the ocean where I'd first landed must seem
like Athens itself in terms of riches and variety to a man
like this. My own father had been just the same. He
knew the valleys and hills of his home like the face of
his mother, but the thought of visiting a large town
turned his stomach inside out.

"I'm sure she'll appreciate having some extra
money."

"And this is for you."

He popped it up into the air and caught it so he
could present it to me over his arm properly, hilt first.
Any smith who didn't know the rudiments of sword-
fighting probably didn't make very good weapons.

This was a very good weapon indeed. The blade
was as long as my forearm but as light as the harpy's
feather. I could see the keen edge as I squinted along the
straight strength of it. No marks of the hammer that had
forged it showed even when I turned it back and forth to
catch the light. Instead, a ray-like pattern seemed to have
been woven into its very making.

"This is a princely weapon," I said. "You should be
making these in Athens, not hammering housewares."

"I didn't make it," Demos said. "It was left here in payment of a debt."

The hilt was handsome as well, leather bound with silver-gilt wire to give a slip-proof grip, while the cross-guards had a curling shape that reminded me of clouds without really looking like clouds at all. The leather was dark as with sweat but not cracked or flaking. The pommel had an indentation on the top, where it would be seen only when worn on the hip. Perhaps a jewel had once resided there, now long gone. A tiny nick, hardly noticeable to the eye, lay half-way up the blade.

"Who left it?" I asked. "And is he coming back for it?"

"I doubt it. It's been hanging up in the shop for Gods know how long. My father remembers when it was left here. He was no more than a lad."

I am not often seized with possessiveness but I very much wanted to keep hold of this short-sword. Partly because I'd lost my own, a good blade but nothing near this good, and partly because to see it was to wish to own it. It fit my overlarge hand as though it had been designed for my use alone.

"What does he recall?"

"My father remembers his father talking about a man passing through here but where he came from and where he was going, no one ever knew. Only that he said he was running late and his chariot had lost the pin that held the wheel on."

"Had he crashed?"

"No. He had good horses. My father remembers hearing more about the horses than about the man."

"Men are all the same but horses are unique," I agreed.

"My father's father was also smith here. He fixed the chariot but the man had no money. He offered this as surety that he'd come back to pay up. My grandfather was doubtful. So the man took it and threw it at my grandfather's feet. It sank in more than half its length just under its own weight. We think that's when it got the nick."

He came with in a thumb-nail's width of touching the blade but he knew better that to smudge that gleaming surface. "The man laughed, jumped in his chariot and drove away. No one saw him come or go; no one except my grandfather and my father who was peeking out the door, as children do. My grandfather would have thought he dreamed it all. Only it took him all day to dig the blade out for pulling it did nothing at all. It was his blisters that convinced him that it had all really happened."

Maybe it had happened that way, though to me it sounded like a mash-up of several other stories I'd heard in my travels. No doubt the man was Phaethon, who had begged to take his father's sun-chariot for a spin around the heavens only to be refused again and again. Having stolen it and in a sweat lest his father should discover that the pin had fallen out, adding damage to theft, no doubt Phaethon had stopped in this remote place to have it fixed. Only Phaethon had been killed by Zeus for driving so close to the earth that Africa had turned to desert and had never returned to claim his sword.

I liked my tale so much that I thought I'd spread it around when I got home again. Plenty of places attract tourists on slimmer connections with the gods than this. A few extra drachmas spent by tourists, extending their journey from Artemis' famous temple, could come in very handy in this village, especially if the harvest had been bad.

"I can't take it," I said. The tourists would be much more interested if they could gawk at the actual sword. "Keep it as an heirloom of your house."

"You must," Demos said. "My father said it is yours."

"I don't want you to go against your father's wishes, of course, but it's too good for me."

"You don't understand. Father recognized your name the moment he heard it," Demos said, his troubled eyes meeting mine. "The man in the chariot also said that if he did not redeem it, Eno the Thracian surely would by some act of courage."

* * *

Sometime later, before the sun had come out behind the clouds that veiled it, I turned to Omphale, walking two steps behind me. She looked pale but clear-eyed. I didn't admit, even to myself, how much I regretted my virtuous refusal of the night before.

"Tell me, is your grandfather...?"

"Is he what?"

"Quite all there?"

She laughed. "Completely."

"Just sometimes when men get old, they get confused."

"Not my grandfather. He's sharp with eyes that can still tell a black thread from a white one long before dawn. He can throw a hammer farther than anyone else, young or old."

"How's his memory?"

"Long. He's told me many tales of his boyhood. He talks about things from fifty years ago or more as though they happened yesterday."

There was a convenient tumble of boulders nearby. I motioned for Omphale to stop and sit. I unwrapped the sword from the hemp cloth I'd picked up on my way out of the cottage. "You've seen this before?"

"That's the sword from the forge. So he did give it to you," she added in surprise. "I heard them talking about it early this morning. Grandfather was determined that you should take it, that it was yours. Father wasn't so sure but he doesn't argue with Grandfather, ever."

Omphale touched the hilt gingerly as if worried it would turn and bite her. "It always hung in the forge, above the chimney, ever since I can remember. My father would stand in front of it, studying it. I've seen him there, oh, so often, his hands behind his back, just watching it. I think he used to try to copy it."

"Not an easy thing to copy, I'd guess."

"He never kept any of his attempts. Then, about two years ago, he took it down and put it in the back, among the junk that always collects, no matter how tidy you are."

That explained why Demos had to go rummage for it. The blade showed not a speck of rust, despite having been intentionally 'lost' for a few years. In the dimness of the morning, the shining blade had bathed in reflected fire.

Here, in the open with the sun coming out, the blade seemed to drip with liquid sunlight. The bright bronze of the curving hilt glowed and tiny colorful flashes radiated along the curves of the cross-guard. I ran my finger over it and felt tiny gemstones set into the metal. They were the same color as the bronze, like stitches in a rich golden seam.

Omphale squinted. "I've never seen it shine so brightly."

I went to wrap it up again in the hempen cloth, though as soon as the sun went in behind a cloud, the dazzling light faded too. I'd have to find a leather worker to make me a scabbard. Something simple to conceal the sword's quality. A weapon that was also a treasure was bound to be used.

"Just a reflection," I said reassuringly. But there had been a surge of power up my arm that had left it fizzing. I decided not to mention it.

"It troubles me," she said. "It always has. My mother thought it came from the Gods."

"Hephaestus' own handiwork?"

"Don't scoff. There are such things. I've heard that the warriors in Troy carry magical weapons."

"There are always rumors about such things in a battle zone. It heartens your allies and frightens your foes. But I have been in many kingdoms and I've handled a lot of weapons. I've never seen one yet that came from Heaven. The Gods are like careful merchants; they know where each piece of their stock lies."

"But this one is so magnificent."

"Not too much so for the hands of a master swordsmith. No offense to your father."

"He never claimed mastery, though he makes some beautiful things." She fished in the neck of her cloak. "See this?"

She had pinched up a chain from within her dress. I took the loop in my hand. The links were smaller than the tip of her little finger, gleaming like silver but heavier by far. "Is this iron?" I asked.

"He made it for my mother when they wed. See how every other link is twisted?"

I looked more closely at the details. "It must have taken him a very long time."

"Yes, he said once...." Suddenly she gasped and clutched my arm. Her lovely face contorted with pain.

I dropped the chain and took her by the shoulders to hold her up as she almost collapsed. "What is it?"

"Can't you hear it? The harpy!"

"Where?" Still holding her, I scanned the sky over her head. I still didn't understand the effect the harpy's scream had on everyone but me. I'd heard it more than once now and, despite Temas' warning at our first meeting, repetition didn't turn my knees to water.

"It's flying around up there somewhere. I can feel it!"

I put my arm around Omphale's slender waist and picked her up. I thought it best to get her into some kind of shelter but the nearest bank of trees was half a mile away at least.

She did not burden me at all, except that I couldn't use my hands for balance when the pebbles on the road slipped beneath my unshod feet.

Then I stumbled and dropped the girl as, for the first time, the harpy's scream resonated fully in my mind.

I have stood dazed in a storm-tossed field of war when Father Zeus struck the earth with his thunderbolts. My hair stood on end all over my body and the impacts shook me like a child in the hands of an angry nurse. I felt so helpless, as if I could weep, while men around me threw themselves to the ground. Several never rose again. A famous captain of Corinth, splendid in his armor, had been struck directly and burned from within, a great black mark charring the hilltop on which he had stood, shouting defiance at us. I had been close enough to see his eyes boil white and the steam issue from his mouth in a long plume.

The harpy's cry took me back there, more vividly than any memory or dream ever had.

My mouth was dry and my limbs as heavy as though I'd fought all day and all night against an unconquerable foe. I could see my enemies around me, thick as flies settling on a wound. Through their insubstantial bodies as through a thin curtain, I saw the harpy wheeling overhead.

She gave one powerful stroke of her wings, folded them against her body and dove with appalling speed directly toward us. As she came, she swung around so that her claws were leading. Her scream blended with Omphale's.

I had just enough wit to throw myself flat, knocking Omphale over with a thrown-out arm as I went. The sword went flying away. If I'd been standing, still dumbstruck, the harpy's claws would have parted my hair. I was never so glad to have it short.

The harpy had to continue on in order to turn about, wings churning the air. I scooped up the girl, over my shoulder, and raced on toward the trees. At least there the harpy wouldn't have a clear run.

Omphale twisted around to talk to me from the level of my belt. Her head bounced, her hair flying over her face. "Stop. Put me down. I can run better than you."

Then the harpy descended again. This time, I fell backwards, as the wind of her passing blew over me. Omphale grunted as she came down on her tailbone, jarring her hard enough to bring tears to her eyes. Despite that, she was on her feet faster than I was.

The girl took off, sprinting like Atalanta, her skirt kirtled up to her knees. I staggered after her, stubbing my toes and bruising my insteps. Why had the harpy changed from being benign, even tame, while I was fighting the snake to vicious now? Could there be two?

Another scream, filled with a kind of aching rage, shattered the sky. It seemed to go by me like a hot wind, scouring but not flaying.

I saw it hit Omphale like a blow from a giant hand. She stopped and swayed. She half-turned toward me, her face slack as a horror-dream took hold of her mind. Her expression did not change as the harpy banked to make another run. She stood, looking up as the harpy passed me and came straight for her.

The scream changed to one of triumph. I pelted full out toward the girl, wishing I were smaller and more fleet for my strength was useless if I could not get there before the flying death over my shoulder.

I threw my arms around Omphale and braced myself against the pain of talons in my back. It didn't come. I didn't see what happened, exactly, but all of a sudden the harpy was tumbling, head over tail-feathers, into the ground beyond us.

Omphale came back to herself with a deep shudder. "I saw my mother...she died in childbirth. I saw her split and bleeding...only it was me. It was me."

"Go into the trees," I said. "You'll be safer there."

She stumbled, still half in a nightmare trance, as I turned her around and gave her a little push in the right direction. The harpy was hardly a dozen feet away but Omphale seemed hardly to notice.

The harpy hissed at her, sticking out neck and tongue. She stood up, shaking out the brass-bright feathers on her wide-spread wings. On the ground, as I'd seen yesterday, she could move smoothly but not swiftly. I stood between her and Omphale. The creature settled back onto her haunches, watching us closely with her large eyes, somewhere between human and bird. It seemed quiet for the moment.

Omphale stopped, with her hands pressed over her eyes. Realizing she was in no condition to be alone, I led her deeper into the woods until we were hidden by the trees from the open sky. Then I took her by the shoulders and gave her a little shake. "You're all right," I said.

"It attacked us. Why aren't we dead?"

"A good question. Would you wait here?"

She nodded. "I'm fine. I won't faint or do anything stupid. I'll just sit here for few minutes."

She sat heavily on a fallen trunk. In a moment, she looked up and smiled warmly if wearily. If it hadn't been for my prior commitment to Minthe, I might have been tempted to sue for Omphale's hand. I'd hardly ever heard of a woman outside of legend who could stand up like this to such harsh events, let alone a slip of a girl.

My heart, however, belonged entirely to the girl I'd seen for but a moment in the agora. No one ever said the dictates of Aphrodite make sense. One can only obey blindly.

I watched the harpy from the safety of the screening trees. Though I was sure she couldn't see me, she stared into the leafy trees as if she could.

Somehow, I'd forgotten how dangerous she was, having been distracted by the beauty of her feathers and the curious delicacy of her face. I'd almost decided, after yesterday, that her reputation had been built more on fearsome appearance than any actual action. Yet now, she'd attacked a human being.

At the same time, I wondered why she hadn't killed me. She could have ripped me to shreds in that last rush but she must have swerved at the last instant, crashing rather than striking.

When I walked out into the clearing, she straightened up, cooing softly. She lifted her wings, high and wide. Her cooing became almost a song.

I walked over and knelt down beside her. Reaching out, I wanted to stroke the shining feathers but didn't want to lose any fingers. I touched her cheek instead. Her skin was smooth as a child's and her eyes glistened as if with tears. She crossed her wings over her face, her shoulders trembling.

Accounting for the difference in species, she looked just as Omphale had. But how was I to encourage a depressed harpy? Shaking her would probably be the worst possible move if I wanted to keep those fingers.

"Poor thing," I said.

Her eyes peeped at me over the curve of her wing. I smiled reassuringly, figuring the tone of my voice and expression would reach her as it would any animal. I only wished I had a little food. Even the toughest warriors always wanted to offer food to wild animals, perhaps to propitiate animal spirits, or just because humans like to think wild creatures need us somehow.

I added, fatuously, "Who's a pretty harpy, then?"

The last time I'd seen an expression like that on a female face was when I'd offered a fully certified courtesan half-price during my first visit to a large town. It wasn't the money so much as the truly execrable poetry I'd composed to accompany the cash.

I could have sworn she rolled her eyes. Then, as Omphale called my name, the harpy hissed again. She glanced at me one final time then, with a massive beat of her wings, she lifted into the sky again. I could hear her cry echoing across the blue and a sadness settled on my heart. Omphale came a few steps nearer. "What in the name of Aphrodite was that all about?"

CHAPTER TEN

As much as I respected Omphale, I couldn't expect her to keep the story of such a wonder to herself. A tale like that would be her password into the bosom of the palace's servants. It would grow in the telling.

I reported to King Temas that his rebel guard problem was over. The lads I'd sent back had appeared, chastened, to confess that they'd been weak and foolish. Temas, a boy himself, had taken their youth into consideration and welcomed them into his home once more. He offered me the job of guard captain. I didn't show how little the job appealed.

"You're kind, sire, but I have one more task to perform for you first."

"The harpy."

"Yes. I believe I will be able to end that burden for you tomorrow."

"It was indeed a great day for Leros when Phandros found you in Piraeus." He poured me a cup of wine. "Shall we drink to your success?"

I noticed that Phandros was watering his wine a little more than half-and-half. He looked pale yellow and his hands shook whenever he released their clasp, one upon the other. He also seemed to have misplaced his appetite. I've never been one to drink to excess but I knew the signs of someone trying to give it up all together.

After the servant girls had served the noon meal, the king dismissed them. He leaned forward across the table and said in a confidential undertone, "Who is the girl you've brought into my household?"

"A brave young woman from a small village. Her father is Demos, the smith."

"Have you any...er...claim on her?"

I hid a smile in my cup. I had been right to bring her. "On the contrary, she has a claim on me."

"Oh?" he said, his expression somber.

"She saved my life, near enough."

I told the tale, giving Omphale a greater part and maximizing the veniality and stupidity of the late Yanni. By doing so, I made Pacci almost disappear from the story. No king wants a brother-in-law that weak.

"And what about Eurytos? I confess I never thought to see you come back alive, let alone unharmed."

"Oh, I have a few bruises and scrapes, sire."

I skimmed over the details of Eurytos' destruction. The king did not need to hear all that had happened nor to know how close everyone on Leros came to being the first step on a road to the end of the world. I did reassure him that none of his accomplices had escaped, describing the avalanches I had caused.

Temas took a drink. "Destroyed all in one go! Marvelous! How ever did you think of it?"

"Rock-slides aren't uncommon on the mountain roads where I come from. It is an easy matter to cause deliberately what happens so often naturally."

"Amazing shooting. Though I could have wished to keep my little rock fortress. It was discovered by some wandering shepherds many generations ago and was always our last resort if invaders ever came. The caves can store much food and water, not to mention people."

"You must warn the citizens not to venture there," Phandros said. He'd been quiet during my recital, not joining in the king's expressions of dismay or glee. "It could be most dangerous, what with unquiet spirits of traitors floating about. There may even be rumors of treasure which is even more dangerous. We mustn't let foolish children go exploring."

"Spread a rumor or two about ghostly appearances," Temas ordered. "That will be more effective than any proclamation."

"Very wise, sire."

It was, too, though I was surprised by Temas' quick understanding of how to mold his citizenry's opinions. He was growing into his authority quickly. A few days of people eagerly agreeing with everything you said would have that effect on even more mature minds.

"Do you have a plan in mind for the creature's capture?" Temas asked me.

"First, I must return to the *Chelidion* to set certain tasks in motion."

"Yes, I saw the cage when I was on board the ship. Is it true you mean to capture the creature alive?"

It would have been very unlike Jori to tell the king more than his own immediate necessity required. Temas must have drawn his own conclusions. I began to wish the girls would come in to clear away the platters and plates. Omphale had distracted him once; why not twice?

"Alive?" Phandros echoed. "Surely that's never been done before?"

"Others have captured all sorts of creatures. Many of our legends describe that kind of thing. I think I can do it too, with a little planning." I suppose it was prideful of me to put it like that, as if I were the equal of Hercules who captured the Erymanthian Boar or Bellerophon who enticed Pegasus. But I'd never been impressed with Hercules' wits and Bellerophon just plain got lucky.

"But no one knows where the harpy will strike next. You'd have to be in just the right spot at just the right moment."

The king nodded at his counselor's words. "We could stake out a young kid. Entice it down with fresh meat."

"That would work," Phandros said. "Then we could have half a dozen men with nets waiting to capture it."

"I think the beast is too wary for that. It would be better to rig a drop-net. I believe old Thryon knows how to make one. He used one to catch that rogue ram, you know, the one with the thorn in his ear."

I appreciated their enthusiasm but this was my operation to run. I already knew how I was going to capture her. "What I need more than anything right now..." They looked at me expectantly. "Is a few hours of sleep. Indoors, for a change."

"Of course," Temas said graciously though he looked disappointed. He clapped his hands to summon the girls.

A very pretty one lit the way to my chamber, giggling like an Aeolian harp the whole way. "Tell me, sweet one...."

"Yes," she said, posing coyly with the candle held low to throw her chest into relief.

"Somewhere in this house is an old woman named Doris. I'd like to speak with her."

"Doris?"

"Yes. Doris. I talked to her yesterday. Very old. Wears black. Thinks everything is cursed?"

I've seen that expression on a kitten's face when a ball of thread rolls by. She was interested enough to look but not about to jump. "I don't know of any one like that."

"She's not in trouble. As a matter of fact, I want to thank her."

"Give me the message and I'll pass it on." She came a little closer. "I can keep a secret."

"I'm sure you can. I'd rather talk to her face to face."

"My face is much nicer than some weird old lady's." I couldn't argue with that. She put it up to be kissed and, having been raised to be very polite, I kissed her. Purely as an expression of my gratitude. If she'd been a boy, I would have handed him an obol.

Before she could drop it, I took the candle out of her hand and lit my way into the room. She started to follow. I pushed the door gently, closing her on the far side. As her face disappeared, I said, "Don't forget to tell Doris I want to see her. Send her up to wake me at dawn."

Her shrug was eloquent. If I was such a fool to pass up what was offered freely, there was nothing to be done with me.

A long time later, I lay with my arms folded under my head in a very comfortable bed, a feather-stuffed pad over a fresh straw pallet. I had slept well in many worse places yet now I couldn't see to bring Hypnos, god of sleep, close enough to throw an arm-lock on him.

From some other room, I heard deep snoring while the giggles of the girls in the maid's quarters was like the tinkling of distant bells. I was thirsty, I decided, but too indolent to seek water. A feather tickled my nose and a piece of straw dug into the back of my calf where it hung over the end of the bed. I kept thinking about the spider I'd seen in the corner of the room, hoping it wasn't going to get curious about me. I writhed and twitched, trying to get comfortable.

"I'd be better off among the tree-roots again," I said aloud.

I didn't have to dig too deep to know what was troubling me. I admitted to myself that I was feeling unusually hesitant about capturing the harpy. If it hadn't been for that feather, I would be dead. True, she hadn't given it to me, I'd taken it from the fallen trash of her nest. But Eurytos would have killed me if that feather hadn't been in my scabbard. I knew it as I knew my own name.

Closing my eyes, I saw the giant crab swimming toward me, that human hand almost pearly in the blue water. Eurytos' mysterious She hadn't done him much good after all. I wondered if his goddess would give him another chance to come into the world of men. Somehow I had a feeling if She could give her tools such gifts, she would have little patience with one who bungled their use.

My mind began to revolve scenarios for tomorrow's efforts. First, I'd have to get the cage landed which could take half the morning. Then to take it up to the Temple would eat up a few more hours, especially if the sailors stopped to dine, chase girls and get drunk. From my experiences with Jori's crews, I could count on that.

Maybe it would be better to have the sailors bring it ashore and then use villagers to take it the rest of the way. No...I reminded myself impatiently that it was doubtful any of the villagers would want to go to the Temple until it was purified. Better use the sailors who wouldn't have heard the story yet.

I sighed heavily. To make matters worse, an owl started hooting outside my window. I couldn't even swear at it, lest it turn out to be a messenger from Athena. Not that she would have much to say to me. I was attentive to all the gods but I had a little less time for her than for some of the others. She watched over soldiers and wise men and I was neither.

I sat up and thumped my pillow. It was sweetly scented with sleep-inducing herbs but it might have been a pile of broken sandals for all the comfort it gave me.

With a snort and a cough, the snorer quieted. The giggling girls had dropped off one by one. I hoped

Temas was sleeping well. He was young, horrors would not leave a deep mark on his soul. Judging by his smile when Omphale had come back, he would heal a little more each time he saw her. I'd noticed her sneaking peeks at him from under her lashes as she moved with a self-conscious grace around the table. Of course, a king is always of interest to a girl but I had hopes they'd eventually find a way to talk to each other. I couldn't very well give him hints about that.

My main objective now was to capture the harpy and leave Leros. I was more tempted than I'd realized by the offer of the guard position. A steady salary, young men to train in my style of fighting and thinking, and pretty island maidens to flirt with sounded like an old soldier's ideal. But I wasn't that old yet. Or was I?

Slowly my eyes began to close. The image of the pretty island girls became to blur and grow indistinct as though someone threw water over a newly painted fresco. I could feel sleep wandering nearer, step by step. Frustrating to know that if I lifted so much as a finger, he'd be gone again. My last thought was to wonder why Hypnos was such a skittish fellow. Maybe he had vicious relations.

My dreams at first were the usual muddle, half-heard words, half-understood imaginings. My mother scolded me for spilling some wheels of cheese on the floor while tiny ants threw huge shadows on the white-washed walls of our home.

Even in my dream I knew that wasn't right. Whitewash belonged to other parts of Greece; I'd grown up in a series of stone huts that look tumbled together by the hand of a Titan child. It was good to see my mother's face again, though. She looked young, as she had when I was a boy.

From there, I passed out of thought to the realm where even the memory of this earthly existence fades. I believe it is there we dream our most ideal lives, which we lose once more as we drift back on the tides of waking. It would be too tragic to remember how beautiful everything is in that dream-world so we forget it all before we ever awaken.

Now there were images again. Omphale, the old crone, some woman I didn't know, high-browed and sneering, the ants, Yanni's amazed look just before he was eaten. Then the crone again. I felt her cool hand on my forehead. It was her voice, her eyes but the face was that of the servant girl at the door. No, it was my Minthe. No, it was the crone. It was all of them, blending and changing one into the other.

It didn't matter which woman it was, they all said the same thing. "Go to Troezen. Hurry before it's too late."

"I am," I said to each in turn. "I am going."

Nothing I said had any effect. They began to change faster and faster until I saw only a flickering blur with only a rare feature recognizable. A nose stood out, then a pair of red lips, or a quick lift of a black curving eyebrow. I began to hear the roar and crash of waves on the shore.

Now I wanted to wake up but you cannot shake yourself awake.

The mélange of faces began to resolve itself. It wasn't just a random eyebrow; it was specific. The same with the mouth, the nose, the deep-set eyes.... Slowly a face was evolving but not one I knew. It was the haughty one, her lips slightly pursed, her dark hair dressed high with jewel-tipped sticks thrust through the looping, gleamless mass.

When she opened her large eyes, made more striking with thick kohl, I suddenly felt wide awake. I tried but could not move so much as a finger. I seemed to hover outside my own body, looking down at my prone self while at the same time seeing this woman very clearly in my dream.

"Oh, Thracian, I am awaiting our meeting," she told me in a voice like caressed velvet. "Do not break faith with me. Come to Troezen. Cross the sea. Come to me."

"Who are you?"

Her smile showed crooked teeth, small as milk teeth but sharp. "I am your future. And you are mine."

She seemed to gloat over me, her tongue churning against her teeth, her eyes burning with lust.

Now, don't get me wrong. I don't mind a woman taking the lead sometimes. It can be fun. But the hunger in her gaze seemed to go beyond mere lust into something foul.

I began to struggle against the bonds she seemed to have cast around me with her gaze. She repeated her claim on me with even greater intensity, her face coming nearer. She raised a bone-white hand as if she could touch me through the veils of night. I saw myself on the bed, sweating, my brow corrugated as I tossed my head from side to side.

"Wake up, Eno, you lout," I shouted from my vantage point somewhere near the ceiling. "Wake up."

I did. For a moment, I stared around mindlessly, disoriented by the sudden change of perspective. I'd returned to my body as quickly as if I'd fallen into it.

Someone scratched at the door. I came to myself, sitting on the edge of the bed. It creaked as I got up and, bleary-eyed, opened the door to see the same girl I'd kissed the night before.

"You wanted to be woken up at dawn," she reminded me as I stood there blinking down at her.

"Did I? Oh, yes, that's right." I yawned, while glancing up and down the narrow hall. "Did you find Doris?"

"I told you there's nobody here named that."

"Did you ask?"

"Yes," she said with a humoring sigh. "I asked Iole. She's worked here since she could crawl and she says nobody named Doris has ever been here, let alone been here yesterday. Do you want something to eat?"

I thanked her and said I'd come down to the kitchens myself. Then I sat on the bed again, my face buried in my hands. Suddenly, I didn't want to go anywhere, let alone far-off Troezen. Death was an ordinary hazard of the business but that woman...I shuddered deeply as if I'd touched something unclean.

When I got downstairs, the girl was gossiping with the others, including, to my dismay, Omphale. "And he wouldn't even let me in..."

One of the others said, "Well, you know what they say about the men in Athens."

"But he's from Thrace. Have you heard what they say about them?"

"No...what?"

I cleared my throat and they scattered like chickens. Omphale gave me a friendly nod. Someone had dressed her hair in a soft knot and she wore a trace of kohl on her eyelids. "How are you settling in?" I asked as I sat down.

"The girls are very kind," she said, putting bread before me. "They talk about things I don't understand, though."

"You'll learn." Had I done her a favor after all by bringing her here? It would be a shame if she became like other girls, giggling and silly. Remembering how she'd insisted on doing her own running when the harpy attacked, I had no real fears that she would.

"They say you'll try to capture that thing today," she said.

"Yes. I don't think it will be too difficult." I started to say something light and reassuring when she cut me off.

"Neither do I."

"Eh?"

"I know it can't stay here. My people will kill it if they can. What will you do with it?"

Temas and Phandros had assumed that I'd kill it outright, somewhere far from Leros where whatever God had sent it would not be displeased. Omphale did not assume that.

"What do you think I should do with it?"

"Take it away and let it go. Find some quiet little island where it won't bother anyone."

I put my elbow on the table, my chin in my hand, and studied her. "Why all this mercy? It tried to kill you."

"Do you think I'm the kind to hold a grudge? Besides, once you understand something, you can't hate it anymore."

"And you think you understand this thing?"

"You understand it too, don't you?"

"No. I don't understand most females of whatever species." I tried a charming grin on for size. It didn't melt her heart appreciably.

"You're not a stupid man, Eno. Don't you think the poor thing has a very good reason for attacking a woman walking and talking with you?"

"What reason could it possibly have? Animals don't reason the way men do."

She gave me that look. All women have it in their arsenal. I think they are born knowing how to aim and fire it. It starts with a sigh, a roll of the eyes heavenward, and then they stare steadily while the unfortunate male hurriedly reviews his entire calendar of crimes, of omission and commission, for the exact one she is objecting to now.

I applied myself to my porridge. After a minute or two and another heavy sigh, she went to make my breakfast. I was so glad to escape that I didn't ask again about Doris.

The dew still pearled on the grass as I went to the edge of the cliff above the bay. I could see the *Chelidion* far below me. The sea looked as calm as a bowl of milk, belying the roiling mass of life that carried on beneath the surface.

It would have been the easy and comfortable thing to walk down to the pier and row myself out as I had when I took the young king to see the ship. But I knew in my heart that the battle with Eurytos had left a fear of the sea like a raised and twisted scar on my soul. I'd known it yesterday when I'd stood at the water's edge, watching the dolphins at play. The old Eno would have dived in and swum out to meet them but I had been afraid.

I care little for what the world may say of me but to stand so accused in my own judgment...that I will not bear. Even in the hint of such fear has driven me to take risks and undergo trials that a simpler, wiser man would decline. I can never be free of the doubt that it is not wisdom but cowardice. That is my weakness, one that sends me to dive, in this instance, into a depthless sea at the prompting of jeering ghosts.

I stood on the cliff, my toes clutching the sandy edge. Raising my arms, I inhaled and exhaled, each breath deeper and wider. Then I reached out, turning my arms into a bowsprit, raised up on the balls of my feet and dove off.

Through the rush of the wind in my ears, I heard the harpy cry, or maybe it was a man, calling out, 'Stop, you fool!"

I dove down into the colder layers until again my breath burned in my throat. A sea turtle stared at me from ancient, wrinkled eyes and I startled a couple of long-bodied fish but that was all. Rising, I broke the sparkling surface, laughing at my folly but powerless against it. I had fought my fears again and won but they would return. They always return.

CHAPTER ELEVEN

When I came back from the ship, Phandros was waiting for me on the dock. "Where have you been?

I grinned at him. "I had to make arrangements with Jori. I'll capture the harpy today and be on my way." I shook myself like a dog, water flying off me. "Where's this taverna I've heard so much about?"

After we were served drinks, sitting at a table under a grape arbor, a pleasant spot we had all to ourselves, Phandros looked grimmer even than usual. He'd watered his wine more than half.

"You said you'd sell the harpy in Troezen. Ever been there?"

"No. Have you?"

He shook his head. "I've heard strange tales, that's all."

"Seems every island tells tall tales about all the others. Apparently, there are stories about Thrace which isn't even an island."

"I suppose you are right. Gossip spreads like milk in water until you cannot separate it from the truth."

"Sometimes rumors are true. You said that Queen Amymone was from Lesbos. Now that's an island with plenty of rumors swirling around it," I said with a wink.

Phandros looked disapproving. "Oh, you mean that old tale about the women there? Nonsense, my good fellow. Pure nonsense, I assure you. Our dear queen was as open and sunny as the day, not remote and cold at all."

"I think we are talking about different stories," I said.

"You do mean the one about Orpheus' head?"

"Do I?"

"You must know it. Every schoolboy knows it."

"My education was neglected."

A true teacher, Phandros could not pass up the chance to enlighten my ignorance, even if he sighed dramatically at my denseness. "You do know that Orpheus was torn to pieces by the maddened handmaidens of Dionysus? In Thrace, actually, according to the legends."

"Really?" I ignored the slur on my homeland. "Why did they do that?"

"The tale varies. Some say it was because he would play only sad songs after Eurydice was returned to Hades and they didn't care for the tunes. Some say it was his indifference to their orgies; others that he refused the worship of the God of Wine to follow the God of the Sun. As you cannot have true revelry without both music and wine, the God slew him for the discourtesy. Naturally, there is considerable discussion among scholars as to which is the true tale. These others are folk-legends or a blend of other tales. Macrites of Corinth, for instance, has suggested that..."

"Where does Lesbos come into the tale?" I asked, interrupting what promised to be a lengthy exposition.

"Ah, yes. Well, the poet's head fell into the sea and was carried to the island of Lesbos where it was recovered by several handmaidens to the queen at the time. It was speaking prophetic verses and continued for three days after his death. These prophecies were so horrific that the maidens and the queen vowed that they would never repeat them, except to their own daughters so that they would not be entirely forgotten. Each woman vows equal secrecy and the habit has so grown on them that they are now famous for their taciturnity and their reserve, rare indeed among women."

"It's said that they are so reserved that they don't even tell their children that they love them."

"As I say, a false tale. Queen Amymone was not like that. A more open-hearted woman never lived. She'd say that she loved her husband, throwing her arms about his neck. He permitted her a great deal of license, more than is granted to most women."

I thought of my Minthe. Would she ever throw her arms around me and declare her love? Did she even know I existed?

Phandros had been musing too. "Though...."

"What?" I poured him a little more wine and he drank it absent-mindedly.

"Perhaps I am being wise after the event. Yet it strikes me now that there was something almost defiant in the way she proclaimed her affection." He poured himself a little more wine. "She would say that she loved him in spite of everything. One naturally assumed this was the result of some quarrel, after they'd made up. Yet perhaps there was more to it than that. She was from Lesbos, after all."

"I wish Nausicaa were still here. I have a lot of questions she might have answered if I'd only known what to ask."

"What did happen up in the temple, Eno? And how did you defeat Eurytos and his men? If you want to discuss wild rumors, start with one of those."

Phandros' eyes were shrewd, if red. If anyone could help me sort through the knotted threads of my tangled thought, he could. I wanted to trust him but he had lived a long time in the midst of what I was beginning to believe was part of a cult of dark magic. "Tell me this first, Phandros. Why is there such a large temple to Artemis on this -- pardon me -- rather unimportant island?"

"Another legend. Our lands are full of legends as Attica is full of snakes. You can hardly move without stepping on one."

"Let's not talk about snakes, if you don't mind," I said, taking a drink myself. "What is the legend?"

We were like two old wives, sitting in the sun, gossiping about our betters.

"A typical tale of the Gods. There are, as you know, seventeen portals to Hades, other than the traditional way of crossing the River Styx on Charon's boat. One is here, so they say, and long ago Artemis came with her arrows to drive back some escaping Titans. She decreed a temple be built over the spot. A typical tale as I say. No one has ever seen anything unnatural here, not until last night."

"I suggest you recommend to the king that a new statue of the Goddess be dedicated as soon as possible."

His eyes had grown comically large. "Yes, yes, indeed."

"There are really seventeen portals to Hades?"

"So scholars say." He began to tick them off on his fingers, obscure cities, most remote or unimportant. I stopped him at a name I knew.

"Troezen?"

"Ah, yes, a very famous portal. It is known as the Poor Man's or the Miser's Way, as you don't need two coins to pay the Ferryman. You can walk."

"Not I."

"No!" he said and spat. "I meant no ill omen."

I wanted to trust Phandros. Despite his dry and stuffy ways, I thought him an honest man who had done his best for an island that was not his native land. But why did he drink so much? What memory or crime was he trying to drown? Perhaps nothing more than a forbidden affection for the late Queen of Leros. She must have been a remarkable woman.

What had Nausicaa said? Something about how the plans had been delayed by a fool? Had Amymone come to open the portal only to find love within her arranged marriage? Had the birth of Temas tied her to life instead of death?

There were too many unanswered questions. I felt I'd give my entire profit from this job for a few solid, indisputable answers.

"A fool like you..." I murmured. "That's what she said. Kept too long away by a fool like you."

"What?"

"Just talking out loud. Let's get another beaker."

Phandros licked his lips but resolutely refused more wine. He waved the taverna keeper over to ask for the reckoning.

What made me a fool, besides the obvious? More questions, fewer answers yet. But there was something rattling around in the far depths of my mind that might make sense if I could only reach it.

The landlord refused our money and made a fuss over wiping the table, which did not need it. "If you gentlemen are finished with your wine, some of the lads are grumbling a bit, sir, about the...well, about the dead ones."

"Never mind," I said, standing up. "They'll be fond enough of me in a couple of hours."

* * *

After the sun had passed the zenith, I felt lower than something smelly stuck to the bottom of a sandal but my prophecy had come true. I was very popular.

The harpy had come to me trustingly, pecking the wheat I held in my hand. When she was near enough, I dropped the grains, threw one arm around her body and flattened my other hand over her mouth. Instinctively, she tried to kick but her claws skittered uselessly over the breastplate of my armor.

I thrust her into the cage and slammed the door closed before she could turn and come at me. I watched, heart-sick, as she threw herself frantically against the bars. "Don't," I said, knowing she could not understand. "You'll only hurt yourself."

Was I afraid or hopeful that she could rip her way out? All I knew is that when the olivewood and iron held, I felt a great weariness settle down on my shoulders.

In a few minutes, she huddled down in the corner, her wings swept over her face in the attitude I'd come to associate with sorrow. She did not raise her face even when I lifted the cage.

My muscles ached as I carried my burden the hundred yards or so to the wagon I'd borrowed from the local oil merchant. The donkeys were placid creatures yet even they shifted their feet and rolled frightened eyes as I lowered the cage into the back.

They showed a surprising increase in energy I drove over the rough track to the ruined pier. Several sailors stood there, waiting for me. I had ordered them not to step foot off the pier and they had obeyed. Perhaps the way I'd picked all three of them up in one fist by the slack of their garments while talking to them might have given them the notion I was serious in my commands.

"You got it!" one of them said gleefully as I drew up beside them. "Way to go!"

"Ugly thing, ain't it?" one of his fellows added.

I didn't glance at any of them. I might have appeared stern but I didn't want them to see the shame I felt lurking in my eyes. "Is the boat ready?"

"Yes, yes, ready and waiting."

They'd rigged a winch while I'd been gone. As is usual with sailors and other men initiated into deep mysteries, there was a certain amount of milling around and unnecessary display of difficulties before commencing on any operation. They discussed weights and shifting beams and balances, even though I'd told them to be ready when as soon as I returned.

"Hurry up," I growled.

"Aye, aye, sir. Just another minute...."

Of course, it was impossible to sneak away cleanly. I'd known that. I stood on the end of the dock, my new sword tied on my belt with a leather cord and a long staff of wood in my hand. Slowly at first, but then with increasing speed as word spread, a crowd gathered.

"Is that it?" a fat woman said in a tone of disparagement.

"Oh, look, Iamos! Did you ever see such a thing?"

"I want to see, Mother. Lift me up. Lift me up, Mother."

The veiled woman were clustered together, whispering behind their hands but glancing far more than at me than at the harpy. I saw merchants, farmers and a couple of faces from the palace. A few high-bellied men conferred near the front of the crowd. Half a dozen young boys were jostling near the sea-wall, daring each other to move closer. I saw one stoop for a loose stone. With a rascally glance at his fellows, he hurled it at the cage.

Some cheered as the stone arced through the air while others applauded, pushing forward. I knew it would only be a moment before all manner of trash would be thrown and I wasn't having it.

I caught the stone. I fixed my eyes on the boy and squeezed. Sand rained down from my fingers. Then I turned my back on them.

The tenor of the crowd's noises shifted from triumph to anger. "Let us have it!"

"Yeah, we know what to do with it!"

"Chicken dinner tonight," called a high tenor voice, followed by clucking noises. Someone else decided it was wittier to crow like a rooster.

I turned toward them again, my hand resting negligently on my sword. One of the town-leaders, his belly as round as a water jar, swaggered forward, holding up his hands for silence.

"On behalf of the people of Leros, I'd like to express my very profoundest...."

From out of the crowd had slipped a narrow-faced, grey-haired man with a beard tangled as a neglected fishing net. Phandros murmured something in the pot-bellied man's ear and I saw the blowhard's eyebrows raise so high they tangled in his hair. "Really? Oh, certainly, certainly."

He silenced the crowd again. "As I was saying, on people loved by Eros of...or rather, I...oh, dear. Gentlemen, the King!"

Temas had brushed his hair in honor of the occasion. He'd flung a bright red himation over his shoulder and his chiton gleamed brilliantly in the morning sunshine. A gold bracelet clasped his right wrist and a large signet carved from a single emerald adorned his forefinger. He wore no diadem but his people parted for him, bowing.

He clasped my right forearm and I had no choice but to return the greeting. "Good people," he said in a clear, carrying voice. "We have much to thank our friend Eno the Thracian for on this day. No other man could have triumphed against the evils that beset us. No more will we be threatened by Eurytos the Criminal and his band."

This seemed to be news to some of the more prosperous-looking citizens. Were they the ones making a tidy fortune selling to the outlaws?

"And now he has captured the beast that turned our days from kindly friend to implacable foe! We may tend our crops, care for our flocks and let our children play without fear of losing any to the terror of the harpy! Let us cheer and rejoice. Phandros...serve the wine!"

The crowd turned from me to see a cart decorated with vine leaves and flowers. No harpy was as interesting as the wine-barrel that rode in the back. Iole, Omphale and several other girls stood by with trays of wooden goblets and cups, all the palace held, I'd warrant. No one had to be asked twice. There was a pushing forward, away from the harpy.

The sailors wanted to accept the king's invitation. I snarled at them. "Get that cage on the boat with no more pissing around or I'll have your liver and lights!"

Temas was staring at the harpy. I felt I wanted to shield her from any more prying eyes. "I'll be off now, sire."

"It's smaller than I thought it would be. How did you capture it so quickly?"

I didn't answer.

With the discretion that would make him not only a good king but a good man, Temas changed the subject. "It's hard to believe that it has been just a few short days since you arrived. And me, standing there, waving those silly red flags."

"You'll fix this pier?"

"That fellow who started to make a speech will fix it. He's got a bit more money than he can account for legally. A good-sized donation to the rebuilding project will just about settle the matter. I'll let him keep a little, just to have a hook in his guts if I need it."

"How old did you say you were?"

He chuckled. "You don't account enough for early training. You only saw my father when he was dead and perhaps have taken a poor impression of his abilities. A more cunning man never lived, even if he lost some of his shrewdness after my mother died. The heart seemed to go out of him and he took no more joy in ruling." He glanced away to where the townspeople were guzzling away happily. "This girl...this Omphale...."

"Sire?"

"Never mind. I'll figure it out for myself." He clapped his hand on my arm. "Don't worry, Eno. My father may have taught me how to think, but it's my mother who taught me to love. I shall not fail of her teaching."

"I am sure of it."

"One other thing my father taught me is to pay my debts." He held out a bag, small but heavy. When transferred to my hand, it gave out a satisfying 'chink'. But the sound brought no joy to my heart or ease to my mind.

I took my leave of Temas. He bade me consider Leros a second home and if ever I wished to settle down to a steady job there'd be one here for me. I thanked him and asked him to drink a cup for me.

One of the sailors, chosen by a quick drawing of lots, approached to tell me all was ready. No one in the crowd noticed as the cage swayed up into the air and was lowered with care onto the boat. The sailors got in, huddled at the farthest end from the harpy, preparing to cast off.

I took a last look at the island of Leros. The citizens were milling around, pledging each other and the king in wine. Temas lifted a cup in my direction and I waved, smiling despite myself. The last I saw of him, he was standing next to Omphale, helping her serve out second helpings.

A disturbance at the rear of the crowd stayed my steps a moment. Here came Phandros, a bag slung over his shoulder and an old straw hat, once broad-brimmed, now drooping with age, falling over his eyes. A stout staff struck the ground with each step. He stopped by me and looked over the edge of the dock. "Rather a small boat," he said.

"Big enough. Going somewhere?"

He handed his bag down to one of the sailors. "Yes, I'm going with you."

"You are?"

"Of course." He turned and held out a hand. "Lower me down, won't you?"

For a moment, I held his eyes, many questions jostling for expression. "Have you quarreled with the king? I swear this was not in your mind last night?"

"No, who could quarrel with Temas? He admits you are perfectly right in your opinion then does what he wants anyway. And I would have discussed the matter with you this morning but you were too busy leaping off cliffs."

"You saw me?" It had been his voice, then, that I had heard just before I made my dive.

"I did indeed, you lunatic."

"It was nothing," I said, but not from modesty.

"Nothing? In good King Theocrites' day, that cliff was measured for a series of experiments in mathematics. It stands one hundred and thirty-seven feet high. I thought I was watching a madman commit suicide this morning."

"And you come with me to prevent further attacks?"

"I come with you because you need a keeper, Eno. Failing that, a friend. I can sing, tell tales, distinguish edible mushrooms from the kind that will send you hot-foot to the latrine, and determine location from the stars. A valuable companion for all eventualities."

"And you can hide yourself in an instant in a pile of leaves," I said.

"That as well. Will you accept me for a companion?"

I did not want to. It wasn't that I was afraid of him or that I didn't trust him. But I wanted to leave Leros with nothing to remind me of my betrayal. "We are going to Troezen first. To sell the harpy for the sacrifice."

He showed no moral outrage but then he didn't know how easily she'd come to me only to be betrayed. "You'll need me, then. I taught in several households there and kept the accounts for one of the banking houses. It's a very wealthy place, Troezen. You have to know how to play the courtier."

"I'm not good at that."

"At last your talents fail? Count me amazed."

"Get in the boat," I said.

Jori accepted the harpy with glad cries and reassurances that he'd had no doubt of my success. The crew were afraid to go near the cage, though the harpy continued to hide her face. I lashed the cage to the deck, made sure she had water and straw, then covered half the cage with a sail so that the sun would not beat down on her, nor the spray dampen her.

Jori's welcome of Phandros was not quite so effusive. "Have you ever worked on a boat such as this? Can you turn out on a black night and take in sail by touch alone? Can you mend rope? Patch a sail? Scrub a deck?"

"I can make soup," Phandros said, holding onto a line with his beard blowing past his shoulder. He looked a little greenish.

"Soup? Soup?" Jori lifted his palms up as he shrugged. "You'll share quarters with Eno and do not complain to me if his shoulders take up more than his side of the bunk."

"Don't worry," I said. "I'm sleeping on deck."

"What?" Jori looked hurt. "You insult my mattresses?"

"Let's get under weigh," I said, in no mood for banter.

"Very well, very well. Ho, there, Minos! Haul up the anchor. Nikko, prepare to make sail. Where's the damned helmsmen gone to? Must I do everything myself? And you...what is your name again?"

"Phandros."

"Phandros. You go...make soup."

I was never more in the way than at the start of a trip. Unless I was called to haul up a fouled anchor, I usually retired to my tiny cabin. Jori wasn't joking about my shoulders. I had finally learned not to crash my head on the low beams every time I turned around.

Maybe my cabin would have been larger if it weren't for all the secret compartments, hide-away holes, and concealed holds on the ship. I knew of several but I'm sure there were more. Jori loved to come up with new tricks to smuggle goods past the sharp eyes of the royal customs agents. Sailing to so many islands, his profits would have been nil if he hadn't taken such precautions. Not to mention pirates, tax collectors and others with a firm grasp of the concept 'what's yours is mine' as well as those who preferred the more oblique, 'nice little ship, captain, pity if anything happened to it.'

However, there was one hiding place in this cabin that I hoped even Jori did not know of, although I was aware he liked to snoop. It was in his nature.

Under the bunk, the builder of the *Chelidion* had made a mistake and hadn't shaved a board down enough. A lost bootlace between bunk and bulkhead had never dropped to the floor. I had felt for it and found it caught on the half-sprung board. I'd pulled out the nails to find a neat little space on the far side of the built-in bed. I now pulled loose the boards on either side, leaving just enough room for the sword, wrapped up again securely. I hammered them back into place with a few blows from the edge of my fist.

Jori's eyes had already been upon the sword, appraising its value and questioning its sudden appearance. He wouldn't ask outright where I'd found it but I could be sure he'd hint. Hiding it seemed safest. Jori wouldn't steal it, though he might try to win it from me with crooked dice. I couldn't vouch for the rest of his cut-throats, however. Better to have it out of sight and hope that kept it out of their minds.

Strangely enough, I didn't feel the same way about the money Temas had paid me. That I put in the strongbox I kept bolted to the wall. If the money went missing, I'd merely hold everyone upside down by their ankles and shake them until all the gold felt out of their pouches. I'd take what I was owed and leave the crew to find out the true thief. It wouldn't be the first time.

I gathered together my belongings. There were a good fewer than when I'd left. Many things had been lost on Leros, including a good-sized chunk of my soul. But I could, at least, change out of this kilt and into my last clean chiton.

Leros slipped away behind us. Jori, thanks to his ancestor's arrangement with a sea-god, didn't sneak from island to island, never going out of sight of land, preferring to cut straight across open water. However, because he hadn't re-provisioned in Leros, he decided to head for Mykonos, less than two days' journey away, for water, bread, and whatever meat was available.

The crew seemed cheerful, happy to be at sea once again. Yet even while they were singing a sea-ditty that night, I saw many curious and uneasy glances falling on the covered cage. I strengthened my resolve to sleep beside it that night and every night until we reached Troezen. As if protecting her weren't reason enough, my suspicions that it was Phandros' snoring I'd heard last night were confirmed very soon after the ship quieted for the night.

"Chimeras with three heads don't make noises like that!" Jori complained, coming to find me after an hour of timber-rattling snores. "And one of them is a goat!"

"Put your fingers in your ears," I advised, sitting up. I never slept well the first night aboard a ship. My time on shore had stolen my sea-legs.

"You have not told me all that you did on that island. While my boys were waiting for you, they talked to the tradesmen. Wild rumors, my friend."

"Too wild, perhaps."

"What? No giant snakes? No clever demons with designs on your virtue?"

"What virtue? That's a tale I've not heard."

"Such things grow with the telling. You chuck a kitten under the chin and the tale says that you slaughtered the Nemean Lion. You argue with your girl and legend says that you attacked a mad Maenad. Such is life. But you, Eno, you really do legendary things, then tell me nothing. Is this kindness?"

"There's nothing to tell. I came, did what I was paid for, and left. Now we'll go to Troezen and be paid again."

"As you say. Rumor says something else. And this Phandros...."

"What about him?"

A noise like war-elephants trumpeting but with the resonance of copper drums rang through the ship.

"Zeus! It's fit to frighten the fish!"

"Nothing to worry about then. That noise would keep off the Kraken."

"Aye, unless it mistakes it for the cry of its long-lost mate!"

The sea was darkness exemplified. Only our torches gleamed against the impenetrable black. The ship's boy dozed near a bucket of pitch, to replenish the torches when they burned low. Maybe one or two of the sailors asleep in the waist of the ship might be cursing our voices but not one would dare tell the captain to pipe down.

"I will be glad," he said, "when the last part of your task is done. I was afraid you would find this task too much for you, this time."

"This isn't like you, Jori. You don't usually worry about me, no matter what I'm fighting. Why were you worried this time?"

"Worried? I? No, I have great faith in your strength, your cleverness, your speed." He waved his hand circularly, as if to take in all the attributes too difficult to name. "What can stand against you? Only the Gods. No disrespect," he added and spit on the deck.

"I almost lost my life this time," I said. "That's near enough. I don't have to prove myself on the Gods."

"Ah, I was right! You did have more adventures!"

"Maybe. But why were you worried?"

He leaned forward and lowered his voice. "A dream, my friend. A very clear dream."

"Was there a woman in it?" I asked, remembering my own very clear dream. I tried to think of my golden Minthe but all I could see was that dream-woman's coiling black hair and kohl-lined burning eyes.

"Of course...but that was earlier. No, I was walking through a marketplace, somewhere I'd never seen before. I passed a house, with an opening in the side where they'd exposed goods for sale. They shone in the sunlight so I went near. They were skulls, Eno! More than a dozen skulls."

"You've seen skulls before."

"These were talking."

"Stop. Can't you see I'm shivering myself to pieces?" I laughed and stretched out on the deck again. "Go back to bed before you give me nightmares."

"Don't you want to know what they were saying?"

"No." I closed my eyes and imitated a snore.

He dug into my ribs with his foot. "I must tell you."

"Tell me, then go to bed."

"They said, "Eno must go to Troezen. Death waits for him there." Who have you so offended that Death sends so many messengers for you, my friend?"

"My death will be of boredom right here. But I won't be going to Hades alone if you don't get to bed."

I didn't have to see him to know he threw his hands in the air before stalking off. He'd killed sleep for me that was certain. I'd turned him off with a joke, not wanting to see how much he'd disquieted me.

It occurred to me that the best way to stop the recurrent dreams would be to go to Troezen and not die. A prophetic dream loses its potency if the prophesy is shattered. Besides, 'Death waits at Troezen' might be interpreted different ways. It could be that I'd like the place so much I'd settle down to live happily ever after there until the day I died. No one had ever dodged a prophecy. Usually trying only made things worse in the long run.

I was a little confused that so many people seemed to want me at some city I'd hardly heard of before this mission. Even now I didn't know much beyond what Phandros had told me, that there, as at Leros, one of the gates to Hades could be found, an open secret.

Even the dream-images of people quite well-disposed toward me had urged me to hurry there, some saying 'before it's too late'...too late for what? Others promised me death or the possibly demonic delights of my black-haired beauty.

I fell asleep eventually, lulled by the splash of the waves and the motion of the ship. No dreams came to me except the usual half-glimpsed nonsense.

CHAPTER TWELVE

When I awoke, the eastern sky blushed with dawn and the sail had slipped off the cage. The harpy sat near the bars, her feathers bedraggled, her face paler than usual, thin gold instead of bronze. She watched me with the steady, fathomless gaze of a very young child.

Her water bowl was empty. I went aft to the cook's area, taking a pitcher of water and a leg of lamb, the last one he said.

I poured the water through the bars into the bowl and then I poked the raw leg in between. She didn't touch it, though soon she crawled over to dip her mouth in the water.

After watching her for a few minutes, I noticed the crew was stirring. I covered the cage and went back to the cook's area to settle a dispute between him and Phandros over soup. Truthfully, Phandros had a gift for creating tasty dishes that the sullen cook lacked. Jori tried to soothe the chef's injured pride but it was evident he preferred Phandros' skill.

I did not leave the ship at Mykonos. The crew would talk, there was no way of stopping them. I didn't want to be pointed at in the streets or questioned for anyone's entertainment. I occupied my time by polishing the weapons stored onboard which had the added effect of keeping off the curious and the potentially violent. One man tried to bribe me with fifty obols for a single glance at the creature.

"There's a minotaur coming in on the next ship," I said, to get him to leave. "Talk to that captain, but you didn't hear it from me. It's supposed to be a big secret."

I hoped the next captain would throw him overboard as a drunken fool when he insisted on seeing a non-existent monster.

Jori came back, full of plans to exhibit the harpy as a curiosity. "The king is coming in an hour, as soon as his wife is dressed. The whole court is thrilled at this chance. If you are wise, you will sell this beast here and now."

"I don't want to do that."

"I will negotiate a better price for you, minus my commission, of course." He pressed his hands together prayerfully. "We could make a fortune, you and I. You capture these beasts and we sell them to royalty. It could be most lucrative."

"I'm not interested in helping spoiled princes set up zoos."

"Who said anything about a zoo? The king here is interested in making a cloak of those pretty feathers. He has some mad idea it would make him fly," he added, chuckling.

"Because you gave him the idea?"

He rolled his eyes. "It was not very hard to do. So you agree?"

"No," I said again. "Get your supplies on board. We'll shove off as soon as we can. And before the king comes down from the palace."

"He has offered good coin." Jori sighed regretfully, knowing when I am unlikely to change my mind. "What can it harm just to look?"

I couldn't answer that. I only knew that I did not want the harpy exposed to prying eyes and gossiping tongues. Oddly protective behavior toward a creature I intended to sell to its death. Surely life in a cage would be better than being sacrificed by a cowardly king to appease a bloodthirsty crowd.

Lifting the sailcloth to peep at her in the soft light of a sunset, I knew the thought of her caged up forever would haunt me. I thought of her in the night sky above Leros, a meteor of flashing gold, setting the heavens on fire. Better to die cleanly than to suffer never reaching the sky again. Perhaps I should even do it myself. A swift stroke with a blade and she would die at my hands, painlessly.

She looked at me with those soft, clear eyes. A chirruping purr reached out through the bars. Abruptly, I dropped the cloth and went to harry the men. They grumbled, having hopes of tasting the fleshpots of Mykonos, but worked willingly enough. It still took longer to get the supplies on board than my patience liked. We pushed off as darkness fell, deep enough to show the torchlight procession leaving the palace on the hillside. Jori spat over the side. "50 drachmas...gone. Gone as though they had never been."

"How much did you get for promising to miss the tide to satisfy the king's curiosity?"

"Ten pieces only. And a small, very small, keg of wine."

"What kind of wine?" Phandros asked. He'd slept most of the afternoon, lying forward with an angled strip of sail over him to keep out the sun.

"What do you care?" Jori sniffed. "You giving up drinking, yes?"

I left them to their bickering. I felt uneasy, as if a storm were approaching over the waves. My skin prickled as if with heat but there was only the refreshing sea air rushing past us as we sailed out of the harbor. We put some miles between ourselves and Mykonos before Jori declared it was too dark and dangerous to go any farther that night.

Once again, I didn't dream as I slept on deck and if anyone else on the *Chelidion* did, they did not mention it. In the morning, the sail was off and the harpy again huddled near the bars, closer this time to where I had slept.

On the third morning, her wing was touching my hand when I awoke. The feathers, razor-sharp, lay over my hand and forearm like a blanket. Seeing I was awake, she lifted her wing with great delicacy and folded it back against her body. Then she crouched down, her wing-joints up to where her ears would be, if she had any visible. I sat up and sighed, my decision taken.

Jori awoke to find me in his quarters, poring over a chart. It wasn't a lot of help, as the names and distances written in a Phoenician code. Phoenician is strange, all lines and angles. Hard enough to read even without adding in the natural paranoia of traders and pirates which made them turn everything, even a letter to their mothers, into ciphers.

"I need an island," I said as he yawned and rubbed his eyes.

"Of course. A very useful item. What kind of an island?"

"Something fair-sized but not so big that it has people living on it. Fifty plethron or so. Lots of trees."

"Are you planning a picnic?"

"No, a sanctuary."

He pushed me to one side and spread out his hands on the map. "I take it this has something to do with that beast out there."

"Exactly."

"You have a heart of surpassing softness, my old friend."

"I just can't take her to be killed."

"Her? It is an it. A beautiful creature, in certain lights, but still an it."

"Be that as it may. I'm not taking her to Troezen to be killed. I can't take her back to Leros; they'd kill her just as fast, though I don't believe she is guilty of any of things they are afraid of. So an island, far enough away so that she can't fly someplace else. There should be water and something to eat...."

"You would like an abandoned palace and lots of sheep?"

"I'm serious, Jori."

"Am I not? Look here...." He pointed to a speck upon the map. "This is Telemenos. Fifty years ago, more or less, there was a plague or a giant or something and everyone was killed or they left. They left in such a hurry, as a matter of fact, that they abandoned their sheep and goats who have been filling in the time ever since by breeding like mad. Your feathered friend would never go hungry here."

"Surely somebody has claimed it?"

"No, no one. The neighboring islands all believe Telemenos is haunted. We mariners stop there sometimes for water, but only in the daytime. Seafarers are superstitious folk. I'd have another mutiny on my hands if ever I tried to remain overnight. And the palace, or at least fortress is still there. Roofless, of course, all the better."

I hadn't told Jori that Eurytos had claimed a history with him. He might scoff at the superstitions of his crew but there were enough votives and images of the gods around, some that I'd never heard of, to show how often he implored this one or that one's protection. Knowing that a former enemy had come back from the Underworld would unsettle him for months. His sword had run red too often to find that thought comfortable. I wasn't any too happy about it myself.

"You won't be the loser by this," I swore. "I earned an extra fee from the King of Leros. I'll split that with you instead of the reward for the harpy. It's not quite as much, but I'll make up the difference."

"Please!" Jori protested, his shoulders and hands working overtime. "Am I such a money-grubber that I would rob a friend? No, no, keep it."

We went back and forth for a little while over the issue. At last he agreed to take an extra third, though he still didn't agree with my decision not to sell the harpy to King Pavlos of Troezen.

We changed course for Telemenos. Two days later, as we ran toward the island, I went forward, eager for a first impression. I stepped up into the bow.

The sweep of the bay was shallow, like a cupped hand turned sideways. There were rolling hills, turned gray by distance, and white cliffs. Trees clustered here and there, dwarfed by the roofless acropolis atop the highest cliff. I couldn't see livestock but I could smell them, an odor wafting out toward us, a little stronger than the sea-smell.

I turned to wave my approval at Jori, standing to the tiller. He nodded back then, abruptly, pushed the tiller over. The boat swung wide, I, to all intents and purposes, stayed put. Only there was nothing under me now and I fell into the sea like Icarus falling out of the sky.

As I came up again, there was a shout from the *Chelidion*. It was not 'man overboard'. I heard the drumming of feet running along the rail and then a splash as Phandros tossed himself over into the water. He coughed and snorted as he came up but didn't seem to be in any distress.

Jori poked his head over the side of the ship. "There you are, my friend. Ai, ai, please do nothing rash!" Beside him appeared the cook, the spear he used to catch fish at the ready. It had an iron barb on the end as long as my hand.

I was floating along on my back, feeling quite at ease. Looking up at the face of my friend, I shook my head. "The money wasn't enough?"

"Your offer was fine so far as it went. But now, you see, I have all your money plus whatever Pavlos will pay for the creature. As for you, there is a fine island here. Perhaps one day you will escape from it if that is the will of the Gods. Come see me at Tyre if you do. I will be so very glad to see you! You can even bring the snoring one, if you don't slaughter and joint him for food in the meantime. Farewell, my friend. Farewell!"

He put the *Chelidion*'s helm over and she spun on her heel like an Egyptian dancing girl. She trailed no ropes for me to grab, no convenient net dragged over the side, not even a piece of laundry. Some members of the crew waved a cheery goodbye to me from the mast where they'd just finished cracking on more sail.

Then, heart-rending, frantic cries arose piercingly from the cage on the deck. The crewmembers I could see clapped their hands over their ears, holding on with their knees to the cross-beams. I saw the cook run aft, spear held high. Would Jori retain enough greed to overcome the harpy's spell and stop him? I had no way to know.

I swam hard but it was useless. I shouted desperately, willing her to understand, "Hush, hush! Don't make them hurt you! I'll come for you. I swear I will come for you!"

* * *

So there I was, in the damn water again. I felt so hot with rage that my only other emotion was surprise that the ocean wasn't boiling for ten yards in every direction. I wanted Jori's head on a platter, nicely decorated with parsley, giant fennel, and saffron flowers. I chose the herbs I knew made him ill or that he just didn't like.

I dwelt lovingly on this image to quell my fears. It would take the *Chelidion* not more than a week to reach Troezen, if the wind blew fair. I could be marooned on this empty little island for months, with no company but sheep and....

"Phandros!" I bellowed. I didn't even know if he could swim.

"Here!" he called back.

The sea was calm, thankfully. I could catch a glimpse of him as the swells rose and fell. He moved through the water more peculiarly than anyone I'd ever seen. For a moment, I thought he must be riding a dolphin, but no sea-brother ever bobbed around like that.

I cut through the water toward him. "What are you doing?"

His beard looked like seaweed and his nose was running. "I can't swim but a philosopher once explained to me that this kind of cask should float. More or less, anyway."

He was trying to stay on top of a small cask, stamped with burnt-in Illyrian symbols, which rolled like a frisky kitten among the waves. Ideally, it would have stayed under his chest, keeping his head out of the water. In reality, it knocked him under the chin, tried to flip over, and popped out of his hands to float temptingly just out of reach. He'd then thrash frantically in the water until he could haul it in again.

"I wish that bloody philosopher was here now, instead of me! His theories are useless."

I took a few strokes and dragged it back to him. It was small but heavy.

"Where did you find that?"

"It's from your friend the Captain's secret stash. I think it's that very special wine they make in Illyria to sell in Babylon."

"How'd you find it?"

"Sneaking around in the middle of the night," he confessed cheerfully. "He had quite the collection of rare vintages." More somberly, he added, "Forgive me, Eno, but I didn't altogether trust your friend."

"Not my friend any more, it seems."

He didn't answer, partly through tact and partly because he was evidently tiring. The *Chelidion* was long out of sight and we weren't floating any closer to Telemenos. I was hating the sea more every minute but that's not the kind of thing you say out loud while bobbing around in Poseidon's domain.

"You should kick off your boots," I said. "They'll just drag you down."

"I would, good sir, but my knife is in the left one. We may need it."

"You're something of a philosopher yourself, aren't you?" That knife could prove to be the difference between our survival and our bones being discovered on the island in thirty or fifty years when the neighboring islanders' fears wore off.

I lashed my belt around the cask, endways. "Hang on," I said, and bit on the leather. Using the full range of motion in my arms was impossible because of how the leather strap crossed my chest but I could still swim faster than Phandros, even while dragging him along.

"Oh, my," he said when we began to build up speed. The waves were crashing in my ears. I could have sworn I heard him say 'Yee-Haw!" when I breasted the breakers over a sandbar. The splash did look impressive, I suppose.

We tumbled onto shore. Even before he checked himself for damage, Phandros checked the cask. "I don't think it shipped any water, do you?"

I looked it over. I didn't have much choice; he'd practically shoved the thing up my nose. "It seems tight enough," I conceded.

"Good. Goat and sheep this island may have, we might even be able to press some olive oil, but wine doesn't fall out of the sky into your hand. You must plan ahead for wine."

I did not heed him. I jumped off the sand and sprinted away. The ruined building, half-palace, half-fortress, sat high on a hill, with a tower still intact. Taking huge strides, heedless of rabbit holes or loose gravel turning beneath my feet, I raced to the top of the hill. The tower took a little more care as the inner stair was all but gone. The exterior rocks protruded handily, however, making it easy to swing myself from block to block.

Far away, as evening stretched her hands over the sea, the ship's white sails caught the last of the daylight, turning her into the swallow whose name she carried.

I hoped against hope that I would see the flashing bronzed wings of the harpy stroking through the sky toward me. She could disembowel me for stupidity if she liked so long as she was safe and free.

I stood there a long time, eyes straining against the gathering dark before Phandros came to the bottom of the tower, calling my name. He bore a lighted torch aloft. I climbed down to him, using the pattern of the stones I'd learned on the way up to get down in the gathering dark.

"You started a fire?"

He looked at the tower, then at me, then back at the tower. He seemed perplexed. I had to ask him again.

"Er...yes, I thought it best. I found some flint and I happened to have a little piece of iron on me."

"Where?"

With his free hand, he fished in his bosom. He held up a square of scratched metal, pierced through at one end to slide upon a long, thin leather cord. "The flint was easy. Half the island must be made out of it. I've started chipping an axe out of it. With that, we can cut down trees."

He led the way down from the cliff to the beach. On the way, he talked about the things he'd found on the island. I hardly listened, depression settling on my shoulders like one of the Furies. What could I do to save my harpy from the hunt? Trapped here on Telemenos, my strength was useless.

"There's the remains of a forge, too," he said. "The bellows gone to pieces but with your strength, fanning the flames for hours won't be a problem. Getting the fire hot enough is the main difficulty."

"Why bother?" I asked. It seemed to me he was talking out the back of his neck. "Are you taking up a hobby?"

"Am I'm right in thinking you could be in rather a hurry to reach Troezen?"

"If they hurt her..." I swore, knowing any promise of mine was futile now.

"Very well. Then we'll need a boat. We could, of course, build it with wooden pegs but I think nails would be more efficient."

I started to pay more attention. "Where do we find the ore? A convenient iron mine? Or shall we just pray for it?"

"I had a look around. I don't know why these people left, if they ever did, but there are iron pots in every house and a tumble-down shed or two full of odds and ends. With a forge, we can melt things down and make what we need."

"It'll take too long," I said despairingly. "They'll have her head off before we ever leave here."

"Not to worry." He raised his eyes to the sky. "The Games at Troezen aren't until the full moon. And look at it now...just a sliver."

I tried to take comfort from the moon, tipped over onto its side like a ship or a smile. Maybe it was an omen that we would build a ship and all would be smiles. I tried to convince myself, but I did not succeed.

I took a little more notice of my surroundings when Phandros led me to the fire-pit, which was properly lined with stones. I still remember one recruit in...never mind. But he decided to build a fire with bituminous shale. When it exploded and the burning bits started falling on the tents, he wished it had blown him to pieces to save him from me.

Phandros had caught and skinned some rabbits, roasting them on spits. Their juices dripped into a pot of soup. I couldn't believe how much he'd accomplished in the comparatively short time I'd been gone. "How did you do this?" I asked, with an especial reference to the rabbits. "Whenever I try to catch wild game, it always takes an eternity and I usually wind up just as hungry as when I started."

This time, he pulled the leather cord over his head. It was thin and tough, knotted at the back so that a long loop hung down over his shoulders, hidden by his clothes. "Hold up your fist."

I raised my clenched hand above my head. With a swift whirling motion, he swung the cord two or three times then the cord flew through the air and settled over my hand. He twitched his wrist and the cord closed tightly. In a moment, I couldn't feel my fingers.

"Amazing," I said. "Can you teach me?"

Nothing ever pleased Phandros more than being asked to teach someone something. "Tomorrow? We'll need daylight. I found some wild garlic which, when mashed in wine, makes a very nice sauce for rabbit."

Several squash were roasting in depth of the fires. "These were on the roof of a building over that way. It's not much of a roof but I guess the goats couldn't climb it. All the rest of the vines are nibbled down to practically nothing."

He told me it would be at least until full dark before the rabbits would be done. Somehow he'd found time to hollow out a couple of gourds into drinking cups. They made the wine taste a little odd, but did not dilute the power. "Good stuff...."

"Go slow. It's quite deceptively strong. That's why it comes in such small casks."

"I wonder how Jori came by it. He's never shown much interest in drink."

"You should probably assume that you know nothing about him. If he can treat a friend so badly for mere money, Gods know what else he might do."

"Well, you know, he is a pirate." Seeing Phandros' disbelief, I added, "No, really. I shouldn't have forgotten that. He's always been a pirate at heart."

The rabbit was tasty, especially when dabbled with the sauce Phandros produced from another damp gourd. "In the morning," he said after eating, "you should take a look around for yourself. It's a nice little island. Pity everyone left. Or died. It couldn't have been a monster; there are too many goats and sheep left."

He sat on the other side of the fire, chipping away at a pointed stone. Little flakes of rock pinged off, hitting the fire-stones, his feet and, sometimes, me. He had a rhythm going. He'd hit the large stone at an angle with a smaller stone, turn the axe he was making to a new angle, hit it again. Hit, turn, hit, turn....

"You're a Spartan, aren't you?"

Hit, turn, 'ow'.

"What?" he said around the thumb in his mouth.

"You're a Spartan. All this, the fire, the iron around your neck, the way you caught the rabbits...besides nobody makes that sauce but a Spartan."

"Don't be absurd. Do I look like a Spartan?"

"What does a Spartan look like?" I asked.

"You know. Burly, muscles on muscles, shouts a lot, can march for days on nothing but unleavened bread and water. More like you than me, in fact. What am I? A scrawny, drunken fool with a head stuffed full of useless knowledge."

"Do I shout a lot?"

He had to concede that I did not. "But look how you climbed that tower before. That's what Spartans do. Never mind the sensible way, taking the stairs. No, climb the outside, barehanded, in the dark."

"The stairs were creaking like trees in a windstorm. They might have held you, but not me."

"To a Spartan, that wouldn't have mattered," he said. "Safety and sense is not the Spartan way."

"When I was a boy," I reminisced, "not long after I'd left home, a Spartan regiment came to support our king, Cisseus, in a war with the Anshanites, across the Hellespont. I'd just come down out of the hills. I thought the Spartans were the men of bronze told about in legends. They marched and drilled as if they were one man, one soul animating many bodies."

"Is that when you started building your body to look like that? In emulation of those Spartans?" Phandros said, gesturing at my chest.

"No, I was this size by the time I was sixteen. We grow large, we Maedi, but I was considered unusually so even among my tribesmen."

"We who?"

"The Maedi. That's my tribe."

"I thought you were Thracian."

"So I am, among you Greeks. But at home, I'm a Maedi." I sighed. "It's a beautiful place, between the rivers. There are lots of mountains, which is where I learned to climb, and much good pasture land. I was a shepherd's son. You Greeks talk of Arcadia as being the most perfect place in the world. That's only because you've never been to my home."

"Home. It's the saddest word in any language when you cannot return to it."

"No, you are wrong. The saddest word is 'hope.'"

"Hope? Surely not. Hope was sent to us as a favor from the Gods. When Pandora...."

I took another drink. "Pandora did us no favors when she shook 'hope' out of her cursed casket. It is easier to bear hardship and disaster when that is all there is. Add 'hope' to the mix and such things become torture. Waiting for release, looking forward to freedom, to happiness. Which is worse? To know you have failed utterly or to hope fruitlessly that something may be saved from the wreckage?" I hiccupped and turned the gourd in my hand, sighting down my nose at it. There seemed to be two bowls, until I shut one eye.

"What is this wine called?"

"It's from Parthini."

"I know this wine," I declared. "It's famous. One draft makes you forget your troubles, two makes you reminisce, three makes you phi...phi...losophical. How many have I had?"

"At least three. I have skipped right to four...dead drunk."

He fell over onto his side, like a ship run aground. I supposed I should not have mentioned the Spartan thing, though it was so self-evident that not to have said anything would have been foolish.

Many Greek states make a fetish of the military. All that gleaming armor, those dashing young men, each a paragon of masculine honor and pride, all with the unquestioning obedience that makes a good soldier, tends to make people proud of the country that can create such men. But most cultures, including or especially Athens, prize other qualities as well. Intellect, mathematics, poetry, wit, all have a place of honor when great men gather.

Not in Sparta. There, service to the state of a very particular kind is all that matters. Their boys have no option but to suffer hardship and brutality in their training camps until they are adjudged fit to join up. Anyone who fails is stripped of their citizenship and turned into a despised member of a merchant class who still serve the military power with a boot to the face if they object. Anyone who wants something else out of life has no place to go. The Spartans tended to make brief but sharp examples of those who try to depart or change the system, so that no others would dare follow in their steps. I began to wonder just how and why Phandros escaped.

I made sure the cask was stoppered, moved Phandros' legs so he wouldn't roll into the fire, and made myself as comfortable as possible. When sleep stayed far from me, yet again, I took up a torch and went to explore.

By night, the fire's light deepening the shadows, there didn't seem to be much left of whatever civilization had resided, however briefly, on Telemenos. I found the remains of the settlement that Phandros had searched.

Abandoned places have an eerie atmosphere, as if the people aren't gone, merely unseen. Shadows move, half-heard whispers sigh, and a muffled drumming breaks the silence until you realize it is the beating of your own heart.

The thatched roofs were long ago fallen in and scattered to the winds. Only one building had a pretense of integrity. Judging by the still-stalwart columns and the remains of a tiled roof, I guessed this had been a small sanctuary. Of what god had been worshiped here there was no sign.

I went inside to inspect some faded painted decoration high on the side wall. Blue and purple curves in an antique style, worn by wind and rain into a meaningless blur, told me nothing.

Turning away, I dropped the torch. It fell to my feet, extinguishing itself. But an amber light, flickering gently like evening sunset through leaves, still filled the sanctuary. The water poured over the lip of the basin, trickling merrily to join a marble-lined channel that dropped away, level by level, down a flowing landscape to join a large lake, blue and silver in the sun. A pavilion wrought of white wood tracery, marvelously carved in the semblance of birch trees, rested by the water's edge.

The ruined sanctuary had vanished, as had Telemenos itself. The light had a golden quality which brought the even the farthest details into crisp clarity. Harps played softly, as if music came from the dancing white and pink petals that drifted from the trees. Delicious fragrances chased themselves like butterflies through the air: apple, fig, orange blossom, lilies. Colors seemed to have an extra dimension here, deeper and richer than any I'd seen since I was a tiny child first learning their names.

I heard laughter and followed it without hesitation or second thought.

My clothes, stiffened by salt and dirty from climbing the tower, had become white as a cloud, of some fabric wondrously soft and fine. My cuts and bruises were healed, even the calluses on both ends of my fist from where I gripped my sword. I put up a hand to scratch my head in wonder and found that my hair had grown back, thick and curly as a lamb's wool. Hastily, I touched my chin. No beard, thank heaven.

Laughter sounded again, nearer, the laughter of happy children. I walked through a drift of small white lilies and saw that if I crushed one to the earth with my sandal, it bounced back immediately, shaking itself all over to straighten petals and smooth out leaves. Glorious butterflies, gold, green, and a shimmering blue, danced over the blossoms, stopping to sip where they wished.

Approaching the lake, I watched as fish, strange to me, leapt from the still water, falling back with a ringing as of silver bells. Birds sang in close harmony from the branches of the trees, long swaying branches that dipped into the water as if strumming it. Harps again, but with deeper tones, blending their notes with that of the air.

"Yo, buddy! Over here."

I heard the thick, rough voice but it seemed to have no meaning here. All was beauty, peace, grace. A voice like that seemed to come from a crueler, more brutal world. So did the small hands that grabbed my hair and pulled, short and hard enough to bring tears from my eyes. I raised a hand to brush the pain away.

"Hey, watch it, ya dumb cluck."

Roused to anger, I looked around and came nose to nose with a short, fat boy. Nose to nose because he was flying or at least hovering right in front of my face.

Little white wings grew from his shoulder blades. They flickered steadily, keeping him off the ground. He had a nimbus of fine white hair on his round head, a pouting lip and eyes older than the Sphinx.

"Snap out of it, boy," he said. "You're wanted inside. Ain't you never heard not to keep a lady waiting?"

"What lady?"

"'What lady', he asks. Where do you think you are, dummy? Come on, come on, step it up. We ain't got all day. Hey, Ducomeos, how's the fruit hanging, man?" he asked as another small, fat boy flew past. That one nodded and smiled at me toothlessly, then made a pumping gesture with a lot of elbow. They both giggled.

As I and my guide approached the pavilion, more of the little bastards started coming around. They were staring at me, pointing and laughing, falling backwards as if to roll on the floor in laughter only never falling. I began to wish I'd brought bow-and-arrow into this waking dream. A few near-misses would have scattered them quick enough.

The intertwining tracery of carved wood was only the outer shell of the pavilion. The walls were made of a pinkish, golden glass, more glass than had been made in Greece for a hundred years. And not the most master craftsman had ever created pieces so fine and smooth, not to mention large. Each piece fitted together perfectly, to form a cylinder. But it was not translucent. I could see nothing inside, only my own reflection coming to meet me as I approached.

"Wait here, fathead. I'll see if she's ready to receive you," the first flying boy said. Two panels slid apart and he entered with a flip of his wings but I could see nothing but darkness within.

I tried to ignore the others, still pointing and laughing, making ever more ribald gestures. I couldn't hear their jokes but it wasn't too difficult to figure out the substance. Those who can't often laugh at those who do.

The first one came back. "All right, all right. Go on in. Try not to trip over your own big, flat feet...or anything else. Mortals. Pfui!"

Afterwards, I knew there were carved gilded couches, gleaming silver mirrors that reflected candlelight, carpets so thick it was like walking on seafoam, bowls piled high with ambrosia, and a bed wide enough for a battalion. At that moment, however, I saw none of it.

She sat in a graceful attitude, reading a scroll, her cheek resting gently on her hand. When she raised her eyes, her smile was all that was kind and benignant, a queen to her suppliant. When I did nothing but stand there, her gaze became a little more intense, her smile a little more amused.

"Have you nothing to say to me?" she asked.

"Pardon, lady...."

"You are permitted to be amazed."

"I am. How did you get here, Doris, and where is here?"

"*Doris*?" It was almost a wail. Throwing aside the scroll, she hastened to one of the mirrors and put a shriveled hand to a wrinkled cheek. She did not blink or wriggle her nose or, indeed, do anything that I could see to make a transformation happen. One instant there stood the withered crone, clad in dusty black, the next she was...

A flat-footed fatheaded mortal like me could never describe what she was like except to say, "Aphrodite."

CHAPTER THIRTEEN

"You have done well, Eno. The events at Leros proved you are ready to be my champion. You showed courage and tenacity in proportion with your strength. Now I ask you to serve me in your next task. My need of you is very great."

Her eyes were not old the way the little fat-flyer's had been. Time had no reckoning in their depths. They were neither old nor young. They measured me from the inside out. I could keep no secret thought, no hidden crime, safe from those eyes.

For the rest, she was beauty itself. I did not desire her, knowing myself to be nothing but the most disgusting worm that crawls and not worthy to touch the floor where she had passed. There was nothing flirtatious in her behavior toward me, not at all what I would have expected from the Goddess of Love. She was beautiful to my eyes but in the way that one's mother is beautiful no matter how she appears to other people. I could see no flaw in face or form so long as she smiled upon me, even if it was the smile of a loving mother to an idiotic son.

"I will serve you to the best of my poor abilities, Lady, but are you sure there aren't others more apt?"

She shook her head gravely. "You are my hero, now, Eno. Thrace came late to my worship but I have no fault to find in you. Listen while I tell you what I need of you."

I knew I would never forget a word. She leaned back on her couch, gazing through me as though I were not there. It seemed a countless span of time before she spoke again.

"Do you know how this war in Troy began?"

When a goddess asks a question, fixing fathomless eyes upon her suppliant, it is impossible to lie, or even to be tactful. Only truth, bitter or sweet, can serve her and you must accept the consequences if she is angry.

"You, er, promised to reward Paris of Troy with the most beautiful woman in the world if he would give you the Golden Apple marked 'For the Fairest'?" At the last possible instant, I managed to lift my voice into a question.

Her full mouth tightened and a sinuous glass vase on a marble tabletop suddenly shattered. In a blink of an eye, it reconstituted itself. Nevertheless, I was warned.

"That's what everyone says! And it's not fair! Who threw that Apple into the midst of the wedding feast anyway, I'd like to know?"

"I never heard."

"Eris, that's who! Meddling wretch! They don't call her 'Strife' for nothing. I've never liked her, you know, not really."

"Why did she do it?"

"Well, that's the question, isn't it?" Abruptly her mood changed again, no longer the furious girl tricked by a jealous enemy. Now she was the housewife, short-changed in the marketplace and determined to prove her point. "I have had time to consider the matter, now that I am cooler. I have looked into the past, tracing each thread of the web. I cannot see the future that is not in my gift but I can make guesses as to what the future holds."

I waited, poised like a piece of gold leaf on the tip of a needle, fluctuating with her breath, her mood.

"Prior to the war, all was peace on earth and on Olympus as well. Heroes like Perseus and Theseus had calmed much of the world, discovering mysteries, building great cities of learning, culture, and wisdom. Who would not want such a state of affairs to continue?"

I didn't feel this was a question I could answer. Peace and quiet is all very well, but how could I make a living from it? If some beast isn't ravaging the countryside or some mad-man trying to overthrow a king, I'd have to go back to shearing sheep. I hate sheep.

She seemed to be waiting for me. "Strife?" I said.

"Yes, Eris. But she could not come up with such a perfect scheme on her own. Her idea of a clever plan is getting two children to tease each other in the back of the cart on a long, hot trip somewhere. She wasn't invited to the wedding and that made her mad but she was more likely to put Pegasus poo in the punchbowl than toss an Apple into our midst. I wished she had."

"That would have caused chaos," I said.

"You are quite right, clever Eno. It caused great chaos among us and, as is so often the way, it has spilled from heaven onto mankind. We were so close to peace and happiness for all until this dreadful war. And who profits from such a thing?"

"The only one I can see is Hades, expanding his kingdom of the dead."

She considered it then dismissed it. "Not Hades. His actions are more straight-forward that this. Besides, Troy is in deadlock right now. The Greeks are on the beach and the Trojans are in their towers and very few are dying. It is not there we must look for answers."

"Then where?"

"Troezen. What is happening there?"

"Don't you know?"

"I cannot go there now, none of the Gods can, any more than we could go to Leros before the king broke off his evil doings with the Nausicaa creature. We have great power, Eno, but if men close their hearts to us, we cannot break in. If they stopper them with greed or hatred or even too much doting on another person or thing, we are kept out."

"But so many people on Leros must have been praying for succor. Why couldn't you help them?" I may have let my tone get a little too demanding. One of the large mirrors cracked, the pieces pouring out of the frame and then falling up in a quick repair.

"The King is the keeper of the will and hearts of his people," she answered primly. "If his heart is dark, the whole nation's is dark."

"Is that what is happening in Troezen? Another king worshiping darkness?"

She smiled at me. I felt like a child who had guessed the answer of a difficult puzzle, half-proud, half-ashamed.

"I think so. That's how it feels anyway. If I could only rouse another God long enough to attend to me...."

"Rouse?"

"I should not say any more." She nibbled on one delicate thumbnail. "Oh, very well. It's simply impossible on Olympus just now. They're all so immersed in this war business that they are neglecting their proper spheres. They all sit around boasting about this champion and that battle. And they are cheating."

"Don't they always?" I said but she didn't blast me into a red mist, only wrinkling her enchanting nose at me.

"Men are supposed to handle their own business unless they pray for help. And even then we're not supposed to answer all the time. Mankind must be left to work things out on their own or they'll get spoiled and do nothing."

"Absolutely." I would have sooner pluck out my eyes than disagree with her on mortal-God relations.

"But we Gods are helping without waiting to be asked. Prophecies and winds and dragons and I don't know what all. I have a few children and children's children in this fight and of course I support them. But I can't make the others see that there's something else going on. I can't even get one of them to look at Troezen or Leros. Why are they so distracted? Why are they eating those orange crunchy things when they have ambrosia? And when I, I, Aphrodite, try to talk to them, they tell me to go away. No one tells me to go away!"

The whole building rattled. A multi-tiered chandelier crashed down. Dirt sifted on to me from a large crack in the ceiling. I could see in one of the mirrors that the door behind me had opened and the flying boys were peering in.

"Hey, boss. This barbarian bastard giving you any headaches?"

She gestured, a mere flick of her hand, and everything was all right again. The flying boys disappeared as if they'd been yanked backwards.

"Orange crunchy things?"

"They are supposed to taste like crunchy cheese. Hera's put on pounds and pounds, not that her figure was anything to boast of. But that's unimportant, though if she doesn't cut back, she's going to look like Silenus. And if my husband doesn't start washing his hands before he comes to bed, I'm going to go live in a cave and be an oracle. That nasty orange dust gets all over everything."

She calmed herself with a few deep breaths. I looked down at my ugly feet, counting the toes until she stopped expanding her chest. "I believe the answer to all my questions lies in Troezen. Will you go there for me, Eno?"

"I will. I am going there already."

"Then I will give you this. Bend, hero," She leaned forward and pressed her lips to my brow, again like a mother. "It is a passport. No one can prevent your entrance if you wear my kiss on your brow. Wit and courage you have enough."

"My Lady, if I may ask one boon...."

"Your harpy?" she said with understanding so warm that it brought tears to my eyes. "I was born of the sea, you know. So long as she is journeying upon the water, I will protect her. More than that, I cannot do."

"And one other thing...."

"Mortals..." she muttered. "What is it?"

"You said something about before about praying to the Fearful Goddess, that the people should pray that she does not attack Leros. Who is she?"

One by one the candles in the room began to wink out, until finally there was only a single shaft, a brilliant beam of light, shining from somewhere above. It illuminated her, making her seem taller and more imposing, more strange. She was not mother, teacher, lover or even goddess now but something beyond the reach of my power to describe.

Her shadow on the ground began to alter, twisting, and evolving. I shut my eyes, knowing that her form was beyond my understanding but not beyond my fears. I realized that the gods took on the semblance of human guise for the sake of our comprehension, not for their own.

"Do you know now who is to be feared?"

I fell on my knees at the sheer power of her voice. I could not speak but an eager, desperate prayer formed in my mind that she should return to her own form and not blast me into nothingness with the blink of an eye. She answered it, dwindling down into the essence of beauty and grace.

"You have much to do, Eno. I fear that Troezen trembles on the edge of crimes more horrible than those you forestalled in Leros. So hurry, my little Thracian warrior, my missionary, my hero, hurry."

I stood again in darkness listening to the distant call of the sea, the sputtering torch at my feet, all the more blind as my eyes had grown accustomed to her limitless light. Picking up the torch and blowing on it to bring the flame back, I looked around. The faded fresco on the wall had been miraculously refreshed, colored so vividly that the artist might have left the sanctuary just a moment before. I now saw before me Aphrodite rising from the waves on a seashell of pure gold. The painter hadn't done her justice, but who could?

* * *

Phandros had been making early-morning-after-a-hard-night noises for a while before he sat up. I lifted his limp hand and wrapped his fingers around a gourd of watered wine. He got it to his mouth without spilling more than a third of it. After a few gulps, he opened sticky eyes. The wine had helped but he still needed a few tries to say, "What...how?"

His eyes opened all the way with surprise when I replaced the drink with a dry sausage. "Is this magic?"

"No, it's a rescue." Now that he could see, I gestured over the water. A fishing boat had run up onto a sandbar in the night. The broken mast dangled over the side, trailing bedraggled sails.

"Who's rescuing who?" Phandros asked, taking in the boat's condition between sips and bites.

"I'm not sure yet. It's a father and his son. The father got sick, the boy didn't know what to do. They've been drifting a while, I think. They were down to about half a cup of water."

"So the boy beached the boat?"

"He saw our fire which, thanks to you, drew them to us. I think they've been sailing around in circles for if they'd navigated in a straight line they would have soon found their way."

Phandros eyed his half-eaten sausage suspiciously. "It's not a plague or anything?"

"They said he was delirious with fever but it left him last night just about the time the ship hit the sand."

"Hmmm. All right then." Phandros tore again into the sausage with remarkable appetite for a man in a delicate condition. "So where are they now?" he said, around a mouthful.

"They're choosing a new mast from the trees here. I discouraged them from waiting for you to wake up. They seemed to think you are Dionysus and want to worship you for saving them. I didn't think you'd care for them kissing your hands and feet so early in the morning."

"Very funny. They think you're bloody Hercules, I suppose. Where's that wine?"

A couple more gulps brought the color back into his cheeks. He staggered off for a pee and a wash. Returning, he stopped short when he got a good look at me.

"Did that hair come on the boat, too?" he asked after a disbelieving pause.

I ran my hand over the thick mass sprouting from my scalp. "You wouldn't believe me if I told you. First place I'm going when we get off this rock is a barber's."

The fisherman and his son were a hundred leagues out of their way. I couldn't help suspecting that there had been a bit of godly meddling in this misfortune. The name written under their ship's painted eye was *Cythereia*, one of the Goddess of Desire's many names.

It gave me a most uneasy feeling, knowing she was watching over me. If I failed, the blame would be entirely mine. Only a mistake so big that my name would live as an example of ultimate stupidity could bring me down. She would find another champion and I'd be a by-word of infamy. I was tempted to run away to hide myself under a very large rock. Only the promise that the harpy would be under Aphrodite's care so long as she journeyed on the sea kept me going. I had to redeem my betrayal or there'd be no rock in the world big enough to hide me from my own conscience.

The fisherman transferred some of his gratitude to me when I plucked out the old mast and stepped the new one into the braces under the deck. This saved us all the bother of rigging winches and tackles to swing it down off the cliff. I don't deny the tree was heavy but ever since my meeting with Aphrodite, I had an unusual amount of energy. I only hoped it would last until Troezen.

After a little more work, the boat was ready to sail. They agreed to take us back to Mykonos where we'd find another ship to travel onward. How we were going to pay for it was in the lap of the Gods, one in particular. The wind filled the sail as soon as the tide lifted us off the sandbar. It blew without change or pause in the right direction.

In exchange for our passage, Phandros decided to teach the boy, Milos, to write his own name and that of his father. As there was nothing to drink on board, it helped to pass the time. The boy, about twelve, went from being a shy, frightened youth to one always underfoot, artlessly confiding. When he completed his name for the first time, he crowed.

"Clever boy," I said, applauding.

"Not clever enough," his father said. "The wisest man avoids troubles. He seems to want to hunt it out and embrace it. It's the excitement, I suppose."

"Sometimes even the wisest man finds trouble on his doorstep and cannot step around," Phandros said. "Then there is my friend, who goes to find other people's troubles."

"And gets paid for it," I added.

"Where is your fee from your last job?" he asked, grinning.

"You have work in Mykonos?" the captain asked.

"Beyond that. Why?"

"Only that I can feel you pushing this little *Cythereia* of mine all the time. We have a wind that a home-bound sailor dreams of and yet you are urging her onwards as though a moment's delay is unbearable. I wondered if it was work. If not, it must be a woman."

"We'll be there soon?"

"You will see the island before the sun sets tonight."

He was as good as his word. This time, though, I watched the shore growing closer from the safety of the waist. Not least among my grievances against Jori was the unfair way he'd jerked me overboard by merely turning the tiller.

Phandros joined me there. "Have we lost too much time, do you think?"

"Less than we would have lost if we'd had to build our own damn boat."

"True. There was one thing I wanted to say...you do know it's just a bird, right? The harpy. If it were a woman, I would understand your anxiety. But this is like running into a burning building to save an almond."

"You don't have to come along."

"No, I don't. But I probably will."

I turned around, leaning my elbows on the railing. "Why are you here, Phandros? Why did you leave your comfy place at King Temas' right hand to follow me?"

With a grimace, he acknowledged the justice of my question. "Orders, I suppose, is as good a word as any."

"Temas gave you orders?"

"I wish. No, it was a dream."

"Oh, yeah, I know about dreams."

"In this one, I was walking along the road to Athens. I've only been there once, when I was quite young, but I recognized it by the hermai marking the miles." He scratched his beard. "You have lived there for some time, I think. Why are they carved only with Hermes' head and genitals? Why not the whole body?"

"I don't know. Budget cuts?"

He laughed shortly. "Anyway, there I was trudging along when one of them spoke to me. I did not stop. I could not. Then the next one spoke, taking up the words where the other one had left off. And the next, and the next."

"What did they say?"

Phandros hesitated, his eyes shifting. "Much of it was unclear or referred to the past. But what I do remember most clearly was the god telling me to turn around and go with you. As soon as I turned, the voices stopped. But each of them nodded approvingly as I passed. It was creepy." He sighed. "After that, what else could I do?"

"We are puppets in their hands...sometimes."

"Then it is for the Gods that you are seeking this harpy?"

"No, that's a side issue. I'm seeking her because I betrayed her. She trusted me and I used her trust to capture her, knowing that once I sold her to King Pavlos she would die. That is not something I want to live with forever. So I'm going to redeem my honor."

"Oh, then I understand. I still think it's a little fanciful. Well, who cares what I think?"

"You have a point," I conceded. "It does seem like folly even to me. But you aren't the only one under orders."

"Oh?" One eyebrow crawled high.

"You are a learned man. What do you know about the Goddess of Discord?"

"Eris?" He gazed off at the white buildings of the island, just now visible above the sea. "She is popularly considered to be a daughter of the Void for she is certainly not known to be an Olympian. Some say she is a daughter or a sister of Ares but I believe that is a mistranslation of an ancient oracles' prophecy. We know, however, that she came from the time before Kronos was destroyed by the Father of the Gods. She delights in conflict and quarrels."

"She said something about that."

"She? Who?"

"A goddess I met on Telemenos."

Phandros took a step back as though unsure whether to flee from a madman's ravings. "Which goddess?"

"Never mind. I'll tell you instead what happened in the Temple of Artemis on Leros."

He fell to stroking his beard and, at the end of my recital, including my chat with Eurytos, pursed his lips thoughtfully. "You say she talked about opening some gates?"

"You'd think I'd remember a bit more clearly what a three-faced thirty-foot tall woman said but I was a little freaked out at the time."

"Justifiably, I'd say."

"Thanks."

"There is much food for thought. I don't believe Eris is the spirit that moved that statue, or appeared to speak through the dead. The tossing of a Golden Apple or the stirring up of unease between lovers, yes, that she might do and often has. But this is plots and plans and a desire to rule the Earth."

"Someone put Eris up to it, someone with an interest in causing as much death and destruction as possible," I said. "If it were Hades...."

"Hades has power enough surely."

"One would think. And generals enough at his command. He doesn't need to recruit me. Besides, Eurytos spoke of a Dark Queen, a 'She'."

"She...I have heard much evil of the Queen of Troezen but a queen cannot command a goddess to do her bidding. Not without coming to a sticky end."

I stared down into the jewel-bright sea, watching some fish jump through our bow wave. So many mysteries in this world, some from the Gods, some of men, some that belonged to neither of us. I sighed and turned to speak my thought to Phandros. But his eyes were closed and his lips moved as though in earnest prayer. As though he felt my scrutiny, he glanced at me and said, "Did she say 'gates' or 'doors', this evil thing in the temple?"

"Doors, I think."

"Doors." He closed his eyes again, mumbling. I thought of the shell-game hucksters in the marketplace, swiftly shifting shells from hand to hand, daring passersby to risk a coin or two on where a pea was hidden. Phandros' thoughts must move like the blurring hands of a games-man.

"Seventeen...chaos...army...darkness. Hades but not Hades...." His voice was low, muffled, like a man talking in his sleep. Then he began to repeat the names of cities, starting with Leros and Troezen. Halfway through, he was watching me. I blinked when he said, "Hattusa...."

"That's Hittite," I said.

"Still, there is a gate to the Underworld there. You seem to know the name."

"A friend of mine -- well, we're in the same line of work -- told me that he'd been hired to take care of a monster by the local king. Some kind of a lava-beast which is strange as I never heard there was a volcano around there."

"Any other cities having those kind of problems?"

"Always. But they seem more numerous nowadays."

"Discord taken to a greater scale. That fits." He shut his eyes again and kept them closed until the fisherman came forward to tell us we'd be berthing before long.

Phandros thanked him then turned to me. A frown carved deep lines between his brows. "How strong are you really, Eno?"

"Strong enough."

"Oh, I know you can lift things and fight things and can carry the weight of the world if need be. But how strong are you in yourself?"

"I don't understand," I said, waiting for the punch line.

"I wish I did as well. What do you think would happen if all seventeen gates to Hades were opened, from the inside?"

"Hell on Earth? But that can't happen. Can it?"

"I hope not. But think of what you have told me. You are not a madman and therefore I must accept what you have said though it frightens me, frightens me badly."

"Me too."

"You say that, but I know you are jesting. This 'She' will not kill you so long as she thinks you could become her creature. But what use would such a one have for me? Or any of the weak things of this earth."

"What do you know?" I asked. "What do you suspect?"

Despite the heat of the day, he shivered. "Terrors beyond what you have already seen. Names I dare not pronounce. Add what you have said to what I have witnessed on Leros...no. No, I cannot say more now. I will study upon these things."

I could see he would not say more than he thought wise. I wished I had studied more of these matters but there was always a living to earn which left little time for anything beyond practical matters. "Don't take too long. I can't fight what I don't understand."

He nodded gravely. "I will help you all I can. But, as a learned man, I must warn you, Eno. When the Gods take this much interest in a mortal, it usually ends badly for the mortal."

CHAPTER FOURTEEN

Milos had been sorry to see us go but I surprised a trace of relief on his father's face. In his first, teary-eyed gratitude, he'd promised a lot and now felt quite relieved that we weren't demanding he follow through. I didn't want all his possessions and certainly not his first-born son.

We had further proof, if any was needed, of the Goddess' interest before we'd gone fifty feet past the pier. Mykonos is in a very useful spot, halfway between Troy and the main body of Greece. Since the war began, it had gone from being a small port to a big one. Building went on all day and well into the night. Ships from every corner of the world stopped there now, bringing useful goods, exotic wonders, pilgrims, and the businessmen who made fortunes from all these things.

"Phandros? Phandros, by all that's holy!"

A man, large even by my standards, had Phandros by the shoulders, gazing into his face with wonder. Before Phandros could react, the stranger threw his arms around him and lifted him clear off the ground. Heedless of grinning passersby, Phandros kicked his feet like an infant.

"Skander?" he squeezed out.

"Look at you!" the stranger exclaimed. "Still skinny as a beanpole!" He slapped his own generous belly. "Can't say the same of me, what ho?"

"I can't believe it's you, not at all." There were tears in Phandros' eyes and not just from having the breath pressed out of his body.

"They do say if you wait on the Mykonosian docks long enough, you'll see everyone you ever knew. And here you are!"

"But what are you doing here, Skander?"

The big man waved a plump hand, adorned by several heavy golden rings, in the direction of the docks. "I own those ships and others besides. I've rented half a dozen pentekonters to the...but hush for that!"

He put his hands on wide hips and laughed, his belly shaking under his long chiton, a chlamys of deep maroon dye tossed over his shoulder. His hair, longer in the back than in the front, was confined by a golden fillet and, even from several feet away, I could smell the expensive musk he used to perfume it. A black ring-beard hedged his full face, accented by straight brows and small, sharp eyes that contrasted with his florid personality.

Phandros was almost too dazed to introduce me. Skander looked me up and down. "I've heard of you! Didn't you do some work for Scambos of Olympia not too long ago?"

"Yes, I recovered an ivory throne that he was having made for Pharaoh Ramses."

"Forgive me! I always check such things. You wouldn't credit the number of times someone has lied to me. Er, well, perhaps you would. Anyway, he spoke very highly of you...when we were still speaking, that is. Had a little falling out over a cargo of vinegar. Soured our relations!"

Skander of Mykonos is the only man I ever met who laughed "ho, ho, ho."

Nothing would content him but that we accompany him to his villa, sitting upon a hillside overlooking the shipping lanes. Skander made room in his litter for Phandros. I glanced at his bearers, sturdy fellows, and declared that I preferred to walk.

"After being cooped up on a small boat, I'd like the chance to get in a little exercise."

The bearers rolled thankful eyes toward heaven. Skander laughed. "Been on a boat, have you? Better you than me."

"But you own ships," Phandros said.

"Own, yes. Visit, certainly. Travel on, never! Mykonos is world enough for me. Anyone wants to talk to me comes to me. Enough about all that! Tell me, my old friend, what brings you to this island?"

From Skander's manner, I would have guessed he'd let Phandros get out half a dozen words before interrupting with some tale of his own. In this, I misjudged him. He drew out Phandros and listened his halting catalog of positions gained and lost, wanderings, refuges and departures as though ten thousand gold minae depended on his complete attention.

"Well, I can see why you are so thin; you must never sit down! Not fear of that now, though. Not as my guest!"

Compared to the villa of Skander, the Palace at Leros was a hut for the winter forage of goats.

A butler so proud one would think he was a master, not a slave, showed us to a large, airy chamber with a view of the sea. The walls were frescoed with beautiful images of nymphs of the sea playing some game with a large yellow ball. I was pretty sure it was an allegory with a dense, religious meaning. I turned to Phandros, to invite him to explain it.

He dropped heavily onto one of the bed. "I never thought I'd see him again. It brings it all back to me."

"All what?"

"Everything. The barracks, the beatings, the constant shouting, the drilling, the drilling, the drilling...."

"Sparta...."

He hushed me, panicked, as though the word was a spike in his ear. "People think there's something noble about the way they train their sons. But it's horrible. Horrible. I can't recall one happy moment in my youth. I was always, always so afraid and so desperate not to show it. You can't understand that, I imagine."

"Oh, can't I?" I didn't want to interrupt the flow of his thought, so I said it to myself.

"There are always a few who can't stand it, who try to flee. They are caught and used as an example...." He shuddered deeply. Then he rubbed his face, thoroughly, as though upon awakening from a nightmare. I knew he was dying for a drink.

"There were four of us. Skander was the biggest and the toughest. They had great hopes of him. They held him up as an example to us all. And he hated it, just as much as we did, the weaklings, the dreamers like me. Those of us who didn't show our weaknesses at birth, so we weren't exposed on a hill. How often did I wish I had been! My mother...."

"What happened?" I said quietly.

"Skander did it, planned the whole thing. They hunted us, of course. We didn't rest for three days or nights. We were half-starved anyway; withholding food was a common punishment. Charillos dropped dead when we were within an hour's walk of our goal. We didn't even stop to bury him. The three of us got away, Skander carrying Nikros on his back. We got away...."

"Yes, you got away." But had he really escaped?

Stepping out, I asked a passing manservant for some wine. It came, pale straw like a child's hair, but Phandros shook his head, even as he licked his dry lips. "I won't drink again until we are finished with what we have to do. I swear it and this time, I mean it."

He kept to that even through the banquet that followed our baths. A banquet seemed to be Skander's normal evening meal. Whatever privations he had suffered as a boy soldier in Sparta, he was making up for it now with plenty. Four husky boys dined with us, in whose faces I could trace their father's heritage. In size, any one of them would have been an asset to a battalion, even the one sniffing listlessly at a white lily throughout the meal.

When the honey cakes and perfectly ripened fruit were served, Skander clapped his hands and a tumbling troop of children came in, nurses carrying the smallest ones. I counted seventeen in all, from the oldest in his mid-twenties down to a pair of babes-in-arms, one of several sets of twins.

"You haven't been wasting your time." Phandros had emerged from his brooding somewhere between the fish course and the meat, drawn out by his friend's unceasing merriment.

"No, indeed. Of course, I am fortunate in my wife. A peerless housewife, a queen among women! If it were not for her, I would be a penniless fool still working as a stevedore in the shipyard. But Aphrodite sent this flower of her sex to marry me."

"They met on the causeway," the lily-sniffing one said and gave a grin that belied his lackadaisical attitude on the couch. Most young men do not loll in the presence of their elders but it was obvious Skander hadn't the heart to be meticulous about such things.

"It was more romantic than that," the huskiest brother put in. "She saw him when her father stopped by the yard to give some orders. She peered out from the curtains and saw him like a young Hercules among the weedier folk."

"Stop them, somebody," said the oldest of them. "Before they start reciting love poetry by the light of the silvery mo-o-o-o-n!"

That, apparently, was the signal for a wrestling match. It was all in fun but when one of the couches broke a leg under the combined weight of the four boys, and the smaller children started wailing, Skander clapped his hands and they all trooped out again, the nursemaids making the twins wave bye-bye with fat fists.

The oldest boys bowed to their father and promised to mend the couch in the morning. "Nonsense...it was old. Take it to Pelemaeus to mend and then give it to him with my compliments and a few obols from you four. That will teach you, rascals!"

When the noise and the litter were removed, Skander slipped off the fillet he wore on his head and rubbed his scalp vigorously. "Now for some serious drinking!"

Skander really was a most excellent host. When he saw that Phandros had refused the decanter more than once, he had a quiet word with his butler. That dour individual's eyebrows raised but he bowed deeply. Soon he brought a new pitcher, poured some of the beverage into a wide-mouthed goblet and offered it to Phandros. "An invention of my own, good sir. The juice of Bergamot oranges, unfermented grape juice and the pressings of a few flowers and herbs. I trust you will find it palatable."

Phandros' nose twitched and he consented to try a sip. I don't know what was in it besides what the man said, but Phandros looked increasingly cheerful as the evening wore on. Finally he drew together all his courage and asked a favor.

"Don't hesitate, my dear soul! Nothing is too much for the friend of my youth!"

"We need to take ship for Troezen as soon as humanly possible. It's life or death for one very dear to my friend here."

"Ha!" Skander pushed the footed decanted closer to me. "I thought I saw anxiety seated on your brow. A fair maiden, is it? She is promised to another and you wish to appear at the wedding, seize her, and ride off? A noble deed, worthy of many of our greatest heroes! A ship, though, a ship...." He scratched his ring-beard thoughtfully.

A raised finger brought his man over. "Tell my son Charillos to attend me."

Phandros spilled his drink. "What...what name did you say?"

The boy came in with haste, wiping his mouth. A few stray crumbs from his snack escaped down his front. It had been, after all, at least half an hour since he'd eaten with us.

"My son, go at once to the docks. Tell the master of the *Doris* that his departure for Troezen is put forward two days. He's to round up his crew from the stews and toss-pots and have them ready for sailing at...is dawn soon enough?" he asked me. I nodded, stunned by the coincidence, if coincidence it was.

"Dawn. If he has to leave half the cargo it matters not, but tell him that he'd better leave no more than that. Oh, and he should prepare a cabin for two special passengers."

"Yes, father."

"My boy," Phandros said, his voice quavering like an old man's. "Tell me, what is your name?"

"Charillos, honored sir. How may I serve you?"

"Nothing, nothing. A good name...a very good name."

"Go now, my son. Take your brothers, Phandros and Nikros with you. Whoever gets there first will win this ring from me." He drew off a ring, a ruby flashing darkly from a golden mount.

Charillos shook his head. "We'll do it for the love of the competition." He kissed his father's hand and was gone.

"You named them...." Phandros' voice choked. The butler filled his goblet with heavy wine and Phandros drained it off in a gulp, not even realizing what it was.

"Yes, I named my sons for the bravest men I'd ever known."

"But...."

Skander leaned back on his elbow. "Men so brave they trusted me to lead them, though I was untested and untried. They followed me in pursuit of freedom, the only treasure worth having. They listened to my plans and, though they knew the price for failure, not one betrayed the others. Though it led to death for one of our number, still they did not falter. Fate led us on separate paths but I could never forget them. How little I have done to honor them. How much more I wish I could still do."

Phandros was too overcome to speak, tears dampening his beard.

Skander sighed and shifted his weight, his couch creaking. "As soon as I could afford it, I sent an expedition to the Spartan and Argonian border with orders to find our friend's poor body. I knew it to be hopeless, of course; too many years had rolled on. So I had them set up a monument, an obelisk of marble from the Northern peninsula, and a poem inscribed on the side. I had a real bard from Athens write it. My sons have memorized it. They say now that when boys flee from Sparta...and they still do, make no mistake...they know when they reach Charillos' Dagger, they are safe." He chuckled deeply. "The Spartans have knocked it down twice but I am rich enough to rebuild it a thousand times!"

* * *

That butler had, I must admit, good reasons for his pride. Before we retired, he had arranged for a barber to come for me, organized another bath, and even offered a girl, guaranteed clean, if required. I returned a civil 'no' and Phandros was already snoring.

Hearing the plaster-rattling sounds with an expression of austere pain, the butler showed me to another room. "I have taken the liberty of packing a change of clothing for you both, sir, as you had no luggage. It will be the pleasure of the household to send you with a basket of supplies as well. Sailors have such a limited diet."

"Thank you. I wonder, could I trouble you for one more thing. It's a little complicated."

He drew a step nearer. "Sir?"

"I need a scabbard, about yay-long and yay-wide." I demonstrated with my hands. "Nothing fancy, though I'll need a belt as well. I will reimburse your master for it when I return." That was my pride speaking.

The butler waved my pride aside in favor of his master's. "Skander of Mykonos delights in offering gifts, the more necessary to your comfort the better in his eyes. I shall send a slave to the leather-makers at once. Do you...er...require a sword as well, sir?"

He knew perfectly well I had none. "Not at present, thank you. Have us called before first light, if you'll be so good."

"I shall awaken you myself, sir, in case you require anything further." He started for the door and then paused. "It was my master's wish that I mix poppy-liquor with your friend's last drink. He will sleep well but do not be alarmed if he is a little less than brilliant in the morning."

"Not that it takes much. Thanks for telling me."

"'Til morning, then, sir. Blessings on your rest."

He was the sort who always had to have the last word.

Not even indigestion kept me awake. The roosters were calling before I was even aware I was asleep. No dreams had troubled me.

To my surprise, not only were Skander and his sons there to accompany us to the water, so was Phandros. He looked better. The bags under his eyes had tightened and his step was lighter. He kept a firm grip on his emotions, even when Skander told him to return to Mykonos as soon as our journey was done. "I need a man who can read and figure and who is honest. The first two are easily bought; the last not so. Promise you will return, brother-of-my-heart."

"I will if the Fates make it so."

"And you as well, Eno the Thracian. I want you to consider working for me, full time. I can offer you pirates, cheats, liars, leviathans, and runaway slaves. It's not losing the slaves I mind, it's what they take with them. What do you say to an annual salary plus bonuses?"

"I would say it is too much honor for me."

"But you'll bear it in mind? I'll want you to teach my boys some of your tricks, mind."

"You have enough sons to start a small school. I will consider it."

The boys sang songs in tenor harmonies as we went down to the docks. I felt like a true hero going off to some fateful quest, instead of a man who'd made a grievous error against his own soul. The empty scabbard by my side reminded me with every step of just what I'd done.

Phandros turned back at the gangway. I saw him slip a closely-written list to Skander and speak urgently. Skander nodded, though his eyebrows drew together in concern. After a moment, he raised his hand as though taking an oath. Phandros skittered on board, nipping the captain's rising impatience in the bud.

As we waved our final farewells, he glanced at me. "It was a list of the fifteen other cities," he said. "Skander has contacts all over the Inner Sea. He's promised to send a warning to every city that holds a gate. Maybe it will do some good; I don't know."

"I hadn't thought of that," I admitted. "Though I doubt any mortal army in the world could stand against what we fear. I've tried to come up with another answer."

"Me too. I told him that I had information that the Egyptians would try to invade one of those cities, but I didn't know which one. I think...I hope he believes me."

"He wouldn't believe the true story."

Skander's captain kept his eye on us the whole way. I don't know exactly what he was told when Skander took him aside to whisper at him. It made him polite but wary. Perhaps he thought we were going to report on his crew's discipline and the handling of the ship. If we had, it would have been a very short report. Once again we had a suspiciously good wind and frighteningly fair weather.

That last day, however, the sun rose as though from a bath of blood. The captain, looking out to the horizon, looked even more grim than usual. "It'll be a bad night. Good thing we are making port today. Last time I saw a sky like that, we were struck by lightning and nearly went to the bottom. 'Tis a bad omen."

We were at least three days behind Jori, at the most generous estimate. Three days in which anything might have happened. Worry wouldn't make the ship go faster but I wished the wind would blow even more strongly.

The crew seemed unusually cheerful, despite the ominous sky and the captain's unease, strange when I considered they'd cut their leave short for this trip. I asked the captain what made them so talkative and good-humored.

"They know tonight's the big celebration in Troezen before the Hunt tomorrow. There'll be free wine, food, and music in the streets. They were afraid we'd miss it because we weren't due to leave Mykonos-port so soon. You're a very popular figure on this ship because of it."

"But not with you?"

He spat over the side. "Coming to Troezen when the Hunt is up is liable to unsettle my men for a fortnight. Running a ship like this is hard enough with a good crew, dedicated and disciplined. With one that's been on a two-day debauch in this black-hearted town, I'll be lucky if we clear the pier without putting a hole in the side."

"Take heart, captain. At least you don't have to run your ship up on the beach to unload her."

"You wait 'til the return voyage. Won't be so pleasant a cruise with every other man-jack so hung over he's puking his guts out over the side."

"I've heard the king here enjoys ritual hunts but I've never heard of it being a festival."

He explained that the Troezenians had always held sacrifices at this time of year to Hermes in his aspect as nekropomtos, conductor of the dead to the Underworld. With the ascension of King Pavlos, the sacrifices had changed.

"Now they release animals, wild boar, bears, wolves, into the walled gymnasium just outside the city where they are hunted down. They can't escape but they do sometimes kill the men hunting them."

"Sounds dangerous."

"Hmph. It's human sacrifice, more often than not. They send in criminals, runaway slaves, men of that ilk.

Eventually men triumph, though at a cost. But the end of the Hunt, that's what the crowd's waiting for."

"Why?"

"The king himself comes down and fights some kind of legendary beast. They had a Griffin one year. Giant scorpion last year."

"And the king fights them...alone?"

"Hades, no. He lets his men torment and wound the poor beastie 'til it's blind with rage and pain. Then he is rolled up close in a large metal box and stabs the thing to death. They claim he has a special treat up at the menagerie for this year."

I would just bet he did. A harpy, no doubt. "Metal box?"

"Do you have a problem with your hearing, man? He had someone make him a metal box on wheels. Slaves drag it out into the arena, then take to their heels. He opens a door, stabs out with a spear, everyone cheers and goes home sated with blood."

He leaned in closer, his face a bronzed mask, his bright eyes stern. "Between you and me, half the crowd is hoping one of those beasts will get revenge some of these days. Pavlos is not so popular as once he was, not since the princess disappeared."

This was the first I'd heard of any princess. He read it in my expression. "What, have you not heard of the missing princess of Troezen? It's a famous mystery."

"Go on."

"She's the king's own niece!"

I still looked blank. He sighed heavily and began as though he were telling a bedtime story. "Not too long ago, the king of the place was Imostratus, pleasant enough for a king. There was none of this bloody business, then. Just the usual lustrations and sacrifices. His wife died giving birth to a baby girl and the king swore he'd not marry again for he and his wife had been brought together by Aphrodite herself. Romantic nonsense, but he believed it. So he ruled for almost fifteen years then he died." He tapped his nose significantly.

"Kings die same as other men."

"Not tearing their own guts out for the burning poison in 'em, they don't. They blamed his best friend from boyhood, saying that the king had debauched his friend in his sleep and this was his vengeance. The king's brother took the throne and his first act was to throw the friend to the bears."

"And the princess?"

"They claim she died of grief shortly after her father's death but no one ever saw the body and the funeral didn't follow for some weeks."

"There was a funeral though."

"Secret one. Not public as it should have been. Who's to say who they burned?" He spat again, more to cleanse a bad taste from his mouth than for luck. "If it were left to me, I wouldn't step foot on this cursed island while this vile business goes on. It is bad enough here when the town isn't full of drunken revelry and extra cruelty. I'll not draw a clean breath 'til we're gone."

"I wanted to speak to you about that," I said. "How long will you be in port?"

"Two days, no more, if I have my way. Are you coming back with us, then?"

"If not I, at least Phandros. I may have more to do here than can be said."

"Keep your secrets, sir, they're nothing to me. If you're here on time, I'll give you passage as my master has bid me. If you're not...." He didn't look sanguine about our chances.

Yet, later, as we tied up, he caught me by the arm. "Listen, Eno...."

"Yes, captain?"

"'Tis none of my affair why you've come to Troezen," he said quietly, not at his usual 'hailing another ship across half-an-ocean of open water' volume. "But there's been bad rumors flying about this place for above a twelve-month now. Rumors of darker deeds than even I've mentioned and many, many dead men. If it should happen that you're late back for the ship, make your way to the House of the Heavenly Twins near the acropolis. My master owns it, though most in the city don't know it. They'll see you make it safe out."

"Thank you, captain."

"Ah, 'tis nothing. But my master is an honorable man and he gave you into my care."

"He chooses good men, does Skander of Mykonos."

The clouds were piling up fast when Phandros and I left the *Doris*. They brought on darkness ahead of night, muffling even the moon. All along the docks, sailors began to hang lanterns out fore and aft, illuminating the large painted eyes and the names of the ships. The eyes seemed to wink and beckon as the incoming tide tossed the ships up and down. They were packed in like grapes on a cluster, spars and oars touching.

That butler had foreseen much. He'd given us chitons dyed a deep indigo, as though we were in mourning. It blended into the night. I only hoped the color wasn't foreshadowing a real death. I don't believe such things but sometimes, on the eve of action, I do.

We were heading toward the portside when Phandros pssted at me. He bent down as though to refasten his sandal. He murmured, "The ship we just passed...is it the *Chelidion*?"

Casually, as if waiting for him, I turned to glance around and to look up idly at the bending prow of the ship behind us. The *Chelidion*'s iris had been painted a deep red, an echo of the red-purple dye obtained from a mussel off the coast of Tyre. Of course, Jori could never have afforded enough purple to paint the eye the color of royalty but he did the best he could. Usually the eyes of ships were blue or verdigris or even brown worn to gray, if they'd not been touched up for a while.

The eye above us was a deep red iris but the name underneath was *Eidolon*, the Ghost. I sniffed for fresh paint, but then docks always smell of linseed oil and pigment like an artist's studio, among other things. "Walk on a little," I murmured back at Phandros. "See if anyone's around."

He nodded, said loudly, "Do it quickly then...I'm thirsty!" and walked on.

I turned toward the edge of the pier as though to answer nature's call. Then, swiftly, I jumped up, raising a hand to touch as high on the ship's side as I could. I timed it right, jumping up just as the ship sank a little on the easy tide. My fingers came back smeared with fresh paint. Looking up, I could just see where I'd taken away the overcoating. I could see what letters it was covering up.

Five minutes later, I'd bluffed my way aboard a ship tied up three down from Jori's. The single guard on board was leaning his elbows on the railing, gazing toward the town. I could hear the music and the sounds of many voices. He wasn't interested in me or my companion's argument that Ormenios and Lapithai shared a common border, though he agreed to let us see a map if we gave him the coin in my hand.

A minute or so later, the guard was sleeping peacefully with a black eye in the captain's armchair and we were sneaking over the railing to the next ship, which was empty and dangerously close. There'd be tangled lines come the morning.

The next had two guards playing at dice with such attention that we could have stepped over them and not interrupted the game. I stole the lantern from their aft-rail as I made my way to the ship we wanted to inspect.

Phandros took the lantern from me and shone it around. He stopped and knelt, peering closely and even sniffing at a large stain on the planks in the rear of the waist. "This is where the cook overturned the egg-and-chive sauce the third day out. It's definitely the *Chelidion*."

Needless to add that the cage was gone. Only a little straw scattered in the corners showed it had ever been there. I forced my anger down into a corner of my soul and told it sternly to stay there. Little pieces of rage kept escaping, though, clouding my thinking.

From somewhere below, a knocking sounded. I held up my hand, indicating that Phandros should stay here. He nodded and drew out his long leather cord, quickly twisting it in his special sliding noose.

I slipped below deck, looking for any member of the crew. I found nothing out of the ordinary except that the door of Jori's private cabinet was swinging as the tide moved. Rhythmically, it hit against the frame, making the knocking sound I'd heard.

The cabinet was empty, not a scrap of paper, but his strongbox was jingling with the coins of a dozen nations and an ivory statuette of Hermes, god of trickery, travel and trade, lay on top. All very portable goods but no one had taken anything, so far as I could tell, except the papers.

I searched the hold, even the secret ones that I knew how to get into because I'd hidden things myself there once or twice. On one memorable trip, a certain hiding place had hidden me. The cargo was still there, chests and barrels and amphorae all muddled together.

I looked in my own bunk. Again, there was nothing much out of place, though there were a few bits and pieces that didn't belong to me. Space being so precious aboard a ship that I'd probably been overboard all of five minutes at Telemenos before the first mate took it over.

It only took a moment, and cost me a fingernail, to get the secret hiding place open. The bundle that held my sword was still there, untouched until I took it out. I unwrapped it and slid it home into the scabbard. Trust Skander's butler. The fit was just a tad off in the width, the length ideal.

It was only as I was climbing the narrow gangway that I paused to stare. In between the boards just below the hatch, a little bead of liquid had run, dry now. It looked as though a line of resin dripped, leaving a thick, bumpy ridge along the wood. In the yellowish lantern-light it looked orange against the graying wood. I'd never noticed it before and I'd been up and down this ladder a thousand times. One of Jori's smuggling holds was behind the wall, a secure strong-room to which I did not know the secret.

I climbed out and held the lantern close to the deck. It was hard to tell but I thought the wood of the deck looked darker than it should after weeks under the bleaching sun. I handed the lantern to Phandros, leaned down and pulled, the wooden pegs screeching as they came out. The two-inch board snapped like a twig when bent back too far. Flies, disturbed at their feasting, dark as the night, spun up past our faces, their buzzing a rasp along my nerves.

Along the sides of the board were dabbled stains, leaving dots along the underside where something wet and dark had gathered and dripped. I did not think that the clumsy cook had also dropped a decanter of wine.

With one accord, Phandros and I looked down into
the hidden compartment between the decks. Half a
dozen bodies, twisted, piled, broken, lay there in a pile.
Sated flies crawled drunkenly over the corpses. The
slack faces were ones well-known to me but of Jori, I
saw only his smooth dark hair.

CHAPTER FIFTEEN

I sat for a long time on a bollard by the sea, watching the wavering reflections of torches in the water. Strangely, though I'd known Jori for years and never met his mother, I thought more about her than about him. He was beyond earthly matters now. She would wait and watch the sea for a glimpse of familiar sails, looking for a ship that would never come. I could tell her he died, of course, but I had a feeling she wouldn't stop waiting for that ship even so.

Phandros had paced up and down the docks for a while before disappearing. He came back, bearing a jug of black wine, resin-flavored and steaming hot. "I don't think this is what I asked for," he said, sniffing dubiously. "But it's definitely alcoholic."

I spilled a little for the souls of the sailors and drank the rest. "We'll find the harpy," I said. "Find the harpy, find the murderer."

Phandros stroked his beard. "Logical. Let's go."

I don't know what the total population of Troezen may be but I'd offer good money that the majority of them were in the street. Small indeterminate children shrieked with excitement or temper, their delight sounding much the same as their fear. Their fathers and brothers capered to the ever-present music, slapping their heels and kicking up their feet, red faces and white teeth a-gleam. The old men tapped their sticks to the beat or used them to nudge someone in the direction of the wine tables to fetch them another beaker. Adding in the visitors and sailors staring about in wonder with no idea where to go or what to do made the streets even more of a log-jam of humanity.

Phandros and I tried to force a way through but our progress was dismally slow. Many people were heading with great energy into the town while streams of others seemed just as determined to go the other way. The cacophony was appalling, shouting, laughing, shrieking, complaining humanity mixed with genuine musicians, with the added irritant of a persistent buzzing from the ram and bull horns that seemed to have magically appeared in every hand.

My head began to throb in sympathy with the increasing sound levels. I wanted to hurtle up the street, knocking everyone over, tossing them aside like straw, but neither violence nor politeness would improve our rate of progress.

For everyone I could have pushed out of the way, there were forty more right behind them, paying no attention to anything but their own entertainment.

There were many young men dressed in kilts, vines or skins, satyr's horns bound on their brows, mooing like cattle. Their bodies were smeared with soot or red paint. They roamed in groups, blocking the narrow streets, or threading their way through, hand in hand, single-file, dancing sometimes, and always, always yelling. One group caught Phandros and me up in a chained dance, grabbing our hands, dragging us back the way we'd come. We no sooner shook loose than another group locked arms and swept up everyone in the street, I no less helpless than the rest in the crush.

I found myself next to a woman, looking into great dark-fringed eyes, her face as fair and flawless as a statue's. When we stood on our own feet again, she threw her arms around me. Her body was lush and full but the skin of her cheek against mine felt oddly lifeless. Her voice quivered with laughter at my expression. "Is that a sword on your hip, or are you just glad to see me?"

"It's a sword," I answered.

She tossed her head. "Hmmph, if you won't, there are plenty who will!" She vanished, swallowed up in the crowd as though she had become one with the night.

Phandros shouted something, for a whisper might as well not have been spoken at all. I put my hand to my ear to show I hadn't understood. This time, I more read his lips than heard him. "They're masks, only masks!"

Looking around, I saw many women disguised as she had been. Animals predominated, cats with life-like whiskers threaded through the masks, birds with great beaks and feathers sprouting, bulls and rams whose heavy horns contrasted sharply with the feminine contours below. Many wore masks of Tragedy or Comedy, mouths pulled square, cheeks round or stretched out. They wore long robes with hoods or scarves to cover their hair.

The very air smelled different to the spring festival where I'd first seen my future bride. The women of Athens maintain their modesty through never exposing themselves to ridicule or disdain. They may compete in games from time to time and participate in important celebrations or religious ceremonials. This sort of Dionysian excess would have been despised as a revolting spectacle no decent woman would dare attend. There was even dancing where both sexes moved together which somehow shocked me more than I understood.

As we progressed toward the upper-town, fighting through to attain our goal, the dancing and drinking of the lower town seemed a mild bacchanal, a sort of bucolic party for native spirits to ensure a good harvest or plentiful nets of fish. I could imagine some of the girls I knew, simple country girls like Iole or Omphale, quite enjoying themselves.

Up here, nearer the acropolis, however, evil was thick in the air, floating like oil on water, leaving a slime behind as much on the soul as on the body. At every step, I felt something like spider webs across my face, invisible but a reminder that there are other motives and forces in the world beside the human.

We heard no wholesome laughter now, only screams or sobbing hysteria. The music had altered, more drumming, more flute, no harp now or delicate sistrum jingling. The flute quavered, a weird melody with no perceptible tune. Many people still danced to it but with a wild, helpless abandon that frightened even sailors.

We passed a few groups of them running back down the street. Phandros bumped into one young man who took a swing at him, sobbing, "I won't, I won't."

I slapped the boy lightly; he was hardly older than the fishing lad aboard the *Cythereia*. The blindness cleared from his eyes and he stared at me wildly. "Who are you?"

"No one important. What ship are you from?"

"The...the *Lotos*." He straightened up. "From Piraeus."

"I'm from Piraeus myself. Do you know the Ram's Head taverna?"

He half-smiled. "My uncle is Bibos the tailor. His shop is near there. I wish...." He stopped, biting his lip.

"Sure, I know Bibos." Really, I didn't know the man from a hole in the ground but it steadied the boy to hear a familiar accent. "Listen to me, son. Round up your friends and get back to your ship. This isn't a night to be wandering around Troezen alone."

He nodded. A moment later, more sailors came by, hurrying, not quite running, held to discipline by the

presence of a couple of older hands. I gave the young
sailor into their keeping. One saluted, looking at me
curiously.

"Get on," I said. "Sail tonight if you can but don't
leave your ships again until dawn."

Phandros and I continued to head up the street,
closer together as the buildings seemed to narrow in
above us. A fog or smoke from the fires burning on
every corner stung my eyes and clouded my sight. The
figures that passed now seemed ever more sinister, and
their glances told me that I looked much the same to
them.

Phandros tugged at my elbow. "Call me an old
fool," he murmured. I could hear him clearly now for it
seemed to me that even the music died away when he
spoke.

"Never mind," I muttered back. "I see it."

"Some of these people aren't wearing masks any
more, are they?"

"Not unless the mask makers here are really, really
good."

Some of the eyebrows were not glued-on feathers,
the whiskers were not black thread, the fangs protruding
over full red lips no longer wooden dentures. Claws and
tails half-glimpsed in the uncertain light spread and
lashed.

Looking at them was bad enough; it got worse when
they started looking back. The hissing I heard wasn't the
criticism a bad actor receives. A hungrier, deeper sound
followed us.

"Let's walk a little faster," I said.

"Excellent idea."

At the top of the street, there was a cross-roads
marker. "Read it for me, will you?"

I wasn't sure when I'd drawn my sword. It felt light
and easy in my hand. Standing with my back to

Phandros, I peered this way and that down the streets
meeting here. I felt eyes upon me.

"It says Palace to the left, acropolis straight
ahead...."

"The left it is then."

"No, wait. Queen's Menagerie to the right. They
must keep the beasts near the arena; that's logical."

"Queen's Menagerie?"

"That's what it says." Phandros squinted again,
holding the lantern up as high as he could. I took it from
his hand, still keeping the sword in my left, and raised it
to shine on the block of wood shaped like an arrow.

"Yes," he confirmed. "Queen's....thank you, Eno."

"Thank you. I can read but right now I have another
use for my eyes."

He sighed. "I feel it too. Somebody's watching us."

"More than one. Top of that roof with the awning
still out. Three streets down -- don't look -- he's behind
a corner. Down at the end of the street, that one's got a
real flair for this, very good, just blending in with the
shadows."

There'd be no shadows in a moment. The moon had
been playing hide-and-go-seek with the clouds all this
time. Now she decided she'd had enough flirtation and
withdrew to contemplation behind her veils.

"What do you suggest, now? Cover of
darkness...element of surprise...spring from hiding...."
He sounded like a small boy reciting his lessons for the
week. Knowing the Spartans, those were probably the
lessons he had been forced to memorize, right first time,
every time.

Before I answered, I threw the lantern to the ground
to burst in a brief flare-up of flame and oil. It
illuminated for an instant the creature that crouched
nearest, a thing of sinew, bone, feather and hide with

only the merest outline of a human being. It lifted up to sniff the air and a low growling whine reached us.

"I have a simpler plan. Run."

"Well, it is a plan...of sorts." The last word had hardly floated across to me when he hiked up his borrowed robe and ran down the street. For a skinny older guy, he showed a nice turn of speed. It was harder to get my mass going but I achieved my top speed at about the same time he did.

One piece of advice I offer free of charge to any young man considering the heroic life as a profession. Sooner or later, you were going to have to run. Keeping yourself fit is important. Not looking back is vital. That may sound like cowardice. So be it. Sometimes you don't want to know what is chasing you. Knowing how close they are won't make you any faster. Run flat out or don't run at all.

A wagon had been pulled halfway across the street. Phandros saw it in time to go around. I took it like a competitor in high hurdles on the last day of the Olympian Games. I heard a thud and a crash behind me as someone else didn't make it over. I knew some of the others would have no trouble. Those kinds of creatures don't.

Then there was no sound except my boots flapping endlessly on the hard-packed road. And heavy breathing, lots of it, from behind me.

We'd reached the outskirts of town. There'd soon be no confining streets where they could only come at us from behind. They'd be able to lope ahead and have room to spring. All the time I ran through those reeking alleys, I kept expecting one to strike from the roofline. Phandros was somewhere ahead but I couldn't see him now. I only hoped they weren't herding us into an ambush. Another cart...I'd never be able to jump that high again.

My throat felt hard, my mouth drying, as I tried to get enough air. I am not built for distance. I had just decided to turn and fight where I'd still have a paltry advantage when I heard Phandros call to me. "This way, Eno, this way."

I skidded around a last corner and found myself on an open plain. The moon came out, flooding the ground with dead light. Not far away was the arena, a tall round structure made up of individual timbers roped together.

Phandros, however, was closer by, standing in front of an open gate in a smaller stockade, the guard of the doorway behind him. I changed course, finding a spurt of speed even I didn't know I had in me.

I saw the staring eyes and gaping mouth of the guard as I passed him. He wasn't looking at me but at those behind me.

Phandros had to jerk the guard in through the gateway or he would have still be standing there agape as they ran him down.

I pushed down on the pivoting bar and it dropped into its slots, holding the gate. Thuds came as something couldn't stop in time. I heard whimpers and then a long, disappointed howl.

"What...what?" the guard gasped.

I clonked him on the head and he crumpled.

"What was that for?" Phandros protested. "He saved us."

"Do you think whoever sent those things will be pleased he saved us?"

"It wasn't just part of the Hunt?"

"With us as prey? I don't think so. They didn't seem to be hunting anyone else. Somebody knows we have come to Troezen and why."

"Do you think Jori told them?"

I shook my head. Taking the unconscious guard by the shoulders, I dragged him over to a shed. It smelled of hay and sweet grass. I dumped him there to have his sleep out.

"I think they killed him outright, along with the rest of the crew to keep them from talking. It's why they took his papers instead of questioning him."

"But why? Why be so brutal?"

"They brought the harpy here...who may not be a harpy. Or at least, may not always have been a harpy. I believe someone didn't want it back."

"It came from here? I thought they came only from the Gods as condign punishment."

"I think it -- she -- was made here. By the same art we met in Leros."

He nodded, scratching his beard. "Ah, I have never learned much about black magic."

"I know more than I want to. And I'm afraid I'm about to learn more."

"I fear you are right." He sighed. "Well, we're not dead...not yet. What's next?"

"We look for the harpy. That's why we came."

The enclosure held cages, pens, and stakes for the more docile creatures. Sleepy growls and murmurs came as we passed among them. I'd taken the guard's lantern and inspected each animal as I passed. There were lions from Nemea, lying on their backs like kittens, bulls who shook sleepy heads at the light, bears curled in big brown balls, large, frightening creatures no doubt, but all of them unambiguously ordinary. No minotaurs, no Stymphalian birds of brass, nothing that couldn't be hunted or trapped by usual means and usual men. Where was the 'big surprise' that was supposed to end the Hunt tomorrow?

After we searched, Phandros and I met up by the front gate. "Not a sign of it," he said.

"They must be keeping her somewhere else. Maybe in the arena itself?"

"It's possible. Other animals might be made uneasy by it...her." He shook his head, tugging on his beard for comfort. "It's a shame. I don't mind the usual sacrifices; they are necessary to keep the Gods happy. But this! All these magnificent beasts to be slaughtered for no reason except the vain-glory of the king. It's not for Hermes' sake, that's certain."

"There's nothing we can do for them," I said all the more reluctantly because I felt the same way. What purpose was served by slaughtering a mother bear and her two roly-poly cubs? "We can't let them out. They'd attack the townspeople. And sooner or later they'd be hunted down anyway."

"True. I only wish...."

I knew what I had to do. By the cold feeling at the pit of my stomach, I knew I was frightened. In my whole life, I'd only ever had one reaction to being afraid. Yet this time, the feeling went clear to the bone, leaving me weak and useless. I could not force the words that I must say past my dry lips.

"Er...no offense, but you'd better stay here, Phandros. It's safe. In the morning, go back to the *Doris*. As soon as you get there, tell the captain to cast off."

"What are you saying? Where are you going?"

"I pray I will succeed and hope I will survive but I may not be able to do both. If I do neither, you will have to convince your friend Skander to buy an army to come back."

"You've gone mad, my friend."

"If I don't succeed, you'll soon know about it. Whoever is doing this had a set-back at Leros, not a defeat. The evil comes from here."

"How do you know?"

My head was swimming with the unclean power in the place. "I'm sure, that's all. It's like a cloud of grease in the air or the sound of gnats. I'm also sure that if I can't stop it, somebody else will have to do it, Gods help him."

"You can't mean to just walk out of this place," he said, grasping my arm. "You can't possibly fight them all."

"Thanks for reminding me." I took off my sword-belt. "Keep that for me until I come back."

I jumped, caught the top of the stockade and pulled myself up for a peek over the wall. "Yes, plenty of them, milling around. If there's a leader, I don't see him." I dropped. "I don't mean to fight them."

"They'll tear you to pieces, the way the Maenads do."

"In that case, I'll definitely fight. But I'm betting they have had no such instructions."

"This is still about the harpy?"

"No. This is about me being afraid." I felt better saying it out loud. "'Bye, Phandros."

I caught the wall again, rising all the way up to put a knee on the top. "Look out below," I shouted and threw myself off like a diver.

***

It took five of them to drag me bodily, all wrapped as I was in ropes and thin chains, to the door. Lifting me up the stairs seemed out of the question. I was either crossing the palace threshold under my own power or I wasn't going.

A delicate foot in a dainty slipper emerged, making no sound on the broad step. I rolled my eyes upward but all I could see was a black column with her head fuzzily atop it. She seemed to float gracefully, but then I'd been hit on the head once or twice before everyone understood quite clearly that I had surrendered.

Her creatures stepped back when she came toward me. I thought that it seemed less in homage than in fright. She looked down on me, gleeful as a small girl with her first kitten. Over her high-piled hair, she wore a black veil and a golden crown. She threw the veil back and I saw her face, serene, smooth and plump as a beauty in her first youth. I recognized her at once from my nightmares.

Despite her lack of wrinkles, she exuded age. A weight of years lay in her flat, empty eyes and coiled in the curiously lusterless weight of her improbably black hair.

Queen Zosime put one embroidered slipper on my chest. "How lowly do the great fall. Here is a hero but I can shrink you, change you into anything I wish. A minotaur, perhaps, to delight my dear husband's heart as he kills you in the arena tomorrow." The way she said 'husband' would have made a thousand pantingly-eager bride-grooms cry off.

"Greetings, Queen of Troezen," I said, my throat working against the cold chain around my neck. They'd tied me up very effectively, considering what paws and claws they'd had to work with.

She cast a cold gaze over the bonds they'd tightened until my flesh swelled around them. "This is absurd," she declared. "Loose him."

A bodyguard, big and muscled enough to give me a little trouble, stepped forward, drawing his knife. He knelt, began to saw, and then paused. "Lady...."

"My will holds him there. His limbs are senseless until I free them."

Maybe her will held me, not the bonds. My muscles did seem more cramped than could be explained by mere bruises. At any rate, it was impressive. Her minions obviously thought so, for they made the same chittering sound that chipmunks do. I wondered if that is how they'd started life, as mice or other small rodent, changed, added to, and cruelly twisted out of all recognition. If Eurytos could do it with ants, this queen, a more powerful servant of his dark task-mistress, could probably do it with anything.

When the bonds were severed, and the chains unwound, my limbs fell limply to the earth as though I had no influence over them. I couldn't even feel my feet. The bodyguard jumped up, his sword at the ready in case I was feigning immobility. I only wished I were.

"Rise, creature," she said, her husky voice like the sound of a snake passing down a tiled floor.

I wanted to obey her, rather badly, but the perfect communication between my mind and my body had apparently been severed for a while. I forced up a hand in a universal gesture imploring a moment's patience. Zosime stepped back, tapping one dainty foot.

"Well?"

"They were a little rough," I said.

"Are you a hero, or a spoiled girl?"

"I've had a hard couple of days," I admitted. "Shipwrecked...storm-tossed...."

"Betrayed...." she added. "Are you angry about that?"

"Betrayed?" I said as innocently as I knew how. "By whom, lady?"

She laughed softly, a charming sound. "I knew you'd come to Troezen. You are that kind of a man, Eno of Thrace. So be it. I have tamed stronger creatures than you."

I met her eyes and received a shock. She had no fear that I'd come for any kind of vengeance. I doubt she'd ever given my reasons for coming to Troezen any thought at all. Nothing in the world mattered to her except her own will, her own desires. I doubted a warm feeling for any other person had ever touched that adamantine heart, for she needed no one except as a tool, to be used, broken, and thrown aside.

Zosime stood there, measuring me as if I were a piece of sculpture in the marketplace, plainly wondering if I would fit the space she had in mind for me. That's sounds morally questionable but for all her beauty, I would have as soon shared a mattress with a thousand scorpions. And throw in a few lethal cat-sized spiders as well. My chances of survival would be improved.

"Help him up," she ordered the bodyguard. "Bring him to my private chambers."

By the time we reached the second floor, I was practically riding him piggy-back, my arms draped over his neck. I may not have felt completely recovered, though my hands and feet were tingling, but I still would rather ride than walk. Exhausting your enemies is good; making them exhaust themselves is better.

Several people awaited the queen in her chamber, a large, all but empty room at the top of the palace. What surprised me was their very ordinariness. An evil queen should be attended by twisted slaves, skin pale and slick from never seeing the sun, hunched and cringing, with long damp hands, bald heads, and shifty eyes.

In Troezen, Zosime was served by a trim maid, accompanied by two small female children. They whisked away the queen's outdoor mantle, placing gently over her head a sheer scarf, spangled with many jewels. It must have been heavy and scratchy even if dazzling to behold.

The maid met my gaze not one whit less proudly than did her mistress. The little girls didn't seem perturbed at all when the guard dropped me onto a bench dragged out in the middle of the floor. I slumped there, still boneless. I noticed, however, that neither of the children dared lift their eyes higher than anyone's knees. They scurried out like mice at a hiss from their superior.

The queen pinched lightly at her earrings. "Fetch a drink for our honored guest, Damalis."

"I have it here, lady." With the unearthly grace of a woman of Lesbos, the waiting-woman knelt beside me, laying aside a tray she'd taken up. She lifted a cup of chased gold and pressed it to my lips. I drank perforce, without any hint from her impassive face whether she poured nectar or poison down my throat.

I began to understand why a man would desire such a woman. What lengths might one go to in order to wrest a natural reaction from her, to force her to acknowledge your existence as a fellow being and as a man.

I drank thirstily, for there seemed nothing in the cup but pure water. And if I were wrong, if poison lurked in the depths, so be it.

"Can I have some too," asked a boyish voice from a dark corner.

Damalis bowed her head with regal humility and poured a cup from another, more elaborate beaker on the tray. She carried to him and I heard him drink thirstily.

"I didn't see you there, my lord," the queen purred.

This thin, frail man was then king of Troezen, far less impressive than his wife's meanest servant. He moved like an elderly man, aching in every joint. I'd heard he was young and I could see that his hair was still dark and thick, his face dreamy-eyed and unwrinkled. For all that, he seemed as old as Tithonius, so loved by Eos of the Dawn that she obtained immortality for him but forgot to include ever-lasting youth. He wound up a cicada. I doubted the king of Troezen would have that much good luck.

He turned the cup round and round in his trembling, emaciated hand, the fingers stained faintly orange. His eyes were young, young and wounded. "I had that dream again, my dear. Seemed very real." He yawned, blinking like a sleepy baby. "She seems such a nice girl...I wish she were real."

"Drink, lord. Drink and forget," Queen Zosime said with a soft but firm note of command. "Damalis, my lord needs his treats."

He shrugged bony shoulders and lifted the cup to his lips. "A brother, a niece and happiness. I don't mind dreaming about these things. No offense, my dear."

"You do have a niece," I murmured.

"What did you say?" he asked, taking a handful of strange orange puffs from the bowl his wife's servant held out. "You shouldn't sit on the floor. We have couches...." He looked around vaguely as if this weren't his home, tossed a few into his mouth and crunched. A faint flavor of salt and cheese reached me. He licked the powder from his lips and ate a little more.

"Come, my lord, you must rest." Zosime coaxed. "You must be ready to perform the sacrifice tonight."

"Sacrifice? Oh, yes. It is tonight?"

"Yes, tonight. Take him to his chamber," the queen said in an aside to the guard. But the king slipped his arm free of the big man's grasp like water through a bracelet. I wondered if they ever fed him or did he so crave those 'treats' that all other food meant nothing to him. He weaved back and forth as he stood looking down at me, like a man beyond exhaustion.

"I dream of a dead brother and a golden-haired child who made me crowns of flowers. Do you dream them too?"

"No. I know she lives."

"She lives?" Slowly, he raised his head to look steadily at his queen. Under his straggling beard, his jaw tightened. "This man says I have a niece."

"He is a prisoner," Zosime said scornfully. "He'll say anything."

"That's true," he admitted, his chin sinking onto his chest. His eyes closed and he swayed like a man asleep on his feet. But even so, he took a few more mouthfuls before he left the room.

They took him away with surprising gentleness, guiding his fumbling footsteps. As he went, I heard him say, "She made me a crown of golden flowers...."

I looked at the queen, her face like a mask of Pride worn in some triumphal pageant. "What are those things you are giving him?"

"A little ambrosia from the Gods' own table."

I remembered what Aphrodite had said. Looking around, I saw the orange dust on the clothes of everyone in the room except for Zosime and myself.

"I believe the Gods are eating it but why do you want them to?"

"They have remarkable properties, these little tasty treats. You eat them almost mindlessly and you don't want anything else. Whatever you are doing, playing a game, say, becomes the most important thing in the world to you. Nothing else matters. Someone could slaughter your children and it would mean nothing."

She brought the bowl to me. "Have some. They're really quite delicious."

They didn't look created by mortal hands that was for certain. For one thing, each one was pretty much identical to all the others. Strangely enough, despite what she'd told me, they did look like something worth trying. Their smell was cloying and as ever-present as the dust that fell from them yet it somehow stimulated both my curiosity and my taste buds.

"It's going to be harder to bend me to your will than that, Queen Zosime."

"Perhaps. Who can say?" She clapped her hands. "Leave me with this man."

The bodyguard said pointedly, "I'll be right outside the door, my queen."

After a moment, she dragged forward a simple folding stool, her every clumsy movement demonstrating how unused to simple tasks she was. She sat down gracefully, though, arranging her draperies, studying me covertly the whole time. "I have waited a long time to see you, Eno."

"And I you, lady."

"Now that I do, I realize what a waste it would be to kill you. Such strength. Such a spirit should not be sacrificed wantonly." Her eyes searched my whole body in a way that reminded me of nothing so much as a housewife planning how many meals she could get out of a haunch of venison. For all her beauty, she had about as much seductiveness as a pool of cold, scummy water.

"You know, there's always a choice to be made in this life. You can choose death or a much more glorious future. What I offer you is a life without limits, a life of absolute power over all the earth."

"If this is leading up to a job offer as head of an army of the dead, I've heard it."

She leaned forward, letting her bosom fall against the opening of her gown. "But have you thoroughly considered all that such a position would entail? Imagine yourself, clad in the finest armor, under a banner of red and black. Armies, unconquerable armies would flock to you. The whole world would tremble at your command. City-states would fall before you. In the end, you wouldn't even have to raise a sword. The mere mention of your name would bring Athens, Troy, Sparta, on their knees before you, all of them begging for your mercy. What is a mere kingdom compared to that?"

"An entrancing picture."

"Isn't it?" she said, her eyes already smoking with the fires of burning cities. Her breasts rose and fell to her heightened breathing. No passion would draw forth such pleasure as her imagining the misery of millions.

Zosime reached forward one delicate hand, her nails shining like pearls, and ran them up from my knee to my thigh. My skin crawled. "And I to ride beside you...."

"You would not like a battlefield. Smelly. Dirty. No place for a lady."

"You'll need me. Only I, by my magic, can raise your enemies to serve in your army forever. The more you kill, the more numerous your own ranks grow, General Eno. My," she said, meeting my gaze, "what a noble sound that has. General Eno."

I nodded. "Not bad."

"She will reward you well once you give up this foolish fight against her."

"Who is that, exactly?"

She laughed in her throat. "The Dark Lady. Once she was queen over all mortals and so she will be again. She serves her brief hour in Hades, dividing the dead souls for punishment or reward. But not for much longer. Soon she will take her rightful place on the Throne of Heaven. Very, very soon."

I tried piecing together these clues. I felt as though there were something I should know but I could not bring it forward. Maybe there'd been one too many clouts on the head earlier in the evening. "Who?"

She looked at me as a teacher instructing a tiny child in the first lisping repetition of the names of the commonest objects. "Hekate, queen of witches, seeresses and enchantresses. You will serve Zosime now and her holy will always."

"Or?"

"Or...?"

"An ultimatum usually has a threat included."

She stood up, her nails digging into my leg as she scraped them down toward my knee again. Then she turned abruptly and went to a chest hung on the wall, unlocking it with a pin she drew from her neckline. A strange reddish glow emerged when she swung open the lid.

Zosime turned, a vial of blood-red glass in her hand. "This is a potion that will bind you to my will and make you forget your foolish opposition. It contains Hypernian wine, the juice of three persimmons, twelve crushed petals from the unholy flowers that bloom along the River Styx, captured vapors from the depths of the Nekromanteion, and five drops from the Waters of the River of Lethe."

"Sounds tasty."

"Join with me of your own free will or drink this and forget there ever lived such a man as Eno of Thrace."

I suppose she was expecting me to shiver, shake and plead. But I was busy with other thoughts. The Waters of Lethe were alleged to wipe the memories of souls passing into the Underworld, forcing them to forget their mortal lives and desires. The Styx and the Nekromanteion were gateways to the Underworld. That this queen possessed the ingredients for such a potion was proof of her service to the Gatekeeper of Hell.

"You already know I'm not going to join. You're not stupid."

"But think! How much better to serve her as her beloved and all-powerful General...than to be a slave, without will, without memories, without hope."

"Was that your choice, Zosime?"

"Mine? I had no choice. No. There was never any choice for Zosime." She turned and poured off the liquid into the goblet.

"You know," I said, "you really need to make up your mind if you want me alive or dead."

"No, not really. Either way you will serve her. If you take my advice, choose to go willingly. It may make things easier for you." She spoke as if she knew.

"Shall I leave you for a few moments to think it over?"

"I'd like that." There was a window behind her. Two seconds alone in the room and I'd be gone like vapor, if I had to crawl.

She laughed again, outright, shaking back her thick hair. "To me!" she shouted.

The door burst open and the bodyguard all but fell into the room.

"Wait," she said when he would have hit me. "Hold him."

She came near again, with that drifting grace both elegant and horrible. "You said I was not stupid, for which I thank you. I'm certainly not stupid enough to leave you to make your escape."

Zosime held out the goblet. "Choose. Life, love and battle...or nothingness."

"I choose...nothingness."

She wouldn't have believed me if I'd said anything else. The bodyguard clasped his hands around my face and neck, forcing my mouth open. I tried to rise to my feet, to shake him off but I hadn't the strength. Only then did I realize that Zosime wasn't boasting when she said she had power over me. I struggled uselessly, feeling like an ordinary man for the first time in my life.

She approached slowly, giving me a chance to change my mind. When I only continued my useless struggle, she raised the cup high in the air, then shot the contents straight down my throat.

The bodyguard stepped away. I saw that he was sweating, so I'd given him at least a little trouble. But that satisfaction was nothing.

What would the potion do to me and how soon would the effects show? I didn't feel any different yet. Would I even know when I forgot, if I didn't know I was forgetting?

These matters were too complicated for me. One thing only I knew. As soon as I swallowed, my strength came surging back. I could have done anything. Break Zosime in half. Throw the bodyguard out the window. Tear the palace down stone by stone til I found the harpy. But what to do first?

When in doubt, play dumb. I let my eyes glaze over and my mouth hung slack. I forced my fists to open. "I don't feel well."

"Don't be afraid. The Goddess offers you a new, glorious life."

"Goddess?"

She laughed again and came closer to inspect me, her dark eyes flickering. If we'd been alone, I'd have sent her with a wrenched neck to Hekate. "Do I know you, lady?" I asked.

Her body-guard knelt beside me. "Are you sure, my lady?"

"The Waters do not fail. He will be nothing but clay for my molding now."

He shrugged broad shoulders, though his eyes stayed narrowed in suspicion.

"Stand up," she ordered.

I stretched, unkinking twisted limbs, yawning. "What day is it?"

"A day of celebration. What is your name?"

I opened my mouth as if to speak but so great was the force of her will, commanding me with unspoken power not to remember, that for a moment I halted, dumb as a bell without a clapper. I ventured the first name that popped into my mind. "Phandros?"

"Phandros. Very well. You will go with this man and he will instruct you in your duties. Serve me well."

I bowed clumsily in imitation of the other man and followed him. I drew a clandestine breath of relief once out of her sight. Queen Zosime seemed to exhale a sweet but evil scent, like some tropical flower luring small creatures to a poisoned drowning within lush petals.

CHAPTER SIXTEEN

I had followed him into the hall when suddenly he pivoted and pinned me to the wall. "I don't trust you."

My eyes must have been as big as eggs with innocent wonder, for the iron-bar of his arm across my wind-pipe lessened just the slightest bit. It was enough. A moment later, he was on the floor, my foot on his throat. "Wise," I said, "but too little, too late."

I stilled his efforts with a kick to the head and dragged him, no less a weight than I myself, into an empty room. No time for fancy knots. I bundled him into a large chest of clothes and put the bed on top of it. I didn't worry whether he'd suffocate.

Then quick as I could, for I didn't know how long it would be before the potion took effect, I went hunting. The palace was large enough to hide an enchanted princess in any dark corner or hidden chamber. As I went upward, I reproached myself for not questioning the bodyguard before knocking him cold. Well, I could always go back and twist it out of him.

From somewhere nearby, I felt a chilly breeze whispering over the floorboards. I found a door and wrenched it open. I found myself on a parapet looking out over the city of Troezen, a city crawling with life the way the soil under a rock teems with frightened, creeping things. I could hear voices and cries, mingling into a pulsing moan, almost a song. If the grubs and worms under a stone could sing a terrified song of praise to the creature that had lifted the rock perhaps it would sound much the same.

Everything that was happening -- from Jori's death to the planned sacrifice of some fantastical animal tomorrow -- had a meaning and a purpose that I could only dimly comprehend. Zosime had hinted that her Goddess was ready to emerge, like some foul creature from a black cocoon. But then, I didn't really need to know all the details. I could wreck all their nasty plans by my ignorance just as easily, if not more easily, than with wisdom.

I smiled, planning mischief, as I ran briskly around the parapet on the topmost tower. On the farthest side from the doorway, a cage hung swinging on a beam cantilevered into the palace wall. I recognized the workmanship for the plans had been mine.

"Princess...." I gasped.

A dark mass huddled in the center of the floor. She couldn't be dead; all my logic said she was destined to die in the morning at the hand of her own uncle. And I had sent her back to Troezen!

I leapt onto the beam in the darkness, guided only by the dim stars. Though it had looked straight, once I was on it, I realized that it was bending under the levered weight of the cage and the harpy. It creaked and swayed under my feet as if I stood on a boom at sea. I inched along, wishing with all my might that I weighed no more than a pigeon. If I could only reach her and open the cage, she could fly away.

She stirred as my weight upon the beam shook the cage. I saw the reflection of her brilliant eyes as she raised her head from her breast. Impossible to say if she recognized me. "You've got to get out of here," I told her, keeping my voice low and reassuring. "Fly to the mountains and hide up there. If I can, I'll get there and we'll find a way to change you back. There's got to be a greater magician some place. I hear there's some smart guys in Samarkand."

I felt the beam sway beneath me as one of the pegs holding it to the wall jumped away with deep-noted 'sproing.' I ducked instinctively and heard another one burst free.

She could fly, of course, but I could only fall.

In the hope of evening out the load, I gingerly knelt, then lay at full-length, face-down, balancing myself on the beam, which suddenly seemed far narrower. I fumbled for the cage door. She didn't cry out or try to slash my hand from my wrist, which I counted as a sign she knew me. I mumbled the reassuring words a man might offer a dog with a sore paw.

The door opened, but she stayed huddled on the floor. "Go on, now," I urged. "You're free."

She sighed but did not move. Had the Queen in her cruelty clipped her wings?

Perhaps it was just long experience that made me feel so jumpy. I doubted the Queen's bodyguard would stay quietly unconscious for long and, though the beam no longer bucked like a runaway horse, I didn't trust my perch to last. A quick scuttle backwards would make me awfully happy but I couldn't leave her and I didn't dare put my hand in to grab her. I was fond of my fingers.

Then I heard that chittering sound around us, as the Queen's minions found me. My attention had been too focused on the harpy. They waited for me, for they could see that to step on the beam meant a long, screaming death for everyone concerned. Even minions don't want to go like that.

Like a tropical sun flooding the sky with golden light, the Harpy's cage filled with blinding brilliance. She spun around, wings outstretched and the cage burst apart, sliced pieces falling away. I was no less dazed than the minions. Had she known she could break free at any moment?

She hovered, fiery wings beating at the air. Her triumphant voice shattered the starry silence, scattering the mutated creatures around us as a hot wind sends leaves flying. Impelled by her courage, I stood up in one move, drawing my sword. It seemed to catch her fire, reflecting into the eyes of our enemies.

Then one came through the rest, larger, bolder, a trickle of red still in the corner of his mouth. The Queen's bodyguard hefted a bow, the razor-sharp arrow pointed not at me, but at the harpy, the string already drawn to his cheek.

I dived, as the arrow flew, while she strove to rise. Without knowing quite how, I found myself lying across the parapet, the stone edge all but cutting me in half, both hands over, scraping against the wall as something swung between them.

Turning my eyes toward the bodyguard, I demanded that he help me. "She's your rightful queen, you ass," I said, in more or less those words. "And you shot her."

"She is a beast and shall die as a beast."

"She? Then you do know. And you're an idiot." At least he didn't try to stop me as I pulled her up. He may have even kept back the minions but I had no further attention to waste on him.

The arrow had pierced her out-stretched wing. She snapped feebly at me for I am sure I caused her great pain, though I gripped her above the wound. Her feathers scraped me, all her dazzling light extinguished, except for one spot that refused to stay still but danced over her body. No matter how I turned my head, I couldn't catch it except from the corner of my eye.

"That's not so bad. You'll be all right once we get that out."

Her eyes were fixed on my face. I am, as you have guessed by now, extraordinarily dense sometimes. It wasn't until I looked closely at the puffy skin where the arrow entered that I realized the spot of light dancing around was coming from me. Specifically, from the place on my forehead where the Goddess had kissed me.

She had called me her missionary. But what is a missionary but one who carries a message from a god? I knew the message wasn't for me. "Bend, princess," I muttered and pressed my lips to the pin-feathers on the top of the Harpy's head.

No sparkling lights, no harpist's strain, no spirits or fat sprites appeared. One instant, I held a wild beast in my arms, bleeding copper-scented blood, the next a girl, red-blooded and naked. The light of Aphrodite's kiss went out so I couldn't see even one glimpse of her face among the shadows of the wall, only the merest outline of her profile.

The bodyguard came up to us. With the princess in my arms, I could neither avoid nor ride the fist he threw at my chin, all his wounded pride and knowledge of his folly behind it.

She and I fell together, a tangle of limbs, her bosom in my face. I pushed her aside and bounded to my feet. He fired again but the arrow went wild as he tried to dance out of range while aiming.

Reaching out, I grabbed him by the back of the neck and shook him as an eagle whips a snake. He cried out and tried to reach me with blind fists. I gave him another vigorous shake for good measure. Then I thrust him down on his knees before the wounded princess.

"This is the rightful ruler of this black and misbegotten land. Obey her or die."

"I will die anyway," he said, gasping. "When the queen finds out."

"Then you might as well die doing the right thing as the wrong one. Help me and be judged for the good you have done."

"Is there such a judgment?" he muttered, hanging his head.

The princess sat up, one hand to the hole in her shoulder. "I, Kissos of Troezen, swear by all the Gods that I will forgive you even this," she said in a voice scraped raw, "if you serve me faithfully from now onward."

He raised his head and wiped his hands across his mouth. "I will. Forever. I also swear by Ares and Hermes that if I am ever foresworn I shall die by my own hand."

It was all very touching but time was gnawing at my heels.

I ripped a strip from his tunic and bound up her arm. Naked, she was as regal as a queen in full royal regalia. Even the minions, copying the bodyguard, knelt to her.

"What is your name? What are you doing here?" she asked me.

"Just a hero for hire, my princess. A wanderer." I didn't know if she remembered me from Leros or not.

"You have wandered into my life with good timing, hero. What shall we do now?"

After a few minutes' discussion, the bodyguard got his chance to take another swing at me. This time, I fell down into a long black slide into nothingness, the princess' too-late cry of 'No!' following me into oblivion.

* * *

When I awoke, still with that 'No!' in my head, I became aware of a strange but familiar sound. It mingled with the roaring in my ears. Searching my recent memory, I remembered. Those animal cries were the sound of the Queen's menagerie, slightly muffled as if by distance or an obstacle.

Testing the limits as usual, I tried to move a hand.
No, I was obviously tied to something, something flat.
Was I an opening act for the sacrificial festival?
Cautiously opening an eye, I saw that it was still night.
The same night?

I raised my head as a booming knock sounded
nearby. That sound had roused me from the sleep I'd
taken, courtesy of the queen's former bodyguard. The
gate creaked open.

"Get out of the way, fool!"

The keeper was muscled aside as five guards in
armor, complete with shields and spears strode in. They
were followed by a covered two-wheeled cart, dragged
by half a dozen human slaves, followed by several
female servants, soberly but richly dressed, carrying
torches. One carried a basket, covered with a cloth that
moved. She kept one hand on whatever it was. Last, and
undoubtedly least, I was wheeled in on a flat-bed cart
which, by the smell, was usually used to carry shit out of
the zoo.

The sergeant lined up his men at the salute, then
strode around to the rear of the cart and got the door
open.

An arched hand, limply elegant, waited for the
sergeant to take it. The queen of Troezen came forth,
veiled head to foot with the finest black linen, and the
sergeant guided her down the three steps at the rear of
the cart. She seemed to float, consciously graceful in
every gesture and movement.

Everyone stepped back when she reached the
ground. I knew it was less in homage than in abject
fright. She paused, as if waiting for something. She
turned her head toward one of the female servants who
gasped. I could almost feel the tingly shock that passed
from the veiled figure to the girl. She handed her torch

to one of the others and stepped up to take away the veil, immediately kneeling at the woman's feet.

The woman pushed her over with the ball of her foot. "Fool," she said, in a low, throaty tone that carried like a deep-tolling bell. It awoke echoes of memory in me, from even earlier than our interview in her chambers. "Where's that gate guard?"

Phandros approached, rubbing his hands together obsequiously. He didn't look at me. "Here I am, my lady."

Her deep-set eyes narrowed. "My lady? Have I been demoted?"

"I beg pardon, my queen."

"That's better." She showed her white teeth in what might have been a smile. "You are not the regular guard."

"No, my queen." He held up his hand, pointing behind him at the town. His hand shook. I hadn't thought he was that good of an actor. "He has gone to the festival. I am substituting."

"Oh, you are substituting, are you? Very well. Show my servants out, lock the gate, then return."

"Yes, my queen," he said, all but bobbing a curtsey.

The maid with the basket and the sergeant remained behind. I wondered if she missed her usual bodyguard who, I hoped, was watching over the princess. If he'd grabbed a fast horse and ridden away, I couldn't blame him. But if he were smart enough to see that a grateful princess was worth more than a doomed queen, he'd stay with the girl. -I had every intention of making sure Zosime didn't return to her palace.

Queen Zosime glanced about her. "It smells," she said, and held her perfumed sleeve to her nose.

The bizarre yet familiar embroidery running around the cuff caught the torch-light, sparkling with gold thread. No doubt it was the dancing fire that gave the illusion that each sigil moved with intention and sinuous pleasure. I felt a hot jumping sensation in my abdomen muscles and had to take several deep breaths to keep calm. I saw a vision of the dead king of Leros as I'd seen him last, shuffling along, one more among the reanimated dead.

"They'll all be dead in the morning," the sergeant said with a coarse laugh.

"Not a moment too soon. I hate all this nonsense even if it does serve my purposes."

Phandros returned alone. "Take the basket," the queen commanded, "and help the sergeant with that."

She tossed her head in my direction, not deigning to point, and swept away, still graceful, hands held high, her feet taking tiny but rapid steps. The maid, Damalis, had trouble staying a respectful distance behind her.

Phandros and the sergeant picked up the handles of my cart. "What did he do?" I heard Phandros whispered.

"Some kind of criminal, I guess," scoffed the sergeant. "Man, what are you, new? What the queen says matters in this land. Don't you forget it, don't ask any questions, and you'll be all right."

The moon had started playing peek-a-boo games among the clouds again. The short parade stopped in the center of the enclosure. No cages were set here, leaving a large empty space. I'd thought, looking around earlier, that it was some kind of training area as the dirt had been swept free of the stones and straw that littered the ground elsewhere. A line of rocks marked the area off.

That thick greasy feeling I associated with dark magic had begun to gather again, wrapping around me like the enervating embrace of a succubus.

"Turn him around," Zosime commanded. "He should see this."

The two men turned me, setting the cart upright. My bonds were tighter this time, but I was tied to the wooden cart's bed which wouldn't be hard to break with a combination of a dead-lift and a cross-pull. I just wanted the right moment.

She came over to me. "How are you feeling?" she asked in a parody of concern.

"I'm still Eno," I said, meeting her eyes.

"Strange..." Then she shrugged. "The power of that potion must have waned. A pity it did not occur to you to pretend that it worked. Now you are my prisoner once more and I will send you in person to serve Hekate."

She walked a few paces off, stopped and suddenly thrust her arms in the air, leaning backward. I could only see her from the back as she swayed and dipped like a young tree in a storm. She did not speak but I saw uneasy glances pass among her witnesses. Phandros' eyebrows tried to hide in the cover of his hairline.

When she did begin to chant, it seemed to have no meaning. Words there were but in a language unknown, strange even in sound, as though not made for human lips and tongues. Humans don't usually bay or trumpet when they speak. Maybe it was a trick of the uncertain light, but sometimes, when she turned her head, it was as if she hadn't turned it so much as sprouted another face. I hoped it was just the light. Had I miscalculated my true enemy?

Far off, lightning illuminated the undersides of clouds with a sickly bluish glow as the storm the captain of the *Doris* had predicted began to make itself known. The thunder was so distant that I felt it through the wheels of the cart rather than heard it through my ears.

Then I realized that the ground was shaking, with a grinding, creaking crash like two long ships smashing into each other. Phandros ran back a few steps as if in fear. No one was paying any attention to him, or to me. They were focused completely on their queen. But even

Phandros paused in the act of cutting me free when the ground before her opened up.

Two large doors rose out of the dirt to stand upright and wide open. A black pit had appeared in the ground. As though this were an everyday occurrence, which for all I knew it well could be, the queen of Troezen walked daintily forward and down into the depths.

Her sergeant was so focused on what Zosime was doing that he didn't even notice what Phandros had done. I saw orange dust on his hands and clothes. After a moment, without a glance at either of us, the sergeant followed her.

Once my hand was free, I took the knife, slashing through the other bonds. "You'd better get out of here," I said.

"I'm staying. This is philosophy and a half!"

He was already a dozen or so steps ahead of me. Before I started down the steps, I chose a large rock, as big as my two clenched fists from among those that demarcated the 'training ground' from the rest. I balanced it on the edge, where one mysterious door would fall. I wasn't about to take the risk of having them closed for good with me on the wrong side.

Though the steps took me down only a few feet below the ground, it felt as if I were in a cave miles beneath the earth. The air, hot and thick like smoke, stifled me. The queen's servants had lit the torches as they passed, each torch burning with a clear but greenish flame. The smoke added to the bad air quality, adding to the streaks of soot on the low ceiling.

There were fissures in the floor, where steam and more varied smells emerged, varied only in their degrees of horribleness. Rotting cheese, the sulphuric effluvia of a nest of dragons, a reek like the stables of Diomedes' man-eating horses were some of the more agreeable ones. From some of the cracks, I heard moans and weeping. The terrifying noises of the upper-town in mid-debauch now seemed like the lilting songs of spring praise in comparison.

I paused, seeing Phandros' back close before me. He was trembling from head to foot, with determination I thought. "Come on, fool," I heard the queen call imperiously. "What, afraid? It is perfectly safe so long as I am here. Stiffen your spine, fool. Come to me now."

As if his body were under some other control, Phandros began walking, lifting each leg high before swinging his weight onto it. I heard him whisper, "Oh, no, no, no...." but he kept moving forward.

Far below us, a pounding arose, forcing everything to move to its rhythm. I felt my heart beat change to fall in with that intense throbbing. Phandros moved to that thundering as well, even his murmured protest matching it beat for beat.

I took a risk and looked out from the tunnel's mouth into a much, much larger cave. The roof looked infinitely far away, a curve on the edge of sight. Only a narrow path lead out from where I stood, the rest empty air.

In the center of the cave, attached to no other wall, attached only by the path, floated a massive piece of rock, smooth on the top but jagged beneath as though torn from the earth and flung away to float eternally between earth and sky. Distance and sizes were hard to judge but I knew it had to be fifty feet or more across.

Upon it stood a circular altar, paved with many tiny tiles, curving and twisting up from the base to the flat surface. On the altar-stone itself was laid a mosaic of surpassing skill, depicting nightmarish figures that wrestled and fought, biting and tearing at each other. This was the source of the bizarre embroidery on the robes of the Leronian king and the queen of Troezen. Changed, simplified for the embroiderers to follow, but still containing the essence of the subtle terror that spread out from the mosaic to touch everyone and everything.

Zosime stood on the very edge of the decoration, her feet not quite touching it. "Give me the basket, then go stand with the others."

She turned to her female servant. "Come, Damalis. Perform the ceremony with due care, though for the last time."

The maid servant bowed. She opened the basket quickly and lifted up a black puppy. Still nearly boneless but with opened eyes, it gave a small yap of protest at being taken from its warm basket.

Damalis cradled the puppy to her bosom. It didn't like it, whimpering and squirming to escape. Maybe it didn't like her perfume, maybe just the hardness of the heart pressed against it. She placed it firmly in the center of that evil mosaic, the queen smiling with more warmth than I'd yet seen.

The maid raised her arms, transformed into a priestess of evil. "For you, Soul of the Darkness! Tomorrow we will sacrifice this creature for you! Ten thousand voices will shout in your praise! Blood will be given to you, much blood. To glorify you, to honor you, grant me this boon that I might make of this insignificant creature a proper sacrifice!"

Damalis began to sway and moan, calling upon the Dark Powers in that weird keening which made the hair on the back of my neck stand up. The puppy, finally realizing that not all was well, tried to move but was flattened against the tiles. It whimpered piteously, then cried out in piercing protest as small black wings erupted from its back.

"Not enough. You are too weak!" Zosime cried out in nearly the same register as the agonized dog. "Come here, Damalis!"

The maid approached, chained to the horrible rhythm. Even from a distance, I could see the sweat shining on her face. She tried to shake her head. The queen's delicate hand reached for the girl's shoulder, nails digging in. Again the swaying, the chanting. Zosime raised her other hand, fingers pointing at the hapless dog.

Then she stopped, choking, her free hand seizing her own throat. The maid sank to her knees, as blood spurted from the fingernails clenched in her shoulder.

"Eno!" Phandros shouted. Five feet behind her, he had both hands up, clenched fists together. He and the queen were linked as if by some force running between his hands and her throat. She was up on her toes, bent back like a bow. She clutched at her throat and I knew that Phandros had thrown his lasso around her neck.

The sergeant was slower than I to break from the hypnotic force of the throbbing power, but he drew his short sword and ran toward his queen. I reached Phandros first, slid under the all-but-invisible cord by sheer instinct, and punched with all my pent-up fury at the sergeant's chin. I heard his neck snap as he went over like an empty bottle.

The queen gasped, sinking to her knees in her turn, pulling Phandros closer. "You'd better ease up," I shouted. "But not too much, eh?"

"Get the puppy...please get the puppy," Phandros begged.

Taking care not to touch that mosaic, seeming to writhe beneath the transformed dog, I scooped it up by the scruff of the neck. It growled, flapping new wings, and snapped at my finger with milk-teeth. I grasped it gently to keep it from flying out of my hand.

The maid, freed from her mistress's painful hold, tried to go for my eyes with her nails. I tripped her in self-defense. She flung her hands out to stop herself and landed with both of them square in the middle of the mosaic. She screamed as her arms sprouted fur, her hands turning into lion's paws. She could still bend them at the elbows like a human but she screamed again in torment as her ears dragged through her cheeks to the top of her head.

Poor Damalis staggered up, her shrieking becoming a deep roaring. Her eye, still human for the moment, stared at me, seeing and understanding the appalled pity on my face. Instantly, with a lion's spring, she bounded to the edge of the huge rock and dashed herself over the edge. A spume of fire exploded upwards as she was consumed. The heat abruptly increased.

Queen Zosime had both hands at her throat, her face swelling. Phandros had tightened up again, involuntarily. I actually admired his self-control. I would have strangled her twice over by now.

"I'll trade you," I said to Phandros, holding out the dog.

He gave me the throwing cord without even looking at it, taking the winged puppy in his hands. "There, now, little lamb. Nothing more to fear."

It cocked its head to the side, one silky ear askew. Then it licked his fingers. I got bit; he got licked. That's life for you.

But I had other concerns now. I loosened the cord, slid it down below her breasts to keep her elbows locked tight against her body, and pushed her onto her side with my foot.

"You will die for this blasphemy," she hissed.

"Yeah, yeah, tell me where have I heard that before."

CHAPTER SEVENTEEN

"What now, Eno?" Phandros asked.

"Maybe her majesty has a suggestion?"

"You will die. Die horribly. I will watch. No, I will drive the dagger myself!"

"Not helpful, if heartfelt."

Phandros stroked the puppy's smooth head. "What are you going to do with her?"

"It's not what I'm going to do with her; it's what she's going to do with me. She's going to take me to see this awe-inspiring Goddess of hers."

Zosime's eyes narrowed. "You are insane. No man may go to Hades and live! Wait a little. She will come to you, oh, yes."

"I think it's more polite for me to call first. You never can tell with goddesses. The last time we met she seemed to take a liking to my charms."

I turned to Phandros. "Go back to the ship. If I'm not there by the time she sails, I'll see you at your friend's house." I didn't want to give Zosime any hints on where to find him later if things went sour.

"Will you?" He smiled sadly. It unsettled me even more than the events of the last few minutes.

"I hope to. I've gotten out of worse messes, though I can't think of one off-hand."

"I wasn't thinking of you." His eyes were shining strangely, as if lit from within. Lines had smoothed away from his face and his chest lifted wide with deep breaths. A kind of peace seemed to have settled on him.

"Phandros. What are you planning?"

He looked up toward the distant roof. "I'm going to let those animals out."

"They'll kill you."

"Maybe. Maybe not. You never can tell." Laughter came into his voice. "I'm not afraid anymore, Eno. For a long time, always really, I've been afraid. It was like carrying a great stone in my gut, filling me with that heaviness. That's why I eat so little and drink so much, I suppose. But it disappeared the day I chose to follow you. Seeing my old friend again helped take it away as well. Maybe it will come back but I don't think so."

"That's all terrific news but what does it have to do with the animals?"

"They don't deserve what's going to happen to them tomorrow."

"They'll just be hunted down anyway."

"Not if the Goddess Artemis comes to protect them. I will pray to her for them. She is the Goddess of the Hunt, yes, but she protects such creatures from man. Only if we hunt for necessity can we implore her aid and this vileness isn't necessary."

I'd heard that distinction of Artemis' role on earth before, of course, as part of the Mysteries taught to every child. "She may protect them, but what about you?"

"Hermes will protect me. I'll pray to him as well. We are, after all, trying to restore this festival to its former purpose, among other things." He turned away before he'd finished, eager to be about his work. I mistrusted his faith. It seemed too much like folly to hold on to any hope in this black place.

"Wait a minute, now. Listen to me! I have it on very good authority that the Gods aren't paying any attention to men right now. They're obsessed with Troy...." I looked down at Zosime. "Did you laugh?"

"I laugh at all vain hopes. That fool will die, torn to pieces as he deserves. But his torment will not end there, oh, no! He will be sent to Tartaros to labor in endless night for daring to blaspheme against mighty powers. You will join him there, chained to a great stone, greater even than you can carry for all your strength."

"Cheerful little minx, aren't you?"

"Do you deny that it was the White One told you that the Gods have ceased to attend to the affairs of mortals while the War in Troy rages on?"

"If you mean Aphrodite...."

She bared her teeth at the name, hissing like a sack of snakes. "Say not her name! She will fall with all the rest, whether the child of that unnatural son or not!"

I felt as if she were giving me all the keys but without labels to tell me which went with what lock.

Phandros waited politely enough during this exchange yet his face told me how much he wanted to be on his way. "They'll kill you," I repeated.

His smile held something uncanny, a confidence not of this world, plagued as it is with fear and uncertainty. "You showed me that I don't need to be afraid any more. Don't try to make me feel that way again. I will see you on the ship. I have no doubt, no doubt for either of us."

His shining eyes fell upon the queen. She shrank away as far as her bonds would let her. "Justice works both ways. It is not too late to turn your heart."

She had just enough saliva to spit at him. He was too far away to be touched, but her message was clear.

He turned back to the tunnel but paused. "Oh, I forgot." Shifting the small dog cradle under his arm, he fumbled beneath his long robe. "You're going to need this."

The sword glimmered in the red light of the altar-place. I caught it and swung it around in the Spartan salute to honor him.

Phandros headed out. I had no idea if I would ever see him again. The number one drawback to my profession is that so often friends don't make it to the end of the job. Look at the Argonauts, for instance, and how many of Hercules' companions ever survived?

I noticed that the deep throbbing had faded into a thrumming like the quivering heartbeat of a gigantic hummingbird. Unsettling but not compelling.

Zosime had risen onto her knees. "None of that," I commanded. If she made any attempt to get to her feet or to put her arms above her head, let alone swaying and chanting, I was ready to tighten the cord until her eyes bubbled.

With downcast eyes, she clasped her hands before her. "Mercy, oh great and terrible warrior. I am much moved by this farewell to your friend. Who will regret Zosime? No one." A tear trickled from her left eye.

"Just one question."

"Anything, lord...."

"Just how dumb do you think I am?"

She sprang for my throat, arms tied against her body or no. I stepped swiftly aside. Her rush would have carried her directly onto the evil mosaic, just like her handmaiden, if I hadn't caught her back with a short sharp jerk on the cord.

Her toes on the edge, she hovered over it, her face just above the heart of the medallion itself. She pressed her hands in hard against her chest or they would have touched.

"Shall I let go?"

"No. No!"

"Is there a way down into the Underworld from here?"

"What? Why...how would I know.?"

I let a little of the cord slip through my fingers. Her weight, greater than I would have guessed from her delicate hands and feet and knife-thin face, strained against my backwards leaning.

The cuff of her robe brushed, only brushed, the surface. The sewn images there that had always seemed to be on the point of moving under their own power now did so – in earnest. It was like watching dormant snakes wake up after a long winter's cold.

There was stern stuff in Zosime. She did not scream. "There is a way down. Save me; I will show you."

I hauled her in, hand over hand, until she could drop safely to her knees again. "Get this cord off me quick," she demanded. When I hesitated, she lifted her forearm as well as she could. The embroidered signs had grown fleshier, twisting and rippling under the fabric, seeking with blind intensity for a way out.

I opened the loop with a shake and it dropped to the ground for her to step out. The instant she was freed, Zosime ripped her robe off and flung it away. It fell half-on, half-off the mosaic. Almost faster than I could see, it vanished, sucked away into nothingness.

I half-expected Zosime to be naked under her robe but she wore the sort of simple garment any modest matron would put on for a visit to a friend. A heavy gold necklet lay at the base of her moderately wrinkled throat, a few dark amethysts flashing with rich purple sparks. The thin line where the cord had dug into her flesh looked like just another necklace. She was female enough to pat her disordered hair into place.

"So...." I prompted.

"It's easy. Jump over the side of the stone."

"As your servant did? I'm not up for a quick suicide today, thanks."

"I have no need to lie to you. Your death is approaching quickly now, every breath is numbered. But you will not die, I grant you, by your own hand. Another wishes to see to that detail. I speak that promise with a voice of power." And for a moment, I heard the echo of the triple-tongued monster I'd met in the temple.

When I still stared at her, trying to tell if she lied, she laughed scornfully. "Coward! I will go with you. I have been before this and returned. Put your cord around my throat again. If I lead you astray, kill me."

"Nice offer, considering we'll both die when we hit bottom." I said it, but I already believed her. Zosime was far too fond of herself to die simply to ensure that I died also.

"Have I not told you I have done this already? I am the very hand of the Goddess. Before I left Lesbos to become queen here, I taught Nausicaa as I trained her mistress, but not everything, only enough to serve Her will. Nausicaa took it upon herself to initiate the king of Leros after the queen died, because she wanted him under her control. I warned her that men are not suited to the tasks we must undertake. And you prove that I am right again, here, now. Coward."

"Well, you know more about that than I would. I do have a couple of other questions." I thought I should try to get some answers while Zosime was in a comparatively good mood. It was common sense, like scheduling grooming time for falcons after they are well-fed so they don't mistake a thumb or an eyeball for their mid-day mouse.

"You want to know if you will be safe," she hazarded. "I've already told you there is nothing to fear. It's the intention that matters. Damalis wanted to die, though I think she was a fool. Her usefulness to me wasn't over just because of one little mistake."

"Little mistake? She turned into a lioness!"

"Does that mean she should rob me of her service? Besides, I was trying to turn that miserable dog into a griffin for my dear husband to kill tomorrow."

"And the spell just spilled over onto her."

"She knew what would happen if she touched the mosaic. It's not my fault; these girls today just don't listen to their elders."

"Right. Speaking of which...you know your niece?"

"Niece? What niece?"

"Your husband's, so I've heard."

"Oh, her. She died of grief. Poor little bud, what a blossom she would have been." Her imitation of sorrow was almost believable, but a little smile of gleeful triumph gave her away.

"Instead, you turned her into a harpy."

She laughed, delighted clear through to the bottom of her black heart. "Dear little Kissos, our little twining Ivy. It's really the king's fault, you know. If he had half the courage he thinks he does, he would have killed her years ago. His brother wanted to leave Troezen to her, can you imagine? I wanted to do it immediately but he swore he'd divorce me and send me to a brothel on the docks if anything happened to her. I should have killed them both instead of transforming her and drugging him. He wouldn't have dared to touch me."

"What stopped you? Couldn't have been conscience."

She laughed shortly. "I won't make that mistake a second time. As soon as I'm done with you...."

"Why Leros?"

"I knew Nausicaa would keep an eye on my little birdie and washed my hands of the business. But you had to come along and meddle. That ridiculous pirate with the cage. At least he had wit enough to cover it when he came to port so everyone couldn't see it and jabber about it."

"You had them killed, I suppose."

"Naturally, I had to," she said as if speaking of cracked eggs purchased by mistake in the marketplace. "I couldn't very well have a bunch of ragtag pirates rattling their tongues about selling the harpy to me even if they did believe it was just for the Hunt. But if they should see that it didn't appear, they would talk."

"Well, I think that's about all my questions."

"Good. It does seem a tiny bit as though you are delaying on purpose. I'm sure I'm misjudging you. Come, hero, wrap your strong arms around me, and we shall jump together."

I walked up to her. I hadn't been close to her before and I didn't want to be now. Though scented and rubbed with aromatic oils like any wealthy woman, there was a deeper odor that came through the attar of roses and cassia flower, a stink like cold wet ashes. I didn't like the glitter in her sea-coal eyes or the shine on her white teeth. Teeth that could come awfully close to my neck with a little effort on her part, effort she'd already shown willing to expend.

I reached out for her shoulders. She showed those teeth in more of a snarl than a smile but stretched backwards to bring her bosom into high relief against me. She put up a hand as if to stroke my face, not noticing or caring that it was still marked with the blood of her late servant. Even if I found her attractive, that would have wiped it out.

I evaded her hand, took her shoulders and spun her around sharply. Then I wrapped my arms around her tight. Lifting her up, I carried her to the edge. "You're sure about this?"

"Perfectly sure, my dearest enemy. Death is only for those who want to die; I have every intention of living forever, in eternal youth and beauty. That is where the real power lies. In a face. Look at Helen. All those ships sinking, all those men dying just for her."

A shudder passed through her, caused by pure pleasure flooding her body at the thought of dead men.

She laid her head on my shoulder. I loathed the touch of her coiling hair on my cheek with all my heart.

"And though this is very delightful...." the wench wiggled her bottom against my thighs! But there was no desire in me to be aroused by the likes of her. "Hekate grows impatient."

"Very well."

I suppose she expected me to take a running jump. But I only needed to take two steps forward and then there was nothing but emptiness under my feet.

* * *

Well, I died.

* * *

Whatever part of me does the thinking had decided to leave off for a while, leaving the husk behind. How long I'd been walking without being aware of it was a question I never would be able to answer. But there I was and so was she. She had my sword in her hand.

That didn't seem right.

I stopped and slipped it from her loose hold. I looked into her face. It was slack and tired, every day of her age showing. She blinked twice, very slowly, like a sleepy cat. Then, like the snap of fingers, she was back in her own head, eyes sharpening, features firming with arrogance and self-will.

"There, you see," Zosime proclaimed. "I was right. You are not dead."

"You'll pardon me if I don't take your word for it just yet." I drew a deep breath and held it, testing. I touched the underside of my jaw. Reassured by the faint beat, I nodded. "Seems to be in working order. So...where is this?"

"I don't know. If we keep walking, we'll arrive."

"Arrive where?"

"Where we are going. There will be nothing until I require it to be called into existence. That is Hades' curse. Emptiness and infinity."

"But you said you'd done this before."

"I was shown the trick of it, long ago. I have gone back and forth, many times. No one except Hades' sad queen has ever done that." Her pride was as thick as a sea-hardened ship's timber and as hard to make an impact on.

"And Orpheus. And Hercules. And Theseus...."

She tossed her head and kept on walking. After what seemed a moment but might have been an eternity or two, she tossed her head again, more coquettishly, giving me a sidelong glance. "Your sword is most unusual. I admire those clouds on the hilt. I have never seen work like that before."

"It's different all right."

"When you are dead, I will make it into hair-pins and a crown. I will think of you whenever I wear it."

"I'll hang on to it the meantime, if you don't mind."

I didn't feel hungry or thirsty or tired. I had lost any sense of the passage of time. The darkness was as deep as a dayless cave, concealed and lost beneath miles of earth. Yet around Zosime and me, there was light, a silvery lambency sharp and clear like the brightest full moon on a cloudless winter's night in my native mountains. I could see her and her shadow clearly. The shadow pointed away from me.

"Let's go back the way we came, or make a turn or something."

"It makes no difference. All ways are one."

"Then humor me."

She sighed in exaggerated affront and turned her face and body. Yet again, I had a feeling her movements were slightly out of phase, as though something I couldn't make out blurred with movement. "Very well."

I walked in a wide semi-circle around her. There was no fixed point anywhere, only black sand beneath our feet, but I noticed that if I used her as a pivot, the shadow at her feet always pointed away from me.

It wasn't until I put up a hand to rub away a headache and the light winked out, that I got it. I took my hand down and the light came on. The light went out when I touched my brow again. "Now that's useful. I was afraid it was out for good."

Zosime sneered. "The Kiss of Aphrodite won't help you here. This is not her domain. Love and all that absurd nonsense is forgotten here. Lovers forget, brothers forget, even mothers forget their children. They drink of the River Lethe and their mortal memories leave them. How else could Hades keep control? The dead would riot if they remembered where they came from and all that they had lost."

The measuring look in her eyes told me that she'd suddenly remembered that I too had drunk of these waters. "Why...." she began to ask.

Suddenly, a river appeared, cutting through the black sand, its twisting banks crowded with the souls of the dead, misty phantoms who knelt to drink.

"There are other rivers as well, aren't there? Pyriphlegethon. Acheron. Styx. Cocytus."

As I said their names, they appeared, snaking among the black sand that fountained up to form banks. Each kept to its own course. Pyriphlegethon swarmed with keening men and women burning in its lava-like stream while the other river of punishment, Cocytus, spread amid the sounds of lamentations into a vast swamp. Bodies floundered in it as well, sucked down by the weight of the hot, sticky mud. Flies afflicted them, buzzing and biting.

Both waters poured ceaselessly into a lake the size of a sea and both poured away at the farthest end, which I could see and hear as clearly as the nearer side.

This lake, Acheron, had many spirits standing on an island in the center, with cool, willow-shrouded banks. I could not see how large it was but there seemed to be gardens there and beautiful houses. It too thronged with people and, faintly beneath the lamentations and entreaties, I heard a drinking song and laughter.

But around the edge of the island stood many with their backs turned on the sufferers swirling around them. The ones in the waters have wronged those on the bank and they can never escape punishment until they are forgiven. Murderers and betrayers and those who lift their hands against their parents, all swirl together in an endless whirlpool of misery and grief. Those who are forgiven arise from the lake and are judged anew. The others go pouring away back to Tartaros to pass another year before they are again permitted to offer their pleas for forgiveness.

It was fascinating to look upon and made me want to live a blameless life forever more so I could join the ones on the island Elysium, taking a boat across the Styx, not swimming. I didn't want to get in any body of water bigger than a gymnasium bath for years to come.

Zosime made some passes with her hands and all these visions faded away. "Why did you do that? These things aren't for you to see."

"You started it." We walked on, still timelessly tireless. "Isn't it about time for your great mistress to make an appearance?"

"She will appear when it is her pleasure to do so. Unlike your foolish gods, she is not subject to the whims and sentiments of mortals."

"Sounds like a great one to serve. Why do you?"

Zosime made no answer.

"You told me her name already. Shall I say it?"

"Silence!"

"Let me think now. Was it...Persephone?"

I had considered calling on one of the more powerful gods, hoping the magic of the Underworld would hold and bring Ares or Apollo in armor to me. But this realm was not theirs. Calling upon Hades would do no good; how could he distinguish my need from the thousands of shades who called upon him every moment. But Hades' wife...if she came, wouldn't she summon her husband? I could only say her name to the darkness and hope.

"Silence! Oh, you fool, you fool!"

A trembling against the blackness that hung around us. Then, as if it were a curtain, it parted and a slender woman, looking not older than sixteen, came through. Her hair was bound low on her forehead and she wore a shining gown of soft red like the deep blush on a peach. Her eyes were beautiful despite the black under-eye circles of one who never slept. "What shade calls upon the daughter of the Fruit-bringer?"

I bowed. "Greeting, Queen of the Underworld. Nice day, isn't it?"

"You're not dead," she gasped, and stepped back, biting her forefinger with indecision. She eyed me with shy curiosity, lit ever so slightly with feminine interest. Her hand rose to toy with her golden hair. Then she saw Zosime and recoiled. "You! What do you want here?"

"Go tell your husband there's a danger in the heart of his kingdom, my lady," I said with a bow.

"Now you've done it," Zosime cried. She made a grab at the unwilling Queen of Hell but Persephone fled back into the nothing.

"That idiot girl; she never could keep her big mouth shut, always whining to someone. Now we must hurry." Zosime ran away from me, flinging her arms up in fanatical abandon. She whirled, stamped her feet, and sang in that inhuman language. Shades began to gather, the misty representations of Olympus-knew who. Some resembled warriors fallen in their prime, others creatures from nightmares too appalling to vanish with dawn.

Their mutterings grew louder until I could understand them. "Goddess of the cross-roads, keeper of the three-fold Ways, come for your prey, Mother of Darkness. Crush this foolish mortal beneath your heel!"

Zosime shuddered and threw back her head. She began to swell and grow. I could hear the cracking of her bones as they broke only to knit themselves anew and the screeching as her skin stretched over the new frame. Her head lolled on a broken neck. One moment there was only a single face. A moment later, she was gazing down on me, her face turned so that she could look with two out of three sides.

"I am here."

If a basilisk could kill with a voice instead of a gaze, if a Gorgon needed nothing but her voice to turn brave men to stone, they would have borrowed hers.

Her three faces revolved, eyes glittered down on me with ever-changing expressions of disdain, loathing and gloating evil. I had destroyed a cheap imitation of this in the Temple at Leros. Now the genuine goddess stood before me. Six times my height at the least, she appeared as an Amazon, armored and armed, bearing a flaming torch in each hand.

I bowed even more deeply than I had to Hades' Queen. I am always careful to mind my manners around loathsome goddesses. They take offense so easily. Considering the last time we'd met I'd chopped her head off, our relationship had nowhere to go but, literally, up.

"Greetings, Hekate," I said.

CHAPTER EIGHTEEN

She lingers on the borders of all tales, unnamed perhaps, always a presence looming over the tasks of the hero. Those I had named to Zosime - Orpheus, Hercules, Theseus - had all faced her.

She'd been a Titan, one of the children of Perses the Destroyer and Asteria, Prophetess, sister and brother, two of the many children of the Earth and the Sky, Ouranos. He had been brutally attacked by Kronos, youngest of his sons and eventual father of Zeus, of Hera, of Poseidon, of Hades, of nearly all the elder Olympian Gods. Of one was he the progenitor, perhaps, but not the father.

Kronos, having emasculated Ouranos, his father the Sky, threw the pieces into the sea-foam. There they floated and, in the fullness of time, Aphrodite, Sea-Born, walked from the water, fully grown and greatly wise.

Ouranos in his torment made a prophecy that Kronos too would be overthrown by his own child. In an agony of mind, Kronos began eating the children his sister Rhea bore him. Grieving, Rhea hid herself when pregnant with Zeus, emerging only when delivered. She gave to her monstrous husband a stone swaddled like an infant and the unsuspicious Kronos swallowed it whole as he had all his other children.

At Zeus' maturity, he came forth from concealment and led his brothers and sisters, vomited forth from their father's swollen gut by their mother's poisons. Zeus did indeed overthrow Kronos, Chaos himself, imprisoning him deep under Tartaros. The Titans chose to support Kronos, finding themselves on the losing side and locked up themselves.

Maybe I'd skipped school that day but I could not quite recall how Hekate had come to be Keeper of the Crossroads. Three roads met in Hades and it was there that the newly dead were first sorted.

It was for Hekate to choose whether the dead went to Elysium, Tartaros or to enter the Avernian Gate. Only those who were not immediately seen to be good or evil were sent on to the Gate for final judgment by the Lord of the Underworld himself and his two fellow judges, Rhadamanthus, always pleading to alleviate Hades' stern judgments, and Minos, always urging greater severity yet. I had a feeling that when my time came to meet Hekate again, she'd make me wait a few hundred eternities before deciding my fate.

"Are you not surprised to see me?" she asked, as feminine and sweet as a new-married bride.

"Well, frankly, I am. Are you really Zosime? Is Zosime really you?"

Her smile was the queen's. "Both and neither. I took her form for my own purposes but she was always my creature to do with as I will. Soon all shall worship me as she has done. From the heights of heaven to the depths of Hades itself, I alone shall rule."

"You know...I'm going to have to stop you."

"Stop me?" Her laughter scraped my ears like sharp shells.

She raised her torches high, the flames leaping upward. They illuminated the throngs of spirits crowding near to her skirts. Pale shades of men and women shuffled their feet and wandered amongst one another, even passing through each other. Though the crowd was numberless, each seemed to believe he or she were all alone. They murmured ceaselessly, words of excuse, of extenuation.

"I didn't mean it."

"It wasn't my fault, not really."

"He made me so angry."

"I had no choice."

"I had to do it."

Lost in their own misery, they made no move toward me. Then there was a stirring among them and two emerged, a man and a woman, their eyes reflecting Hekate's torches as though burnished within. "Hear us, great Goddess!" they called as they pushed through the swarming dead.

Nausicaa, haughtily humble even now, with the bruises from the priestess's lifeless hands still showing upon her throat, gazed at me with undying hatred. Eurytos stepped beside her, returned to his fully human form. The great wound I'd sliced in his chest gaped wide, as if I'd inflicted it while he was in this body, not his crab form.

"Hear us, great Goddess," they repeated. "This man killed us. Let us take our vengeance. Make us mortal again!"

I lifted my sword, though they were dead already and presumably now impervious to sharp objects.

None of the faces of Hekate seemed pleased to see her servants again, though they had perished on her behalf. "You are useless," she stormed. "Now you want your lives back. You, Eurytos, have already had one life restored to you. And what did you do with it? This single mortal defeated you and all your mongrel rabble. Tartaros for you!"

She threw a torch at him, even as he raised his hands in supplication. It passed over his head, spinning end over end. I watched it subscribe a turn and fly back to Hekate's outstretched hand. When I looked to where Eurytos had stood, he was gone, banished to some farther corner of Hades.

Nausicaa instantly sank to her knees. "I had no orders, Great Mother!"

"No, but any but a fool would have seen this man is dangerous to my plans. And instead of poisoning him quietly, sending him to me to be my servant, you let him fight the dead...my dead...and win. And win!"

"Let her try again," I said boldly. "She didn't have a fair go the first time."

Nausicaa's shining eyes seemed now to have small fires of their own burning in their depths. Her fingers crooked into claws and I knew she was measuring the distance to my face. "You won't be so cocky at the back of the line."

"Seems to me that's in the future for me and more of an immediate problem for you. Long line, and more joining in all the time."

Persephone must have had time to rouse a dozen husbands by now, I would have thought. I didn't know how much longer I could stall. What weaknesses did a Goddess have, let alone a dead woman who hated my guts?

"Come on, then," I said, wanting to know her best angle of attack. "Or are you scared?"

"I'm dead, Eno. What can frighten me now?"

"Ask your boss."

Nausicaa flew at me with a screech. She didn't jump up or anything, she just propelled up and forwards, claws headed for my face. I misjudged my timing for I'd been anticipating some kind of preliminary movement. She sailed into me and right on through.

If you've ever eaten thick cold fat congealed on a pot of greasy soup for breakfast because you let the fire go out in the night, you know what it felt like. The way the fat sticks and clogs in your throat is the way Nausicaa passed through my chest and out my lower back. I gagged with my whole body.

Far above me, the triple-goddess laughed, harmonizing with herself. "Doomed, doomed, doomed!

You are no general, Eno! I will keep you as my jester when I am Queen on Olympus, laughing as you preen yourself on your empty courage!"

"Since when," I shouted back, "do they let hideous monsters into Olympus? With or without a jester."

Hekate's torches exploded into furnaces that burned not with heat but with the frigidity of her rage. "Strike again, my daughter! Squeeze his heart 'til it bursts in your cold hands."

Cackling with laughter like an insane pigeon, Nausicaa soared around and started toward me. As she dove, I did a snap barrel-roll forward. Nausicaa's clammy, insubstantial skirts brushed my cheek as she passed by my head.

"Clever, clever Eno!" Hekate said, applauding. The third face chimed in late, soberly. "Not clever enough. Mortals. So weak. So brittle. What good are tools like these?" A faint shade of disgust lifted one of her lips. "Fight it out amongst yourselves. I will make use of whichever one survives."

"Choose me, Great Goddess!" Nausicaa screamed. "I will turn all the cities of the world into temples for you. You will stand over the world with flail and whip...."

"Give it up," I told her, crouching low to prepare for her next attack. "She doesn't care about you or your promises. Pray for mercy from another God."

Nausicaa laughed bitterly. "I have blasphemed, I have been cruel when I should have been kind. I have traded love for power and now have neither. I have served one who plots to overthrow Heaven itself. To which of the Gods can I look for redemption now?"

"Nowhere," Hekate proclaimed. "Nowhere at all."

I'd had enough. I let the hatred and loathing I'd felt for all these works leave my heart and mind with hardly a struggle. I thought about what Phandros would do.

"Here. She can find it here. I forgive you, Nausicaa. I forgive you."

With that word, I ran her through. Blood had not been spilled in this black land since Time was born to slay us all. Though she was a spirit, red life dripped from the end of my sword. The black sand fled from it, leaving us standing on a nothingness as deep and as limitless as that which surrounded us. The Light of Aphrodite showed me something, immeasurably far below us, that gleamed white as it moved in the depths.

Nausicaa pressed her hands tightly against the wound in her belly. "What have you done to me?" Then she was gone, even her spirit now beyond the touch of any god or goddess. I wasn't sure I'd done the right thing, but it had seemed right at the time and that's the best any mortal can do.

"Eno the Victorious!" Hekate shouted, and would have softened her voice if she could. "I'm glad you won. From the first moment we met, I had high hopes of you. You are the kind of man I need. Women are powerful but to lead an army one needs the right sort."

"Don't you get it?" I asked tiredly. "I'm never going to be working for you."

"Work for me? Am I some butcher looking for the one who stole a few sausages? Or a fool menaced by some witless beast?" She laughed and it was like a bitter roar of a volcanic avalanche. "You will join me willingly. My wishes will be yours. You who have attempted to match your puny will against mine will embrace me as consort and serve me all the days of your life...and even after."

"You know I can't do that."

"But it is foretold. You will serve the greatest goddess of them all, the one whom even the Gods themselves must serve. I am that goddess."

"Foretold? By who?"

"You know of the Graeae?"

"Sure. Three women, one eye, prophecies while you wait."

She sneered at me. "That humor of yours...they swore you would be serve the greatest Goddess who ever lived, she who rules all. So you must belong to me for that is who I am."

I felt the crushing weight of her inexorable will bearing down on me. It increased yet I still stood just as before on the black sand in the middle of nothingness. "Is something supposed to happen?" I asked after a bit.

It was morning and I opened my eyes in a bed of softest down, covered with blankets so smooth and fine I could hardly believe they were made of wool. A stirring beside me and a sweet-faced girl sat up, throwing her arms above her head with a giggle of glee. It was Minthe as I'd seen her in the marketplace, only with heavy gold ornaments around her throat and in her ears. She wore nothing else.

Then I was riding a splendid bay horse as glossy as rocks in a riverbed. My sons, five of them, rode along with me, young men so ideal as to make Skander's boys look like gammy-handed numbskulls. The eldest rode with his spear at the ready and I realized that, of course, we were going boar-hunting. I rose in my saddle to look back at the sweep of my lands below, green and fertile as the Nile valley. My white, columned house sat on a promontory, overlooking the seas, calm and blue.

Soon came the wedding and the dancing. Orange firelight flickered on rejoicing, laughing faces as my guests wove in an out in patterns half-as-old as time. The wine flowed fast. Everywhere I looked, I saw flowing bowls in one hand and handfuls of food in the other. My wife came up with a golden bowl for me. I raised it to my lips to toss off the wine, but orange things tumbled out and down the front of my best robe.

"What are these?" I demanded, hearing them crunch beneath my sandals.

"The new cook made them; aren't they delicious!" Then she was off, caught up by two of my sons into the dancing. Other women were there too, sly faces looking away as soon as I glanced at them. One wore a black veil over her head, an insult at a wedding. Something about her head was the wrong shape...or was it the firelight, the same firelight that seemed to show lips and fingers stained with that peculiarly bright shade of orange, unlike any I'd ever seen. Who had warned me against this strange food?

I set off in pursuit but the music was getting louder, the dancers more raucous, and I lost her. I stood among them as they spun around me like the heavens around the Unmoving Star. I heard a voice in my ear or did it come from within? "All this can I give you...and all this can I take from you."

I grew dizzier and dizzier until I fell down to the laughing cheers of my friends. I hit my head on a stone and heard nothing more.

When I awoke, my sword gleamed red in my hand, I felt the stickiness of dried blood upon my face and chest. My sons and all my guests were slain and I knew, beyond any doubt or question, that I myself had done all this. Like Hercules, I had murdered all those I loved in my madness. I saw Minthe standing the doorway of my shattered house, a firestorm turning the sky to red as it consumed everything I possessed. Her eyes grew huge and she fled from me, choosing to burn alive rather than die at my bloody hands.

I found myself upon my knees before Hekate, the torches she held too bright for my streaming eyes. Bowing my head to the black sand of Hades, I groveled, knowing that I had no choice but to worship Hekate as my only goddess. My defeat was absolute and I sent a prayer away begging for Aphrodite's forgiveness, though without hope that it would ever reach beyond the Pit.

"What do you want me to do?"

The three faces turned ceaselessly, smiling down with contempt, hubris, and vile superiority. I couldn't see how they moved, what arrangement of bones and muscle permitted this oddity but that's why she's a Titan and I'm not. On no face was there any pity or humanity.

"You must understand. It is only justice that I want." Abruptly she shrank down to my own size. I was glad of it. Discoursing with forty-foot tall women takes a toll on the back of the neck. I did not make the mistake of assuming she'd cooled off. The torches said otherwise.

"Justice?" I asked numbly, so worn by grief that I hardly cared.

"The Thunderer promised me that I would be his queen and sit at his right hand on Olympus. Instead, he married that bosomy sister of his and stuck me down here. I'm sick of the dark and the dead. I want what I was promised."

"You want Father...."

"Don't say their names!" she ordered, her faces snapping around to look fearfully at the nothingness. I felt as if the nothingness were crowding in, like bed curtains of blackest velvet smothering a sleeper.

"You want the king and queen of Heaven to part so that you can take her place?" I said, rousing myself from despair into disbelief. "That's what all this is about? A long-ago love affair?"

"I was promised," she said fiercely. "I helped Z...him to overthrow his own father. My reward was to be queen over all the gods, not a gatekeeper for a lot of mumbling, shambling fools! I have waited all this time and now it is my turn to be avenged. I don't just want that cow-eyed bitch gone, I want them all gone!"

She'd begun to grow again, the torches as bright as burning magnesium. Gods would be easier to talk to if they stayed the same size for more than five minutes consecutively. "I will rule Earth and Heaven without pity, driving gods and men before me like cattle! And you will be my herder, driving them to their doom. Pledge your sword to me, Eno, and I will make you a god over the Earth!"

I could see it, as I had when Eurytos had first proposed it. I rode a blood-red horse, my armor spotted and stained with blood and rust, my army, shambling, stinking, and unstoppable. Every man I killed would be a new recruit until my army swallowed all the lands, all the seas and mounted like a wave to Olympus itself. Even I perished in the first battle, I would ride on. I could hear the screams, smell the burning buildings, and taste the grit of battle.

My heart had already begun to turn. Soon I would be her willing slave, giving up all my human qualities to serve her and her alone. I closed my eyes tightly. I did not pray for I already knew no one from Olympus would hear me. I looked within my own shrouded heart and there, in the last hidden, black corner something stirred. The tiniest hope, the merest shred of all that I had denied, still lived.

And it inspired me -- not to some great deed of honor -- but to a question. I looked at Hekate, trying to meet her shifting eyes. "Why didn't the Waters of Lethe work on me?"

For an instant, her implacable will was taken aback. I saw the merest hint of a doubt. "What?"

"You gave me the Waters of Forgetfulness to drink up there," I said, pointing to the hardly-glimpsed roof of the Underworld. "But I have not forgotten anything. Not my name, not my position in the world, not why I came here. I'm going to give up in a minute. You might as well tell me why the Waters didn't work."

I have tried my level best throughout this account to be as honest as is consistent with a good story. So let this testament state that Hekate backed away from me, her three foreheads equally creased. "I don't know. I should know that, but I don't. The Waters cannot not work; it's impossible. Unless...."

"Unless?"

"They only work once per soul. If you have drunk them before, they will not remove memories a second time. That means...that means...but that's impossible." She straightened up, growing again, her torches brightening. "It doesn't matter now. You are mine."

"What's going on here?"

In my own defense, I have to admit that, of all the Gods, Hades is my least favorite. I think most people feel that way. There are fewer temples to him, fewer honors, fewer festivals, than to any of the others. We know that, sooner or later, everything belongs to him anyway so why give it to him early?

Seeing him striding forward, staff in one hand, scroll in the other, glints of red volcanic light popping around him like starry sparks on a summer's night, I changed my mind. The very first temple I found with his name over the door was receiving a very large donation.

"Hekate," he called out reprovingly, reading the large scroll he carried in his hand. "What is going on? There are no souls coming before us in Averna. We have a quota, you know."

He looked up, his eyes as piercing as a spike. "What is this mortal doing here? Is that blood on his sword? And why is he glowing with a heavenly light?"

He lifted his staff and it had a sharp spear-point on the end. "I want answers and I want them now."

Hekate threw open her arms, her torches flying wide to fall unheeded to the shifting black sands. "Uncle!" she cried aloud, despair cracking her voices. "Uncle, help me!"

The wind died, the dead stopped whispering, and the blackness swirled and moved, as a vault opened in the midst of it. Something white moved there, gleaming like snake-skin, sliding out bonelessly, liquid yet solid. As yet formless, heaped flesh twisted and tumbled, trapped and struggling against a transparent caul, giving birth to itself. I swear I saw a rolling eye, as big as the full moon when it rises.

The Lord of the Underworld and I exchanged glances, mine comprised of terror and awe, his rather world-weary. "What is that?" I asked, though I guessed that the gruesome answer that had come to me was correct.

He studied it with enviable dispassion as it oozed out into his kingdom. With breathtaking speed, the thing took form, two legs, two arms, the rest of him more or less like the rest of us bipeds. He was hairless, naked, huge and hideous, covered with pulsing red and purple veins, clutching at emptiness with attenuated hands. He opened a red maw and bellowed a wordless challenge to the universe.

Hades frowned. "It's my father."

"What?"

"You know," he said. "Kronos, Chaos Himself. Father to us all, devourer of us all, mortals as well as Gods. And he looks hungry. As usual."

CHAPTER NINETEEN

With those words, Hades disappeared, leaving me alone with Hekate and Kronos.

"You can forget about that donation!"

Kronos resembled some loathsome insect, born in lightlessness, so pale that every system under the skin could be traced by its pulsing. But Kronos was not blind. His bloated face held flat grayish eyes and a toothless gaping mouth, one just as hungry as the other.

Hekate ran toward him, the inner fire that had powered her torches now covering her entirely. "Uncle, help me. The others are coming; I can feel it!"

He picked her up with a swoop of his hand. Holding her before his face, he examined the burning goddess as if he'd never seen her before. Her flames lit his hollow eyes.

Shaking her twice, her flames going out, he popped her into his mouth. She screamed as the fleshless lips closed, cutting off the sound. He swallowed. It reminded me of a man eating a sausage that had fallen into the fire, right down to his expression as he decided it wasn't too burnt.

I had a feeling, however, that this family squabble was far from over. Nor was my part in it, as I was still there. In Hades. Facing something so old, so corrupted and slimed with ancient crime that even the Gods had locked it away rather than face it down.

Kronos stood up, belched a little smoke ring, and bellowed, "More!"

Without Hekate, the milling dead were at a loss. They fixated on me. But with a starving god bearing down on me, the only edible thing in sight, I fought my way clear of the clinging, confused spirits.

Kronos swept his hand through them, moaning his disappointment when he couldn't grab anything to eat. Some went down under his huge feet.

I ran, sand spurting and sliding, giving me no purchase to gain speed. In all that featurelessness, the only direction to run was away.

As I ran, I panted out the name of every god I'd ever heard of from Zeus the Mighty all the way to down to Lips, god of the South-West winds. I wasn't about to stand around waiting for rescue but if anyone cared to lend a hand or send a sleep-inducing mist or an oversized stuffed eggplant to throw behind me...apparently no one did.

I knew it was hopeless but tried to keep that a secret from my legs. If only Zosime had chosen to give me wings instead of that poor little dog.

The ground changed character, becoming white and spongy, no easier to run on. Had I arrived in some new section of the Underworld unknown to the tellers of tales? I glanced behind me. Kronos no longer pursued me.

A pit opened up right before me, red light issuing from it as though from the volcanic bowels of the earth. I stopped on the very brink, arms windmilling for balance.

From the pit, a bulging cratered creature lashed out blindly. I dodged as it flicked toward me. Some offspring of Ouroboros, the snake endlessly swallowing its own tail far beneath even the Underworld? It looked more like the tongue of some leviathan.

I realized I stood on the edge of Kronos' lipless mouth. I turned, sat down hard, and started to slide down his cheek toward his knurled ear when he plucked me off his face as if I were a flea.

My legs had finally gotten the word. I kicked and thrashed but it was all useless.

Kronos held me as he had Hekate, between thumb and enormous forefinger. Lifting me before his eyes, he seemed puzzled by me, like a man presented with his wife's newest taste sensation, raved about by all her friends.

His slate-colored eyes seemed to have no pupils and no depth. For all their flatness, a mind moved slowly behind them. Infinite, ageless, marked by horrible crimes and eternal solitude, it brooded on the world. Not even his own immortal children could understand that their lives, to him, were as brief and pointless as my own which must seem like that of a moth that lives but one day.

His voice echoed weirdly under the vault of the Underworld. "You...Smell...."

"Well, I've been running...."

"Like...A...God."

"No, no, just a Thracian, son of a shepherd. Have you ever been to Thrace?"

"I...Eat...Gods."

I had a feeling he'd eat anything. The mouth opened for me. I twisted violently from side to side, his fingers all but pinching me in half as he raised me up to toss me down that red gullet. I swung my sword blindly, hopelessly.

He howled in pain and missed the drop. I fell on his sticky chest, bounced out far enough to miss everything else, and landed on one of his feet, sword point down. He howled again, and kicked me off.

I fell hard on the black sand. Dimly, in the distance, I saw Kronos hopping on one foot, shaking his hand as if he'd been stung by some small biting fly.

My sword lay near me. I got up, painfully, and went to get it. On the edge of the blade, a golden stain etched the silver. I felt my eyes stretch as I looked at it. I had to convince my hand that it was all right to pick up the sword.

I held it in front of my face, like Kronos inspecting a snack. Faintly, I smelled a perfume compounded of a thousand flowers. If a brutal god's blood smelled like that, what divine essence must breathe from a more beneficial one?

"Thracian!" Kronos' voice sounded like a wounded bull's. "Thracian! Your...Life...Is...Over."

In all that featurelessness, the only direction to run was away. And still there was only one direction to walk.

If I could scratch him, I told myself, I can dispatch him. He was no longer a god to me, no longer a menace, everlasting and unforgiving. He was just something that I wasn't going to be running from any more.

"Eno the Thracian...hero for hire," I muttered as I strode along. "All monsters dispatched from carnivorous geese to Minotaurs. Special rates for Gods."

The light on my forehead faded, slowly, leaving me to the darkness. I could see Kronos though, glowing like the sickly light that hangs over marshes, luring men to drowning deaths. He had the curve of the stretched skin between thumb and forefinger in his mouth. His eyes over the rim of his hand were boring into me like twin awls.

Then, like the flashes one sees behind closed eyelids, tiny lights began to move, swirling and dancing, blinking and growing stronger. I could not follow one with my eyes, lost in the growing pattern of a hundred, a thousand, an uncountable number. They began to cast enough light to see a shadow and not just mine.

I looked to the right and there, driving a white chariot drawn by half a dozen of the little winged bastards, rode Aphrodite. The lead boy thumbed his nose at me but I laughed because I was so delighted to see her. "You're doing very well, Eno," the Lady said. "I'm afraid I've been bragging about you."

Beyond her, fierce as a lioness in mid-spring, drove Artemis. Her chariot was of rougher make, wood unstripped of bark, and was drawn by four deer, their coats shining like silk and their hooves made from gold.

She turned her stern face toward me. "I bear you no malice for the destruction of my temple," she said. "It will be cleansed and Leros will not suffer for it."

"Thank you, my lady. And Phandros? Will you answer his prayer?"

She looked forward again, her strong wrist controlling her deer easily. "I have heard no prayers from a Phandros."

Someone cleared his throat, noisily, on my left. I was almost afraid to look.

Eagles were harnessed to his chariot which was painted in broad swirls of black and white like the clouds of an angry sky. The spokes on the wheels were golden thunderbolts. Zeus drove, beard flowing past his shoulders, looking just like his statues.

He held out a hand to me. All the chariots, pulled by whatever animal, went at the same speed I was walking.

"Come," he said.

I vaulted over the basket to stand behind him. I heard a deep, male laugh. "A new shield-bearer, my father? Lend him to me; I have need of such warriors."

It was Ares, driving eight black horses bridled with gold. Painted flames and bright brass decorated his car, and his helmet bore a large silky plume. A pair of dice, large and strangely fuzzy, hung from the front of the black basket weave.

"No, Eno drives with me."

Ten had come. Demeter would not venture into the domain where her daughter lived with her fearsome husband, even for such a cause as this. Hephaestus, lame and thoughtful, would not be of much use in a battle, even if he hadn't been so busy making the chariots of others that there'd never been time to build his own.

Kronos had seen his children approaching. He knew why they had come. He threw back his head in titanic laughter. "Come...Then. Lay...Hands...On...Me. Bear...My...Curse."

They circled him, going round and round, faster and faster. Zeus spoke quietly. "Return to your rest, my father. Give up your vengeance. You are not Master here."

"I...Am...Master...For...All...Time."

He exhaled. A blast of eternity blew by. I saw the cracks grow and splinters spring out as time ate away at the chariot's wooden panels and pitted the silver mountings.

"Jump!" I shouted as the magnificent chariot crumbled to dust.

Zeus didn't fall. Larger than he'd been, he stepped clear of the wreckage. I began to wish I hadn't come. The chariots were whipping around Kronos faster and faster, until I could hardly distinguish Ares' black from Dionysus' purple from Hermes' gold. The black sand swirled around in a tornado.

Ares' was the next to break down. He sailed over my head, past Zeus' shoulder and landed, spread-eagle, on Kronos' naked stomach. Like two acrobats on a tilting board, Ares flew in but Hekate, disgorged from Kronos' belly, flew back.

Above all the tumult I heard Aphrodite laugh. I wondered what they'd do with Hekate, as if being covered in Kronos' interior juices wasn't punishment enough.

Then I had no more time to think about her as the battle began in earnest. They all had the very best weapons but seemed oddly reluctant to use them.

Kronos snatched at the chariots of the Gods, smashing one with his fist, stepping on another. When all were afoot, except for Artemis, who kept her distance, he began groping in the sandstorm for them, sifting the black sand with his long, interwoven fingers.

He found Poseidon first. The sea-god tried to keep his father's hands at bay with jabs of his trident but only used the threat. I don't believe he pierced Kronos even once. Surely if my little sword had made the giant screech, the fierce trident should have elicited some response.

"Sea...Food...."

Down the gullet went Poseidon. That sobered the Gods. They must have known what would happen.

I ran forward, almost without realizing what I was doing. I hated Kronos more violently than I'd ever hated an opponent since the days when my uncle had defeated me so easily during my earliest training.

Bumping into a form amongst the blowing sand, I would have run on if he hadn't gripped my arm. Contrary to popular opinion, Hermes doesn't always wear wings. Nor is Dionysus drunk all the time. He wouldn't be so popular among the Maenads if he were.

"We can't hurt him, you know," dark-haired Hermes said as if continuing a long-carried-on conversation. "He is our father and to raise a hand against a parent is a vile sin."

"Practically the only one," Dionysus said. The leopard-skin across his well-muscled shoulders looked the worse for wear...or time. An hour's practice with me every day would have tightened the bags under his eyes and reduced the slight potbelly the leopard-spots weren't quite disguising. Nevertheless, he was handsome in a dissipated, life-among-the-fleshpots kind of way. "Of course, it's blasphemy for a mortal to attack a god. Under ordinary circumstances, I'd never recommend it. The effects are unforeseen."

"These circumstances couldn't be more extraordinary," Hermes said with a lift of an eyebrow.

"How did you capture him last time?" I asked Hermes.

"A sleeping potion in a shipload of wine. He swallowed it off in a few gulps, the greedy pig."

"You can't blame him," Hades said, appearing at my elbow. "He'd just finished vomiting us all up...how I love remembering that! If you are quite finished standing around, I'd like to get him out of my domain."

At once, Dionysus untied his triple-strand golden belt. Unbraided, it was much longer than needed to go around him. "I'll try tripping him up with this. Hermes, take the other end. When he goes down, be ready to tie him up!"

"Sounds like a plan," Hades said approvingly. "I can't believe my brother thought that just the sight of us would make Father behave. He loathes us and always will."

Black-browed Hades clapped me on the shoulder. "You're a good fellow, Eno. I look forward to meeting you again. We always enjoy hearing a few good stories during the long evenings when my wife's in residence. We'll have you over some time...but not, I hope, for a long time yet."

I thanked him, but he didn't wish that any more fervently than I.

The golden strand of Dionysus failed to hold Kronos. He snatched the cord in the center, hauling up both the God of Festivity and the Olympian Messenger. Down they went, into his terrible maw. He then looked distressed. Everyone held their breath. I saw the bulge as his tongue sought in his cheek for something. He drew out the long golden ribbon.

He flicked it away like a used toothpick. I was already angry but something about that carelessly dismissive gesture really put my back up. Kronos was having things too much his own way. If his children and their children were reluctant to injure him, unwilling to commit the blackest crime in the calendar, then I had every reason to.

My sword in my hand, I ran full tilt toward the huge white columns of his ankles. I heard Aphrodite cheering me on. "Run, my sly young fox, run!"

The wind seemed to be lifting me up. I made sure my sword was in my hand. I had evidence that my sword, mysteries of mysteries, could injure him.

Artemis, the only god still in a car, raced up beside me, her fleet-footed deer flecked with sweat-foam. "I will carry you, if you wish, mortal man."

"I decline with thanks...." I took another breath. "It will be dangerous when he falls."

"Athena and Hera have the girdle of Dionysus. When Kronos falls, they will bind him. Good hunting...mortal." She grinned at me as carefree as if she rode at ease in the cool-scented morning. She turned her chariot aside, neatly avoiding Kronos' stomp.

I braked hard and threw myself on my knees. As I slid past, I sliced deep into the tendons of Kronos' pulsating ankle. He let out a bellow they must have heard up above as an earthquake.

I reversed my grip, brought my hand up and over, stabbing sharply into the hollow behind the ankle on the other side. The sword was almost torn from my grasp as he pulled away from the sudden pain shooting up his leg.

He began to collapse like a house built on sand. Sinking to his knees, he began to vomit from the pain, bringing up Hermes, Dionysus and Poseidon, reversing the order in which he'd swallowed them.

I ran out from between his knees, avoiding blood, vomit and wedding tackle but not his swift hand. He bellowed my name, cracking the vault of the Underworld, letting a trace of blue sky in upon that bitter place. He cupped me in both hands, gazing up at the sky, his own father whom he'd tried long ago to murder.

"Father," Zeus called. "Let him go."

Well, so he did. He closed his hand over me. I held my sword ready to drive him off if he should squeeze. He rattled me like dice, then, I presume, threw me with all his might into the darkness beyond the darkness.

How long I fell or how far I traveled, I cannot say. Tumbling end over end, I lost all sense of myself. I felt sicker than Kronos ever had but there was no way to stop or control my precipitate flight. The miseries of my situation were nothing compared to the uncertainty that tortured me. What would happen? Would the Gods triumph? I wouldn't know until I returned to earth, if it and I survived.

At first, I thought I had gone back. But in all my comings and goings, I'd never arrived anywhere like here. I didn't land on sand; I rose up through it from underneath, first black sand, then white pouring off my body.

I realized I was on a beach, with a gentle surf washing the sand not a body-length away. Except for that susurration on the edge of hearing, there was no sound at all. Not a bird sang. Not a leaf rustled. Not a fish leaped from the water to splash again.

Lying there, I felt no need to move, not even to glance around for my location. I was warm, the sand conforming to my body, the sea whispered of sleep, of rest, of surcease.

After about five minutes, measured by my pulse, my nose itched, my foot had fallen asleep and I was pretty sure from the tickling that a spider was shopping my ear as a potential new house. Nothing like minor annoyances to let you know you're still alive.

I sat up, rubbing my ear. No spider. Only sand, white instead of black, powder instead of grains. The sea was a uniform greenish-blue as far as I could see. Behind me was a grove of trees, not many, that stood straight and motionless. Except for the soughing of the sea and the green of the clump of trees, there was nothing. The whole place seemed to be waiting to be brought to life.

Since I had no idea how long I'd be there, I started to explore. I was stymied at the start. Though the ocean seemed a few strides away, I couldn't reach it. There was nothing between me and it but I never got any closer. Same story with the trees. They were there, a little farther away apparently than the sea, yet they might as well have been on the other side of the moon.

The only path I could actually walk along was a narrow one. The beach curved and I could walk around the curve in a lane not more than three paces wide. "Strange...."

Keeping an eye on the sand prevented me from kicking the head of the only other person there.

"Jori?"

He was lying down, hands folded behind his head, staring up into the blank sky. No sun or cloud ever crossed that expanse, the hot flat white of an endless summer afternoon.

Sitting up, he squinted at me a moment. "Oh, hello, Eno."

His voice held no hint of surprise. He turned his head to look out at the featureless sea. After a moment, as if remembering his manners, he said, "How have you been?"

"Well..." I sorted among my thoughts. I didn't think any of my recent adventures would interest him now. "You know. Not much is new."

I sat down beside him on the sand. Jori picked up a handful and let it pour from his fingers. It was so fine there wasn't a grain left to cling to his skin. He looked out to sea again.

"What are you looking for?"

"The *Chelidion*. I'm waiting here until she comes."

I couldn't ask him how he came to be here; I already knew. The Judges of the Underworld and their enforcers, the Furies, are endlessly inventive in their punishments. Sisyphus and his ever-rolling rock, Tantalus and his ceaselessly unsatisfied appetites, the forty-nine daughters of Danaus who are forced to carry water eternally in sieves for the murders of their cousin-husbands were the best known. But to doom a sailor to wait on shore for a ship that will never come seemed too cruel even for the Kindly Ones.

His eyes, so empty of all the merry trickery that had made him my best friend and an enemy both, turned again to the ocean. "I'm waiting for the *Chelidion*."

After a while, he stood up and walked down the narrow path to the other end. I dozed. When he came back and sat down, he seemed to have forgotten that I was there. He could be spoken to but his attention never strayed from the barren sea for very long.

Then I was drawn up and away. I saw Jori growing ever smaller and realized the limits of his prison. There was no sea, except in front. It was just a blob of dirt set down in the midst of that same featureless black sand that formed the rest of Hades' dominion.

CHAPTER TWENTY

All honor to the Gods and all that but I was getting pretty tired of being yanked around, without so much as a 'if you wouldn't mind....'

I had been returned to Hekate's secret place of sacrifice in Troezen. The tiny tiles in the center of the floating rock were cracked and scattered. I picked one up and rubbed my thumb over the surface. The thick coat of white glaze was impenetrable and permanent. Kicking my foot through the pieces, I saw that they were all white, no trace of pattern or meaning left.

Red fire glowed on the walls and the stone began to tremble even as a great wind will shake the sturdiest foundations. A low rumble rose all around me. I started to run back toward the tunnel. A thunderous crack struck through the chamber as the aisle of stone split clean across.

I leapt the crack, even as it widened under my flying feet. Just as the narrow way snapped, I reached safety. The great floating slab had gone, dropped into the Pit Itself. There wasn't even an echo of the fall. I knew as soon as I turned away, the tunnel's mouth would be gone as well.

"The Gods are thorough indeed...."

Maybe in time someone would use the tunnel to store feed out of the rain and sun. It would be a better use for it than any it had ever been put to. I had begun to climb out when I heard a tremendous commotion bouncing off the tunnel walls. I glanced behind to see if the echoes had finally caught up to the crash but those roars and cries came from living throats.

"Phandros!"

Not even when Kronos chased me had I shown a better turn of speed. I emerged at the top expecting a scene of absolute massacre. But Phandros' head was still on his shoulders, his guts in place, or so I presumed, and the basket still in his hand. He presided over a congress of wild and violent creatures.

I'd heard that someday the lion will lay down with the lamb. Traveling entertainers have been known to show it, though I understand they have to replace the lamb fairly often.

And here, in the menagerie where they'd awaited death, Lion sat with sheep, Bull let Bear Cubs ride on his back, and Bear Herself was enjoying a leisurely ear-scratching from a bemused Phandros. She only growled when he stopped so he, naturally enough, didn't stop.

"Eno!" he said with joy as I came toward him tentatively. "I'm so very glad to see you, alive and unharmed. What happened?"

"It's a long story, something to fill the long hours on our trip back to Mykonos."

"We're going back there?"

"Maybe. What's going on here?"

"I have no idea. They seem to like me." Considering that four hundred pounds of Bear was pressing her great head against his side would seem to be evidence of that.

"I thought for sure you'd get eaten. Forgive me for my lack of faith."

"You were almost right. The Lion seemed to have a grudge against whoever put him in that cage. He was so glad to get out that he knocked me flat. When I sat up, he was sniffing my feet. I thought my last hour had come but he seemed to conclude that I wasn't the one he was looking for."

"How long do you think it's been since we parted?"

He glanced up at the moon. The storm had either passed or changed its mind. "About half an hour, maybe. Why, is it important?"

"Probably not. So what happens now? You can't take them all on the *Doris*. The captain would hurl us both overboard."

"If you'll take over here," he said, guiding my hand to the spot just under the rounded ear, "I'll find out."

"Wait...." But when a huge head tosses under your hand, demanding attention, and that mouth is bearing a full set of very unsympathetic teeth, ear-rubbing rises to its own importance.

For all the strange and heart-twisting things I'd seen and done, I was missing only a spare half hour out of my thread's length. I wondered how many times lately the Fates had raised the scissors, thinking 'ah-ha, now we've got him.' Maybe Aphrodite distracted them, sharing beauty secrets or what-have-you with Lakhesis, Klotho and Atropis, until I'd scraped through.

Artemis had heard his prayers now and Hermes the Trickster was, as usual, way ahead of the game. I had no doubt that he'd enchanted the animals so that Phandros met no harm. He was the protector of travelers and Phandros had traveled a long way.

A darkness surrounded me and the great weight of the bear's head ceased to press against me. The reek of the lion faded and I no longer heard the snuffling of the bull's breathing. All the sheep and goats were gone as well when the cloud lifted again.

Phandros was still on his knees, his lips moving in prayer...or conversation. I waited for him to be done.

Hearing a few little sounds from the basket, I took a quick peek. A small black snout lifted and sniffed, then yapped. "Hungry, little fella?"

I slipped my hand under his soft belly and lifted him up to eye-level. The black wings were feathery, too thin yet to get him air-borne but they flapped in concert with his wagging tail. He could scratch under them too, just like his ears. "I wonder what Phandros will call you?"

"Griffin, of course. In memory of what could have been."

I wondered if Phandros could see the same glow in my eyes, the glow of one who has conversed with a god, that I could see in his. "All well?" I asked.

"They have been returned to their proper places. I only hope they've all learned their lessons and won't be captured again."

"Not by Troezen, at any rate. I'm going up to the acropolis now to make sure of it. Do you want to come along?"

"Yes. This little guy needs some milk and bread and soft-cooked meat. I'm more likely to find that at the fortress than on the ship."

So, after a pee for the pup, we headed up the hill. Silence had fallen over the town. No flute, no drum, no voice could be heard. We came across a man, half-dressed in a leopard-skin, his head on a doorstep. "Is he dead?"

I felt the corner of his jaw. "No, just asleep."

"Drunk then?"

"I don't think so. Enchanted, maybe."

Farther on there were more, just fallen over wherever they'd been. Some smiled in their sleep; others twitched and groaned. Of the ones who had hunted us, of the many minions, there was no sign at all. I wondered if they had vanished when Hekate vanished and what had happened to her 'niece', my harpy princess. I hoped there was at least one physician sober enough to see to her arrow wound.

The guards at the acropolis gate slept too. The long period of peace prior to the start of the war in Troy had encouraged many city-states to abandon the stern acropolis for a pleasanter palace. But most fortresses still had quarters for the royal family in case of attack.

Phandros headed for the kitchens. I ascended the narrow winding stair, finding soldiers sleeping at their posts, an elderly maid passed out on her own laundry pile, and an interestingly posed group that sleep had caught in mid-orgy. There would be some red faces tomorrow.

At the top was a large wooden iron-enforced door. Symbols of a nature well-known to me were carved into the panels for protection. When I touched the door, it crumbled into sawdust, the iron-hasps shattering like pottery on the stone floor.

"What? How did you do that?"

The King of Troezen started up from his chair. Maybe the symbols had kept Morpheus out of this room for he didn't look sleepy. Nervous, anxious, near-starved...but not sleepy. His large eyes were almost popping from his thin, aristocratic-looking face.

"I bring a message from your late queen...."

That's as far as I got. "Late...late? You mean...late? Not   just   delayed?" He began to laugh, rocking back and forth, his arms crossed over his belly as if to keep his interiors in. "Zosime is dead...she's dead...and I'm not!"

"Steady on, man," I said, hoping I wouldn't have to slap him. A jug of wine was empty but there was water in another. I shot it over him and he fell back into his chair, gasping.

"How dare you!" he demanded, just as if he hadn't been hysterical.

"I'll do it again if you don't shut up."

"Who are you?"

"Eno the Thracian." Now that I didn't have to contend with him, I glanced around the chamber. It was large but comfortless, not even a fire or much in the way of furnishings, except two standing lamps. "Where's your niece?"

"My niece?" he said, his eyes shifting. "Is this a trick? One of Zosime's tricks? I won't tell you anything...you can't make me."

"Of course I could. But relax, will you? Zosime is dead. I sort of killed her myself. At any rate, I helped."

"Prove it," King Pavlos demanded. "Show me her body."

"That's complicated too." I thought about explaining that his wife had actually been a rather nasty Titan in disguise but decided to skip it.

"I believe you are a madman. Guards...."

Before he could call again, I picked him up out of the chair and dragged him by his weedy beard to the crumbled remains of the door. His guards were slumped in their niches, snoring lustily. "If you can wake them up, arrest me. If you can't, head down to the kitchen. There's a man there and, if I know him at all, he's cooking something. Maybe soup."

There was an inner door in the chamber. It did not obligingly crumble when I touched it. I had to set my shoulder to it. The lamps in the room behind me shed dim illumination. From somewhere in the darkness, a quiet rustling came to my ears.

Out of the darkness, a sword sang free of a scabbard. I parried it blindly, my instincts more aware than my eyes. A sweetly sharp voice called out. "Herodias! Stop that!"

"Kissos? Princess? Harpy?"

There was the patter of feet and my arms were suddenly filled with a woman, soft-skinned but firm in all the places that counted. Maybe my resistance was low through exposure to Aphrodite or just from all I'd experienced lately, but I didn't exactly push her away.

Well, not for a while anyway. When I did, there was plenty of evidence that my doing so was not caused by any repugnance on my part. "Slow down," I said, a little breathlessly.

"I'm very happy you've come back," she said. "Where did you go? Is Zosime dead?"

"Yes." I half-expected her to break out into a song or something, considering the king's reaction to the news. But Kissos was made of stronger stuff.

She stood with downcast eyes, her arm tightly bound. "I always felt that she hated me but I never knew why. When she first married Uncle Pavlos, I thought she was so wonderful. I know my father hoped she'd stand as a mother to me. But she always hated me."

The light gilded the thin gown over her perfect body. She had the 'vase' figure, the ideal, a waist slender as a vase's neck and her hips flaring full. Her face, now that I could see it clearly, had the straight nose and full cheeks so beloved by our sculptors.

"It's all over now," I said. "She won't be coming back and the evil she did has passed with her."

"I will mourn the woman I wished she had been," Kissos said, her voice as soft as a dove's. Then she looked up at me and smiled more enchantingly than any spell. "You were so kind to me when I was...changed. Even though I didn't have any memory of my life as a woman, I remember that you were kind."

"I betrayed you," I said, the coldness of my tone directed at myself. "I used your affection for me to capture you."

"And you saved me too. I think the people of Leros would have killed me, sooner or later."

She came closer and touched my chest. "My uncle will abdicate in my favor. I will have much to do to alleviate the evils of the last dozen years. It goes deeper than just my aunt. She has been twisting the running of the city, lying to our allies at Argos, and putting wicked men in place to collect taxes and police the city. All that must be changed. Together, we can make Troezen a measure by which all other cities will be judged."

I pressed her hand against my heart, tempted as much by her vision of doing good as by her remarkable beauty. She was everything any man could dream of and what did I have? A glimpse of a pair of eyes, the flicker of light on pale gold hair, and about a half-a-smile. Not much to build on, there.

"Glorious Kissos," I said, "compared to you, Helen of Sparta is an old shoe. I only hope Paris never catches a glimpse of you or he'll realize what a bad bargain he's made."

Her beautiful eyes narrowed slightly. She was nobody's fool. "This sounds not like acceptance."

"I am the son of a Thracian shepherd. I am not fit for palaces and great counsels. My natural place is on a sylvan hillside, piping songs for sheep."

"Men rise to greater heights than their birth every day."

"You are a queen and I am no king. It is not in me to rule. Not even over you."

She turned away from me then, picking up an over-dress that lay over a clothes-chest. Donning it, she proceeded to do up her hair, though her hands trembled. "When will you leave?"

"Soon. There are a few things I must do first."

"Whatever you wish, will be given to you. See to it, Herodias."

The queen's former bodyguard bowed to me but he would never trust me. "What do you want?"

"Well, there's this ship in the harbor...."

When morning came, the city awoke. The announcement from the palace that the Hunt had been canceled due to the sudden passing of Queen Zosime caused little grumbling. Troezen seemed ashamed of itself. The sudden reappearance of Princess Kissos and the abdication of King Pavlos brought new smiles to a lot of faces and the number of magistrates, guards, and professional witnesses that absconded from the city shortly afterwards lightened many hearts.

Business was up and running again by noon. I confess I took advantage of some lingering headaches when I auctioned off all the goods, hidden and open, that Jori had on the *Chelidion*.

With the backing of Queen Kissos behind me, no one complained even when I sold embargoed goods from cities associated with Troy. Actually, those goods went for the highest prices as it had been so long since any had been seen there.

Kissos was a good sport. She made no overt overtures yet every word she said and every gesture of her elegant hands made clear just what I was rejecting.

After sounding every board and measuring every corner of the *Chelidion* to be sure I'd missed nothing I could sell, I took her out alone beyond the mouth of the bay. I climbed the mast, out of the smell of the pitch I'd spread around, a torch in my hand. I balanced on one foot on the crossbeam, the ship as gentle under me as an old horse.

"Hades!" I called at the top of my voice. They probably could hear me on shore. "Hades! This ship is for Jori the Phoenician, who languishes in Tartaros. If you cannot let him go to Elysium, let him sail the eternal seas in her!"

With that, I dropped the torch. It fell, end over end, landing on the pile of shredded rope I'd laid there. For a moment, I thought it had gone out, a sign that the Lord of the Underworld refused my demand. Then the flames spread out like vines seeking light, blossoming swiftly with crimson flowers.

I dove into the water just as the *Chelidion* exploded. There must have been one hold of twice-distilled liquor or turpentine that I'd missed. I headed deep as the sea above me turned to molten gold.

I came ashore at a deserted cove as the sun touched the clouds with pink and red. Shaking myself all over like a wet dog, I hopped first on one foot and then the other, clearing the water from my ears. A linen towel hit me in the face.

A short man, muffled in a cloak, stood a little way off. 'Short' wasn't quite the right word. If his legs had been straight, he would have been as tall and broad as I am. His reddish beard was singed at the edges.

"A nice gesture," Hephaestus said, pointing one of the sticks he leaned on toward the black plume of smoke still rising into the sky.

"Will it work?"

"Probably. They are very fond of grand dramatic gestures, my family. Especially my wife."

"But not you?"

"I have too much work to do, magic armor, mechanical owls, and Talos, my man of Bronze, is always breaking down. It's the knees, mostly. Speaking of work, may I see your sword?"

I handed it over. He tut-tutted over the seawater on the blade, blowing the drops off with a powerful breath. "This dispatched some shades, if what I hear is true."

"And cut Kronos."

"Indeed." He lightly flicked the edge and nodded thoughtfully as he stuck the wounded finger into his mouth. "It is good workmanship. Where did you come by it?"

I told him while the shadows deepened. By his nature, Hephaestus was always more interested in objects of craft than in people so I kept it brief.

"So you think it might have belonged to the one who fathered you." He held up his hand. "Don't bother telling me he was just a simple shepherd. Your recent activities may have left you wondering if we Gods are all we are cracked up to be but about some things we do not err."

"I have no quarrel with the Gods. But I have questions. Why didn't the Waters of Lethe work on me? Hekate said...and Kronos said...."

"Don't ask me," he commanded, but then he smiled, a sad, twisted smile. "These are things you must learn on your own, Eno. You are well on your way, if the answers are indeed what you desire."

"But...."

"My wife is very fond of you. She says you make her feel quite maternal." He chuckled at my expression. Smiles sat oddly on his austere face. "Not what you wanted to hear, perhaps? Take it and be glad. It's much safer to have her as a mother than as...anything else. Even as a wife."

"She's the most powerful goddess of them all, isn't she? Hekate was wrong to think the prophecy referred to herself."

"All of us, even the Father of the Gods, bow to her whims, that is true. But she is seldom as whimsical as she would like us to think."

Seeing he meant to keep his counsel, I changed the subject. "What became of Hekate?"

"She is banished to the same fate as my grandfather, Kronos. Though he is banished for all eternity and my father has decreed that she need only serve three thousand years. She has taken her poisons and her 'treats' with her. I will miss those evil crunchy cheese bits, even if my wife objected to my eating them. They were the key to keeping us docile. Zeus has sent them into nothingness as well. Beware if you meet with them again!"

"What will happen now in Troy?" I asked.

"We will meddle. That's what we do best." He drew his cloak around him as if feeling a chill. His voice came out of the darkness. "Your sword comes from the East. Seek there."

I was alone.

* * *

Phandros sat on the bottommost step of the Palace's entrance, Griffin on a string beside him, pouncing on the pebbles his master tossed. "I told Her Highness that you weren't likely to be caught in the explosion. Are you going to marry that girl?"

"No."

"Too bad. She's very pleasant."

He fell into step beside me as we went inside. "I'm going to get married myself."

"This is sudden," I said. Had someone slipped him a love philter? "To who? Some girl from Leros?"

"Oh, I haven't met her yet. I'll work for Skander 'til I have a nest-egg saved up. Then I'll marry a poor girl from a large family...or a large girl from a poor family." He stopped Griffin from lifting his leg on a statue. "Then we'll all move to Telemenos and settle it. I liked that island."

"What about the ghosts and the monsters?"

"If they trouble us, we'll call on our old family friend, Eno, to dispatch them for us."

"I'll do it. No charge."

We left Troezen on the morning tide. The captain actually smiled as the last rope was coiled.

There'd been no time for a private good-bye to Kissos. She was already surrounded by those who wanted 'just a moment' and those jostling for a 'single word'. So she handed me a large bonus with some formal words about my service and the lasting friendship of the House of Troezen. By neither sign nor inflection, did either of us make reference to her visiting me in the night. She'd wept and pleaded but that was not good for a queen to remember.

I'd wept a little myself but I don't mind remembering.

I never did tell Phandros all that had happened. There would have been time, perhaps, if he'd asked. But Griffin had learned to fly before we'd been out of port a day and he kept both Phandros and me, as well as a good portion of the crew, dodging air-borne puppy teeth. He found it great fun to swoop down unexpectedly and nibble ears. Flying puppy poo was a whole other kind of menace.

Skander gave us the reception of a lifetime...or as it is known in his house, Sunday. He agreed to send the money I'd made from the *Chelidion*'s cargo to Jori's mother in Tyre. I gave him all the information about her that I could recall.

"I have a ship leaving for Tyre in two days. I shall send Charillos and Phandros the Younger. The trip will do them good. But where are you going, my friend?"

"I return to Athens, to pay my debts and deposit funds. Then I must visit my mother in Thrace."

"You always have a passage on one of my ships. I will write you a letter, good anywhere."

"You're the soul of generosity, Skander. By the way, thank you for the job offer. I...."

"Oh, I know, I know. Independence! A free hand! All well and good while you are young. But when the mighty arm grows stiff and the monsters get too large, come and tell me you've changed your mind, eh? Or even sooner? There are some interesting and rather frightening rumors coming out of the East. If true, they'll affect trade. I need someone to go and investigate what is happening out there."

"The East?" I asked, remembering Hephaestus' words.

"Aye. Egypt. Well, think it over. Think it over!"

My landlord was glad to see me. I was behind on the rent. A scoop from the bag that held Kissos' generous reward widened his eyes. He sent up the better wine with my evening meal. He also sent up a message that had been left with him some weeks earlier. I thought I recognized the handwriting so laid it aside until after supper. I didn't want to ruin my appetite.

Minthe's father wrote to say that, upon further thought, he decided my profession made me too great a risk for his precious flower. She'd been married the week before to one of her other, more boring suitors. I laid the letter aside and laughed until my stomach burned. So much for all my faithfulness and virtue.

I had taken my meal on the roof. The sounds of the street and the city, familiar to me as a lullaby, floated up to me there. I set my chair so I could rest my feet on the coping. Beyond them, I could see the brightest star in all the heavens, a wanderer that, for the moment, hung low in the twilight-shaded sky. It is named Aphrodite.

THE STONE GODS

Read on for an excerpt from Book Two in the Eno
the Thracian series by C. B. Pratt.

After the third week of a one-week cruise, the sea
had lost its sparkle.

I stood atop the mast, feet braced on the cross-bar.
The *Idyia* wasn't the largest ship afloat and, sailing alone
in the midst of a watery desert, she seemed even smaller.
The mast transcribed circles with the motion of the sea
below me. As I spun slowly, I surveyed empty sky and
empty sea.

From time to time, I caught sight of the deck,
crowded by the crew, muttering, clutching staves, knives
and axes. Some few clutched their heads, taking no
further interest in me. Considering that the water ration
had been cut the week before so that there was no more
for washing, I was just as glad to be up where the air
was fresh, even if they hadn't been trying to kill me.

By the second week of our one-week cruise, their
camaraderie had begun to fracture. One or two had
determined that the voyage had somehow incurred the
wrath of some Sea spirit or other and, in time-honored
fashion, had looked about for a scapegoat. As usual,
they'd picked on the only stranger on board -- me.

When the water ration had been cut the first time,
they'd found ears willing to listen to their theory.

Today, with their captain face-down drunk on the
deck, the knives had come out. It was climb or swim. I
was secure enough for the moment, though I couldn't be
sure that they were sane enough to refrain from
chopping down the mast.

"Come down, Thracian!" The first mate, Nacrolos, had joined with the crew rather than be tossed overboard himself. A burly-chested man, he had a voice like the roaring of a lion, easily heard over winds and storms.

"You should see this view," I called back.

"We won't hurt you, if you come down."

True, that. Nobody wanted to anger a sea spirit or god further by spilling blood on the deck. They'd agreed that be best thing to do was to throw me overboard and leave my fate in the hands of the Fates. Those three alone knew whether my thread of life foretold my death on this day or another. If I drowned, my blood would not be on the crews' hands as it was evidently my lot in life since before my birth. I had objected for several reasons, not least among them was that drowning was no death for a fighting man.

The sun was a blurred white dot in the height of a pale sky. The sea dazzled with a thousand glittering shards until eye and mind alike were wearied. But beyond all that, I thought I glimpsed something else. I gripped the mast tight between my knees, to bring up a hand to shade my eyes, straining to bring what I saw into focus.

"You can't stay up there forever," Nacrolos said, adding to the others, "Thirst'll bring him down soon enough."

"I'm serious," I shouted back. "You should see this view. Send somebody up here."

After a certain amount of bickering and shoving, Nacrolos himself started up, climbing like a monkey or a sailor bred to the sea. Certainly better than I could do.

Clinging to the mast, braced against me for balance, he snarled, "What game are you playing, Thracian?"

He wasn't as tall as me, so at first he couldn't see it. Then I got a hold of his broad leather belt and hoisted him up, raising him with one arm above my head. He gasped, scratching and beating at my hand like a fool. The crew below cried out, thinking I meant to dash him down.

Then I felt right through his belly the start he gave as his wildly rolling eye caught sight of what I'd brought him up here to witness, a thing that haunted the nightmares of sailors since the dawn of time. "Do you see it? Do you?"

"By the mother of the Gods...."

"Gods or not, that's the mother of all whirlpools," I said, lowering him 'til I could look him in the eyes. He'd gone green under his walnut-colored tan. "And we've been riding the rim for days, I'd wager."

"Aye. What's to be done?"

"We start by not throwing me to the waves."

"Of course not," he said, mindful perhaps that I had plenty of strength left. "Let's call that a joke, eh?"

"Let's call it a bloody stupid idea. The only thing keeping us riding the edge of this whirlpool is that somehow -- by the luck of Heaven -- our weight is neither too much nor too little. Throwing a weight like me overboard would change that by enough and then you'd really know what a curse is."

Nacrolos wasn't a fool when his thoughts weren't clouded by fear of the unknown. As we climbed down, he was already planning our escape. He thrust a meaty fist into the jaw of the first crewman who charged at me. Even as the poor fellow went down like a felled ox, Nacrolos shouted orders.

"We man the oars, boys. And row, damn your eyes, as you've never rowed before."

They cut extra holes in the hull, carefully husbanding the wood to make extra oars. Though the crew continued to throw suspicious glances at me, having something tangible to do gave them heart to work with a will. They'd make a port for every man, saving no one for a second shift.

Pausing a moment in his work, Nacrolos took me aside. "I'm uneasy about this. If it goes wrong, we've had it."

"We've got to do something. Can't just keep sailing in a big circle 'til we die of thirst."

"I wish the captain were awake. He's a clever man; I'm just an old salt."

"At least you're still on your feet." I clapped him on the shoulder. "We'll be all right. I'll get back up there and tell you which way to steer."

"If there were only two of you...I'll need your strength at the oars as well."

In the end, we sent two men up the mast, one to sit on the other's shoulders so he could see the dark, swirling pit of water on the very edge of the horizon. We dared not steer for even one instant in that direction. As soon as we were broken free of the current that carried us endlessly around, we might meet any kind of wild water. If we were unlucky, we'd be swept down into a crushing oblivion of roaring sea and splintered wood.

I did not speak my fears to Nacrolos. There are two things in this world that cause a whirlpool. One is an influx of mixing waters. The other is a monster. We were far from the narrow strait haunted by Charybdis the Vast but there were other creatures almost equal to her brutality.

Of course, monsters make up a good deal of my business. My sign in the Athenian acropolis says it all really. *Hero for Hire. All monsters dispatched from carnivorous geese to Minotaurs. Special rates for multiples. Eno the Thracian at the sign of the Ram's Head, one flight up.*

But this brief journey from Athens to Kalithanos wasn't supposed to be for business. I'd taken down my sign and told my landlord to send any clients to Kyex, a nice fellow and a good fighter. If they didn't want to see him, they'd have to wait until I got back from visiting my mother.

Frankly, I'd rather face a hydra with a head-cold.

Not because she was so formidable - though she could fell an ox with one glance - but because the questions I had for her could easily be interpreted as insulting. Just how did one go about asking a decent woman whether she'd made a slight mistake and passed her infant son off on her husband, knowing he was not the father? Even my extra time on the *Idyia* hadn't given me an answer to that.

An hour into our labor, the captain woke up, staggered to the side and vomited like a volcano. Straightening up, he wiped his mouth with the back of his hand. Nacrolos started toward him to explain what we were doing. Before he reached him, though, the captain spewed again.

There's nothing more eye-catching than a man being deeply and thoroughly sick, as much as we might feel our own throat burn with a sympathetic gagging. Everyone watched him for a brief space of silence, then we all felt the change in the ship. A deep lurch as the ship, lightened by just so much, changed position toward portside, where the vortex awaited. "What in Hades' name was that?" Captain Eosphorous demanded.

Nacrolos explained urgently. The captain rubbed his no-doubt aching head as he tried to understand. "So what you're saying is...I should try to hurl on the deck?"

The lookout shouted down that we'd changed position and not for the better. The sailors redoubled their efforts, driven harder by their new fears than by their hope of escape. One by one, the thudding of axes ended as the sailors stood by at their ports, little more than a row of holes in the fabric of the ship. Captain

Eosphorous, pale and sweating but in command, took his position where all could see him. He raised the padded drumsticks above an empty barrel laid on its side and gave the beat for the rowing.

The beat was low and urgent. We threw ourselves on the oars, driven by that thrumming which seemed less in the ear and more from someplace inside that warned us to 'hurry, hurry, or you'll be caught!'

At first, it went well. We broke from the current that had held us in place for so long. Two or three men raised a ragged cheer when word came from the lookouts that we seemed to be putting more distance between us and that swirling mouth of doom on the horizon.

The muscles stood up on our arms and backs like armor-plate as we strained to force the *Idyia* onward. Some men gasped for breath while others groaned with each pull. Their hands, sea-hardened though they were, began to run with blood, the red trickling over their bodies as they leaned back with the stroke, but not a man faltered. Even the two ship's boys, sharing an oar, fought with every bit of their power against the sea.

One of the lookouts came down to tell the captain, face to face, that they were losing. The whirlpool was nearer, close enough to be seen to port without even raising on tip-toe. We were wasting our time and our strength to no purpose.

I shipped my oar. Ignoring the inquiring cries of my shipmates, I went forward. Nacrolos followed me. "What are you doing?"

"Tie a loop in this rope for me," I said, pushing the coil into his hands. "I like to travel by ship, but I have no idea how they work."

"D'ye mean to hang yourself?" He tied a loop like a noose and held it out.

"Make it bigger, man. I'm no bean-pole."

I stepped up into the bow. The *Idyia* was a newer vessel and lacked the high prow of the old ones. The front end extended farther from the ship and still bore the traditional 'living' eyes on either side. I could only hope that she would watch over me as I tried to save her life.

"Tie each end to those bits over there."

"Very well," Nacrolos said, his eyes busy with questions.

When I slipped the loop over my head and around my chest, the excess rope coiling on the deck beside me, he tried to stop me as one confirmed in his estimate of my mental health. "It's suicide, Thracian. Come back to the oars where your strength is useful. With you, we might succeed. But if you do this, you condemn us all to die."

"It's in the hands of the Fates, don't you think?"

"Gods! Is this your vengeance?"

I shook my head. "Shout to tell me which way to go," I said and clapped him on the shoulder.

I dove over the prow, swimming fast to get ahead of the ship. The ropes grew taut as I found the proper distance. Then I began to plow through the water, throwing my arms forward without stinting while I kicked like a dolphin. With every stroke, I prayed as hard as ever I had in my life. To Poseidon, to Amphitrite, to Tethys, to every god, goddess or Titan who'd ever so much as admired a seashell. "Let there be no monster, let me be strong enough, let this damn well work."

Above the roaring in my ears and the splash of my efforts, I heard Nacrolos bellow that I should turn to starboard. "Not too much!"

I tried to make myself as mindless as a sail, as biddable as a rudder. I emptied myself of thought, aware only of the harsh voice crying instructions.

They told me later that there'd been a solid wall of water forever circling the whirlpool, that we broke through it as though it were made of glass. But don't believe it. We passed through no such wall on the way in. Legends grow like that, though. One day, no doubt, I'll hear the tale told and won't recognize myself at all.